Favored

JOHN FUJA

Northwoods, Illinois

Favored by John Fuja

First printing August, 2013.

ISBN13 978-0-9777226-5-5
ISBN10 0-9777226-5-1

Additional resources and author contact:
www.FAVORED.info

Cover design by Sherwin B. Soy
me@sherwinbsoy.com
www.sherwinbsoy.com

Published by Byron Arts, Northwoods, Illinois, USA.

Visit www.ByronArts.com for quantity discounts of this and other Byron Arts publications.

Copyediting by George August Koch
GeorgeAugustKoch@aol.com
www.GeorgeAugustKoch.com

This novel is dedicated to my wife Mary Ann. Without her support and constant encouragement, *Favored* would never have been written.

PROLOGUE

It was the last quarter of the first century B.C. In a small town in the Middle East, Zillah, who had been married to a habitual drunk for the past five years, sat by her fire pit, adding thorn branches to the hungry flames. The masked sun was about to set on this chilly March day. The slate-gray sky began to darken even further as the young woman's labor pains intensified. The latest one was so painful that she moaned.

Zillah turned away from the God of Abraham two years ago. In His place she had begun to worship Asherah, the goddess of fertility. She made an idol and burned incense to it every night. If the Jews in her town found out what she was doing, they would have her stoned to death. Jewish law forbade idol worship, sorcery and witchcraft. The woman promised the goddess that if she became pregnant, she would dedicate the child to the spirits of the air and of the netherworld. All Zillah wanted was a child to love and cuddle, and then she wouldn't care if her husband was ever sober again.

The soon-to-be mother was the type of person who found fault with everyone. She had a vicious

1

mouth and loved to start rumors. That's probably why no one who passed by that evening paid any attention to her. Soon the only light she could see came from the dancing blaze before her. Taking a stick, she held it over the leaping flames until it caught fire. The pregnant woman shielded the struggling flame with her hand, for a cold breeze now blew in from the north, chilling her to the bone. Zillah entered the house and lit the night candle. The severity of her labor pains caused her to lean on the wall as she moaned much louder this time.

Seven houses away from Zillah's, Jacob and his pregnant wife, who was a month from term, ate their evening meal. "The baby is really active tonight," the young carpenter said as he watched his wife's tunic move. "Must be a boy!"

"Girl or boy, whichever God gives us, as long as it's healthy," his wife replied with a smile.

Jacob rose from his place and went toward his wife. He knelt by her side and kissed her abdomen. "Be good tonight; let Mommy get some sleep," he said to the child within her womb. Then he added, "…son!" His wife laughed.

About midway down the hillside in the same vicinity, in a stand of scrub oaks, an old hag named Zaddu walked from her cave to her fire. A pack of rats trailed close behind. One rotting brown incisor was the only thing that kept her mouth from caving in over her gums; it distorted her mouth in a hideous fashion. Her weather-worn skin was as wrinkled as a prune, and her bloodshot eyes, sunk deep into her bony head, only amplified her ugliness. The rat that nested in her tangled, matted gray hair began to squeak loudly. She grabbed it with her long, dirty nails and put the rodent into her filthy, ragged tunic, near her shriveled bosom. Tonight, she had to hear everything clearly. Zaddu then sat down by the fire.

It appeared she was talking to herself, yet two separate, eerie voices came from her mouth. A hoarse, gravelly male voice dictated instructions, while the witch's shrill, high-pitched voice sought clarification of the orders. As soon as the conversation ended, the sorceress reached for her staff. She supported herself with it as she rose slowly. The hag then hobbled off toward the town. Her back was hunched so badly that she could only see the ground in front of her when she walked. No one knew how old the witch actually was. The great-grandparents of the town's younger residents said that Zaddu must have been over a hundred years old when they were children.

While the two voices still emanated from the witch's mouth, Jacob laid next to his wife. With his arm around her he said, "I'm sorry, but I don't think this marriage of ours is going to work out." Her eyes opened wide as she looked at him, shocked. His statement startled her. "Yep, something's come between us," Jacob said as he lowered his hand to her abdomen, and began to rub it and laugh.

"Silly goose!" his wife said. "You frightened me there for a moment. You sounded and looked as if you were serious. I thought I was going to lose you."

With his hand still on her belly, Jacob brought his face up against his wife's, and rubbed his nose against hers as he snickered. He kissed her on the cheek and said, "Do you really believe I could live without you? *Now* tell me who's the silly goose, huh?" She put her hand under his arm and began to tickle him in his most vulnerable spot. He laughed so heartily that she joined in too. Jacob tried to roll away from his wife as he said between chuckles, "Stop it, you're gonna kill me, please!" They laughed so hard they cried. When there was no laughter left in them, Jacob snuggled up next to his wife once again. With his hand still resting on her abdomen, the young couple fell asleep.

Zillah's husband, in a drunken stupor, laid no more than an arm's length above her head as she pushed with all her might to force her baby out. She felt as if she were being split in half. Her nerve endings were overstimulated, and the receptors in her brain kept warning her she was near the breaking point. *One last push,* she told herself as she bore down one last time. Zillah heard the *pop!* as the baby's head was delivered; a few moments later she was tying off the umbilical cord and cutting it. She held her little son, whom she named Joshua, in her arms, and suckled him as she passed the afterbirth.

He nursed gently at his mother's breast while Zillah, filled with contentment, kept touching her newborn son with her free hand. When he finished nursing, she checked him over thoroughly; all his parts were where they should be. The new mother swaddled the babe and set him in a reed basket she had previously padded with a quilt. Zillah took the afterbirth and her idol, and went to the fire pit. She threw the useless tissue onto the flames as a sacrifice of thanksgiving to the goddess. She was told to do so by the followers of Asherah. After adding more kindling to the fire, she tossed the idol into the roaring flames and said, "Bye-bye, sweetie! I guess I won't be needing you around anymore, will I?" The flames licked at the idol as Zillah walked back into her house and finally fell asleep. She didn't bother to lock the door from the inside.

As Zillah suckled her son, the witch reached the opening between the last house that formed the town wall, and the rocky hillside. There was just enough room between them for a child to slip through. The old hag was extremely thin. By facing the hillside and sidestepping, she managed to get through without too much difficulty, despite her hunched back. Once she reached the street, she knew exactly where to go.

Click, click, click, went her wooden staff as it struck the pavement and echoed through the frosty night air. The battened-down window coverings in the homes emitted shafts of candlelight every time the wind blew. The flapping sound intensified the eeriness of the dark night. Zaddu loved it! She finally arrived at Zillah's house to do Satan's bidding.

As Zaddu approached her destination, flames from Zillah's fire shot high up into the air. The witch slowly opened the door, and saw the newborn lying in the basket. His mother was sound asleep, weakened by her ordeal. The sorceress picked up the basket and laid it on the low table close to the

5

door. Because the frame of her body was so bent, her face was now directly over the infant's. She turned the basket so that the baby's head was perpendicular to her face. Zaddu then lifted her head and expelled all the foul-smelling air from her lungs as she faced the western horizon, the direction that stole the light. The old hag then placed her gaping mouth over the newborn's nose and mouth. Her rotted incisor scratched the baby's face, and the infant began to stir. She clamped her mouth more tightly over his and sucked the breath of life right out of him. She held it within her lungs until they ached, and the baby stopped moving.

Zaddu shook from head to foot; the child's innocent life-breath was now captive in her lungs. She couldn't wait to rid herself of the sweet innocence that now filled her. When she broke the seal formed by her mouth, her long, ugly nails clicked as she rubbed her hands together in glee. She was overjoyed; the baby's lips were turning blue, and his chest no longer rose and fell. She expelled the infant's breath of life from her and didn't stop exhaling until her lungs ached and were clear of the goodness that had filled them. Zaddu watched with amazement as the breath of the innocent seemed to sparkle in the air above her like sunlight on rippling water. She continued to watch it as it drifted upward, and eastward to where light is restored.

The minute the witch entered Zillah's house, Jacob's wife awoke. Her baby was so active now that she couldn't fall back asleep. She placed her arm under her head, looked down at her belly, and whispered, "What, are you doing somersaults in there?" Though her husband was a sound sleeper, she worried the constant activity of their unborn child would wake him. So she gently raised his hand from her abdomen and put it over his hip. The young mother-to-be then raised her petticoat and watched as her belly moved. "Your father will have to chase after you," she said. "He can run faster than me. From the look of things, though, he'll always be out of breath." The baby just wouldn't stop moving that night.

Zaddu unwrapped the swaddling cloth from the lifeless baby, then took out a small dagger from her waistband and made a slit on the edge of her thumb. She cursed under her breath at the stinging pain. She faced west again and breathed in the cold night air that contained the acrid smoke from the now-smoldering idol. Her lungs burned. The hag placed her mouth over the lifeless child's nose and mouth once more and breathed her fetid breath into him until his lungs filled with the pungent, foul-smelling air. Her bloody thumb pressed up and down over the baby's heart. The infant's eyes popped open; he stared at her and then seemed to look at his surroundings. Zaddu put her dirty, bloody thumb in his mouth until her gnarly fingernail went down his throat. He sucked on it, then clamped his gums around it so tightly that she cursed the baby and the resulting pain. The witch tried to swaddle the baby again, but her long, curving nails thwarted her efforts, so she left and went toward Jacob's house.

Jacob's wife gently rubbed her abdomen in the hopes that it would calm the baby within her womb, but the child was still restless. As the mother-to-be lay next to her husband, she thought she heard a child's voice calling for help.

"Please come and help me," the voice said. "It's so cold, and I haven't had anything to eat today. Please help me!" Her motherly instincts wouldn't let her ignore the child's plea. Jacob's wife left the bed and went to the door. She opened it but couldn't see anyone, so she decided to step out into the night and find the child. The moment that she did, her bare foot touched the cold slippery stone, and she slid. Her legs flew out from under her. The poor pregnant woman landed with a loud thud. Her head struck the grease-covered threshold and she was knocked unconscious. A dark-red spot began to spread on her fresh white petticoat. The young woman was hemorrhaging. Jacob's wife would never live to see the beautiful son she would deliver.

Zaddu cackled under her breath as she watched Jacob's wife fall. She couldn't resist saying, in a childlike voice, "I'm not hungry or cold anymore, you gullible fool!" The witch had accomplished all that her master had told her to do. She returned to her cave, wiping her grease-covered hand in her ragged tunic as she hobbled along.

Zillah woke as her baby screamed at the top of his lungs. She crawled out of bed and picked up her son. The woman wondered how he could possibly have kicked himself free from the swaddling cloth she had tied so tightly around him. She thought he might be wet or hungry. Carrying the baby to the low table, she placed him nearer the night candle and loosened the cloth. That was when Zillah

8

noticed the small scratch-like mark near her son's mouth. "Did my widdle wuv scwatch himself?" she asked in baby-talk. "I'm a bad mommy. I should have bound you tighter so those little nails wouldn't scratch your tiny little face." When the swaddling cloth was completely opened, Zillah noticed a blood spot over her son's heart. "I think I missed a spot when I cleaned you up earlier, my dear," she said. The new mother took a washcloth and began to dab at the bloody area. The cloth turned a rusty red color, but the red spot still remained. "You, my little one, have a birthmark that looks just like a thumbprint. I'm surprised I didn't notice it before. Don't you worry; no one will see it there."

Zillah changed and re-swaddled her son. She held her baby close to herself to suckle him once again. Joshua took hold of his mother's breast and clamped his gums down on it so tightly that Zillah recoiled in pain. She tried to force him to let go by pulling away, but he wouldn't release no matter what she did. The new mother realized her baby wasn't interested in nursing. He was just interested in biting her with his strong gums. Joshua opened his black, eerie eyes and stared at her. She sensed her son enjoyed inflicting pain. Zillah saw his evil eyes gleam even brighter in the candlelight as he bit down even harder. The babe wouldn't release until his mother passed out from the unbearable pain.

CHAPTER 1

The eastern sky began to turn from deep gray to blazing red as dark billowy clouds rolled across the heavens from the great sea. The sun hadn't yet risen, but its pre-dawn light still caught the perimeters of the cloud forms, framing their edges in a brilliant gold. A rather tall, somewhat portly woman carrying a water jar upon her head walked hand-in-hand with her little daughter. The silent, deserted street was still shrouded in semi-darkness.

"Hmm, red skies in the morning," the woman said under her breath.

"What did you say, Momma?" her eight-year-old daughter asked.

"Oh, I was just thinking out loud, dear," Anna replied. "It's going to rain today! You can see it in the sky and feel it in the air."

"I don't see any rain in the sky, and I can't feel the air, except maybe when the wind blows," the little girl said as she extended her free arm and began to swing it in an arc. "It sure doesn't feel wet to me, Momma."

"What I said is just an expression, dear. Sometimes though, like today, the air feels a lot

11

heavier than it usually does. When the sky is red at daybreak, people say, 'Morning sky red and gloomy, the day will be stormy. If we have red skies at night, tomorrow will be sunny and bright.'"

"Oh," the girl said. She thought for a moment, then added, "You know everything, Momma. You're a very smart woman." The child's mother said nothing; she just smiled.

The pair reached the entrance of the town well. Since Anna could not tilt her head, she probed the edge of the first step with her bare foot. Memory and instinct would take over from there. Anna had performed this task for the past thirteen years. She knew every crack, indentation and worn surface of every stair tread. Anna thought it was about time for her daughter to start learning this part of a woman's daily chores, so she took her with her every morning.

As they began to descend the curving staircase, they could smell the pungent odor of smoldering candlewicks drifting up the shaft on the humid air. Some of the candles that had been placed in small coves in the wall the night before still struggled to maintain their glow. They too would soon surrender and become but glowing citrine embers and pirouettes of white wispy smoke. Anna favored coming to the well at daybreak before droves of loquacious women would gather and detain her from her daily chores. She was not a gossip and detested the practice. Her main goal in life was to live so as to please her God and raise her daughter to do the same.

The sky began to lighten, but the interior of the cavern was still in dark shadow. The new light of day, however, seemed to add its glow to the chamber with each descending step. Anna carefully balanced the water jar on her head while placing one hand on the stone wall and the other extended behind her as guidance for her daughter. "Walk in the middle of the stairs," she instructed. "Keep one hand on the wall and hold my hand with the other."

Children have the ability to turn everything into a game, even steep, narrow stairs in a dimly lit stairwell. The woman began to notice there was an ever-increasing distance between the child and herself. The little girl would wait until they were at least two stairs apart and then jump to the next step. Anna scolded her daughter, warning her of the inherent dangers in such reckless behavior. She stopped jumping but never shortened the distance between her mother and herself. As Anna was in the process of putting her other foot on the cavern floor, her daughter saw that there remained only two stairs on which she could enjoy her new game. Unable to resist the temptation, the child jumped. As she did, she slammed into her mother's side, throwing the woman off balance.

Anna felt her arm being jerked forward, followed by a sudden blow to her hip. Instinctively she raised both of her hands to the vessel atop her head, in an effort to keep it from falling. Her feet twisted and turned at strange, unnatural angles as she tried to stabilize herself, but her efforts were in vain. The woman's right shoulder slammed into the wall, just as her ankle gave way and snapped. Searing pain

13

shot through Anna's body like a fire bolt. The intensity was so great that she unintentionally screamed. The woman felt weak and thought she was about to pass out. Miraculously, though, she managed to keep the water jar upon her head. Anna transferred all her weight to her good ankle as her bruised shoulder and stone-scraped arm leaned against the cold damp wall for additional support.

The little girl was startled and frightened by the result of her frivolous behavior. She began to sob while saying, "Oh, Momma!" over and over again as tears streamed down her cheeks. Her mother thought it sounded like some strange litany. Just then they both heard a voice calling out. The voice tried to stay baritone but drifted to tenor.

"Hello! Is everything all right down there?"

While Anna bit her lower lip to try to control the pain, the little girl shouted back, "Please come down here. My mommy's hurt! Don't jump, though; just take one step at a time." Had Anna not been in such agony, she would have burst out with one of her hearty, contagious laughs over her daughter's cautious instructions. Before the little girl's voice could become an echo, they heard the sound of bare feet hitting the stone stairs. They looked up and saw the strong legs of an adolescent boy coming down toward them, and then finally, he came into full view.

The boy was tall for his age. He already was about three inches taller than Anna. The youth was thin but muscular. His thick curly black hair strained to release itself from under his tight-fitting cotton cap. He had dark, piercing eyes that were a perfect match to his olive complexion. When the boy saw

Anna and her daughter, he asked, "What happened? I heard someone scream. Is there anything I can do?"

"Everything's all right," the woman replied, as her daughter began to cover her eyes and sob. "As you can see, my daughter is a little emotional. I lost my balance and fell into the wall. I just twisted my ankle and bruised my shoulder a bit, that's all. I think I'll be fine," she said as she pushed against the wall in an attempt to stand erect.

Anna tried to put a little pressure on her injured foot, but as she did the searing pain returned with a vengeance and a deep moan escaped from her lips. "I guess I was wrong. I spoke too soon; I may need your help after all."

"Here, Ma'am," he said as he reached for the jar. "Let me take that from you, and help you to the stairs, so you can at least sit." The boy placed the vessel by the mouth of the well, then went back to Anna. He offered her his arm. "Here, lean on me, Ma'am." Anna grabbed hold and they slowly moved toward the staircase. "Don't you worry now. After we get you settled on the stairs, I'll fill the water jar and carry it home for you."

"That would be wonderful," Anna replied. When they reached the stairs, he gently grabbed Anna's forearms and helped her lower herself to the step. His strong biceps bulged from her weight. "You just be careful so you don't hurt yourself. I'm not a feather," she said jovially. "And I don't want to have your broken back on my conscience." The boy chuckled.

When the woman was settled, the boy turned his attention to the sobbing child. He knelt before her and said, "You don't have to cry anymore!" Her deep sobbing stopped, but she still continued to rub her eyes with her hands. "Your mother is going to be all right." He took the end of the sash that he wore around his short tunic and said, "Here, dry your eyes with this. It's clean. I just put it on this morning."

The girl took it and wiped her eyes and her tear-stained face. When she finished, she let go of the sash and said, "Thank you." Then she looked at the boy. The instant he saw her eyes, they mesmerized him. They were almond-shaped and heavily lashed. He was totally enthralled by their dark golden, honey-like color. He had never before seen eyes so captivating.

His trance was broken when he heard Anna say, "I can't thank you enough for what you're doing for me. The One Who Always Sees will surely bless you for your kindness."

"And may He bless you as well, and your little daughter too," the boy said as he left the girl and moved closer to the mouth of the well.

Anna motioned to her daughter to join her by the stairs. She whispered in the girl's ear, "Such a fine boy, such a fine boy!" The woman tried to move her injured foot slightly and grimaced in pain.

Her daughter saw her expression and said, "I'm sorry, Momma, I'm so sorry."

"Pshaw! Pshaw!" her mother said. "Next time, listen to what I say, dear, then you won't have to be sorry. I don't want what happened to me to happen to you." Even though the woman's words were a reprimand, the boy could hear gentleness and love in her voice. He wished that he had a mother to care for him the way Anna cared for her daughter.

The boy took the wooden well-bucket, knelt, and began to draw water from the well and fill the large water jar. "You're Jacob's son, aren't you?" the woman asked.

"Yes, I am, Ma'am."

"Do you know your father made that bucket you're using over ten years ago?"

"No, Ma'am, I didn't. I've never been down here before; we always use the upper well that's closer to our house."

"Your father was such a talented carpenter," Anna said as she shook her head from side to side. "It's too bad, too, too bad. Your father was such a good man." The boy understood; that was what everyone said. "You're a blessing to his name and you're growing up to be just like him, so thoughtful and considerate."

"Thank you, Ma'am. That's what my uncle tells me," he said as he blushed and continued, "This Sabbath I'll read from the Sacred Scroll."

"And you will be a man to all of Israel and a true son of the promise," Anna interrupted.

"That's right, I turned thirteen this week," he replied as his face beamed.

"Well, congratulations!" Anna said, and then gently nudged her daughter until she did the same.

The boy finished filling the jar and then started to lift it. The woman watched him as his muscles strained from the heavy load. "Whew, this is heavier than I thought," he said. "I don't know why they say this is women's work."

"That's why we wear veils—because if we didn't, everyone would see our flat heads," Anna jokingly replied. They all laughed. "We better get going," she said. "I don't want to detain you any longer; I've been enough of a burden to you already."

"It's been no burden, Ma'am. Here, let me help you up."

"You have enough to handle with the jar. My daughter can help me, and together, I think we can manage." Anna looked down at her daughter and said, "You, my little darling, will have to help me up these steps. You're my crutch until this ankle heals."

Anna placed one hand on the wall and began to lift herself up while she gently placed her other hand on her daughter's shoulder for additional support. She led off with her good foot, centering all her weight on it. Just standing up caused immense pain even though her injured foot hadn't yet touched the ground. She gasped as the pain coursed through the rest of her body. "This is going to be some procession," she said jovially. As she turned to face the stairs, the boy laughed at her comment and her daughter giggled.

The girl moved closer to her mother as the boy said, "You and your daughter go first, Ma'am. I'll follow, just in case you have any problems."

As they started their ascent, Anna said to her daughter, "No more jumping, Princess, do you understand me?"

A sheepish look came over the little girl's face as she answered, "Yes, Momma, I know, and I'm sorry for before."

"Let's forget about before; now just move along and be careful. These stairs are very narrow and there's no wall on your side." Anna tried to support most of her weight by leaning on the wall rather than on her petite daughter's shoulder. But the pain was almost unbearable. Her whole leg throbbed as she felt a strong pulse in her ankle. The pounding beat was so powerful that it echoed in her head like a bass drum. An uncontrollable deep gasp escaped from her lips as her injured foot touched each stair.

When her daughter heard it, she said, "Oh, Momma!" That was followed by the clanking of the water jar as the boy moved it from stair to stair. Even in her pain, Anna found humor in the repetitious sounds. The litany of "uh," "Oh, Momma" and *clank* was repeated with every step they took and caused her to smile despite her discomfort.

As they neared the middle of the flight of stairs the boy asked Anna how she was doing. "I'm doing fine," Anna replied, "but I think you would be doing better if you carried the jar on your head. It would be less of a struggle for you."

"Not on these stairs, Ma'am; I've never carried one of these things before. Maybe when I get to the top I'll try it, but not down here. I think it would be a little too risky, and I wouldn't want to drop your jar."

When they reached the street, the boy squatted and raised the heavy vessel to his head. Using his strong leg muscles, he began to rise as he stabilized the jar with his hands. His head swayed back and forth and side-to-side as he tried to find the right balance for the movement of the water in the vessel. As he walked, some of it sloshed over the jar's rim, drenching him. He attempted to maintain his stride while he snorted to free the water from his nose. The little girl snickered at the sight.

Anna for the first time was somewhat grateful for the pain; otherwise, she would have laughed too. She didn't want to embarrass the boy. The youth kind of chuckled and said, "I'll get this yet, I will!" as his head continued to sway. He walked at a snail's pace, so Anna and her daughter were soon able to pass him despite the woman's infirmity.

Night's slumber had ended as the sleepy town began to come to life. Little children were perched on their doorsteps, rubbing the sleep from their eyes as their parents prepared for the day ahead. The boy asked Anna, "How do you ever get used to this? It feels like my head is going to sink right through my neck into my chest."

"Practice, practice and more practice," she replied. "Next week you could be running up and down the well steps without even holding onto the jar."

"Not me, Ma'am," he answered emphatically. "I won't be around here long enough to learn this fine art. Anna asked him why not. "After this Sabbath, I'll be leaving town for about five years of apprenticeship with my Uncle Achim. He's a carpenter, like my father was."

"You're going all the way to Banias?" she asked.

"Yes, Ma'am, I'll leave with a caravan on Sunday morning, but after I learn the trade, I'll come back here and reopen my father's shop. My Uncle Eleazer said that I could learn a lot there, and there's plenty of wood so I can make a lot of mistakes." They all laughed. "Anyway, my aunt and uncle—well, really my aunt—she wants to move away from here. She always wanted to live in the Holy City. So if I didn't go to Uncle Achim's, I'd have to live here by myself, and they don't think that would be a good idea." Anna inquired as to when they would be leaving. The boy replied that his uncle planned to put the property up for sale as soon as he left Sunday. Anna expressed her regret at hearing the news and told the boy how she and her family would miss not only him and his family, but also his uncle's excellent cheeses. The boy graciously accepted the compliment and said that he'd pass on her remarks to his uncle.

They continued on their way and came upon a group of adolescent boys who were tossing pebbles into a ring they'd dug into the earth. The leader of the group, who had just turned thirteen, was using a slingshot to do the same. When they saw the boy carrying the water jar, they began to mock him. Males of any age never went to the well in this town; it was considered woman's work. They whistled and shouted taunts at him.

One of them called out to the boy, "Hey, pretty lady, I'm thirsty! How about some water here?"

Another mimicked the boy by raising his hands to his head and swishing his hips as he walked while asking, "Which one of us is prettier?" The boy ignored them, but not Anna. She was furious. The girl looked up at her mother. Her face was turning a bright red as her brow furrowed. She had never seen her mother this angry before.

The woman lifted her hand from her daughter's shoulder and began to point and shake her finger at the boys. With a voice more stern than her daughter had ever heard before, she began to chastise the group. "Go home, you brats. Go do something useful! I know your mothers, and when I tell them what you're doing, they'll take a switch to you. You won't be able to sit for at least a week."

Joshua, the group leader, sassed her back by saying, "Listen, lady, men aren't supposed to carry water jars! That's women's work."

Anna's voice got louder as she said, "He's more of a man right now than you, Joshua, or any of your friends here will ever be. The Almighty blesses those who show compassion on people in need. You should all be ashamed of yourselves. He's an example that all of you should follow. Now go home, all of you!" The boys fell silent and returned to their game, all except for Joshua, the ringleader. He continued to stare at Anna with malice in his eyes.

"You can't tell us what to do. You're not our mother! Why should we listen to you?"

Anna could feel herself shaking as she said, "Keep sassing me, Joshua, and I'll take a stick to you myself!"

The helpful boy convinced the woman that they should leave. The little girl agreed. The children's wise advice prevailed over the woman's raging emotions. So Anna turned from Joshua and started to walk away. As the woman put her hand back on her daughter's shoulder, the child could still feel her mother trembling with rage. "Those boys are nothing but trouble. They'll never amount to much or ever get anywhere in this world, especially that Joshua." The girl had an eerie feeling that the ringleader was still staring at them, so she turned her head to look. She saw the boy stick his tongue out, put his thumbs in his ears and wiggle his fingers at them. The child quickly turned her head and looked forward. She didn't dare tell her mother what he was now doing.

The tension Anna was feeling caused the pain in her ankle to flair up once again. She tried to calm herself down by talking to the boy. So she asked him what had brought him out so early. He replied that his uncle had lent his donkey to a fellow townsman to help him clear some land, and the boy was going to retrieve the animal. As they neared Anna's house, the westerly breeze turned into a stiff wind and the sky blackened. The woman was concerned that she was delaying him. He would have to return home in the rain since a storm was brewing. The boy assured her it wasn't a problem. He enjoyed walking in the rain. The little girl chimed in and said that she loved the rain too, especially when she could twirl around in it.

"Just don't start twirling around until we get home," Anna said. The boy snickered at the remark. When the little girl heard him, she was embarrassed. Her face turned the color of a ripe pomegranate. She said nothing for the remainder of the trip.

They finally reached the courtyard of Anna's home. It was a rectangular shape formed by Anna's house on one side and her brother-in-law's on the other. Her husband's leather-smith shop and their stable completed the bottom of the U. They passed under the branches of the old twisted olive tree that grew in the center of the yard. The woman pointed to a grassy surface close to the tree trunk and told the boy to leave the water jar there. Her husband would carry it inside later. She also asked the boy to stop by on his return trip home and pick up some extra goat curd that she had. Anna had more than she possibly could use. The boy thanked her on behalf of his uncle. He insisted that he be allowed to carry the water jar into the house for Anna. He was concerned the debris from the olive tree might fall into the water jar when the storm hit. He reassured her he'd be happy to do it.

"Oh, that's so nice of you," Anna said, "but I don't want to get you in any trouble with your uncle."

"When I tell him what happened, if I hadn't helped you, I'd be in far more trouble," he replied.

If only all the women in Israel could be blessed with a son like this, Anna thought. "By the way, Ma'am, I can make up for the lost time," the boy said. "I run pretty fast, and with a handful of feed in front of him, the donkey can run pretty fast too." The woman laughed as she visualized the scenario he just described. Her outburst was so hearty that she pressed her hand to her chest to try and control it. Her deep laugh was so contagious that the children joined in too.

Laughter almost caused Anna to forget about her injury, so she put a little too much weight on her injured foot as she took a step forward. She again cried out in pain, then said, "I think I better get inside now, before that storm does hit. You can go in first. Just set the jar by the winter oven." The boy agreed to do so as he walked to the doorway.

Before the teenage boy entered Anna's house, he first kissed the tips of the fingers on his right hand and touched them to the small wooden box attached to the doorframe. The box contained a small clay tablet on which the Ten Commandments had been inscribed. As he touched it, Anna could hear him whisper: "Hear, O Israel, the Lord Your God Is One!" By this time, Anna was so overwhelmed with admiration for the boy she kept thinking over and over again, *He's so pious and such a blessing, such a blessing.*

The boy was tall, and the added height of the water jar upon his head made it impossible for him to enter the house standing. He squatted, with his knees severely bent and his legs spread apart, as he waddled through the doorway. The little girl giggled because to her, he looked like a duck. The very moment they got inside, the sky exploded with blinding brilliance as lightning struck and the deafening thunder rumbled. It startled them as the house shook violently. Raindrops the size of pistachio nuts pummeled the roof and quickly turned the courtyard into a sea of ochre-colored mud. Suddenly, out of nowhere, a huge bat-like object blocked the little light that had been filtering in from the open doorway. The boy recoiled in fear and almost dropped the water jar he was lowering. The puzzled, frightened adolescent drew back further.

The center of the black thing in the doorway seemed to be splitting in two. A small wrinkled head with dim, watery eyes popped out of the opening and began to shout in a shrill voice, "What's happened, what's happened to you, Anna? What kind of mischief has this rascal been up to? What has he done to you?" The boy sighed deeply as his racing heart finally slowed down a bit. He realized that what he perceived to be a huge bat was only an old woman with a long black shawl draped over her head. Her arms were extended upward and out to her sides like huge wings.

Anna quickly answered, "I'm all right, Tamar. I just had a little accident. I seemed to have sprained my ankle. I don't know what I would have done without his help."

The old woman stared coldly at the boy as she lowered her wet shawl, shook the rain from it and said, "Are you sure? He looks guilty to me!"

"Of course I'm sure, Tamar. Would I lie to you? He's a fine young man. He's Jacob's son."

"A blessing on your head then," the cantankerous old woman said to the boy.

"Thank you! And shalom to you, Ma'am," the boy replied, as he turned to Anna and said anxiously, "I really should be going now."

"Why don't you at least wait until the rain lets up a bit," Anna pleaded. "You'll be as wet as a swamp rat before you even reach the street."

"I really can't, Ma'am," he said as he moved quickly toward the door. "As you said before, I'm running late already, but thanks for offering.

Shalom!" He bolted from the door and ran to the street before Anna could say anything else.

"Tamar, I think you frightened the boy," Anna said to her sister-in-law. "I didn't even get a chance to thank him properly."

"Pshaw!" The old woman said. "You'll see him around town. You can thank him then. He won't die because you didn't thank him properly. When I saw you limping and holding your chest, I thought you were having a heart attack or something. I couldn't see the boy in front of you, and from a distance it looked like the jar was on your head. Forgive me for worrying about you; forgive me already!"

"Tamar, I meant no insult by what I said. I appreciate your concern. You know that!"

"So, tell me what happened already." Anna quickly related the experience, omitting her daughter's complicity in it. She knew that even though Tamar and her husband Azor doted over the child more like grandparents than the aunt and uncle that they were, Tamar at times had a sharp tongue and could easily bring the child to tears.

Anna was still standing near the doorway, supporting herself by holding on to the wall. "So let's see that foot already," the old woman said as she boldly lifted up Anna's tunic above her knees and gazed down at her ankle. "Your ankle and foot are ten times the size they should be and they're turning black and blue. I think it's broken! Can you move it? Never mind, don't try," she continued. "We'll splint it." Anna knew her sister-in-law always tended to exaggerate, so she took what she said with a grain of salt. The confused girl just stood there listening to her aunt rattle on. "Is it painful?" Tamar asked.

"Almost unbearable. I can't seem to put any pressure on it!"

That was all the old woman needed to hear to take full charge. She began to bark orders. "Bring the straw mats and the goatskin blanket so your mother can sit down. Put them here by the door so your mother can get some fresh air. Hurry, hurry, your mother needs to lie down." The child didn't know where to turn first, so she grabbed the blanket and ran toward her aunt. "No, no! The mats first." She leaned forward and grabbed Anna by the elbows as she forced her to the ground almost before the little girl was able to slip the mats under her mother. Anna landed with a thump and gasped with pain as her ankle was jarred again. "Oh, you poor dear," the old woman said as she stooped and probed Anna's ankle with her index and middle fingers. "Go get me some thorn branches from the woodpile," she told the child as Tamar stood and went to get a knife and skein of yarn. The rain had stopped, and the sun began to peek through the clouds as the girl ran to the woodpile. She returned with an armful of branches. Tamar took them from her niece and deftly removed the thorns, then cut them to size.

With the skill of a weaver she wrapped the splints in yarn and bound them to Anna's ankle. "Just try not to move your foot now," she said as she grabbed her niece's hand. "Get some rest, Anna. We're going to pick some herbs for a fine poultice. Don't worry, I'll take care of the child and the meals. You just breathe in the fresh air, take deep breaths. Fresh air is the best medicine for healing." Tamar almost dragged the little girl out the door as the child looked back at her mother with bewilderment. It was as if she was pleading with her mother to explain what was going on. Everything was happening so fast since her aunt had taken over that she was confused. Anna shook her head in a laissez-faire attitude and gave her daughter a comforting smile. When the old woman and her niece reached the street, Tamar said commandingly, "Hurry, hurry, we have to get that poultice made so your mother's swelling will go down."

The child was swept by a whirlwind of emotions as she asked, "Will Mommy die?"

"No, silly, not for a long time, I pray. She'll be laid up for awhile, that's all. The sooner we get that poultice, the sooner your mommy will get better." Although Tamar was 72 years old, she moved with the speed and agility of a young mountain goat.

CHAPTER 2

Their small town was nestled on a hillside. The storm clouds had rolled away and now were barely visible on the far eastern horizon. It would be about two hours before the hot sun reached its zenith in the hazy blue sky above. A fresh aroma from the cleansing rain perfumed the spring air as Tamar and her niece made their way down the hillside in search of healing plants. When they reached the vegetation, the delicate scent of early spring wildflowers wafted on the slight breeze as tiny sparrows fluttered about. The aroma was intoxicating. "Don't let go of my hand, Princess," Tamar said. "The hill is steep, and the ground is still wet and very slippery. You can easily lose your footing."

"May I pick some flowers for my mommy?"

"Only if you're careful and watch out for the bees. Don't let go of my hand, though." The old woman moved quickly along the steep hillside with her back bent and her head lowered, looking for the plants that she needed. As the child was dragged along, she tried to pick some flower stems with her free hand, but because the moisture-laden soil was shallow, she harvested the whole plant, roots and all. Tamar continued her search, undaunted in her quest for her precious healing herbs.

The girl walked beside her, as the dirt covered roots from the flower stems rubbed against her white tunic. "Are all the stories that Uncle Azor tells us true?" the little girl asked. (Her uncle was a raconteur and often entertained them with his anecdotes.)

"Of course they are; why do you ask?" The girl wondered how her uncle knew about the men with the funny red hats and white coats with tails that twirled around for a long time. Tamar told her niece that when he and her father went to market their goods in David's city, they met caravans from all over the world that come and trade there. They exchanged stories when they did.

"I wish my daddy would take me where they live so I could see how long they can twirl," the girl said. "I like twirling around in circles with my eyes closed, too." Then when I stop and open my eyes, everything still spins around me. If I twirled for a whole day, how long would it take for the spinning to stop?"

"If you twirled for a whole day," Tamar replied, "the brain in your head would turn upside down and then you'd start seeing things that weren't there and start hearing things. Oh, and you'd probably start talking backwards too."

"Then I'll just twirl a little bit every day."

"Better that you don't twirl at all; you could fall down and hurt yourself like your mother did." They were having this conversation while Tamar was still bent down, facing the ground as the child walked beside her. The old woman finally finished collecting herbs. When she straightened up and turned toward her niece, she noticed the stains on the tunic. "Look at all that mud on your clothing. I thought you wanted to bring your mother some flowers, not the whole hillside. How am I ever going to get that clean?" Tamar took the flowers and skillfully severed the roots from the stems in one successful wrench. "I don't know if I'll ever be able to get your clothes white again; your mother's not going to be happy, child." Tamar kept shaking her head, mumbling something unintelligible under her breath as they walked back to town. The late-morning sun beat down on them as the temperature kept rising. It was turning into a steamy hot day, but the old veiled woman still took long, quick strides and never even broke a sweat.

As they climbed the road to the town gate, the girl asked the woman, "Aunt Tamar, how does the sun know when to come up and when to go down?" Her aunt had never pondered the natural occurrence before.

The woman thought for a moment, then said, "I think the Holy One must have His angels set it in the sky in the morning and then tuck it into bed at night."

"Then how does it move across the sky?"

"Maybe His angels roll it across the heavens," her aunt replied.

"Well, why don't we see them doing that then?"

"Perhaps it's because the sun's so bright that we can't look at it long enough to see them," Tamar said.

The child thought for a moment, then commented, "But it's not so bright just before it falls behind the mountains, when the sun turns orange and the sky's all pink. You can look at it then! Have you ever seen an angel, Auntie Tamar?"

"No, I haven't, dear, but maybe the angels fly ahead of the sun before it starts to lose its brightness, and by then it's so low in the sky that it just falls right into bed by itself."

The girl pondered her aunt's answer. "If the sun goes to sleep there," the girl said, pointing to the western ridge of hills, "and comes up over there," she continued, pointing toward the eastern plains, "how does it get to the other side?"

"So many questions, so many questions all the time. Girls don't have to know about such things. Questions like that are for men and rabbis to figure out, not women."

"Why not?" the girl asked.

"See! There you go again!" Tamar said. "It's just because, child, that's why. Just because that's the way it is." Tamar at this point was more perplexed by her own lack of inquisitiveness than she was by the child's questions.

"Just one more question, Auntie, if you don't mind. Did anyone ever see an angel?"

"I don't know, Princess, but there's this pool called Bethesda in the City of David, where the God of Israel sends His angel to stir the waters. They say that the first sick or lame person who jumps into the pool when the waters are moved is healed. I don't think you can see the angel, but your uncle told me that he himself once saw the ripples on the water."

"I wonder what angels look like," the child said.

"Maybe they look like us. That's why we don't recognize them when they're around." The old woman was pleased with her witty answer.

Tamar and her niece reached the courtyard of their homes. As the woman was about to enter her house, she said, "Take the jug that's by the rain barrel and fill it with water for me, Princess, while I sort through these plants. Then go and check on your mother while I prepare the poultice. You be sure to change that dirty tunic, too, so I can launder it. If your mother is sleeping, don't bother her. Just let her rest."

The girl did as she was told and fetched the water. She then picked up the little bouquet she had left by the door and began to skip across the courtyard to her house. As she did, she saw the boy who had helped her mother earlier that morning. She giggled because he looked so silly. He ran with his arm extended behind him while he held a handful of hay. The donkey trotted close behind, never quite able to reach the fodder that the boy held just out of reach. The girl's giggling turned to full-blown laughter, for when he brought his arm forward, the donkey stopped dead in its tracks and immediately sat, right in the street.

The boy came toward the girl while she was still giggling and said, "He's pretty smart for a donkey, don't you think?" The girl nodded in agreement as he continued, "I almost forgot that your mother asked me to stop by on my way home to pick up some goat curd. By the way, how is your mother doing?"

"I think she's sleeping. I went with my aunt to pick some flowers to make my mom feel better," the girl said. She shoved the flowers toward the boy and said, "I picked them myself, and I have a lot of them; would you like some?"

"No thanks," he said. "My donkey would only try to eat them." Anna, who was sitting so close to the door that she could overhear their conversation, grinned from ear to ear.

The little girl ran past the boy and entered the house first. She threw her arms around her mother and planted a kiss on her cheek. Anna warned her daughter to watch out for her injured foot. The child handed her mother the bouquet and said, "These are for you, Mommy. I picked them myself."

Her mother looked at her daughter's stained tunic and said, "Oh, really, Princess? I would never have guessed! Thank you, dear." She took the flowers as the boy knocked on the doorframe. "Come in!" Anna said. Before he entered, the boy once again paid proper reverence to the Law that was mounted on the doorframe. *This boy really knows what respect is,* Anna thought. She was growing fonder of him with each passing moment. When he entered the house, the boy inquired as to the condition of Anna's ankle and asked if she was feeling any better. "Not quite yet," she replied, "but my sister-in-law is making a poultice that should help take down the swelling."

"Maybe I shouldn't be bothering you then, Ma'am."

"Nonsense!" she replied. "My daughter can get the curds for you. Dear, please get the curds and also get a horsehair bag from the cupboard." The little girl went over to the ground silo that was dug into the floor and slid the wood cover from the opening. She reached down into the pit and struggled to raise the clay vessel.

The boy immediately said, "Here, let me help you with that." He moved toward the silo and knelt down beside her. He grabbed the vessel by its mouth and hauled it up to floor level.

The girl lifted the lid from the clay jar and said, "Phew, that really stinks bad."

"If you think this is bad," the boy replied, "you should smell the place where my uncle makes and ages his cheeses." Anna and her daughter chuckled. "I'll take this outside, Ma'am, and separate the curds from the whey out there. That way the smell won't stay in the house here."

"That would be wonderful," the woman said as her daughter found the horsehair bag that her mother had requested. "Go outside with the young man. That way you can hold the bag for him while he fills it." The boy beamed with pride because Anna had referred to him as a man.

The girl followed the boy into the courtyard, carrying the horsehair bag. He found a spot of bare earth beneath the olive tree, tipped the jar and placed his hand over its mouth to hold back the curds while he poured the whey into the ground. "That even stinks worse out here than it did in the house," the little girl said. "Your hand is going to smell really, really bad." He chuckled as the little girl curled up her nose in revulsion.

"I'm used to this. I have to do it all the time. Watch this!" He pulled a handful of grass blades from a nearby tuft and vigorously rubbed them between his hands until they stained his fingers and palms a bright green. He extended the open hand he had used as a strainer until it almost touched the tip of the girl's nose. "Now smell this," he said as she hesitantly took a sniff then beamed with a smile.

The chlorophyll residue had magically changed the horrid smell of spoiled milk into the sweet smell of newly sheared grass. A look of amazement appeared on her face as her captivating eyes grew even wider with delight. Their beauty again intrigued the boy. Reluctantly, he looked away and took the clay vessel to the rain barrel. After he ladled a sufficient amount of water into the empty jar, he sloshed it around a bit, then returned to where the girl was still standing and poured the water over the spilt whey. "You won't get too many flies if we wash this into the ground," he said. Needless to say, the little girl was very impressed with him and everything he had shown her so far.

The boy carried the empty jar into the house as the little girl followed close behind. As he entered the doorway, Anna said, "I hope I haven't gotten you into any trouble by delaying you so long."

"Don't worry, Ma'am," the boy replied. "I'm sure my uncle will understand. I think I should be getting back though, now."

"You're a fine young man, and a true son of Father Abraham. Congratulations on your bar mitzvah tomorrow."

The boy again beamed with pride. "Thank you, Ma'am, and may the God of our fathers, Abraham, Isaac and Jacob, send His blessings on you and your home, and may He make your ankle and foot well again. Shalom!" He then turned and left.

Anna sat there nodding her head in approval, as she said, "Shalom to you also! Young man." She whispered under her breath the same phrase she had been using all day: "Such a fine boy, such a pious, good boy." She turned to her daughter and said, "There goes a true Son of David and a real pride of his people Israel."

"He's a really, really nice boy," the girl said. "A really nice boy." Anna smiled as she thought to herself, *My daughter is beginning to sound just like me.* As soon as they completed their verbal exchange, the girl went outside and watched the boy leave. He went to his donkey and tied the bag of curds to the leather blanket that was draped over and tethered to the animal. He walked back to the corner of her house and picked up the handful of hay he had previously left there. The little girl started to giggle again as the boy stepped in front of the donkey with the handful of feed stretched out in back of him and started to run. In a split second the animal stood up and began to chase after him.

CHAPTER 3

After the boy left, the girl returned to the house. Anna asked her daughter to place the flowers in some water and then go change her soiled tunic. She told the child that she would launder it as soon as her foot felt better.

"But Mommy," the child said, "Aunt Tamar said that I should bring it to her and she would wash it."

"All right, do as she says, but fold it neatly anyway."

The girl changed quickly, folded the garment and returned to her mother with her arms outstretched and the neatly folded garment lying on the upturned palms of her hands. "Should I take it to Aunt Tamar now?" she asked.

"Go ahead," her mother said. "And be sure to ask Aunt Tamar if you can be of help to her; she's out in the courtyard right now."

The little girl planted another kiss on her mother's cheek and asked, "Will you be all right, Momma?"

"I'll be fine," Anna replied. "Now go, go ahead, child, help Aunt Tamar if you can." When she left the house, the girl carried the soiled tunic on outstretched arms as if it was something precious that she was about to present to her aunt.

Tamar knelt by the outdoor fire-pit, striking a piece of flint that she held in her gnarled fingers. The heat of the day had become so intense that she removed her outer cloak. Except for her sagging bosom and deep wrinkles, the old woman still had not lost the curvaceous figure of her youth. With her narrow waist and full, graceful hips, from a distance she could pass for a young maiden. Although her once-beautiful face was now wrinkled and dried out by the elements and the passage of time, age had not diminished her stamina. She looked up and saw her niece coming toward her and said, "Oh, is it Chanukah already? How nice of you to bring me a gift!"

The child looked at her quizzically as she answered, "No, Auntie, it's just Thursday, and this is my dirty tunic that Mommy told me to fold nicely. You told me to bring it to you, that's all."

"I know, Princess, I was just teasing you a bit. Just take it inside and put it in my wash hamper. You know where it is! I need to get this fire started. Otherwise there'll be no poultice for your mother's ankle and no dinner for us tonight. So just drop that off inside and come back here. I'll need you to go to the animal's pen and get me some dry straw. This one is a little too damp for a spark to catch." The little girl did as she was told and returned with a handful of clean, dry straw. She handed it to her aunt. The woman took it and placed it on top of the damp material. "Thank you! You're a real angel."

"I can't be, Auntie," she said. She turned her back to the woman. "See, I have no wings."

"I didn't mean that you are a real angel. That's just an expression people sometimes use when someone does something nice for you, silly."

"Oh, you mean it's like when people say 'clumsy as an ox,' they know that the person doesn't look like an ox, or smell like one, they just don't watch where they're going or they drop and break things, right?" the girl said.

"That's right," Tamar replied, as she bent even lower and struck the flint again. This time a white-hot spark landed on the dry straw and it began to smolder. The woman gently blew on the pile of tinder until a flame was born, and the fire moved rapidly through it until it began to consume even the damp straw well beneath the flame. The gray smoke that it produced drifted toward Tamar. She began to fan it away from her face with her hand, as her eyes stung and began to tear. "Would you please be a dear and get me several bundles of thorn branches from the kindling pile?" the woman asked.

The girl skipped to the woodpile then returned with her arms full of dry branches. She handed them to her aunt and said, "I don't like these things. They scratch and pinch too much."

"I don't like to handle them either," her aunt replied, "but we have no choice. Wood is too scarce around here to burn, and thorn branches aren't good for anything else, except for the thorns themselves; we use them for needles sometime. They're so sharp they can almost penetrate anything."

Tamar tented the dry branches around the flames, then sat cross-legged next to the fire pit and continued to feed it more fuel until she could see waves of heat rippling in the hot, humid air. She reached up and swung the iron arm that held the pot she had previously filled with water and various plants over the now-roaring fire. As she brushed her hands together to remove the soot, she looked up and noticed how antsy her niece was. "Now why is our Princess so restless today that she can't even keep her legs still?"

"I miss going to Synagogue school," the girl replied. Though classes only lasted three hours a day, six days a week, she had the opportunity to play with other girls her age after school until about the time of the midday meal. Furthermore, she loved to learn.

"What's your favorite subject?" her aunt asked.

"I really like reading and writing and learning about God's Law. But you know what, Auntie? There are so many laws, I don't know how people remember them all. I guess I like the stories the best. You know, the ones about Father Abraham, Moses, King David and King Solomon. Oh, but my most favorite of all are the stories about Deborah, the Judge of Israel, and also the stories of Ruth and Queen Esther. Uh-huh, those are my favorite ones!"

"Well, the rabbi should return today, so you'll be back in school the day after the Sabbath."

"Where did he go?" the little girl asked.

"To the Holy City, where the holy name of the Unseen God dwells. You know, to Jerusalem, the City of David."

"Aunt Tamar, if nobody ever sees God, how do they know He lives there?"

"Because He told Moses that His Holy Presence would always be with us and that the glory of His name would always dwell behind a very heavy curtain in a special part of a very dark room," Tamar said. "A long time ago the Ark of the Covenant was in that room with Him, but now the Ark is gone and God alone is in there. We call that room the Holy of Holies or the Most Holy Place. At first that room was in a special tent called the Tabernacle, but now that special room is in the Temple."

"Auntie, what do you think are in His holy presents?"

Tamar smiled at the girl. "No, no, not 'presents' like gifts; it's 'presence,' like in being there, child. Like, uh, right now you're here with me, so you're in my presence. Do you understand?" The girl nodded affirmatively. "Anyway, the priests can go into a part of the room to offer incense, that part is called the Holy Place, but only the High Priest can go behind the heavy curtain into the Most Holy Place, and only once a year, on the Day of Atonement. He can only enter that sacred place with the blood of the sacrificial animal in his hand. He mustn't look up because he might see the glory of the Lord."

"What would happen if he *did* see it, Aunt Tamar?"

The old woman stammered before answering. "Uh, well, uh—his brain, or, well, his eyes—well, I think his head would blow up or something like that. All I know is that he couldn't see God and still live."

"Doesn't God get lonely in that room all by Himself, all the time, Auntie?"

"How would I know, child? He's never told me, but then I guess I've never asked. I talk to the Holy One all the time, but so far He hasn't talked back to me yet."

"Then how do you know He's listening, Auntie?"

"Because, child, I know; I just know," the old woman said. "Even if everyone in the whole world talked to Him at the same time, He'd still hear me."

"I wouldn't want to live in a dark room all by myself, even if I was able to hear everybody talking to me at once. Would you, Aunt Tamar?"

"No, I guess I wouldn't, Princess!" Tamar slapped her thighs with both hands. It was her way of signaling that the conversation was over and it was time to get back to work. She arose and said, "Enough questions for now. More work and less talk." When the girl stood up, her aunt put her wrinkled hands on the child's shoulders and followed the girl to the doorway of her home.

They entered the house and both sat cross-legged on the straw mats that were around the low granite table. While her niece had been with her mother, Tamar chose the root vegetables she planned to use for her stew. She handed them to the girl and asked her to wash them. The child placed the vegetables in a clay bowl filled with fresh water and scrubbed them thoroughly with a stiff reed brush. The vegetables had been harvested last fall and were now reaching the end of their usefulness. "Make sure you get all the mold off of them," Tamar said. "What you can't get off, I'll have to cut away, so scrub very hard; otherwise, it's going to be more of a soup than a good hearty stew." As she finished scrubbing each one, she handed it to her aunt, who then chopped it and placed it in a fire-blackened cauldron. The child was hungry, so her stomach growled. Her aunt heard it and said, "Is that a mountain lion I hear?"

"No, Auntie, that's just my stomach. I think it just needs a little food, that's all."

"We'll be eating as soon as I get this stew on. It's been such a crazy morning that I don't know what to do first. If I don't get this over the fire right now, the men's stomachs will growl louder than a whole pride of lions." The child's scrubbing was a little slower than her aunt's chopping, so Tamar decided to break away and start the preparations for the midday meal. As she stood up to gather the things she needed, she said, "These old bones don't want to move as fast as they once used to."

"I don't think you're that old, Aunt Tamar; when you walk, you take such big steps that I almost have to run to keep up with you. No! You're not too old." And with childhood innocence she continued, "Maybe a little wrinkled, but not too old yet."

Tamar laughed heartily. "I think you meant that as a compliment, dear, so I'll take it that way. Wrinkles are God's way of telling us that He's keeping us alive a lot longer than He originally intended to do, so in some way they're a blessing, I guess!"

Once the woman had straightened up, she moved like a flash of lightning. Her hands flew as she cut wedges of cheese, poured honey from a pot into a clay bowl and tossed a salad of dandelion greens. Tamar then stacked into a wicker hamper six pieces of flatbread she'd made earlier and carefully added all the other items she had just prepared. She came back to the table with a large clay canister of raisins and said, "When you finish the scrubbing, you can make us some raisin cakes while I finish off the stew."

47

Tamar sat down and started chopping vegetables again. The girl asked, "Why do vegetables get moldy, Auntie?"

"I guess it's because nothing that has life within it lasts forever," her aunt replied. "That's just part of God's plan."

"Rabbi said that's because of Adam and Eve. If Eve didn't pick the fruit, and if Adam didn't eat it, everyone would have lived forever. Is that true, Aunt Tamar?"

"If Rabbi Asa says that, then it's true. But I'll tell you what I think—if Adam or Eve hadn't picked that fruit, I'm sure one of their kids would have done it and we'd be in the same predicament. Ah! But when Messiah comes, things will be different, child. We, God's chosen people, will never have to die. No! No! And when Messiah will reestablish the kingdom of David, his father, even our people who are dead will rise from the grave."

"I don't think I'd like that," the little girl said. "That sounds pretty scary to me."

"No, it won't be scary at all," Tamar replied. "Everybody will look just like they did when they were alive, except there will be no deformities in them and no one will ever be sick again. The walls of the Holy City will reach out to include our town and almost the whole world too. The Gentiles, they probably won't be able to live in the Holy City, but they'll be able to come to the Temple and worship our God." Tamar prided herself on the fact that she had remembered the stories her father had often told her. They really seemed to impress her niece. The little girl listened to them as she sat with her jaw dropped and her mouth wide open.

All that her little niece could say when Tamar finished was, "Wow!" The child was silent for a few moments, then said, "That boy's aunt and uncle shouldn't move, then, neither should the boy."

"Whose aunt and uncle, and what boy?" Tamar asked.

"The boy who helped Mommy today and his aunt and uncle," the girl answered.

"You mean Jacob's son?"

"Yes, Auntie, he's the one."

"Where are they moving to?"

"I didn't hear where he's going. It's some place with a lot of trees. He said his aunt and uncle are moving to the Holy City, but if Messiah is going to move the city walls, why are they going anywhere? They'll all be in Jerusalem anyway."

"Hmm! I wonder why your mommy didn't tell me?" was the only response the girl received. Shortly thereafter, the girl continued with a myriad of other questions until she finally finished scrubbing the vegetables. When she handed her aunt the last of them, the woman said, "Now you can make the raisin cakes, and no more questions for awhile. I'm getting a headache already from thinking up all the answers." She pushed the canister of raisins toward her niece.

The child took a handful of the dried fruit and formed them into a circular pile, then flattened them into a cake-like shape about the height of a sparrow's egg. "I really like making raisin cakes," the girl said. "They're more fun than making mud pies, and they taste better too."

"They sure do," her aunt said. "Now make three for each of us."

"That makes nine, right, Aunt Tamar?"

The woman had to count on her fingers before she answered. "That's right, child, nine it is." Her niece's intelligence intimidated her at times. Tamar had now placed all the ingredients she needed for her stew in the cauldron; she just had to add the water. "Why don't you take the hamper over to your house now? As soon as I put the stew on the fire and finish making the poultice, I'll join you. Carry it level, though, and no skipping or twirling, or else everything will spill out or get jumbled together. You've been such a help to me today. So before you leave, take a couple of figs from the jar and you can have them for dessert." The girl did as she was told and then left the house with their midday meal, while her aunt carried the cauldron out to the fire pit.

When the girl entered her home, she saw that her mother was sleeping. Anna was still sitting with her head tilted to one side, resting against the wall. The woman's mouth was slightly opened, and a faint snore gave her daughter the assurance she needed to know that her mother still was fine. The child tiptoed into the room, being extremely careful not to disturb her mother or cause her to move her ankle and have more pain. She placed the hamper on the floor next to Anna and opened the wicker lid. The girl was pleased with herself, seeing that nothing had spilled in transit. She busied herself by fetching three reed mats and setting them around her mother—one for her, another for her aunt, and one in the middle for the food. They would eat right where her mother sat; there was no need to try to have her mother move to the table, she reasoned. As the girl began to remove the food from the hamper, her mother awoke with a jump. "Princess, you startled me! I didn't expect to see anyone when I opened my eyes."

"Are you all right, Mommy?" her daughter asked. Her mother reassured her that she was fine and asked her if she was off help to her aunt. "Yes, Mommy, I was. Aunt Tamar is finishing the poultice. She should be here real soon."

Just as Anna finished speaking, Tamar entered with her dripping-wet poultice. "Is my patient doing any better?" she asked her sister-in-law.

"It doesn't throb as much as it did before, and I napped a bit; that seems to have helped," Anna replied.

Tamar knelt down by the younger woman's foot and took a close look at the injury. "It doesn't look any better to me. As a matter of fact, it looks a lot worse." She gently moved the edge of the splint she had previously made, and Anna gasped. "Oh, it hurts that much. I'm so sorry, dear. I'll try not to move your foot at all while I apply this." Tamar attached the odiferous wet poultice to her sister-in-law's ankle and foot. Anna bit her lip to redirect her pain so she wouldn't cry out, while Tamar tied it to her foot and ankle with bands of cloth.

Tamar finished her act of mercy and went outside to wash her hands. When she re-entered the house she said, "Let's give thanks so we can eat; I think we're all famished. You just sit there, Anna; the Holy One doesn't expect you to stand." Anna lifted her hands up to the Lord as Tamar and the child stood. They turned to face the Holy City, and lifted up their hands as well. The old woman prayed the prayer her father taught her many, many years ago: "Blessed are You, O Eternal our God, King of the Universe, who is always worthy of our praise and thanksgiving. We thank You for this food that You have provided by Your goodness. Hasten, O Lord, the days of Messiah and free Jacob's house from foreign rule forever. Reestablish David's kingdom as You promised of old. We praise You and give You glory." All responded, "Halleluiah!" Tamar then said, "All right! Let's eat!"

When they finished their meal, and as the little girl munched on her dessert of figs, Tamar said, "Your daughter was such a blessing to me today, such a blessing. That's why I gave her a special dessert. She really worked hard for it."

"I'm glad to hear that," Anna replied. The girl looked down at the ground as she continued to munch away. As she did, Tamar would look at the child then nod her head toward the door. She did this about three times before Anna realized that it was a signal.

"Princess, did you feed the animals and milk the goats today?"

"No, Momma I didn't. I forgot."

"Well, why don't you go and feed them now and milk them as well. We don't want the goats to get milk fever, do we?" The child immediately left the house, choosing to use the outdoor stable entrance. She was still chomping on the figs as she left.

As soon as she was out the door, Tamar began to speak. "I'm glad our husbands didn't make it home in time for this meal. I have something very important I want to discuss with you. As surely as the Lord lives, we love your little one very, very much, and what I'm about to say, please don't take it the wrong way, my dear." She reached over and grabbed Anna's hand and began to pat it. "But you know, my dear heart, your daughter asks too many questions for her own good. No man will ever want a woman who's smarter than him, my dear. Men have to be looked up to by their wives and they shouldn't know more than their husbands do, so they can feel more important, you see. Otherwise, they'll feel demeaned and divorce them, and you wouldn't want that, dear heart, would you? So, my dear, maybe you should talk to our little princess and tell her to save all of her questions for her husband one day. Like I said, I mean no offense, no offense at all, my dear." The old woman continued to pat Anna's hand.

"I'm sorry, Tamar, but I see nothing wrong with an inquisitive mind that searches for knowledge, be it in a woman or a man." Tamar's smile changed into a pout as she withdrew her hands. Anna continued, "I pray that one day my daughter would have the wisdom of Solomon, the determination and leadership abilities of Deborah the Judge, the dedication of her ancestor Ruth, and the beauty and bravery of Queen Esther. Times are changing, Tamar; you and I both know that at times we are smarter than our husbands, but we say nothing. I don't think that will last forever. Wasn't Abigail smarter than her boorish husband Nabal? If not for his wife's keen mind and quick actions, King David would have destroyed Nabal's prosperity. And didn't that earn her such favor with the king, that he married her when Nabal died?"

"Well, my dear, I didn't mean to upset you," Tamar said.

Anna replied, "I'm sorry if I came off as sounding upset. I know that you really tried to help, and not to harm my daughter. There was no offense taken, Tamar; I'm a strong believer that knowledge is never wasted. I only pray that one day my daughter will find a husband who will respect her intelligence and value her input. That would be a great blessing not only for her but for me and my husband as well."

"Maybe I'm too old to change my way of thinking, but I still think the old way is best," the older woman said. Tamar slapped her thighs and stood up. "Well, I've got work to do." She began to pack her things in the hamper and collect the mats.

Anna grabbed her sister-in-law's hand. "Don't be angry with me. I meant no disrespect when I disagreed with you. You know I love you and value your opinions."

With a hurt look on her face, the old woman said, "So when were you going to tell me about Eleazer and Rebecca moving?"

"I'm sorry, with all the confusion today I just forgot. They're going to move to Jerusalem as soon as they sell the house and business."

"And the boy, what about him?" Tamar asked.

"He's going to apprentice with Achim."

"So I guess we won't be seeing him for a while," Tamar said.

"For five years. It's a shame that he has to go; he's such a fine boy, such a pious boy. He plans on coming back and living here again, though."

"From your lips to God's ears," Tamar said. "We sure could use a good carpenter in this town."

"So all is forgiven?" Anna asked.

"All's forgiven," her sister-in-law replied. Anna squeezed Tamar's hand even tighter as she said, "I can't thank you enough for all you've done for me today, and by the way, this poultice of yours seems to be helping, so thanks again." Tamar bent low and kissed her sister-in-law on her forehead.

"All I ask is that you think about what I said, that's all."

"I will," Anna promised.

"As soon as our men come home and the stew is finished, I'll bring dinner over so that you won't have to move."

"Tamar, you're a real blessing on my head, and I thank the One Who Always Sees, that He gave me a sister-in-law like you."

CHAPTER 4

The little girl entered the house through the inside stable door that was at the back of their living quarters. Anna heard the click of the hasp and said, "Pour the milk into a clean jar, dear. I'll scour out the old one as soon as I can."

"I think I can do it for you, Momma."

"Thank you dear, but I think I'd rather do it myself. Did the boy rinse out the curd jar after he emptied it?"

"Yes, Momma, he did."

"Well, just leave it where it is, then. When your daddy comes home he can store the milk in the silo. I saw you struggling before, when you tried to lift the jar out, so just leave it close to the opening for now." The girl did as she was told. Then her mother said, "Princess, bring the hairbrush and sit by me. I'll brush your hair now." The child did so and then sat down in front of her mother, carefully avoiding the woman's injured foot.

Anna loved to brush her daughter's auburn hair. She enjoyed watching the sunlight play on the varying strands of red, brown and golden tones. Her hair color was the same as her paternal grandfather's and her

Uncle Azor's. That was quite unusual for people of their race at that time. Anna took the brush from her daughter and said, "Now count with me." They began to say in unison, "One, two, three." Her mother found the exercise very relaxing. "Four, five, six." Before they got to seven, the woman caught a glimpse of someone out of the corner of her eye. She looked up and saw the town's rabbi standing in the door opening.

"Shalom to you and your daughter. May the blessings of the Lord, the God of Israel be on you, your family and on this house," he said as he kissed his fingertips and touched them to the little wooden box on the doorframe. The woman returned the greeting as she tucked the hairbrush into the folds of her garment while her daughter stood up and bowed as a sign of respect.

"May I come in, Anna?"

"Forgive my lack of courtesy, Rabbi. By all means come in! It's just that I was surprised to see you. By no means did I intend to insult you by not welcoming you into my home myself."

"I should be seeking your forgiveness. I could have knocked on the doorframe or at least made enough noise so you could hear me coming," the rabbi said jovially. He looked down at Anna's outstretched leg as he carefully crossed over it. "I see you have greater problems at the moment than courteous manners," he said, nodding to her injured foot. "What happened?"

"Just a silly accident, that's all," Anna answered as her daughter looked sheepishly at the ground. "I either sprained my ankle or tore something down there."

"Ooh, that sounds painful," he replied. "May I be of any help to you, Anna? Perhaps I can move you further away from the door. That way your foot would be better protected."

"As surely as the Lord lives. My sister-in-law would never forgive me if I moved from where she planted me," Anna said. "That dear woman's cure for everything from a hangnail to a consumptive cough is plenty of fresh air and an odiferous poultice. I must admit, though, since she applied it, the pain has decreased somewhat."

The rabbi stepped further into the house so he wouldn't block the sunlight. "Please get a mat for the rabbi," Anna said to her daughter.

"No, no, thank you! I won't be staying that long. I haven't even been home today yet. I've been to Jerusalem and haven't seen my family for a few weeks now. I just thought I'd stop by to see if Heli is home."

"No, he's not, Rabbi, but I expect him to return shortly. He and Azor went to the tanner to buy more leather."

The little girl stared wide-eyed at the rabbi, and as he opened his mouth to speak she said, "I missed having school, Rabbi, and I missed the way you tell us stories and sing with us. You have a good voice. You tell stories better than your wife and you sing better too, but I like the way she teaches us reading."

Anna was embarrassed by her daughter's audacious interruption. "Children should not interrupt adults when they're speaking," she told her. "Don't you know that children are to be seen but not heard? I'm so sorry, Rabbi. Now, apologize to the rabbi."

"There is no need for an apology," the teacher said jovially. "Praise be to Yahweh. I finally have an admirer. Usually people tell me I'm too windy and talk too much. Don't be too harsh with the child, for Scripture says that out of the mouths of babes comes perfected praise." The little girl apologized anyway. The rabbi patted her on the head and said jokingly, "I think you miss playing with my daughter Leah more than you miss school, though."

"Oh, no, Teacher, I like playing with your daughter very much, but I really, really, like school too."

"I know," he said. "I was just teasing you. My wife and I both know what an excellent student you are. She often tells me that when classes are held outdoors, under the sycamore tree, you're the only one who really pays attention and answers all the questions. But now I must get to the main reason for my visit, and that's to see if Heli would be interested in making a new leather cover for the Sacred Scrolls. He does such beautiful leatherwork. I wouldn't trust anyone else to do it."

"Why, thank you, Rabbi," the woman said. "I'm sure my husband would be honored to do it. I'll send him over as soon as he gets back."

"There's no need for him to do so today. Tomorrow will be just fine. I know that we both will be tired from our travels, and my wife wouldn't take too kindly to my working as soon as I get home," the rabbi said. "Well, I had better be going. And may the God of Abraham, Isaac and Jacob extend His Mighty Arm and heal you. Shalom!"

"Shalom to you also, Rabbi!" Anna replied, as the teacher took his leave. The girl wanted to say shalom as well, but she knew she was in enough trouble already.

When the rabbi left, Anna once again scolded her daughter for interrupting. The girl began to sob, so Anna reached out, took hold of her daughter's

60

hand and drew her to herself. She leaned forward and kissed her daughter's forehead. "Now, now, no more tears! You've learned a lesson today. There's no need to cry. Everyone makes mistakes; that's how we learn. I'm sure you won't ever do that again." The child stopped sobbing and clung to her mother. Anna reached for the hairbrush and the child sat back down in front of her mother. The woman once again began to brush her daughter's hair.

The wheels of an inquiring mind never stop turning, so after a few moments of silence the child asked, "Mommy, why does Rabbi Asa call my daddy 'Heli'?"

"Because that's really your father's name," Anna replied.

"Then why does everyone else call Abba 'Joachim'?"

"Well," Anna said, "it's a very long and complicated story, dear."

"I like stories," the girl said. "Please tell it to me, Mommy, please!"

"Well, your Grandma Naomi was a very determined woman who liked to have things her way. Your Grandpa Matthat always liked your grandma's father; he was a leathersmith like your daddy, Uncle Azor and your grandpa. Grandma Naomi's father's name was Heli, so when Great-Grandpa Heli died, Grandpa Matthat said, 'If we ever have another boy I want to name him Heli, after your father whom I loved very much.' Grandma said, 'I loved my father too, but I think we already have too many Helis in our family, and our town is full of them too.' When your Uncle Azor was 17, your daddy was born. Grandpa Matthat was overjoyed. He picked up your daddy and held him up high and said, 'Thank You, Lord! You have finally blessed me with a new son I can name Heli, to honor my father-in-law.' Grandma Naomi asked, 'Are you sure you want to name the boy Heli? I'm telling you we already have too many Helis in this town.' Grandpa said, 'Woman, I've made up my mind, and nothing you can say is going to change it.' Grandma said, 'Okay, have it your way,' then under her breath, she said, '...for now!'

"So when the day came for your father to become a true Son of Abraham, the rabbi asked your grandpa, 'By what name should this Son of Abraham be called?' Your Grandpa said, 'Heli,' so the rabbi recorded your daddy's name in the book of the Sons of Israel as Heli Bar Matthat. Grandma just shook her head from side to side and kept muttering something under her breath.

"Several years later at the Passover, Daddy's two brothers with their whole families, as well as Uncle Azor and many of Daddy's aunts and uncles and all of their children, got together."

"Was Aunt Tamar there too?" the girl asked.

"Yes she was," Anna said, "They had just gotten married, but they didn't have any children yet. So Grandma thought to herself, *This is the perfect time to show Grandpa how foolish it was to name your daddy Heli.* When everyone had finished eating, Grandma called out, in a loud voice, 'Heli!' When she did, five boys stepped forward and said, 'Here I am!' Grandma just looked at your grandpa and shook her head as if to say, 'I told you so.'

"'I'm only calling the youngest Heli,' Grandma said. She stomped her foot and said, 'All you others, go away; I didn't mean you!' She then sat down next to Grandpa and said, 'See, I told you so!' Your grandpa just grumbled."

"The next day, after all the relatives left, your daddy went out to play. When Grandma Naomi wanted your Abba to come home, she went to the door and shouted, 'Heli!' Eleven boys came running, but your father wasn't among them. The boys all gathered around Grandma's door, trampling her garden under foot, and they all said, 'Here I am!' Grandma didn't see your father there, so she stomped her foot on the ground, and said, 'Go home, I didn't mean you!' So all of the boys left.

"The day after, Grandma did the same thing, but this time only seven boys named Heli showed up, trampling your grandmother's garden even further, and once again your father wasn't with them. They all said, 'Here I am!' Grandma was even angrier than she was the day before, so she stomped her foot twice and said, 'Go home, I didn't mean you!' So those boys left too. Grandma was so frustrated and angry that when your grandpa came home she said, 'You had to have your way and name our son Heli. Every time I try and call him home, every boy in town named Heli comes to my door! Look at my garden; it's almost ruined. So, talk to your Heli, and find out why he doesn't come home when I call him, while every other Heli hears me and comes running to my door.'

"Grandpa sat your father down and asked him, 'Why don't you come home when your mother calls you?' Your father answered, 'All I hear is someone calling Heli, then I see everyone with that name go running to answer, so I know whoever's calling doesn't mean me. If they did, why would all the other Helis answer?' Grandma just gave your grandpa an 'I told you so' look again, while Grandpa just shook his head in disbelief. The next day, Grandma went to the door and shouted out, 'Heli!' Nine boys came to the door and said, 'Here I am!' But this time, your father was among them. All the Helis trampled her garden into the ground, and there was nothing left of it. So Grandma grabbed your father by the ear and dragged him into the house. She then stomped her foot and said to the rest of them, 'Go home, I didn't mean you!' After they were inside, Grandma closed the door and said to your daddy, 'You're not leaving this house again until I find a new name for you.'

"When Grandpa Matthat came home that night, Grandma said, 'We must change that boy's name. I'm sick and tired of having half the boys in town come to my door every time I call my son home. There's nothing left of my garden. I'll have to plant it all over again. Seeds cost money, you know, and my back is already breaking from bending. As surely as the Lord lives, if I call Heli again, all the boys who come running will just ruin everything I plant once again.' Your grandpa replied, 'What?! I named him Heli, and a Heli he will always be, woman!' Grandma just shook her head from side to side, but she didn't say anything."

"Your grandma was a very strong-willed woman, and she wasn't afraid to insist on having things done her way. The next day she made your father stay inside the house. Grandma went to the door and shouted out the name, 'Jehu!' Four boys with that name came running up to her door and said, 'Here I am!' Grandma stomped her foot and said, 'Go home, I didn't mean you.' Later that day, Grandma stuck her head out the door again and shouted at the top of her voice, 'Samuel!' This time seven boys came to her door."

The little girl broke in, "And Grandma said, 'Go home, I didn't mean you.'" Mother and daughter laughed together.

Anna continued, "For several days Grandma did the same thing, and each time she shouted out a new name, more than three boys would come to the door and say, 'Here I am!' And Grandma would say, 'Go home, I didn't mean you.' The girl joined her mother as they said the line together. They laughed again. "Finally, your grandma stuck her head out the door and shouted, 'Joachim!' No one came, so she shouted the name again as loud as she could, 'Joachim!' Still no one came. Grandma drew her head back in and went over to your father and said, 'Listen to me, there are so many Helis in town that when I call your name, practically all the boys in town come running to my door. My whole garden is ruined. From now on, every time I want you home, I'm going to stick my head out the door and call for Joachim. There's no excuse for you not to come. I've already checked, and there are no other Joachims in this town, so when you hear me call that name, you better come running. Do you understand me, Joachim?'

"So every time Grandma stuck her head out the door and called for Joachim, your father would run home and say, 'Here I am!' Soon all the people in town started calling him Joachim because they heard Grandma calling him that. Even your grandfather finally gave in and started calling him Joachim too. Rabbi is the only person I know who still calls him

Heli. That's how his name was officially recorded in the Synagogue. It's like when your daddy and I, or Aunt Tamar and Uncle Azor, call you 'Princess.' We usually only call you by that name when no one else is around. But if we called you 'Princess' in front of other people, soon they'd think that was really your name. Eventually, everyone in town would be calling you 'Princess' instead of calling you by your real name."

"Am I really a princess, Mommy?"

"No, dear, you're not. Princesses live in palaces and their fathers are kings and their mothers are queens. Your father is a leathersmith and I'm a housewife. I don't think that you could call our house a palace, do you?"

When her mother stopped speaking, the girl said, "That was a really good story, Mama. It's almost as good as the stories Uncle Azor tells." Anna thanked her daughter for the compliment and told her to run along and play outside for awhile, then go and see if her aunt needed any more help. Before the girl left she had one more question. "Where does that boy who helped you out today live? I've never seen him before."

"He lives on the hillside at the other end of town with his aunt and uncle."

"Why doesn't he live with his mommy and daddy?"

"Because they died when he was just a little boy."

"Both of them?"

"Yes, both of them, dear," Anna said. "That vacant house across the street belonged to the boy's father, Jacob. Now that house belongs to him. When he's older, I'm sure he'll live there too."

"Why doesn't he live there now, Mommy?" the little girl asked.

"Because he's too young to manage a house by himself."

"But you said he'd be a man tomorrow!"

"Yes I did, he might be a man according to our law, but he's a very young man who can't manage on his own yet. He's old enough to start learning a trade, though. That's why he's going away for a while."

"Well, why don't his aunt and uncle come and live in the house across the street, then the boy could live with them in his own house."

"Because they have their own home on the hill where there's plenty of fresh air. You see, dear, the boy's uncle is a cheese-maker, and cheese is made from spoiled milk. You know firsthand how badly spoiled milk can smell. If they lived here in the middle of town, people would complain about the odor. Furthermore, the house across the street is suited for a carpenter, not a cheese-maker."

"Momma, just one more question, please. What's the boy's name?"

"His name is Joseph," her mother replied.

"Joseph. Jo-seeph, Jo-seeeeph. I really like that name, Momma. The last part of his name is like the sound the wind makes when it blows through our olive tree." The little girl bent down and whispered in her mother's ear, "Don't tell Daddy, but I think it's a better name than Heli or Joachim."

Anna chuckled and said, "Now run along and play for a while." The girl kissed her mother's cheek and skipped out the door, whispering the boy's name over and over.

The girl skipped to the street. With all the sound the larynx of an eight-year-old could muster, she shouted, "Joseph!" She looked up and down the street, and waited a few seconds before shouting the name again. No one responded to her call. "Yes!" she said aloud. "Grandma Naomi should have named my daddy Joseph; that's a much nicer name." She wondered why her mother was laughing. Anna realized her daughter liked the boy far more than she liked his name. Her daughter had her first childhood crush.

The girl returned to the center of the courtyard and began to spin and spin and spin, until she almost lost her balance. When she opened her eyes everything before her continued to move. She had to hold on to the trunk of the olive tree to remain erect. When the little girl regained her equilibrium, she skipped across the courtyard to her aunt's house while whispering the boy's name over and over again.

CHAPTER 5

After leaving Anna's house, Joseph continued to run as the donkey cantered close behind. The hot sun had dried the streets, but the heat of the day was so intense that it kept most people inside, seeking the coolness of shade. The boys who had taunted him earlier were still grouped together. They had resumed their game once the rain stopped. Joseph saw them as he ran by, and increased his pace to avoid them. He knew they were nothing but trouble. The leader of the group caught a glimpse of Joseph as he passed by. The minute he saw him, the leader took his slingshot, picked up a stone and began to swing it around above his head. The loaded sling made a swishing sound as Joshua shouted, "Hey, orphan girl, get out of our side of town!"

One of the other boys yelled, "Your smelly uncle shouldn't send his prissy niece here. Something very bad could happen to you!" The rest of the group laughed at the remarks. Joseph ignored them. He raised his right foot even higher to increase his stride just as Joshua sent the stone flying from the sling. Joseph heard a popping sound and felt something strike his right shoulder with such force that it knocked him to the ground. A fraction of a second later he felt searing pain in his shoulder and could feel something wet and thick running down his back. The projectile that had struck him ricocheted off his shoulder bone and hit the donkey right between its eyes. The animal stopped dead in its tracks and sat down on the roadbed. The stunned donkey then began to bray loudly.

With Joshua in the lead, the group ran to the fallen boy. Joseph jumped to his feet and turned quickly, facing the group just as Joshua reached him. The group leader threw a right uppercut at Joseph's chin. The boy tried to duck, but he wasn't fast enough. The stinging punch landed just below his eye. Joseph retaliated by throwing two strong, swift punches to the ringleader's abdomen. Joshua fell to the ground, groaning in agony. As he lay there, the rest of the group could hear his pain-laden voice saying, "Go get-um!" Three of the boys charged Joseph and knocked him to the ground. When he fell, his head struck the roadbed and dazed him a bit. With his sight slightly blurred and his head throbbing, it was easy for the three of them to subdue Joseph and pin him to the ground. One boy knelt on each of his arms, while the third sat on his legs. Joseph's head began to clear, and he struggled to free himself, but the odds were not in his favor.

When Joshua recovered from the ache in his gut, his anger burned like a flaming torch within him. He ran to Joseph and said to his comrades, "Make sure you keep him pinned down!" He straddled his victim, and with one hand he gripped the crown of Joseph's head, then grabbed his chin with his other. He viciously pounded Joseph's head into the roadbed and would have possibly killed him had it not been for the fifth boy who found the bag of curds on the donkey.

"Look what I found on the cheese girl's donkey," he shouted. Joshua, who still straddled the boy, stopped the pounding and turned to see what his friend had discovered.

"What's that?" Joshua asked.

"I think it's a bag of smelly curds," the boy answered.

"Good, bring them here to me," Joshua said as he stood up and stepped over Joseph's body. The boy handed the bag to his leader. Joshua opened the flap and sniffed its contents. "Phew, this almost stinks as bad as you and your uncle," he said, as he began to pour the small amount of whey that still remained in the bag on his victim's face. Joseph mustered all the strength that was left in him as he tried to buck himself free while turning his head to the side to prevent the liquid from running down into his nose. Joshua then poured some of the goat curd on Joseph's face and started to rub it into his nostrils and mouth with his dirty, bare foot. Joseph couldn't breathe. He struggled to snort out the curds that filled his nose and spit them out as well, but Joshua kept forcing more of them into his mouth with his foot.

The boy who found the bag said, "Hey! Save some of that for me; I found it!" Joshua grudgingly handed the boy the bag and its remaining contents. He took it, then bent over Joseph and began to lift his tunic, as he said, "Let's see what's really under there. Whatever's there probably could use a little of this to grow a bit, too." He was about to lift

Joseph's tunic all the way up and expose the boy, humiliating him even further, when just then two men with their pack mules rounded the corner.

As Joachim and Azor turned onto their street they saw the group of boys abusing their victim. "What's going on here?!" Joachim, the younger of the two men, shouted at the top of his voice. The older man started yelling at the boys to break it up. The three boys who had pinned Joseph to the ground jumped to their feet and fled. Joachim grabbed Joshua by the back of his head and practically lifted him up off the ground with his strong arms. Azor, the older man, grabbed the boy who was holding the horsehair bag by the back of his tunic.

As if it was orchestrated, both men moved their hands to the back of each boy's neck and knocked their heads together. In unison the boys shouted, "Oww!"

"You two are very brave. Let's see, five against one, that's pretty fair, isn't it?" Joachim said. "Let's see what the two of you can do against the both of us, okay?"

The men banged the boys' heads together one more time as Azor said, "Now get out of here. If we ever catch you two or any of your friends doing something like this again, you'll not only answer to us, we'll take you before the Town Elders as well."

The boy who held the partially filled bag of curds dropped it as he said, "I'm sorry, I apologize." Joshua just stared at the older man with raging hatred in his eyes.

"Don't apologize to us; apologize to your victim," Azor said.

72

The boy looked down at Joseph and said sarcastically, "Sorry!" Joseph, who now was sitting and pulling down his tunic, nodded his head in acceptance of the apology. Joshua just glared at Joseph.

Joachim took the slingshot that was tucked away in Joshua's waistband and said, "Now get out of here! Both of you!" The boys ran away as fast as they could.

The two men turned their attention to the young man, who still sat half-dazed in the street. Joachim extended his arm to Joseph and said, "Here, take my hand; I'll help you up. Get up slowly, though. You're pretty banged up, and you don't want your blood rushing up to your head."

"Thank you, sir! I could've taken them, even if it was two against one, but I couldn't handle all five of them at once."

"Azor and I both know that," Joachim said as he helped the boy to his feet. He then began to untie his own sash; Azor did likewise. The younger man walked toward his mule and said, "I think there's some wine left in our wineskin. It acts like an antiseptic." Azor took his sash and began to wipe away the cheese curds that Joshua ground into the boy's face. Joachim returned with the wineskin and a small leather bag that still had some raisin cakes and flatbread in it. He soaked his own sash with the wine as he said to the boy, "This will sting a bit, but your wounds should be cleaned out."

Joachim removed Joseph's blood-stained cap and handed it to him. He cleansed the head wounds as the boy winced. Carefully he peeled the teenager's tunic from the gaping wound on his shoulder and began to dab it with his wine-soaked sash too. The boy grimaced but said nothing. As the two men tried to care for Joseph, Joachim said, "Have you had anything to eat yet?"

"No, sir, I haven't had time today."

"Well, here's a little something to tide you over until you get home." The boy thanked him as he took the raisin cakes and bread; he ate them with delight because he was famished.

"You might want to clean those wounds again when you get home and put some olive oil on them," Joachim said. Then he turned to his brother and asked, "Azor, would you please take the mules back to the house while I walk the boy home?"

"I appreciate all you've both done for me, but I don't want to inconvenience you any further, sir. I think I can walk home by myself."

"I'm not going to chance that," Joachim said. "Joshua Bar Abbas is a very vindictive boy. He's liable to try and come after you if we leave. Furthermore, your head and your shoulder are pretty banged up. I don't want you passing out or anything like that. I'll just walk you to the hillside and watch you walk up from there by yourself, if you like."

"Thank you, sir! Once again I want to thank both of you for all you've done for me. I'm glad you both turned that corner when you did. Otherwise, I don't think Joshua would have stopped."

"That boy's bad seed," Joachim said. "One of these days, if he doesn't control that temper of his, he's going to kill someone." Joachim returned to the mule and tied the wineskin to its strap.

74

Azor came over to Joachim. "Joshua never really stood a chance, with the town drunk as his father and the vicious town gossip as his mother. What do you expect?"

"I know. It's a real shame, but that doesn't excuse his behavior. Does it?" Azor shook his head "no."

Joachim coaxed the boy's donkey to his feet as Joseph picked up the horsehair bag and said to Azor, "Shalom, sir, may the God of our Father Abraham bless you for your kindness."

"And shalom to you my son," Azor replied. Joachim and Joseph then walked toward the boy's house with the donkey following behind them, while Azor led the mules in the opposite direction.

Joseph tried to put his cap back on his head. Good Jews always kept their heads covered in respect to their God. When Joachim saw what he was trying to do, he said, "I'd leave that cap off if I were you. God understands. The wounds on your head are pretty fresh, and if your cap should stick to them, they'll just reopen, and that'll delay the healing." So Joseph rolled up his bloody cap and carried it in one hand, and the horsehair bag in the other. Passersby stared curiously at the beaten boy who wore no cap as Joachim and Joseph walked through the market area. Joachim put his arm over Joseph's shoulder for moral support. The boy found the weight of the man's arm to be rather irritating, as it rested on his open shoulder wound, but he said nothing, for he knew that Joachim was just trying to give him some moral support.

Joseph said, "By the way, sir, I never introduced myself."

"I know who you are," Joachim replied. "You're Joseph Bar Jacob. I've seen you with your uncle at Synagogue. If I hadn't seen you with Eleazer, I'd still know who you were. I knew your father since he was about your age, long before my wife and I moved here, we would visit my brother. Azor and I would see your dad helping his father. If your dad were able to stand next to you right now, you'd pass as his identical twin. You're as handsome as he was at your age."

The boy's face reddened with embarrassment as he smiled from ear to ear and said, "Thank you, sir!"

"So why do you think Joshua and his gang attacked you? As if that evil delinquent ever needs a reason." Joseph relayed his experience with the woman at the well and their journey back to her house, omitting the girl's involvement in the accident.

"Do you happen to know the woman's name?" Joachim asked with great concern in his voice.

"Yes, I do, sir! Her name is Anna," the boy answered. He added, "Her little girl has very beautiful eyes and reddish-brown hair, like the other man who helped me. The girl's hair was a lot nicer and there was no gray in it."

"Anna's my wife!" Joachim said. "Are you sure she's all right?"

"She seemed to be, sir. Your sister-in-law and your daughter are taking very good care of her, from what I could see."

"Well, you helped my wife, and now my brother and I were able to help you," Joachim responded. "The Eternal One sees to it that one good turn deserves another."

"He sure does, sir!" the boy replied. Joseph could see the worried look on Joachim's face, so he said, "I'll be fine from here on, sir. I can see you're worried about your wife. Why don't you go home to her now?"

"No!" the man replied, "I said I'd walk you home, and so I will. A few more minutes won't change my wife's condition." Joachim tried to allay his fears about his wife's condition by keeping his mind occupied through further conversation, so he said, "How come I never see you on my side of town except when you go to Synagogue?"

"My aunt and uncle—well, especially my aunt—keep me pretty busy. I don't have too much free time."

"Well, I'll tell you what—whatever they're doing, they seem to be doing it right. You bring honor to your father's and your uncle's name." The boy thanked him.

"No, thank you for what you did for my wife today; I really appreciate it." Joseph responded by saying that anyone would have done the same.

"Would they have?" Joachim asked. "I think you have some cuts and bruises that prove otherwise."

"Well not everybody, I guess, but most everyone," Joseph said. The two laughed.

They reached the path that led to Joseph's uncle's house. Joachim hugged the boy heartily, forgetting about the boy's wounded shoulder. The boy involuntarily said, "Oww!" Joachim realized what he had done and apologized. "I'm sorry, I forgot about that wound on your shoulder. I just wanted to let you know how grateful I really am for what you've done for my wife today."

"I know, sir. I didn't mean to sound like a baby, but that sore on my back really stings."

"Believe me, it's more than a sore," Joachim said. Once again he thanked the boy for helping his wife. Then he left.

Joseph waved goodbye to Joachim as he neared the house even though raising his arm caused him more pain. Joachim waved back. He whispered under his breath, *Such a fine boy! If only my little princess could find someone like him one day.* Joachim looked up to the heavens as he said out loud, "From my lips to Your ears, my Lord!" Then he hurried home to check on his wife.

As Joseph reached the corner of his uncle's home he prayed, "Lord, God of Israel, please let my uncle be home now." The boy's aunt had never been too fond of her nephew. Rebecca resented the fact that the Lord had never allowed her to conceive. Now that she was in her late forties, she knew she would never have a child of her own. Her sister-in-law, Joseph's mother, had died in childbirth. Instead of Rebecca's motherly instincts responding to the situation, she resented the baby boy, and wouldn't even hold him. She was angry with God. She was alive; a child could have come from her body, she told herself. Why was God so cruel in giving a child to a woman who was destined to die? Yet she, who was destined to live, would always be barren. She tolerated the boy at family gatherings, but that was as far as it went.

When Joseph's father was killed in a tragic accident, her husband took his nephew to live with them. Eleazer, her husband, loved Joseph and treated him as if he was his own son. Rebecca felt threatened. The boy drew the attention of her husband away from her. When Eleazer was around, Rebecca pretended to treat the boy kindly, but when he wasn't, she was mean, even cruel to the boy. Joseph never complained. He always tried to please his aunt. She usually had such a foul disposition that the boy actually pitied her. He prayed often that God would change her embittered heart so she could find some happiness in life.

Rebecca's heart was so hardened that she was egomaniacal. Everything she did was for her own benefit. When the boy came to live with them, it ruined her plans and shattered her dreams. She thought herself too cosmopolitan to live in a small town like Nazareth. Her dream was to live in the City of David. She wanted to have servants and fine clothes. Rebecca had a large wicker hamper that contained her precious personal treasures. Every day, when she was alone, the woman would open it and take out the exotic fabrics and heavy brocades she had purchased in Jerusalem. She would gently stroke the fabrics with her hands and press them to her cheek, and run her fingers along the ridges of the costly brocades. In the very bottom of the hamper was an alabaster vile with a stopper held in place by beeswax. Rebecca would separate the wax with her fingernail, just enough to smell the captivating scent of nard, the costly aromatic perfume that filled the vile. She then would press the soft wax back into place and repack everything into the hamper.

The woman could picture herself strutting through Jerusalem's streets, while the people commented on her finery. Rebecca was a very conniving woman. She knew she could manipulate her husband into doing almost anything, even moving to the Holy City. He could've already established a very profitable business there, were it not for the boy. No more would they have to be peddlers, taking their cheeses from town to town. She imagined her husband would open a huge cheese factory. The residents of Jerusalem alone would buy enough of his product to make them wealthy. She continued to dream big. They would hire foremen for the factory and buy slaves to work there. They would live away from their business, in the wealthiest section of the city. No longer would she or her husband have to live with the awful smell of aging cheese. Servants would run her household. Oh, and yes, handsome slaves would carry her through the streets of David's City on a gold-covered litter when she tired of walking. She just knew she would be the envy of every woman in Jerusalem. "Just one more day, and my nemesis will be gone forever!" she said as she heard the *clip-clop* of donkey hooves. She knew that the boy finally had returned home.

Rebecca, who was still in menopause, resented the boy more today than she ever did before. The anger that had built up for the last eight years peaked as she heard him approaching. He should have been home hours ago, and in her mind, she now had a reason to justify her anger. She grabbed the broom and ran toward the door. With her shrill, nasally voice she yelled at Joseph, "Where have you been? How long does it take you to cross this stupid town? You should have been home hours ago!" She walked out the door and saw the boy standing there in his bloodstained tunic, with his bloodied cap in hand and the horsehair bag tucked under his arm. He had already tied off the donkey.

Joseph's left eyes had turned a deep purple and his head was pounding. The woman showed no compassion. She grabbed the boy by his ear with her free hand and began to drag him toward the shed, still yelling at the top of her lungs. "What have you gotten yourself into now? You're not coming into my house until you wash those filthy clothes." She personally hadn't cared about Jewish law or tradition in years, yet all of a sudden it now mattered to her. It gave her the opportunity to scream at the boy and further torture him. "Put that cap back on your head! Now!" Joseph knew it was useless to try to explain anything to his aunt when she was so enraged. He just put the cap, which had stiffened from his dried blood, back on his head. He felt a burning pain as it rubbed against his open wounds. "If you think I'm going to get you a clean tunic, you're crazy! You got it stained, you launder it, and you better get all that blood out of it, and out of your cap too. Otherwise, you're going to wear it that way tomorrow to Synagogue. I'm sick of you. For eight long years I've put up with you, and I can't wait until Sunday when you'll be gone from us forever!" she screamed hysterically. His aunt only yelled like that when his uncle wasn't around to hear it.

When they reached the shed door, Rebecca let go of his ear and pushed him forward. As Joseph entered she whacked him on the back with the broom. "Don't come out of there until your uncle comes home, and I don't expect him until tomorrow morning!" the crazed woman said as she headed back to the house, still enraged.

There was a water trough in the shed. Joseph set down what was left in the bag of curds and removed his cap and tunic. The material had already attached itself to his open wounds. It stung badly as he peeled the fabric from them and exposed the raw, sensitive tissue to the open air. He trembled as his weakened arms drew some water into a washbasin. Joseph proceeded to soak his stained clothing in it. The boy found two large, smooth stones and vigorously rubbed his soiled clothes between them. The water turned a reddish brown as he scrubbed, and the stains began to lighten. Joseph had hoped that his aunt would at least let him have some fresh water to bathe in. He wanted to remove the dirt and small bits of cheese curds that still clung to him, but he didn't want to provoke her any further. The water in the trough wasn't very clean, but it was the best he'd have for now. After he changed the water in the basin, he re-soaked his clothing, then began to wash himself. It seemed to refresh him somewhat.

No matter how hard the boy scrubbed, he still couldn't get all of the bloodstains out of his cap and tunic. He finally gave up and hung the garments on the shed gate to dry. Joseph sat there, wearing only his undergarment that covered him from waist to about mid-thigh. Like all the Jewish people of his time, he was very modest. He wouldn't leave the shed without being fully clothed, even if his aunt hadn't confined him there. His aunt knew that too.

Joseph's uncle had always encouraged him to follow in his father's footsteps and become a carpenter. Every time Eleazer found a sizable tree branch or a good-size tree trunk, he would load it onto his ox cart and bring it home for the boy to work on. He'd tell his nephew, "Don't just see it as a piece of wood, my boy. Visualize what a carpenter's hands can make it become." Eleazer even brought many of the tools from his brother's house over to his own, so his nephew could experiment with them and have a head start when he became a carpenter's apprentice. The boy spotted a rather thick tree branch, just about his height, toward the back of the shed. Joseph dragged it out, leaned it against the wall and stood next to it. With his fingernail, he scratched a line in the branch about four finger-lengths below his armpit. Even though his body ached and his head still throbbed, Joseph thought he could overcome the discomfort by working. He gathered the necessary tools and began to saw away. His aunt heard the sounds of chopping, sawing and pounding, but she paid little attention. She didn't care what the boy did as long as he stayed out of her way.

Rebecca stopped praying a long time ago. If God couldn't answer her prayer, to her that meant He didn't exist. When she was alone she never prayed before her meals, so she just sat down cross-legged on the mat and ate a hearty evening meal all by herself. *The way the boy came home today, he doesn't deserve any supper,* she thought, thereby justifying her cruel behavior. Rebecca could treat him as poorly as her heart desired. She knew Joseph would never say anything about her mistreatment of him to his uncle.

Eleazer surprised his wife by returning that same evening. She panicked when he walked through the door and saw her eating by herself. Rebecca was enjoying the meal so much that she didn't even hear him approach. He walked up to his wife and kissed her forehead and then asked, "Where's Joseph?"

His wife almost choked on the bread in her mouth as she tried to think up an excuse for why the boy wasn't eating with her. She regained her composure and began her set of lies. "The poor dear is in the shed working on something. You better go to him. I think he got into a fight while he was in town. I tried to comfort him. He has a black eye and some cuts and bruises."

"That doesn't sound like our Joseph," Eleazer said.

"I know!" Rebecca said, and then continued, "Don't be too hard on him, though, Eleazer. Boys will be boys, you know! I tried to get him to change his clothing so I could wash and mend his tunic, but the poor dear was too ashamed to have me do it. He just told me he'd rather do it himself. He wouldn't even let me clean or dress his wounds. The boy just walked over to the shed to sulk a little, I guess. It looked to me as if he must have lost the fight. Maybe that's why he had such a sour disposition. I called him to supper several times. I even offered to fix him a plate and take it out to him, but he said he wasn't hungry and didn't feel like eating. He just wanted to finish what he was doing. Go talk to him, Eleazer. Perhaps he'll open up a little, you know, one man to another. I'll prepare your plate and make one for him too. Please try to coax him to eat. I'm really worried about him. Tomorrow's his big day, you know!"

Eleazer thanked his wife for her concern and went out to the shed to see his nephew. He immediately noticed the boy's tunic and cap that hung over the shed gate to dry. The last golden rays of sunset reluctantly surrendered to the purplish hue of twilight. The little light that still remained filtered through the high windows of the shed. The boy, however, was still working. It was too dark inside for Eleazer to see his nephew clearly. "Good evening, Joseph!" The boy returned the greeting. His uncle then said, "Don't you think it's a little dark in here? How about if I get some fire and we'll light some of those lanterns so you can see a little better. I don't want you to be straining your eyes. They have to last you a lifetime."

Eleazer left and returned in no time with a flaming taper. He lit all three of the lanterns, and the shed was soon filled with the warm amber glow of firelight. He blew out the taper and turned to his nephew. The boy's left eye was swollen shut and his face was swelling from the beating. His uncle also noticed the open wounds on Joseph's shoulder and those on the back of his head. "My heavens," his uncle remarked as he saw the injuries. "I only hope that whoever did this to you looks a lot worse. I'm going to go into the house and get some things so we can take care of those wounds for you. Then, if you feel up to it, you can tell me what happened." Tears welled up in the boy's eyes; he knew his uncle really loved him. Joseph bit his lip so he wouldn't cry. After all, he was supposed to be a man now.

Eleazer gathered the things he needed and was about to return to the shed, as his wife said, "I'll go with you, dear. I've fixed two plates, one for you and one for Joseph. I also have a clean tunic and cap for him. We'll just take these to him together, and perhaps I can help you tend to his needs." The woman feared that she could have pushed the boy too far this time, and that he might have reached his breaking point. She wanted to be within earshot of him so she could defend herself if need be.

Eleazer said, "I'd appreciate it if you would just carry the things to the shed gate for me. I'll take it in by myself. The boy had enough humiliation today. It would be far too embarrassing for him to be seen by a woman without his tunic on."

"I understand, my dear!" Rebecca said. "It's just that I feel so sorry for him that I thought I might give him the comfort of a woman's touch, that's all." She followed her husband to the shed and placed the tray to the side of the building, out of the boy's sight. "Tell him I love him, and how concerned I've been. Will you?"

"Of course!" Eleazer said. "I'm sure he already knows that."

As soon as his uncle entered the shed, he began to cleanse his nephew's wounds with wine. He then applied a light coating of olive oil over them. After Joseph changed into a clean tunic, his uncle said, "Do you think you'd like to tell me what happened today, son?" Eleazer started to bandage his nephew's wounds with a new roll of cheesecloth while Joseph reluctantly recounted the day's events. He omitted the callous greeting he'd received from his aunt when he arrived home. Rebecca had remained at the corner of the shed, listening to hear if her nephew would say anything derogatory about her. When she was fairly certain that he wouldn't, she left quietly and returned to the house. The story of the boy's heroic deeds didn't faze the cruel woman one bit.

When Joseph finished telling his story, his uncle hugged him and said, "I'm very proud of you, Joseph." He kissed his nephew on his bandaged head and said, "You're a righteous man. I knew that from the day you first moved in with us. The Eternal One will one day bless you for what you did today. The God of Israel never forsakes a righteous person." Eleazer brought in the meals his wife had prepared for the two of them. They stood and faced the Holy City. As they were about to give thanks to their God, Joseph reached for his clean cap and was about to place it on his head. His uncle stopped him, saying, "Joseph, I think the bandages cover your head enough to satisfy the Lord today. Why don't you wait until tomorrow to put it on? Some of the swelling should go down by then, and no one will even be able to notice the bandages. I don't think we'll be able to do anything about your eye, though; it's already turning purple." Eleazer and his nephew chuckled. They then prayed, thanking the Eternal One for all of their blessings and asked the Lord their God to hasten the coming of Messiah. When they finished eating, Joseph asked his uncle if he could buy two rounds of cheese from him, one for each of the men who came to his aid. Eleazer replied, "Just take them! Their help was a blessing on my head as much as it was to yours."

Joseph said, "I'd like to pay for them myself, Uncle Eleazer. I'd rather show my own gratitude to the men." Eleazer knew that Joseph had some money of his own. He often slipped the boy several copper coins, without his wife's knowledge, for all the work he did around the house and shop. (He suspected but could never prove that his wife pushed the boy a little too hard.) "So how much do two rounds cost, sir?" Joseph asked.

"You caught me at the right time," his uncle said. "I was running a special this week—two rounds for four copper coins." In reality, Eleazer could sell them for at least ten times that much. The boy was rather skeptical and asked if that was enough. He didn't want to short his uncle's profit. In his mind Eleazer thought, *Forgive me for lying, Lord,* then said, "Joseph, that's more than enough."

"May I also shave some hair off the belly of one of your goats and use some of the cheesecloth too?" Joseph asked. "I'll pay for that also."

Eleazer finally figured out what Joseph was making and said, "The Lord doesn't charge me for the goat's hair, so why should I charge you? As for the cheesecloth, I think you'd be better off with sackcloth. It's more durable and there's plenty right here in the shed. I take it you'd like to get back to work now."

"If it's okay with you, Uncle, I'd like to. And if you don't mind, can I sleep out here tonight, and may I run the cheese rounds over first thing in the morning."

"If that's what you want to do, it's all right with me. Just make sure you get enough sleep. Remember, you have a big day tomorrow."

"Oh, Uncle, I almost forgot. I still have some of the cheese curds that the nice woman I helped today gave me. Should I put them in the forming bin?"

"I'll do that on my way out, and I'll leave the bag by the goat's pen. You can get it when you shave the goat. Then you can return it to Anna tomorrow morning when you deliver the cheese rounds. By the way, since Anna gave me some curds, the cost for the two rounds is only two copper coins; otherwise, I'd feel as if I was stealing from her. Now don't stay up too late, Joseph." His uncle grabbed his nephew by the chin and gently shook his head side-to-side in an affectionate gesture. "Good night, Joseph!" His chin began to quiver as he thought about his nephew leaving Sunday morning. He turned quickly so the boy couldn't see the tears forming in his eyes. "Don't forget your nighttime prayers," his uncle said, his voice cracking with emotion.

"Goodnight, Uncle. May the peace of the Lord be with you! Thanks for everything you've done for me."

"No need for thanks, Joseph. You've been God's blessing to me and your aunt." Eleazer left quickly. He didn't want his nephew to hear him sobbing.

Joseph went to the gate and retrieved his stained tunic and cap. He ran his hand over them to check if they were dry. They were, so he removed the tunic he was wearing and changed into the stained one so he could complete his tasks. He took a lantern to the goat's pen and shaved the underbelly of one of the goats. Finding the empty curd bag where his uncle said it would be, he took it and returned to the shed to complete his work. Joseph worked quickly; his muscles were starting to stiffen from the beating he had taken.

CHAPTER 6

After Joachim left Joseph, he walked at a very fast pace so he could get home to see his wife. The late-afternoon heat was still rather oppressive. Just past the spot where the boys had attacked Joseph, Joshua's mother Zillah approached him and said, "I just want to thank you for rescuing my Joshua today from that vicious nephew of Eleazer's."

"Oh, is Joshua still able to speak?"

"Yes, he can! Why? Did that troublemaker hurt my boy's mouth too?"

"No, it's just that your Joshua's tongue is so full of lies, a normal mouth wouldn't be able to form any intelligible words with a tongue so huge, that's all! My advice to you, Zillah, is to look for the hardest, strongest branch you can find, then bare his buttocks and start beating him with it. When you're all tired out and can't do it anymore, give it to your husband Abbas. If he's sober enough, let him use it on your son as long as he can too. And as for you, Zillah, you should tie your lips shut with a piece of string—or better yet, sew them shut with some thread so you won't be able to spew your vicious lying gossip around this town anymore. Wake up,

Zillah! You and your husband have spawned a real monster. Good day, Ma'am! By the way, I think there are enough people in this town with complaints against that evil son of yours to bring him before the Town Elders. As a matter of fact, I'm going to do so myself tomorrow morning, and I'm sure Azor will join me, as well as many others. He could have killed that innocent boy today!"

Zillah looked at Joachim with contempt. She threw her head to one side and said, "Hmm! My Joshua is a good boy!" She turned to leave and spat on the ground and mumbled, "A curse on you and your brother's houses." She then ran off to spread her vicious lies. Now Joachim and Azor were included with Joseph as the aggressors.

Joachim finally reached his house, paid his respect to the Law, and entered his home. He saw his wife as she dozed with her head against the wall. He carefully stepped over her injured foot. Joachim didn't want to wake her, so he crouched down in front of his wife to look at her injury. The man couldn't see much, though, since the poultice covered not only the ankle, but also most of her foot. What was visible was covered with dark bluish-brown bruises that now even encompassed her toes.

Anna, in a twilight sleep, could sense a presence in the room. She opened her eyes and saw her husband crouching before her. "I was dreaming that you had come home," she said. Joachim grabbed her hand, kissed it tenderly and asked her how she was. Anna smiled and said jovially, "I've been better."

"Eleazer's nephew told me all that had happened at the well this morning. Did Azor tell you how the poor boy had to pay for his kindness?" Her husband regretted the question as soon as he asked it. Anna told him she hadn't seen Azor yet. Joachim hesitated. He didn't know if he should say anything else, for he knew the tenderness of his wife's heart.

"Please don't keep me in suspense," Anna implored. "Tell me what happened to that fine boy."

Joachim told his wife everything that had transpired between Joshua, his little gang of thugs and Joseph. As her husband spoke, all that Anna could do was hold her face between her hands and shake her head in dismay. When Joachim finished, he could see tears in his wife's eyes. "I feel so responsible," she said. If it weren't for me, none of this would have happened to him."

"That's not true, Anna, and you know it! What did Susannah the widow do to deserve being pelted with stones by that evil seed, causing her to lose an eye? What did Nethanel the cripple do to have Joshua kick the crutch out from under him and then beat him with it? It's just a terrible shame there weren't two witnesses to prove what he did then. Otherwise, we could have brought charges against him to the Town Elders a long time ago. The boy has been deviously clever, though. He's at his worst when he thinks nobody is watching, but now at least he made a big mistake. Azor and I can both testify against him, and Susannah and Nethanel can have their testimony included too. Our Elders will finally render the justice demanded by the Law of Moses. I just hope they banish that boy from this town forever. He's nothing but trouble, and as long as he's around, nobody will be safe. The few times that I've had the misfortune of looking that boy straight in the eyes, all I'd see was hatred and pure evil staring back at me."

"As surly as the Lord lives, may the people he's wronged get the justice they deserve," Anna said. Just then their little daughter skipped across the courtyard to their home.

Joachim, with his knees bent, was still crouched opposite his wife as their daughter entered. She flew at him with open arms. The force of her sudden embrace knocked the thin man off balance. As her father fell to the floor, his daughter landed on top of him; the cotton cap slipped off his balding head. "Whoa!" her father said. "Watch out for your mother's foot, Princess!" Anna began to laugh at the comical scene. Her husband and daughter soon joined in the laughter. Joachim was skinny, but he was also very strong. He lifted his daughter as if she was light as a feather and tilted her legs up toward the ceiling until her forehead reached his lips. He kissed her, then set her down beside him and tickled her a bit as she giggled. The girl then stood up and straightened out her tunic. She went to her mother and kissed her too. Anna turned her daughter around and began to brush the dust from the child's tunic. Joachim stood up and brushed himself off as well, since the floors of all the houses in town consisted of nothing but hard-packed, oiled clay.

"Mommy, did Daddy tell you what that bad boy did to Joseph? Uncle Azor told me what happened to him."

"Yes, he did, and it was a horrible thing to do, don't you think?"

"Yeah, Mommy, it was," her daughter replied. "I think his mommy and daddy should punish him, don't you, Momma?" Anna agreed with her.

"And if they don't," her Father added, "Uncle Azor and I will see that someone else does."

"That's good," the little girl said. "But you know what, Daddy? I feel sorry for that boy. He must be very sad." Her father asked why. She replied that if you look at him up close, you could see that he had very, very sad eyes. They should all pray for him. At her tender age, the little girl couldn't tell the difference between sadness and pure evil. Her mother and father agreed that prayer was the best answer.

Joachim could see Tamar and Azor as they crossed the courtyard, carrying the evening meal they were about to share. Joachim asked his daughter to set the table as he lifted his wife and carried her there. He could see the pain in Anna's face and saw her wince and heard her cry out softly as her foot dangled freely in the air. As Tamar and Azor entered, Joachim lowered his wife to the floor as gently as he possibly could. They both asked Anna how she was feeling and then exchanged some pleasantries. After that, the three adults and the child stood and faced the city of Jerusalem. They raised their hands in prayer, and so did Anna; Azor led them. When he finished, the little girl added, "And please make my mommy better, and don't let Joseph hurt too much; and help that bad boy so his eyes won't be so sad." Joachim and Anna smiled at each other while the older couple looked confusedly at their niece. They then joined Anna at the table and enjoyed Tamar's stew.

While Joseph worked on his project in his uncle's shed, Zillah was busy packing Joshua's clothes and some food for travel. She said to her son, "You go to your Aunt Ruth's house in Sepphoris; you should know the way. We've been there many times. You have to leave before sunset; otherwise, the town gates will be closed for the night, and that old fool Eliud won't re-open the gates for anyone after sundown."

"But why should I leave?" Joshua asked snidely.

"Because some fools in this town are jealous of you and the fine man you're growing up to be. They have no sons of their own, so they're envious and trying to demean you because of their jealousy. They're making up lies about you, and they want to take their falsehoods to the Town Elders tomorrow morning."

"So! I'm not afraid of anybody in this stupid town," the boy said boldly.

His mother patted him gently on the cheek. "I know, dear, you've always been such a brave boy. Lies can hurt, though. My poor ailing heart would break if I had to watch you being flogged, or if I was forced to see you being led from this town in disgrace. My failing heart would just stop beating and split in two if I had to watch something like that." (The woman was actually very healthy and would feign a heart condition to elicit his sympathy, but he never showed any.)

"Yeah, yeah, yeah!" Joshua said. "How long do you expect me to stay there? Hmm!"

"Maybe for a year or two," Zillah said. "Just until all this blows over." She kissed her son on the cheek.

Joshua slapped her and wiped the spot where she had planted the kiss and yelled at his mother, "Don't you have any ears? How many times do I have to tell you to stop kissing me? What are you, deaf or something? Or are you just too stupid to understand what I say to you?!" Zillah didn't even flinch; she was used to such treatment from her son.

"I know you're just a little upset, dear; who could blame you after all those nasty lies."

"Are you that dumb, that you think I care what people are saying about me?" Joshua snarled. "Boy, you're a bigger idiot than I thought you were."

"Just say goodbye to your father, love, and let's get going. We don't have much time."

The boy's father was lying on the floor in a drunken stupor. Joshua kicked him and said, "You're even more pathetic than your crazy wife is, old man." Abbas, his father, moaned, then mumbled incoherently as the boy kicked him again. He then left the house with his mother.

"It's suppertime now," Zillah said. "Everybody should be eating. No one will see you go."

"As if I care!" the brazen boy answered.

They reached the gate just as the remaining sliver of the sun still blazed brightly over the ridge of the distant western hills. Eliud, with his old bent frame, moved slowly as he began to close the town gate. Joshua yelled, "Hey, you old fool, if you're too blind to see that I'm leaving, maybe you should quit this job and just go home, die and rot." The old man pretended he couldn't hear too well and didn't understand what Joshua had said. He kept the gate open just wide enough for the boy to pass through. Eliud then pushed his head through the opening and spit on the ground where the boy's feet had trodden. It was an old curse that called down misfortune on the person whose footprints were spat upon. It was supposed to prevent them from ever returning. It wouldn't work, though.

"Be safe, dear," his mother called out to him as she waved goodbye and blew him kisses. "I love you." Joshua turned and put his index finger to his temple as he rotated his hand in a circular motion. He pointed that same finger at the gatekeeper and then at his mother. "He's so shy!" she said softly through her tears, almost as if she was talking to herself. "I guess all boys his age have trouble showing their mothers how much they love them." She dried her tears with the edge of her veil as she walked home in silence. For the first time since she had moved to this town, she didn't try to look for someone with whom to share some vicious gossip.

Zillah wouldn't see her son again for several years. This gave her enough time to transform him into a national hero to any of the townspeople who would listen to her lies. Soon, the fabrications concerning her son's fame were carried far beyond the town by travelers who didn't know of the woman's or her son's reputations. The lies would even reach Jerusalem one day. Every time Azor or Joachim heard the stories of Joshua's fame, they would laugh hysterically and try to set the record straight.

After they had finished eating, Tamar and her niece began to clear the table. Joachim carried his wife to bed. He feared that someone would accidentally stumble over her foot and further injure his wife's ankle. Their house, like all the other homes in town, consisted of one large room, so even though Anna was in bed, she still could converse with her sister-in-law and her daughter.

Azor and Joachim quietly discussed something in the opposite corner of the house. They kissed their wives and the little girl as they prepared to leave. It was their custom, after sunset, to meet with the other men of town and discuss the events of the day. Each visitor or caravan that passed through kept them abreast of what was happening in the outside world. This evening, though, they had a real purpose in mind for going. They would ask the town's Senior Elder, who was always at the gate at twilight, to convene his group on the morrow, so they could formally bring charges against Joshua, to the Council of Elders. As they were about to leave, the little girl said, "Uncle Azor, may we make a fire tonight and maybe roast some grain, and then maybe you can tell us another one of your stories?"

Joachim said, "It's a little too hot outside for a fire tonight, don't you think, Princess? Uncle Azor is probably tired from our trip."

"No, no!" Azor said. "These old bones of mine are always cold. A fire tonight sure sounds good to me, and a little roasted grain will help me sleep better. That's a wonderful idea, Princess! While we're gone, you just think about what kind of story you want to hear, okay?" Joachim and Anna just looked at each other then shook their heads and smiled. Azor and Anna usually would do anything the little girl asked of them, even if it meant spoiling her a little.

Pain always seems to worsen at night. Tamar could see that her sister-in-law's discomfort was increasing. It was evident when she looked at the expression on Anna's face. "You're really suffering, my dear, aren't you? When I first saw your ankle and foot, I knew you'd be having a bad night. I could just feel it in my bones." Tamar reached into her outer robe and fished for the leather bag she had tied to the sash around her waist. The woman was a walking apothecary. She opened it and began to extract medicines. She asked the girl to bring her the pestle and mortar, so she could make something to ease her mother's pain. The girl brought the requested items. Tamar took some Valerian root, along with several various-colored powders and the dark-green leaves of an herb even she didn't know the name of. She added a little bit of myrrh for good measure and placed them in the mortar and crushed them. Tamar asked the girl to bring a cup of wine. The child poured one from the wineskin her father had hung on the wall, and brought it to her aunt. Tamar then added a clove of garlic to the mortar and blended it with the rest of the ingredients. She mixed the mash she had prepared with the wine and some honey and brought it to her sister-in-law. "Just take a few sips of this now and a few sips each time the pain gets too strong for you to bear." She turned to the little girl and said, "And make sure you don't drink any of this, child; it's only for grown-ups."

"Don't worry, Aunt Tamar. It smells pretty bad. I don't think I'd like it anyway." Tamar laughed as she handed the cup to Anna. "Drink! Go ahead, drink! I'm telling you, it'll help you!"

Anna tried to hold her breath so she couldn't smell the odiferous medication. When the foul liquid reached her taste buds, she had to let go of her breath and swallow hard to keep herself from spewing the liquid back into the cup, or worse yet, vomiting. Tamar produced, seemingly from nowhere, a small piece of flatbread dipped in honey and vinegar. She took the cup from Anna and immediately shoved the morsel into her sister-in-law's mouth. "Chew on this. It will kill the bad taste." The sweet sour bread did in fact eliminate the unsavory drink's horrible flavor. "Don't be afraid to wake Joachim during the night so he can give this to you. I'll show him how to do it." Anna thanked her sister-in-law and told her what a blessing she was. "You should start to feel a bit groggy in a little while. I'll stay with you while the men and the little one have their campfire and roasted grain. But," she said to her niece, "you better be sure to bring some in for your mommy and me." The child heartily agreed to do so.

Tamar was the type of person who always had to keep busy. She could never just sit by idly and relax. She noticed a basket full of raw Egyptian cotton that Anna had purchased recently. "I see you haven't combed this yet. Your daughter and I will do it for you." Anna replied that she had done enough. "Never you mind, dear," Tamar said. "Don't you know that idle hands are the devil's workshop? Come, child!" She walked the girl to the other side of the room, where the basket of cotton was. The woman put her index finger to her lips to indicate that they should speak quietly as she said, "We can both do this for your mother until the men return home."

101

Tamar found the two brushes that were needed for the combing process and made a game out of the work. Her gnarled fingers quickly pulled the cotton out of its prickly dried pod and placed it in the middle of the stiff reed-brush she held in her hand. She handed the other brush to her niece and told her niece to pull up while she pulled down. The girl did as she was told, and the wad began to thin into fibers. When it was fully stretched, Tamar told her niece to hang it on the wooden dowel next to the spindle. The child ran her hand over the combed cotton. "This is so soft, I bet if you could touch the clouds they'd feel just like this, Aunt Tamar." Meanwhile, Anna struggled to keep her eyes open. *Tamar's remedy must be working,* she thought to herself as her pain started to subside. She then drifted off into the deep dark void in our existence that we call sleep.

When the two men returned home, Joachim immediately asked Tamar about his wife. His sister-in-law raised her index finger to her lips so everyone would speak in hushed tones. She whispered that Anna was sleeping since they left, and that she had mixed her a potion. She then asked what Jakin the Elder had to say, and if he'd agreed to convene the council tomorrow. Azor told her that there was no need to do so now; Joshua had left town at sunset. Eliud had said that he witnessed the boy leave town just before locking the gates for the night. His mother was there to see him off. He carried his belongings with him.

"I bet she sent the boy to her sister Ruth," Joachim whispered. He knew of Joshua's aunt because he and

Anna had lived in Sepphoris until both of their older daughters married. They had moved to Nazareth just five years before their youngest daughter was born. Joachim agreed to partner with his brother in Azor's leather shop because his older brother's arthritic hands could no longer do fine leather detailing. "The boy has no other relatives," Joachim whispered. "After I spoke to Zillah this afternoon, she knew the handwriting was on the wall. Knowing her, she'd rather send her son away than face the embarrassment of him being censured by the Elders."

The little girl listened to the exchange between the adults, and waited for a break in their conversation, so that she could ask her uncle if they could go out and build the fire. As she was about to speak, Tamar reminded her husband about the roasted grain. She told Joachim to stay behind so she could show him how to administer the elixir if Anna awakened.

Azor and his niece left the house. The girl skipped to the woodpile and carried back two bundles of branches while her uncle stoked the ashes in search of any live embers that remained in the fire pit. The girl knew the routine. She ran to the stable, brought a handful of dry straw and sat on the large boulder. The moon and stars hid behind a heavy cloud cover. In the total blackness of the night, it was easy to find the glowing embers that still remained from the fire his wife had made earlier in the day. When Joachim joined them a few minutes later, they already had a roaring fire going. He could tell the brightly glowing sparks that rose above the fire had already mesmerized his daughter. They danced straight up on the waves of heated air. Since there was no breeze, they couldn't be diverted from their straight upward path. Azor had to back away from the blazing flames. The high nighttime temperature combined with the intense heat of the burning branches made him rather lightheaded. His old bones weren't really as cold as he had previously claimed. Joachim noticed his brother's ashen face and told him to move farther back; he would roast the grain. The old man took off his outer robe, laid it on the ground and sat on it. He felt cooler immediately. He kicked off his sandals and placed his bare feet on the cool grass; it revived him and his head cleared. The child offered him her seat on the boulder, but the elderly man declined.

The heat of the fire was proving too great even for Joachim. He stoked the flames, opened the second bundle of branches and slowly added them to the blazing fire. He too removed his outer robe and set it down next to his brother. Using a poker, he dragged some glowing embers to the side of the fire pit. He set the grain-filled clay bowl into the white-hot embers so the kernels would roast slowly. The bright firelight illuminated his little daughter, and caused her to stand out from the surrounding darkness. The light from the flames highlighted her ivory complexion, and the heat from the fire caused the cheeks of her cherubic face to turn a rosy red. The glow of the dancing flames gave a captivating sheen to her beautiful long auburn hair.

Every parent likes to think that each of their children is attractive. Joachim always tried not to favor one daughter over the others, but he had to admit to himself that of his three girls, the youngest was by far the most beautiful. Stunningly so, as a matter of fact. Joachim wondered how a person as homely as he could have such a beautiful daughter. He wasn't aware that his wife asked herself that same question daily.

"Have you thought about a story you'd like to hear tonight?" Azor asked his niece.

"Mommy told me the story about how my daddy got two names, and about all the boys who kept saying, 'Here I am.' I liked that story, would you tell it to me again?" The girl knew that her uncle could embellish any story and make it even more humorous and interesting than it originally was. She wanted to hear her uncle's version of what she already considered a hilarious incident. The child was all prepared to add her "Here I am!" to her uncle's version at the proper time. The very moment that his daughter asked to hear the story again, Joachim looked at his brother, and they both began to laugh. The truth of the matter was that the story their mother told of her son, and the difficulties she had with his name, had no basis in fact. The woman just devised the tale so she would have the liberty to call her son "Joachim" in her husband's presence. The woman never cared for the name Heli. She had called her son Joachim since his birth whenever her husband wasn't around. When the little girl saw that her father and uncle were laughing, she just thought that they found the story as humorous as she did. She was surprised when her uncle began to tell a totally different tale.

Azor began by saying, "Well, Princess, since you already heard the story about your father's name-change, I'd like to tell you about another little boy who heard a mysterious voice calling him in the night. His name was Samuel. When the boy was sleeping in the tent where the Ark of the Covenant was housed, he heard someone call out his name. He got up and looked around, but he couldn't see anyone, so he ran to the only person who was in the Tabernacle beside him, an old priest by the name of Eli. Samuel woke the man and said, 'Here I am!'

"The old priest said, 'I didn't call you, son. Go back to sleep.' So Samuel did as he was told." Azor told her that the incident was repeated again. After the second time Eli realized it was the Lord who was calling Samuel, and so the old priest told him that if he heard his name called again he should answer, 'Speak, Lord, your servant is listening.'"

Azor could see his niece's beautiful eyes widen as he continued the story of Samuel and segued into the story of David the shepherd boy whom Samuel anointed King of Israel. "Some people think that our auburn hair—at least yours, Princess; my hair is more gray than auburn now—is the same color as our ancestor, King David's, was," Azor said with pride. He continued his story. Toward the end he drifted into the Days of Messiah. "And when Messiah comes, and that will be any day now, you'll take your place as a real princess. And you may even be invited to live in His palace because He will be a son of David, and all of us who are of David's line will be considered royalty."

Azor's story was no more far-fetched than any other Jewish person of his time. The nation had waited so long for its deliverer that the times of the Messianic reign were only limited by the imagination of the individuals who spoke of the event. Azor continued to speculate further as he said, "And Messiah will ride out of the sky on a white stallion, and an army of angels will follow Him. The Temple mount will immediately rise up so high that the Temple itself will touch the clouds, and the streets of the city will turn into pure gold. And at His mighty shout the walls of the city will turn into precious stones so hard that even the hardest metal wouldn't be able to cut through them. One of the angels will call out to the great sea and gigantic pearls will roll out of it all the way to the old Jerusalem gates. They'll be three times as high as your house, and then the angel will cut the pearls into new gates for the city. Caesar will have to come to Jerusalem and kneel before Messiah to pay Him homage and bring Him tribute."

The little girl added, "And the walls of the city will move so that all the children of Abraham will live inside the city walls and none of us will ever have to die."

"I see you've been talking to your Aunt Tamar," Azor said. He continued, "And if Messiah decides to marry, He'd want a wife as beautiful as Esther, and we all know that there is no one more beautiful than you, Princess, so one day you may be queen."

Joachim smiled and shook his head from side to side. Azor's tales of Messianic times became more preposterous each day. Joachim removed the roasted grain from the embers and set the clay bowl away from the fire to cool. "I think your 'would-be queen' should be going to bed now," her father said to his brother.

"But Daddy," the girl replied, "I didn't even get a chance to eat any of the roasted grain yet."

"We can all have a bit when we get into the house. If you put too much food in your stomach you won't be able to sleep and you'll be awake all night. You can have the rest of it in the morning." Joachim grabbed the bowl with leather pads and took the grain into the house with them. Just before they entered, they felt a cooling breeze. As the sky began to clear, the full moon started to peek through the gaps in the clouds, painting the town a silvery blue.

When they entered the house, the trio saw that Anna was still asleep and Tamar was dozing. She still held the combing brushes in her hands, and her mouth was slightly open. The light of a single tallow candle danced in the evening breeze, and its flickering light barely illuminated the large room. Azor motioned to his brother to give the child some grain as he whispered, "I'll just wake Tamar and we'll go right home. From what she's told me, she's had a pretty busy day. I don't think she'll eat anything now; she'll just want to go to bed." Azor gently touched his wife's shoulder as he called her name softly.

The old woman's body quickened as she opened her eyes and said, "Hmm!" She shook her head to clear it, then she continued, rather loudly, "You startled me! What? Was I sleeping?"

Azor put his finger to his lips and said, "Shh! Anna is still asleep. Let's just go home and get you to bed." Azor took the brushes from his wife's hands and placed them in the basket of uncombed cotton. The little girl picked up the strands that her aunt had already turned to fiber. She kissed her aunt's forehead and whispered goodnight.

"Goodnight, little one!" her aunt replied softly.

Azor bent his head toward the little girl and bounced his index finger on his cheek as he whispered,

"What, no kiss for me?" His niece gave him one of her heart-melting smiles, then kissed his cheek twice.

"Two for you, Uncle Azor," she whispered. "One for goodnight and one for the story." Her uncle smiled and then extended his hand to his wife to help her to her feet. After saying goodnight to Joachim, the old couple left.

Joachim handed his daughter a little roasted grain and told her to chew it very well so it wouldn't lie in her stomach that night. Then it would be bedtime. They'd all had a busy day. Joachim took a few grains for himself; when he finished chewing, he said, "Let's wash our feet, then we'll pray." The little girl fetched the pitcher as Joachim brought the basin and towel. They washed the day's grime off of their feet. Joachim was about to take the pitcher and basin to the bed where his wife lay, then remembered that Tamar had told him she had already done so earlier, when she applied the poultice. He did, however, go over to the bed and take a long, hard look at his wife's injured foot. As he did so, he shook his head in disbelief. The swelling was worse, and now the entire foot had turned bluish-black. He tried to lift the poultice a bit more and look under it, but Anna stirred and groaned. Joachim withdrew his hand quickly. He knew it made no sense to wake his wife. Joachim gently kissed Anna's forehead, and let her sleep. The girl and her father then turned to face the Holy City. He prayed in hushed tones so he wouldn't wake his wife. When his prayer was finished, Joachim and his daughter both said, "Halleluiah, amen!"

Their bed was similar to all the beds of the townspeople. It was a rectangular mound of hard-packed clay less than an arm's span above the floor. Anna had sewn together several goatskins to cover the clay and to add some cushioning to the bed. She then had overlaid the skins with thick-woven mats of straw. The little girl hugged her father and gave him a sloppy wet kiss on his cheek. The child always slept between her mother and the wall. As she hopped up on the head portion of the bed and slid across its surface, the mats moved a bit; her mother stirred and groaned. The girl was about to lean over and plant one of her wet kisses on her mother's cheek too. Joachim knew it would wake his wife, so he raised his index finger, then turned his head side-to-side several times. He sent her a message in pantomime. Joachim raised his opened hand to his mouth, kissed it, pointed it toward Anna, and blew on it. The girl understood. She too blew her mother a kiss and laid down next to her. Joachim lowered himself down on the opposite side of his wife and stretched out next to her. As soon as he laid his head on the mat, he fell into a deep sleep.

The little girl tossed and turned as she waited to be certain that her father was asleep. She turned away from her mother and with her index finger she began to draw imaginary Stars of David on the wall. Her invisible triangles that formed the star's points grew larger and larger as she waited to hear the familiar sound of her father's snoring. There was something the little girl needed to do before she fell asleep. She didn't want anyone to hear her doing it.

At the first faint snore, the girl turned on her side, braced herself on her right arm, and began to rise and leave the bed. As she did, she saw that her mother's eyes were open and that Anna was biting her lower lip. The pain was intense once again. "Mommy, do you need your medicine?" the girl asked. "If you do, don't wake Daddy up. I'll get it for you."

"Yes, dear, I think I could use a little more right now," her mother said.

"Are you feeling any better, Momma?"

Anna didn't want to alarm her daughter any further so she whispered, "Yes, dear, I am. Be as quiet as you can be when you go get my medicine, though, so you won't wake Daddy."

"Okay, Momma! I remember what Aunt Tamar did, so I know how to do it," the girl said softly. The child scooted across the bed, went to the cabinet and quietly brought the liquid and the dipped bread to her mother. She stretched her small arms over her father's sleeping frame, being very careful not to wake him. The little girl administered the medication and then returned to bed. She whispered, "I'm so sorry for making you hurt yourself today, Momma."

"It's over and done with, dear. It was just a silly accident, that's all. Now let's just forget all about it, and go to sleep."

"Momma, may I just ask you something? This afternoon you said you just call me 'Princess,' but Uncle Azor told me that I really am one. Who's right?"

"Was Uncle Azor telling you about the Days of Messiah?" Her daughter said that he was. "Well, your uncle believes, as do many others, that Messiah will restore David's kingdom just as it was when

King David was alive. If that's true, then I guess you could possibly be considered a princess, or at least royalty of some sort." Anna didn't want her daughter to think her uncle was a sophist, so she tried to take a position somewhere between fact and fiction.

"Momma, Uncle Azor also said that maybe I could be a queen someday. Do you think so too?"

"Well, I don't think that's very likely. To be totally honest with you, dear, I don't think that a girl from a humble town like Nazareth stands much of a chance to have a title with such distinction." Anna struggled to keep her eyes opened. She could feel the effects of the elixir so she whispered to her daughter, "Give me a nighttime kiss, close your eyes, and get to sleep. The rest of your questions can wait till morning." The child kissed her mother and closed her eyes. She opened them again as soon as she could hear her mother's breathing become shallower. She couldn't leave the bed for a while yet; she first had to be sure both of her parents were sound asleep.

The little girl laid on her back and looked up at the ceiling. She saw the thatched ceiling's shadows overhead dancing in the light from the flickering flame of the tallow candle. The moon's glow was rather strong as it filtered through the high windows. The lulling sound of chirping crickets almost caused the girl to drift into sleep as she struggled to keep her eyes open. All of a sudden, a loud snapping sound tore through the night's calm. It startled the girl, and she shot up abruptly. A wind gust had caught hold of the end of a rolled up rawhide shade that hung above the window. The gale snapped the covering against the wall with a loud slapping sound that echoed through the entire room. Neither of her parents heard the noise, so the girl knew they were both sound asleep. She could finally leave the bed undetected. She scooted across the straw mat in silence. The child then tiptoed to the door, lifted the hasp, and stepped out into the pleasant night air.

The silvery glow of the moon made the world outside her door appear surreal. The dark velvety shadows beneath the olive tree swayed with the branches overhead as they moved in the night breeze. The moonbeams appeared to dance between them. Now a gentle wind whispered as it passed through the willowy olive branches. *Sefffff, sefffff,* was the sound it seemed to make. She thought of another game she could play, but this one wouldn't be as dangerous as the one she had invented that morning. She waited for the breeze to cease and for the branches to stop swaying. The girl then watched the top of the tree for the first sign that it would stir again. When the gentle gust came she was ready for it. She whispered, "Joe." *Sefffff,* the stiff breeze completed the name as it passed through the tree's branches again. She giggled softly. The child and the wind played their little game several more times and then the wind stopped. Her little game was over. Now she needed to do what she had planned on doing since her aunt had told her about the special room where God's earthly presence dwelled.

The little girl sat down with her back against the outside wall near the door. She drew her knees up to her chest, wrapped her arms around them, and cradled her chin on the valley she had formed between her knees. For the first time in her life the child began to converse with the God of Israel. Before this night, she had only spoken with her Maker in the rote of formal prayer. "Holy One," she said, "I feel bad because You have to live in that dark room in the Holy City all by Yourself. Dark rooms can be scary, especially when there's no one there with you. I don't like to be outside when it's real dark, either, because sometimes you can hear funny noises and then you get more scared.

"I think it was a real good idea that You made the moon because if You didn't, it would always be real dark at night. Then I wouldn't ever want to come out alone. Then I wouldn't be able to talk to You like right now. But maybe it would be better if You made the moon so that it never got any smaller because then it would be bright like this every night. Anyway, Aunt Tamar said You always see and never sleep. That's too bad because sleeping is good for you, and sometimes you have good dreams too. And if You could sleep, then the time you stay in that room wouldn't seem like it was so long. I thought I'd wait till it was night to talk to You because it must be hard for You to listen to all those people talking to You at once in the daytime. When everybody talks at one time it must sound like a bunch of bees, kind of like this, *bzzz, bzzz, bzzzz.*

"Anyway, there's another reason why I wanted to wait to talk to You until nighttime. It's because everybody else is sleeping, and I didn't want You to be too lonely. I thought maybe You could use some company. I was thinking all day about what Aunt Tamar said. I don't know what Your glory is, but if

114

You'd stop using it just for a little while, maybe people would be able to visit You without having their heads blow up and then You wouldn't be lonely. They could bring You some candles so You wouldn't have to sit in the dark anymore. Oh yeah! And they could bring You some raisin cakes and some bread. Yeah! Some bread dipped in honey, a lot of honey. I like it that way and I think You would too. Oh! And maybe when Your glory is off You could come out of that room, and then everybody would be glad to see You. Everybody would see how nice You look, and You could talk to them and they'd listen to You too. Then You could walk in the sunlight and see the birds and the flowers and watch the bees making honey. Even though my mommy says You always see, I still think it's good to feel the sun making you warm or smell the flowers and not just look at the birds but to hear them chirping too. I really, really think that all the people would like You because people are good. I mean there're some bad ones like robbers or like that bad boy who beat up Joseph today. I heard that there's some people who kill other people— You know, people like Cain, who killed his brother. Once You told everyone who You are, though, I'm sure nobody would do anything bad to You."

"I just have two things to ask that You'd do, please. Would You make my mommy's foot better and make Joseph feel better too. My daddy and Uncle Azor said he was pretty beat up by that boy Joshua. I know that I was to blame because if I didn't play that silly game, Mommy wouldn't be hurt and then Joseph wouldn't have been beaten up

115

either. I'm so sorry I did that. And one more thing. Would You please help that boy Joshua so he could be happier inside, then maybe his eyes wouldn't look so sad. Well, I'm getting tired now, so I'm going to go back to bed. Maybe You should try to see if You could sleep too. Rabbi said You could do anything. I think everybody is sleeping, so if You tried to sleep for a while, You could wake up as soon as You heard someone talking to You, and nobody but You would know that You were even sleeping. Oh! I almost forgot, I think Aunt Tamar was wrong about the holy presents, because Rabbi Asa said You like it when people bring You lambs, goats, turtledoves, and flour and olive oil. I didn't want to say anything to her, though, because my mommy and daddy said it isn't right to disagree with your elders. Well anyway, goodnight! I love You! I think I'm supposed to say 'Halleluiah, amen,' when I finish talking to You, but I guess I just did that. Oh! Just one more thing, I'll try and talk to You every night so You won't be too lonely when everybody else is asleep. Okay?"

The girl was about to stand up and go back to bed when all of a sudden she heard someone calling her name. She had never before heard a voice that sounded so beautiful. The tone was softer than the combed cotton she had pressed to her face earlier, and it was as gentle as the fluttering of a butterfly's wings. At the same time it had the chiming sound of many tiny bells, like the ones attached to the reins of camels that passed through her town in caravans. She jumped up, ran to the street, and looked both ways in search of the source of the melodious voice as she

116

said, "Here I am!" a little too loudly. The moment the words left her, she put her hand over her mouth. She feared that her loud response might have awakened her parents. The girl returned to where she had been sitting and looked up at the olive tree. She knew it was impossible for the branches to duplicate the sound of her name. Furthermore, there wasn't even a slight breeze now. The puzzled child stood where she was for a few moments, hoping she would hear the melodious call again, and she did.

"Mary!"

She heard the beautiful voice call to her once more. "Here I am!" she said as loudly as a whisper would allow. Mary stood there in confusion for several minutes, hoping to hear the voice respond; there was only silence. "Maybe I twirled around too much today, that's why I'm hearing things," she said disappointedly. Little Mary was very happy, though, because to her it didn't sound like she was talking backwards as her aunt had warned.

The girl finally gave up and went back into the house. Mary quietly made her way back to bed by her mother's side. She was happy to see that both her parents were still sleeping soundly. When she settled, in Mary chided herself for not remembering to say, "Speak, Lord, for Your servant is listening!" just as the boy Samuel had to do before he received a response to his reply. If she ever heard that beautiful melodious voice again, she'd remember what to say, and Mary hoped it would be soon.

What the little girl or the rest of the world couldn't possibly fathom, at that point in time, was that in her meandering prayer, some of her childhood logic was actually attune with the Divine Plan that had been in existence before time began. For in the not-too-distant future, that same little girl would rock the great "I Am" in her loving arms. She'd gently kiss His tiny forehead before tucking Him in for the night. Mary would actually watch Him sleep. She'd make sure a candle would always burn during the night so He would never have to be afraid of the dark. Mary would smile as she'd watch Him eat raisin cakes that she would make for Him, and she'd watch Him smile as He ate bread dipped in honey, yes, a lot of honey, like His mother. Mary would laugh when He would wrinkle His nose then shudder after taking a bite of overly ripened cheese. He would hold her hand as they would walk along the hillside and she'd teach Him the names of the birds and the flowers that His own word had created, for she was highly FAVORED by the Lord. She had made one mistaken assumption, though. The truth was, when He would tell them who He was, a lot of people wouldn't believe Him, and they'd hurt Him too.

CHAPTER 7

While Mary cuddled up close to her mother and drifted off into a deep sleep, Joseph completed his project. He then spread some old burlap on the floor of the shed and laid down to sleep. The pain in his stiffening muscles was increasing. The boy turned on his side so the battered part of his head wouldn't have to feel the pressure of the earth below him. Joseph drew his knees up to his chest and laid in the fetal position, hoping sleep would come quickly. But the soreness he was feeling would keep him only on the rim of sleep, where all the doors of the subconscious are opened wide for pleasant dreams or horrendous nightmares. As soon as somnolence came, the teenager entered that strange world of distorted reality.

Joseph began to dream the recurring nightmare he had dreamt almost every night for two years after his father's death. However, new characters and different scenes were added from the events of the past day. The rusty-red water he had seen in the washbasin was probably the key that unlocked that part of his subconscious that kept the death of his father trapped there for the last six years.

In his dream, Joseph saw himself walking next to his dad, but he wasn't the five-year-old boy he had been on the day his father died. He saw himself as the teenager he was today. His father pointed to a very tall, sturdy cedar tree that grew in a cleft of the steep terraced hillside. Jacob said, "Today, son, we're going to fell that cedar. It's going to make some fine sturdy roof beams. I've been watching it for years now, and we're finally going to bring it down." Jacob took hold of his son's hand; with his other he led the pack mule along the narrow path.

When they reached the tree, Jacob tethered the mule and led his son to a much-wider location on that same terrace. It was a safe distance from the tree yet totally within Jacob's range of sight. He handed the adolescent several wooden blocks along with a small knapsack filled with dates, figs and olives, and a skin filled with fresh water. "Sit right here, son; you can build things with your blocks or watch me chop the tree down. Whatever you do, don't move from here; otherwise, you're going to get a good spanking." Jacob pointed to a lower, wider terrace on the hillside below and said, "Now watch—if I make the right cuts on the tree trunk it should fall right there. Then it'll be much easier to get a team of oxen onto that wider terrace so we can haul the tree back to town."

"Uh-huh!" Joseph replied, and wondered why his father gave a 13-year-old a set of wooden blocks

to play with. He pretended to enjoy playing with them as his father watched from a distance.

The next thing he knew, he was standing next to his dad by the tall cedar. Joachim was standing beside them with his little daughter. He said, "Now you have to pick out which one of the two is really Joseph." The girl couldn't decide. Jacob scolded Joseph for leaving the safe area. Suddenly Joachim and his daughter were gone. Jacob then led his son back to the wider section of the terrace. Somewhere along the path, Joseph turned into a five-year-old again, and the girl reappeared with her mother. Little Mary was playing with the blocks while Anna swept the area with a broom. His father had returned to the tree that he would fell. When she finished sweeping, Mary's mother opened a napkin containing goat curd, and the three of them ate.

Jacob kept smiling and waving at his son as he removed his tools from the pack mule and tethered it farther away from the tree. As soon as Jacob started chopping, Joseph saw a huge black bat flying toward him. He waved his arms rapidly above his head to try to keep the bat away from the little girl and himself. Anna came to their rescue. She began to swat at the bat with her broom. Mary just kept playing with the blocks as if she was totally oblivious to what was happening around her. Anna had her back to him as she fought off the bat, but when she suddenly turned around, it was no longer Anna—it was his Aunt Rebecca. She began to beat him with the broom. He crouched over to fend off the blows. The teen could see that his father had a look of horror on his face. Joseph knew what was coming next. The boy could hear the rumbling sound of a huge boulder that had broken free from its footing

121

and now rolled toward him. His father was yelling frantically and pointing to it as he ran toward his son. Joseph didn't move. He just bent over even lower as his aunt continued to beat him mercilessly.

All of a sudden Joseph felt himself being lifted up as he was tossed away from the path of the rolling boulder. He landed with a thud. The boy looked up as he saw the massive rock strike his father's back and knock him off the terrace. The boulder rolled right past the spot where Joseph had been sitting, and bounced down the hillside. Jacob landed face-up on a tier below Joseph, just out of the boy's reach. The terrified child walked over to the spot directly above his father. He laid down and pushed himself forward just far enough to see his father's battered, bloody body. He stretched out his arm, but he couldn't extend it far enough to reach his dad.

Jacob was barely able to speak. "Get help!" he tried to say. Joseph understood. He was about to get up and go for help when a sudden strong gust of wind whipped at the hillside, bending the tree towards the boy. The thin layer of wood that still held the huge cedar upright snapped. Instead of falling directly forward, the strong wind gust blew the tree in Joseph's direction. The trunk didn't break freely from the stump, and never fell the way his father had intended it to do. Instead, it pinned Joseph under one of its heavier branches. It didn't hurt him, but he couldn't dislodge himself from under it. He thrashed in his sleep as he saw himself lying there helpless, once again watching his father die a slow, painful death.

Joseph shot up and awoke from his sleep by the renewed horror of that tragic day. His tunic was wet with perspiration. The teenager's breathing was so rapid that he was gasping for air. His whole body trembled as he tried to stand on wobbly legs. Joseph doused his face and neck with water; it seemed to calm him a bit. As his adrenaline level returned to normal, his soreness increased. He took a rough stone and continued to sand his project, even though the wood was already smooth as silk. The increasing pain kept him awake until morning. He didn't want to fall asleep anyway. The boy didn't want to risk the chance of repeating the nightmare again tonight. Once was enough.

In the early-morning darkness Joseph went for some fresh water. He washed up, changed into his clean tunic, and pulled his cap over his bandaged head. He winced as the dressing pressed into his open head-wound. When the moon was about to fall behind the western ridge of the hills, he went to the aging room and chose two rounds of cheese. He'd pay his uncle for them later. The boy returned to the shed. He picked up the horsehair bag and his nighttime project, and headed down the hill toward the main street of the town.

When Joseph reached the lower part of the sleepy hamlet, the sky began to lighten slightly. He would be back home by the time the sun's blazing rim was visible on the eastern horizon. *I sure hope it's going to be a better day today,* he thought to himself as he neared Anna's house. When Joseph accomplished his mission, he quickly walked home.

As he neared the path that led up to his uncle's house, he heard a rooster's crow salute the new day.

Little Mary heard the crowing too. The girl always rose early. She sat up and rubbed the sleep from her eyes. Mary saw that her father was already up and about, but her mother still slept beside her. Joachim busied himself with the morning chores that Anna usually did. The little girl crawled out of bed, went up to her father and tugged on his tunic. Joachim turned and bent low so his daughter could give him a good-morning kiss. It was a daily ritual they both enjoyed. "Good morning, Daddy!" the little girl said.

"Good morning, Princess!"

"Is Mommy okay? She's usually up before you are, Daddy."

"She's fine, Princess. Mommy will be sleeping for a while yet. I had to give her another dose of her medicine not too long ago, so I'm sure she'll sleep a bit longer than usual. I did check her foot when I got up, though; it looks like the swelling went down a bit. You'll have to help Mommy all that you can today. I don't think she'll be able to walk on that ankle for a few days. I know Aunt Tamar will help out, but she has her own house to take care of. So be a big help to Mommy and your auntie too. Okay?"

"Sure, Daddy, I'll help Mommy. I'll do whatever she wants me to do."

"I'm sure you will, Princess. Now would you please fill the kettle with water for me? I'll start a fire so we can wash up and have a little something to eat."

Mary took the kettle from her father and walked outside to the rain trough. Within seconds she came

124

running back into the house, shouting, "Daddy! Daddy! Look what I found!"

With his finger over his lips, Joachim turned to face her and whispered, "Shh! Mommy is still sleeping." Joachim was surprised to see his little daughter enter with a round of cheese, a horsehair bag and a sturdy crutch. "My!" he said with a smile. "I wonder where that came from."

"I think I know, Daddy."

"So do I, dear!" her father replied.

"I think that boy Joseph; he must have left these things here. You know why, Daddy? This is the bag Mommy gave him for the curds yesterday, and his uncle makes this," she said as she handed her father the cheese. "But I don't know where he got this from," she said as she handed her father the sturdy crutch.

Joachim took it from his daughter and examined it carefully. "I believe Joseph made this himself," he said. "And it looks like he did a mighty fine job too. It's been carved out of a single piece of wood. I think Joseph is a good carpenter like his father was. He's way past the apprenticeship stage. Don't you think?"

Mary looked in awe at the crutch. "You mean Joseph can make things like this?" She ran her hand over the finely sanded wood and asked, "How did he do it?" Joachim didn't answer; he just put the crutch under his armpit and used it as he walked around the room. It was a little too high for him, so he couldn't keep it perpendicular to the ground. It gave him solid support, though. It would be the perfect height for his wife, since she was taller than him.

While Joachim practiced walking with the crutch and Mary watched curiously, Joseph finished climbing the hill. When he reached the top, he saw his uncle standing there waiting for him. "Good morning, Uncle Eleazer!" he said.

"Good morning, my boy! I see you ran your errand already."

"Yes I did, sir! I wanted to drop the cheese off before anyone was awake. As soon as we get into the house, I'll pay you for the rounds."

"There's no big hurry," his uncle said. "How are you feeling today? I bet you're pretty sore."

"Yes sir! I am, but moving around helps a bit. I don't feel as stiff as I did before."

"Well, why don't we go into the house for a bite to eat. There's some fresh bread, and I brewed some of that herbal tea that you like."

"That sounds great to me," Joseph said. Eleazer put his arm over his nephew's shoulder as they walked toward the house. Joseph knew his uncle was trying to show his affection. He didn't want to hurt his uncle's feelings by telling Eleazer how much the pressure on his arm hurt his injured shoulder blade.

"I want to take another look at those wounds of yours and put some fresh bandages on them too. You take the rest of the day off. You deserve a little break and your body needs some down time so it can heal."

"I'd rather keep busy, Uncle." the boy said. "That way I won't have time to worry about how I'll do with my reading tomorrow."

They paid their respect to the Law on the doorframe and entered the one-room home. Rebecca was still sleeping. Joseph noticed a woven reed chest on the table in the place where he usually sat. "Let's sit down," his uncle said. They both sat cross-legged as the boy stared curiously at the chest. "Go ahead, open it!" Eleazer said. "It's for you."

Joseph lifted the lid and saw a pile of cedar shavings. He looked dumbfounded. He had no idea what he was supposed to do with them, but he smiled at his uncle and said, "Thank you very much, Uncle Eleazer." So far both of them had been whispering in deference to the sleeping woman. When he saw the look on his nephew's face and heard the boy's heartfelt gratitude for what his nephew perceived as nothing but wood shavings, Eleazer burst out laughing.

"Quiet, I'm still trying to sleep," Rebecca said.

The man got his laughing under control. As he wiped tears of laughter from his eyes, he said, "Take the shavings out of the chest, Joseph. There's something between them."

The boy carefully removed the shavings; about midway into the chest he uncovered some white wool material; as he dug deeper he could see the blue stripes that were woven into the fabric. Joseph's eyes lit up as his face beamed with joy. He knew what it was. "It's my father's prayer shawl. You saved it for me! Thank you, Uncle!" The boy shook off the remainder of the shavings and placed the shawl over his shoulders.

"Tomorrow when you read from the Holy Scrolls, a part of your father will be with you, and I know that he's as proud of you as I am. Now, just put that aside for a while and we'll eat," Eleazer said jovially. "I was going to wait until tonight to give it to you at our Sabbath meal, but according to our law we'd have to leave the shavings and the chest on the table until Saturday night. Your aunt wouldn't like that at all."

"May I be excused for a minute? I have to run to the shed. I have gifts for you and Aunt Rebecca too."

"Go ahead, Joseph, but it's your celebration tomorrow, not ours."

When the supposedly sleeping woman heard her name mentioned in conjunction with the word *gift*, she immediately crawled out of bed and said, "Good morning!" They returned the greeting, and then the boy ran off to the shed.

Joseph's body ached as he pulled away some of the burlap and began to lift the heavy wooden objects he had been working on for the past two years. He made them to show his gratitude to his aunt and uncle for all they'd done for him. The teen carried the lighter gifts he had made for his uncle to the side of the house, and left them outside the door. Joseph stuck his head inside the doorframe and said, "Please stay inside until I'm done." Returning to the shed, he struggled as he dragged the heaviest object to the side of the house too. Joseph poked his head into the house and asked, "Is everybody ready?"

"Yes we are," Eleazer answered.

"Would you both mind closing your eyes just long enough for me to get these things inside?" When they did, Joseph brought into the house the four objects he had crafted. They were still draped in burlap.

"You can open your eyes now," Joseph said. He uncovered the first of his gifts and handed them to his uncle. He had carved two sturdy cheese-paddles for him. "Your old ones are rather worn, so I thought you could use a couple of new ones."

His uncle beamed with pride as he examined his nephew's handiwork. "This is great. You're already a good carpenter. Maybe you shouldn't go apprentice with Uncle Achim after all," he said jovially. Rebecca was about to chastise her husband for even suggesting Joseph stay with them, but she thought better of it. Instead, she craned her neck to see if she could get a better view of the largest item, which was still covered. She wondered whom it was for. Rebecca could care less about the cheese paddles or the workmanship that went into them. Joseph then unwrapped the smallest of the gifts.

His uncle couldn't believe his eyes when the boy handed it to him. "Joseph, did you really make this?"

Yes, Uncle Eleazer, I did. Do you know what it is?" the boy asked.

"Yes, I do, and it's the most handsome and detailed cover I've ever seen."

"Let me see that," Rebecca said.

"Do you know what it is, dear?" Eleazer asked as he handed it to his wife.

"No," she said, "but it's beautiful." She examined the fine workmanship in disbelief. "This is a real work of art, whatever it is."

"It's a new cover for the Commandments on our doorframe," Eleazer said. "See, the words, they're written in Hebrew."

"What, don't you think I can read?" his wife asked. "It says what you always say when you enter the house: 'Hear, O Israel, the Lord your God is One!' Those letters look like they'd be easy to carve

129

in comparison to the designs that border it. You couldn't have made that, Joseph. You're only thirteen. You bought it from someone, didn't you?"

"No, Aunt Rebecca, I really did make it myself, from the wood that Uncle has been bringing me."

Rebecca was more anxious than ever to see what the largest gift was. She knew it had to be for her. Eleazer said, "Come with me, son, and let's put this up now."

"It just snaps right over the old one, Uncle. It's a real tight fit, so you won't need any nails. You can just tap it into place with your fist."

"Eleazer, don't be so rude," Rebecca added. "Can't you see that Joseph has another gift?"

His uncle looked at Joseph then shrugged his shoulders. The teen smiled at his uncle and then said to his aunt, "Please close your eyes one more time, Aunt Rebecca, and don't peek."

"Okay!" she said rather sarcastically. Rebecca was anxious to see what was under the burlap. She tried not to show her annoyance at the boy for making her wait longer. The woman closed her eyes tightly and put her hands in front of her face.

Joseph uncovered the last of his gifts. Rebecca heard her husband say, "As surely as the Lord lives, I've never seen anything like it. You actually made that, Joseph?"

"Yes, Uncle Eleazer, I did."

Rebecca couldn't wait any longer. She dropped her hands and opened her eyes. The woman couldn't believe what she saw. Her eyes filled with tears as she said, "Oh, Joseph! I can't believe you made this for me!" She was absolutely thrilled. She couldn't understand why Joseph would make her such a beautiful gift after the way she had treated him. Her hardened heart was softened by her nephew's unconditional love. She went up to him and took him in her arms. It was the first time she ever hugged or kissed him. "Please forgive me for yesterday," she whispered in his ear. It was the first time in his life he felt the tenderness of a woman's lips touch his face. His mother hadn't lived long enough to hold her son, let alone kiss him.

Tears welled up in Joseph's eyes too as he asked, "Do you really like it, Aunt Rebecca?"

"Joseph, it's gorgeous! It's so lovely. I have never seen a chest like it in my life. Look, Eleazer, it's raised off the ground on legs that are carved like clusters of almond blossom, and Joseph carved the same flowers on the lid. And look at this filigree around the edges and down the sides. I don't think anyone has a chest like this one."

"Open it, Auntie!" Joseph said.

Rebecca did, and at once she could smell the fragrance of the cedar wood that the boy had used as an interior lining for the chest. "This is priceless!" Rebecca said. "Something this beautiful would cost a small fortune at the bazaar in Jerusalem."

"I made it the same size as your wicker hamper. I don't know what you keep in there, but I thought if there's any cloth, the cedar will keep the moths away."

Rebecca hugged and kissed her nephew again. "I still can't believe how talented you are. Woodworkers twice your age couldn't make something as detailed as this," she added.

"I think Joseph has sawdust running through his veins just like his grandfather, his father, and his Uncle Achim," Eleazer said. The tenderness of the moment was broken as they laughed at the remark.

When they stopped laughing, Rebecca said, "When we move to Jerusalem, I want my chest to be in a place on the wagon where everyone can see it. And don't you think of covering it. I'll be the envy of every woman there." Eleazer just looked at Joseph as he raised his eyebrows and smiled.

"I almost forgot to pay you for the cheese," Joseph said. He went to his small hamper and picked up his bag of copper coins. He noticed it was lighter than it was before. After paying his uncle, he'd have only two coins left. There should have been twenty times that amount in the pouch by now. Joseph knew that his aunt kept taking them from him every time his uncle was generous enough to give him a little something for the extra work that he did. Joseph never complained, though. He felt she deserved it for washing his clothes, fixing his meals, and letting him live with them.

Joseph installed the new cover on the doorframe as his uncle stood back to admire it. Rebecca just sat on the floor, running her hands over the beautifully detailed blossoms on the cover of the chest. *They look so real,* she said to herself. *I can almost smell them.* Rebecca was very anxious for her husband and Joseph to leave so she could transfer her treasures to her new wooden chest. "You two eat," she said. "I have bread to bake and the Sabbath meal to prepare. I haven't even washed up yet." Eleazer led them in prayer and the two men sat and ate as Rebecca rushed off to the upper well for fresh water.

Joseph cleared off the table, then placed the prayer shawl in his hamper. After his uncle cleaned and re-bandaged his wounds, Eleazer and his nephew went off to the aging room of the cheese shop. There were rounds of goat cheese that still needed to be dipped in wax before the Sabbath.

While Eleazer sat by the kettle, waiting for the wax to melt, he watched his nephew stack the cheese rounds that needed to be coated. Joseph had grown into a fine young man and had come a long way from the frightened, traumatized little boy he had brought home with him eight years ago. He remembered that tragic day when he finally located his nephew trapped under the branches of the huge cedar. The poor boy had been there for two days with his father's corpse almost within his reach. Little Joseph couldn't get to the food or water. He was dehydrated and starving. His clothes were soiled, and his small hands were bloodied from digging in the sandy soil to throw dirt and rocks at the small animals and the birds of prey that tried to feed off his father's corpse. Had it not been for Jacob's mule chewing through its reins and wandering back into town, no one would have suspected anything.

Jacob always took his son with him whenever he went in search of lumber. Fortunately, Eleazer remembered his brother had recently spoken about the huge cedar and had told him he would be chopping it down soon, before someone else did. Since the tree was downed, it was hard to locate the precise spot where the cedar had been located. The townspeople searched for Jacob and his son by torchlight the first night. They finally found him in the evening twilight of the second day. From a distance they could already tell that Jacob was dead but his son was still moving. As night fell, they freed the boy from under the heavy branches, and Eleazer lifted Joseph into his arms. The boy kept trying to call for his daddy. His throat was dry, and his voice was hoarse from screaming for help. The sound of the air moving through his larynx was louder than any of the actual words he tried to say.

The townsmen had thought they would find Jacob and his son alive, so they didn't have the forethought to bring anything with which to cover Jacob's blood-stained body. Consequently, they had to carry his corpse into town uncovered. The flickering light from the torches made the boy think that his father was still moving. Joseph kept screaming, with what little was left of his hoarse voice, "Wake up, Daddy, they found us! Wake up, Daddy! Please! You don't have to sleep anymore."

For the next couple of years, little Joseph would wake up screaming from the nightmare in which he was forced to relive that terrifying experience over and over. Eleazer would take him in his arms and try to rock him back to sleep. Some nights he was more successful than others. Rather than hardening the boy's heart, the accident drew him closer to the Lord God of Israel. Joseph grew up with a heart full of compassion for the misfortunes of others. His uncle couldn't have been more proud of him. At 13, Joseph was already more of a man than most grown men were. It was fitting, Eleazer thought, that all of Israel would finally recognize that fact tomorrow afternoon.

Joseph looked into the large kettle and saw that all the wax had melted. He knew if it overheated, the extreme temperature might ruin the cheese. The teen saw that his uncle was lost in thought. "Uncle Eleazer!" Joseph said, rather loudly.

His uncle jumped as he heard his nephew call his name. He left his memories behind as his mind returned to the present. "Yes, yes, what is it, Joseph?"

"The wax, Uncle Eleazer, it's about to overheat."

"Oh! Thank you my boy; my mind just wandered a bit. The older you get, the more it happens." The two of them then finished the dipping process. Eleazer would sorely miss the boy when he was gone. He didn't want his nephew to think he wanted to be rid of him, so he said, "Joseph, I hope you know you don't have to leave on Sunday if you don't want too. The agreement that Uncle Achim and I made wasn't carved in stone or written in blood, you know. It's just that the oldest son usually pursues the trade of his father. You could make a very good living just making things similar to the gifts that you made for your aunt and me. People will be amazed when they see your work just like your aunt and I were. Stay right here if you'd like, and follow through with your talent, or for that matter, you could always join me in my business."

"No disrespect, Uncle, but I'd like to be a full-fledged carpenter someday," Joseph replied. I have to learn how to install roof beams, build solid walls and even dress out large timbers for building. I just don't want to be a woodcarver. I'd like to be a real carpenter so that someday I'll build something great and be able to support a family. And if I don't enjoy that line of work anymore, or if my back or hands fail me, then you sure have taught me enough to go into the cheese-making business like you. Not that it's a trade less honorable than carpentry; I didn't mean to imply that. I'm grateful for all you taught me and for everything else you've done for me, Uncle Eleazer. I know I could never repay you. You're like a father to me."

His uncle turned his head away. He didn't want his nephew to see the tears in his eyes. Eleazer stirred the melted wax with one of his new paddles as he said, "Joseph it's been my privilege and my pleasure. You're a blessing from the Lord. I have had more joy in raising you then if I would have had twelve sons of my own like our patriarch Israel." Joseph blushed.

Eleazer had to leave for town, as he was planning a combination bar mitzvah and going-away party for his nephew. His friend Nabu, a Hittite who was not bound by Sabbath laws, would prepare the food for the feast on Saturday. The celebration would be held in the common area, close to the town gates. All the townsfolk usually participated in such events. Eleazer had to purchase the food and beverages for the event.

Nabu was not only a neighbor and good friend, but he also worked for Eleazer when he needed additional help. He helped Rebecca run the business when her husband went on the road to peddle his cheeses. Eleazer also had another non-Jewish friend, named Ali, who was an Ishmaelite. He led caravans throughout the Middle East. Joseph was to join his caravan on Sunday morning to go to his Uncle Achim's. Eleazer would trust Ali with his own life, and knew he would watch over his nephew, making sure that Joseph would reach Achim in safety.

As Eleazer headed down the path to the town below and Joseph re-stacked the newly waxed cheese rounds, Anna awoke and saw Joachim walking around the house on a crutch. When little Mary saw her mother move, she couldn't restrain herself any longer. The girl ran to the bed. "Mommy! Mommy! Look what Joseph made for you." Anna slid to the edge of the bed. She grimaced as she lowered her throbbing foot to the floor. Anna was surprised to see her husband was at home. She could tell by the position of the sun that it was the latter part of the morning.

"Joachim, did you injure yourself too?" she asked.

Her husband chuckled as he said, "No, dear, I've just been trying out this crutch that Joseph made for you. It sure is sturdy."

"The dear boy made that for me?" she asked.

Joachim was about to answer when little Mary said, "Yes, Momma, that's what I was telling you. I found it outside by our door with a round of cheese and the horsehair bag you gave Joseph yesterday."

"That dear, sweet boy!" Anna said. "Joachim, may I use it now, please?"

Before she stood up, Joachim insisted on checking her foot. His wife jokingly said that she didn't think he wanted her to stand up yet, because he was enjoying using the crutch a little too much.

"Was it that obvious?" Joachim replied humorously.

"Nothing usually keeps you away from work, so I thought it must be your new toy."

"Now my feelings are really hurt," he said with a smile. "Here I did all of the housework, and you say that I'm playing. I'm devastated by your remark."

"You'll get over it!" Anna said jokingly.

Joachim assisted his wife from the bed and handed her the crutch. Anna asked if Tamar had been over yet. He replied that she had been there earlier and that Joseph had left them some cheese also. His sister-in-law then left for the market to purchase some things for tonight's dinner. "So you see, my dear, I was already working today. I just took a break to have lunch with my wife and daughter. Now who owes whom an apology? I can't help it if some people try to sleep the whole day away. I'm not mentioning any names, of course, but there's no limit to what some people will do just to lie in bed and do nothing."

Mary took her father's playful banter seriously and said, "Daddy! Mommy didn't do that on purpose. It was just a silly accident."

"I know, Princess. I was just teasing Mommy." As he checked her ankle he said, "Well, the swelling is down a bit, so I'm going to remove the old poultice. Tamar said she was preparing a new one." Joachim cut the poultice free and saw how badly the bruised area actually looked. He said he thought it would be best if she still stayed off of her foot for a while. Then he added, "Now wait until you see the delicious lunch our Princess has prepared for us." Mary smiled at her father as she carried the tray with her mother's meal on it to her bedside. The little girl removed the cloth that covered it. Anna saw that there was bread and honey, salad greens and honey, barley cakes and honey, and last night's roasted grain in more honey.

Joachim smiled at his wife as she lathered her daughter with praise for the culinary delights before her. "I'll just have a few bites now and finish the rest later, dear. After I wash up a bit. You go out and play for a while so Daddy can help me. And thanks again for this delicious lunch."

As soon as Mary was outside, Joachim handed Anna the jug of vinegar. "Some of it isn't too bad if you cut the sweetness," he said. "I snuck some vinegar when Mary wasn't looking. I think she emptied the whole honey pot, though." The couple laughed.

The little girl started to twirl as soon as she stepped outside. She thought that if she did so for about the same amount of time as she did yesterday, perhaps the beautiful voice would call her name again. This time she'd remember to answer correctly. When Mary thought she had spun around enough, she grabbed hold of the olive tree and opened her eyes to see everything still move before her. To her surprise, she saw her Aunt Tamar and a stranger with a cask under each of his arms moving in the blur. "What did I tell you about twirling?" her aunt asked.

Mary waited until everything stopped spinning, and when she regained her equilibrium she said, "I just did it a little while, Auntie. See, I'm not talking backwards yet." The man who was standing next to her aunt looked at the girl quizzically. He didn't quite comprehend Mary's response to the question.

"This is Joseph's Uncle Eleazer," Tamar said.

"And you're the girl with the beautiful eyes that my nephew told me about," Eleazer replied. Mary blushed and looked to the ground as he continued, "And I see that she is a beautiful little cherub too, as captivating as my nephew said she was."

"I'll go get my Azor. Mary, go tell your father that Joseph's uncle is here to see him. You'll have to excuse me, Eleazer, but I have these chickens to clean and prepare for our Sabbath meal."

"No need to apologize, Tamar; I have a very busy afternoon too. By the way, you do know that my nephew's bar mitzvah is tomorrow. I hope you and your husband will join us to celebrate."

"Yes, my sister-in-law told me about it yesterday. You can count on us to attend."

"And I hope to see you there too, Mary." The little girl smiled at Joseph's uncle, then skipped toward the door.

Mary opened the door slowly just in case her mother and father still wanted privacy. No one rebuked her, so she entered and told her father of Eleazer's visit. She took Joachim's place by Anna's side and got her first good look at her mother's injury. "Mommy, does that hurt much?"

"It's still sore, but the pain is not as bad as it was yesterday."

"That's good, Mommy. I asked God last night if He would please make you better, so I think He listened, don't you?"

"Yes, dear, I do! He always listens to us when we speak to Him."

"Mommy, do you think I could go to Joseph's party tomorrow? His uncle said we should all come."

"We'll have to wait and see, dear."

"Aunt Tamar said that she was going."

"I would like to go too, dear, and I'm sure Daddy will go. If Aunt Tamar is going, you can go also."

"Oh, thank you, Mommy, he's really a nice boy. And you know what, Mommy?"

"What is it, dear?"

"He told his uncle I have pretty eyes." Anna was amused and smiled from ear to ear at the coquettish way her daughter looked when she said it. Mary definitely had a childhood crush on the teenage boy, and Anna could see why.

Meanwhile, Eleazer presented two casks of olive oil, one to Azor and one to Joachim, in gratitude for helping his nephew. As was custom, they declined the gift at first but good manners insisted on them accepting it with deep gratitude. It would be rude of them not to ask their benefactor to join them for a while, so the three men sat under the olive tree and talked. Both men complimented Eleazer on the wonderful job he had done in raising Joseph. Eleazer then expressed his melancholy over losing his nephew. The two men understood. They both had to bid farewell to their daughters when they married, so they could empathize with him. "My two older daughters both moved away from us," Joachim said. "One lives in Tarsus; the other is married to a merchant and lives in Rome. I have eleven grandchildren, maybe even more by now, but I never get a chance to see any of them because they're so far away. My daughters can't travel because it's hard to do so with children, and I could never leave the business for the amount of time it would take to go and see them. That is, not unless we wanted to starve without my income. That's why I said to my wife, when our youngest daughter marries; she'll marry someone local who will keep her here in town or at least within a day's journey from us. I want to be able to at least bounce one of my grandchildren on my knee; even if my knee joints won't be able to move by then." The three men laughed.

Azor said, "My daughter and her husband live outside of Jerusalem in the Judean hills. We very seldom get a chance to see her either. My brother here complains about not being able to see his grandchildren, but as for my wife and I, we will never have any. My daughter, our only child, is barren and way past her childbearing years."

"Only the Lord God knows what's in store for each of us," Eleazer said. "As our people always say, 'The Lord may give us sorrow tonight, but He brings us joy in the morning.'" Joachim and Azor nodded in agreement. "I better get to the other reason why I came to see you both before the Sabbath is upon us. I'd like to purchase some leather saddlebags and a leather apron or two for my nephew." The three men got up and went into the shop just as Mary and her mother came to the door.

The little girl stood close to her mother so she wouldn't fall as Anna experimented with her new crutch. Little did Mary know that if her mother lost her balance, she was so tiny that she wouldn't be able to do anything about it anyway, except perhaps call for help. The boy had made the crutch to fit perfectly under Anna's armpit. She didn't have to put any pressure on her injured foot. Tamar, who was bringing out the dressed chickens for baking, saw Anna and began to scold her for walking too soon.

Mary said, "Don't worry, Aunt Tamar. I talked to God last night, and see, He's made Mommy all better already." The women just smiled at each other.

By sunset Anna had mastered the crutch. She was able to walk from the bed to the table. When the family had gathered to celebrate the Sabbath, Joachim lowered his wife to a sitting position. She found a comfortable place, and Tamar brought her a lit taper. Since the meal would be eaten in Anna's home, she had the privilege of lighting the Sabbath candles. When they were lit, she rotated her hands three times above the flames, placed her hands over her eyes for a moment, and then prayed. "Praised are You, Lord our God, Ruler of the Universe, who has sanctified us by Your commandments and commanded us to kindle the lights of the Sabbath. I pray that the brightness of these lights may inspire us and bring spiritual joy and promise us all until Messiah comes." And all replied, "Amen, halleluiah!"

CHAPTER 8

Rebecca went about preparing the greatest Sabbath meal Joseph had ever seen. He couldn't believe how much his aunt's attitude toward him had changed. She was not only civil; she was downright loving. Rebecca paused in her preparations and asked her nephew to help her pull the wagon to the side of the cheese shed. She actually assisted him in loading it with a variety of cheeses that she herself chose. Together they placed wet straw between the layers. Rebecca complimented his work and thanked him often; she had never done so before. Joseph thought he was dreaming. *This can't be happening,* he said to himself.

Joseph's aunt apologized at least three times for her behavior yesterday. She even asked him if he would like her to cleanse and re-bandage his wounds. Joseph, however, was too modest to remove his tunic in her presence. When they had finished loading, she hugged Joseph and kissed his cheek. She said that she didn't want his uncle to know they loaded the wagon for him today. It would be their little secret. Joseph thought nothing of it. He was accustomed to his uncle leaving on peddling trips on Sunday mornings. Rebecca told Joseph that there was fresh water in the house, and that he should go inside, clean up and eat his lunch while she finished cooking. The woman returned to the outside fire pit and basted the lamb she had been roasting for their Shabbat dinner.

When Joseph entered the house, the aroma of fresh-baked bread filled his nostrils as his stomach growled. His aunt had prepared a fine lunch for him. He washed quickly, ate, and then went to join his aunt by the fire. Joseph thanked her for the noontime meal. He had really enjoyed being with her today. "Joseph," Rebecca said, "would you mind watching the lamb and turning the spit if it starts charring. Your uncle should be home any moment now, and I'd like to freshen up before he gets here." Joseph said he would, and asked if there was anything else he could do for her. "You've done enough today," Rebecca said. Joseph was stunned. He was used to his aunt telling him how lazy he was. "Remember, don't tell your uncle that we packed the wagon." His aunt grabbed his cheek and pinched it in a gesture of affection. "You're a good man, Joseph," she said as she walked toward the house. The boy couldn't believe his ears.

Joseph was sitting by the fire pit, turning the lamb, as Azor came home. Joseph stood and kissed his uncle on the beard of his chin. His uncle returned

146

the greeting, kissing the boy on the peach-fuzz-like facial hair on the boy's chin. "My! That lamb really looks good," his uncle said. "I could smell the aroma all the way from the bottom of the hill."

"Wait until you step into the house. Aunt Rebecca baked some fresh bread, and that smells great too."

Just as Joseph finished speaking, Rebecca came through the doorway with a very large platter in her hands. "The sun is about to set. We better bring the lamb into the house before it's too late, or we'll have to eat out here." It was the first time he could remember his aunt ever so concerned about strictly observing the Sabbath laws. She went up to her husband and kissed him on the cheek. "Welcome home, dear! Did you get everything taken care of?"

He winked at his wife as he said, "Yes I did, but I left the mule on the plateau to graze since the grass was pretty high there."

"I can go down later and get him for you," Joseph said.

"That won't be necessary! I'll just let him graze there until Sunday morning; there's a full trough of water and he can roam a bit. It'll be good for him to be free for a while." In reality, the mule was in the small cave at the base of his property. Eleazer didn't want his nephew to see the leather goods he'd purchased. They were still on the mule. He wanted Joseph to be surprised when he gave them to him Sunday morning.

The three entered the house. Eleazer immediately went to get his prayer shawl. Rebecca said, "Joseph, why don't you wear yours tonight. It's only a few hours to your bar mitzvah; I'm sure the Lord wouldn't mind if you used it right now." When

Joseph went to his hamper, he found four pouches filled to the brim with copper coins. He couldn't believe his eyes. Joseph knew his aunt must have returned everything she had taken from him plus some. He said nothing. The boy didn't want to embarrass her. Joseph took out the shawl, placed it on his head and closed the hamper lid. When he returned to the table, he smiled at his aunt. Rebecca understood that it was his thank-you. She was grateful that Joseph said nothing and saved her the shame of having her husband find out what she had been doing.

Rebecca seemed more reverent than ever as she lit the Sabbath candles and began the prayer. Her hands trembled as she raised them high above the candles in the traditional manner. As she covered her eyes with her hands, she started to sob. She had a difficult time completing the prayer as her sobbing intensified. Joseph and his uncle were a bit surprised by her emotions and intense reverence. They just looked at each other, and then bowed their heads. They didn't want to embarrass her.

As Rebecca prayed, the guilt of her anger at God overwhelmed her. The Lord had opened the eyes of her soul so she could see the egotistical, selfish, uncompassionate, manipulative person she had become. She had realized earlier in the day that she had defied God's mercy, love and goodness by not accepting the boy as the blessing he was. She had been too blind to see that Joseph was given to her by the Lord to compensate for her inability to conceive. God gave her the opportunity to experience motherhood without the pain of delivery and to raise a child from birth. The boy had no other mother.

148

She had refused to even help her brother-in-law with the boy after his mother died. Consequently, Jacob always had to take his son with him wherever he went. Today, for the first time, she realized Joseph could have died upon the hillside with his father, and she would have been partly responsible for his death because she had refused to watch him. Since he came to live with them, instead of nurturing the boy, she'd showed him nothing but resentment and contempt. Today, Rebecca saw Joseph as the warm, loving child she could have cared for and loved. It was too late now; she missed the opportunity the Lord had given her to be a real mother to a wonderful, caring, respectful son.

There wasn't much they could do after dinner; it was the Sabbath, a day of rest as commanded by God and Jewish law. Work of any sort was forbidden from sunset to sunset for any Jew who practiced the faith. It was a little chillier tonight than yesterday, so Joseph, his aunt and his uncle went out and sat by the fire pit. Eleazer and Joseph reminisced about the past eight years they had spent together. Rebecca was rather maudlin. As uncle and nephew laughed and exchanged anecdotes, her eyes began to tear. Joseph noticed that his aunt seemed deeply troubled. She just stared down into the glowing embers with watery eyes.

"Rebecca, is something wrong?" Eleazer asked.

"No, dear!" she replied. "I think the heat from the glowing coals is just making my eyes water a bit. I'm going to go for a walk."

"Joseph and I can join you, if you like."

"I don't think so. Enjoy your reminiscing. I'm not going to go far, perhaps just to the shed and back."

When she left, Eleazer said, "I think your aunt is going to miss you as much as I will. That's what's making her so melancholy tonight."

"I'm going to miss you both too," Joseph said. "This is the only home I've ever really known, and to be honest with you, Uncle, it's kind of scary thinking about a new family that you don't really know that well."

"Your Uncle Achim and his wife are good people, Joseph. Believe me, if I thought for a moment that you wouldn't be happy with them, I wouldn't let you go."

Joseph replied, "I know that, Uncle." They sat there in silence for a while, watching the glowing embers. Eleazer could see his nephew's eyes closing and his head bobbing up and down. Joseph was fighting off sleep.

"Why don't you go to bed, Joseph; you have a big day ahead of you tomorrow."

The sleepy adolescent said, "I think I'll do that, Uncle. Shalom and goodnight; tell Aunt Rebecca I said the same to her." He kissed his uncle goodnight and weaved from side to side on his way toward the house. His body still ached from the beating.

Eleazer walked toward the shed. As he neared the building, he could hear his wife sobbing loudly. He entered and took his wife into his arms. "What's the matter, dear? Is it that you're going to miss the boy? I'm going to miss him too. I know he's going to be missing us as well."

When Eleazer said that, her sobs grew louder, and her tears increased. "You don't understand, Eleazer. I don't know how the boy could miss me. I

150

treated him abominably for the past eight years; I never showed him any love. I was constantly picking on him and couldn't wait for him to leave."

Eleazer was shocked to hear his wife's confession. "I think you may be chastising yourself too much. Joseph never complained. As a matter of fact, he told me to tell you goodnight."

"That's why I feel the way I do, Eleazer. He never complained. The boy had ample opportunity to tell you how despicably I treated him, and he didn't. And what does he do—he makes me that beautiful chest. Did you know that I would steal the copper coins you gave him and keep them for myself?"

Eleazer looked at his wife in disbelief as she continued to speak through her sobs, "And yesterday, when he came home all bloody and beaten, I made him go to the shed and wash his own clothes. I beat him with a broom and refused to give him anything to eat. How could I have been so cruel to him? He always showed me respect and love. Tell me, how could I have done the things I did? What kind of witch am I?"

Eleazer didn't know what to say to his wife. He couldn't believe his ears. Anger welled up within him; he didn't want to lose control. He buried his face in his hands as he said, "As surely as the Lord lives, I have failed my brother and his son. What am I supposed to do? Men have given their wives a writ of divorce for far less than this. What do you want me to say, that I forgive you? The forgiveness is not mine to give; that has to come from Joseph and the Lord. I don't know how much of a fool one has to be in order to be duped by his wife for eight years. I must have been deaf and blind not to have heard and seen what you were doing."

151

"Hear me, please, my husband. Tell me what I have to do to erase my shame and the shame I brought upon you. Whatever it is, I'll do it."

"It's too late now," Eleazer said. "Joseph leaves tomorrow. How could you remedy eight years of deplorable behavior in one day?"

"I was going to wait until tomorrow night to tell you this," Rebecca said, "but I just had to tell it to you now. My conscience wouldn't allow me to be silent any longer. Joseph and I packed the wagon with cheeses; I want you to go with the boy to Achim's. Maybe you could try explaining to him how sorry I am on the way there. And you can peddle your cheeses as well. I'll take care of the shop, and if I need Nabu's help, I'll pay for it myself. I'll sell some of my things if I have to. Please forgive me, please!"

She fell to her knees and clung to her husband's legs. She continued to sob deeply as she pressed her head against his knees and said, "I know you may not believe me after what I told you, but I'm afraid for the boy. With his cuts and bruises, he could look like easy prey for other members of the caravan. I know Ali is a good man, but he can't keep an eye on Joseph all the time. But you could. I've heard tales about marauders who attack caravans just for handsome, strong boys or beautiful girls so they can kidnap them and sell them into slavery. Believe me, I wouldn't want to see anything like that happen to Joseph. He's suffered enough abuse at my hands. He doesn't need any more from anyone else. You could stay with Achim until Ali makes his return trip and come back with him then. That'll give you time to decide what I can do to rectify the wrongs I've done, and how I can be worthy of your love again." She still sobbed as she said, "Please forgive me! … Should we go inside and go to bed now? We have a big day tomorrow."

"I need some time to think," Eleazer replied. "I'm going to sleep on the roof tonight." All the houses in Nazareth had flat roofs with an outside staircase leading up to them. Most families slept on their rooftops on hot nights.

"But it's rather cold tonight. It's not as warm as it was last night. You're liable to catch cold or something. Please come inside with me."

"No! I need time to think. I've got to sort through a lot of things. I'll leave with Joseph on Sunday morning. That's all that I'm certain of for now. What will happen after that, only the Lord knows." Rebecca went into the house as Eleazer climbed the stairs to the rooftop. Moments later, she came up after her husband with a goatskin comforter. "If you insist on sleeping up here, please cover yourself with this." Her husband said nothing as he took the comforter and turned away.

Rebecca made her way down the moonlit staircase and entered the house. The warm glow of the two Sabbath candles bathed the room in mellow light. She prayed silently at the edge of the bed. The woman hadn't prayed in years. Rebecca cried as she asked the Lord's forgiveness and asked Him to help her change. She also prayed that her marriage would survive after her confession tonight.

When she was about to lie down, she noticed that Joseph, who slept opposite her bed, was having a restless night. He had kicked off his covers. Rebecca got up and gently pulled the comforter back over her nephew. It was the first time she had

153

ever tucked him in. That action tugged even more deeply at the motherly cords that were still very much alive in her heart. Rebecca realized the joy that could have been hers, and felt the pang of knowing that the opportunity was gone forever. Kneeling by the sleeping boy, she gently kissed his bandaged head. The woman sobbed harder as she returned to the bed. She sat on its edge and buried her face in her hands as she continued to cry.

As he tossed and turned, Joseph landed rather heavily on his bruised and injured shoulder. The sharp pain that accompanied the movement awakened the boy. Hearing his aunt's sobbing, he asked, "Are you okay, Aunt Rebecca?" His aunt nodded her head yes, but she couldn't stop crying. The boy got up from his mat and handed her a washcloth to wipe away her tears. Rebecca couldn't stop her sobbing. Joseph had never seen his aunt like this. As a matter of fact, until tonight, he had never seen her cry. Joseph sat down beside his aunt. He put his arm around her shoulder, and drew her closer to himself. As she leaned her head against his chest, her sobs became so loud and deep that he was afraid she would hyperventilate.

Joseph was very concerned now. He thought something might have happened to his uncle, since he wasn't in the house. "Is it about Uncle Eleazer? Is that why you're crying? Is he okay?" His aunt couldn't speak; she just nodded yes.

"Aunt Rebecca, where is he then?" Through her sobs she managed to tell him that his uncle was up on the roof. "Why is he up there? It's pretty cold tonight."

She continued sobbing as she said, "Joseph, I told your uncle about how I've been treating you all these

154

years, and what I did to you yesterday. I couldn't keep the guilt inside me any longer. Joseph, please forgive me! I don't think your uncle ever will."

The boy gently reached out and took her hand. He kissed it and said, "Aunt Rebecca, I don't think you treated me that badly. I would've been a lot worse off if you and Uncle Eleazer didn't give me a home. I could've ended up a street urchin or something like that. It must have been hard for you, because I know how badly you wanted to move to Jerusalem. I know that because of me, you had to stay here and give up your dream. It was different for Uncle Eleazer. I'm his brother's son, and people might've looked down on him if he didn't take me in since we're blood relatives. But you and I aren't related by blood, and I don't know if anyone else would've done any better if they had to raise someone else's child. Don't be too hard on yourself, Aunt Rebecca. Every one of us makes mistakes; even Father Abraham and Moses did, and somehow God forgives us all. If God forgives, we should too. Don't you think? I knew it was nothing personal, and you really didn't treat me as badly as you think. Let me go up and talk to Uncle Eleazer and see if I can get him to come inside."

"Joseph, I can't believe that you'd do that for me, now that your uncle knows everything," she said in amazement.

"I'll go up there right now." He squeezed his aunt a little tighter. Rebecca gave Joseph another kiss on his cheek. "Now dry your eyes and I'll have my uncle back down here in no time," he told her.

"Joseph, I really am sorry for all that I did to you."

"I know you are, Aunt Rebecca. Now let's just forget all about that." The teen, in an effort to stop her crying, asked, "Would you walk with Uncle Eleazer and me to the Synagogue tomorrow?" She replied that she'd be honored to do so. She finally stopped sobbing and dried the tears from her eyes.

While Joseph worked to negotiate reconciliation between his aunt and uncle, little Mary snuck outside again. She told her Lord she would talk to Him every night and wanted to thank Him for making her mommy better. Deep within her heart she was hoping to hear that beautiful voice call her name once more. It was much colder than it was last night, and Mary soon began to shiver. Her little talk with God was shorter than it had been the night before— because, she told Him, "my teeth are starting to chatter." After she said her "Halleluiah! Amen!", she continued to gaze at the massive display of bright celestial bodies that filled the night sky and waited a short time to hear her name again, but she heard nothing. The disappointed girl crept back into the house and slid under the goatskin comforter at about the same time Joseph and his family went to sleep.

The teenager was successful in convincing his uncle to forgive and make peace with his wife, and to leave the roof and sleep inside for the night.

CHAPTER 9

The rim of the sun broke through the twilight as it colored the cloudless sky a brilliant shade of pink. It was Saturday morning. Joseph awoke, stretched, and went outside to watch the sunrise. His big day finally had arrived, and with it came the jitters. *Will I read and pronounce the words correctly?* he asked himself. His nervousness caused his hands to turn a bit clammy. Everyone spoke Aramaic, and today he'd have to read in Hebrew. Furthermore, he didn't like to be the center of attention and he knew everyone would be watching him. He asked the Lord to help him with the reading, and to calm his nerves, as he looked up and watched the sky turn from pink to lavender and then to a bright blue. It was still rather cool outside. He could see his breath, and could feel the goosebumps popping up on his bare legs. The teen still wore the shorter tunic that children traditionally wore. When he dressed today, he would put on the longer tunic of a man.

Joseph's body quickened as he felt something land on his shoulder. He didn't hear his aunt who had come up behind him; her touch took him by surprise. "Oh, I'm so sorry, Joseph. I didn't mean to startle you."

157

"That's okay, Aunt Rebecca, I guess I was just pretty deep in my thoughts."

She asked him if he was nervous. He said that he was. She assured him there was no need to be. She had heard Joseph practice with his uncle, and his pronunciations were flawless. He thanked her for the compliment and said the rabbi had told him the same thing. Since the sounds were so guttural in Hebrew, he questioned whether he was using enough "oomph" when he spoke them. She laughingly assured him there was no need to worry, and there was more than enough "oomph." Joseph laughed at her remark.

"I shouldn't be laughing, though. When I get up there with everyone looking at me, I'll probably do worse than all of them put together."

"Nonsense!" Rebecca said. "You'll do a great job. It'll be the best reading any of us have ever heard." Joseph still couldn't believe the woman who now spoke to him was the aunt he had lived with all these years. He thanked her for the compliment that boosted his morale. Rebecca told him to come inside because the morning air was a bit too nippy. The two of them entered the house just as Eleazer was rising. He stretched and yawned. "Gooo—maw—ning!"

"Now, if you sounded like that, *then* you'd have to worry about your pronunciation," Rebecca said. Joseph laughed.

"Wha—arr—yoo—taww—king about?" Eleazer asked between yawns. Joseph and Rebecca laughed even louder.

"Just about pronunciation, dear, that's all."

"Well, what's so funny?" Eleazer asked.

In unison, Joseph and Rebecca said, "Nothing!" and they burst out laughing.

Eleazer just shook his head as he rose from the bed. "I guess you have to get up real early to enjoy the humor. So, your big day is finally here! Are you excited?" Joseph said he was more nervous than excited. His uncle assured him he would do fine. Rebecca reinforced her husband's remark. Then Eleazer said, "Now, son, why don't you go outside for a while so we can wash up and change?" The boy did as he was told.

Even though Eleazer had forgiven Rebecca, their relationship was a bit strained. They avoided eye contact and didn't speak much. As he began to wash, Eleazer panicked. "The boy is choking!" He turned and began to run to the door in his undergarment. Rebecca grabbed his arm and reassured him that Joseph was fine. He was just practicing the low, throaty, guttural sounds of Hebrew for his reading. Joseph heard the two of them laughing and was glad they had made up. He surely didn't want to be the source of marital problems for the couple he loved.

When the pair was finished, Eleazer called Joseph back into the house. His uncle said that his aunt had something for him. Rebecca smiled as she handed Joseph a new, long tunic. A gift that was made out of a sense of duty was now given as a gift of love. Joseph took it from his aunt, thanked her and kissed her cheek. She took him in her arms and kissed him back as she whispered, "No, thank *you,* Joseph." Her eyes filled with tears once again.

"Enough of this emotional stuff," Eleazer said. He tried to hide the fact that he had just wiped away his tears as well. "The man needs to get dressed now, and we have to get something to eat. It's going to be a long day, and we wouldn't want our stomach growling in front of the whole town now, would we?" They all smiled, then Joseph's aunt and uncle went outside so he could do his grooming.

As Joseph washed and dressed, little Mary crawled out of bed and went outside to welcome the new day. She stepped out into the courtyard and began to twirl in the chilly morning air. Mary knew the approximate amount of time she had spun when she had last heard the voice. Today she would count her spins and adjust her turns daily until she reached the magic number that would allow her to hear that melodious sound again. Midway through a turn, Mary heard her mother's voice telling her to stop spinning and come into the house. She grabbed hold of the olive tree to steady herself and waited for her head to clear. She then skipped to the door and entered.

Mary was surprised to see how well her mother was walking with the use of the crutch. Yesterday she seemed to have struggled with it. Joachim was still asleep and snoring. Even her mother's call had not awakened him. Mary went up to her mother and gave her a good-morning kiss. Anna returned the greeting. The little girl put her hand to her mouth and snickered as she pointed to her father with the other. "I know, and your father says he doesn't snore, but we know better, don't we, dear?" Anna said with a grin. The girl nodded and giggled.

"Is your foot better today, Momma?"

"It sure is, dear, and thanks to this crutch that Joseph made for me, I can go to Synagogue to witness his bar mitzvah."

"I heard that," Joachim said as he sat up. "I don't think you should be going anywhere yet."

"Pshaw! I should know my own foot, and I'm telling you I won't have any problems walking that short distance."

"Okay, let me see that ankle of yours," Joachim said as he swung his legs over the side of the bed. "I want to see this miracle firsthand, the near-broken ankle that can heal itself in just two days." Anna hobbled over to him and raised the hem of her tunic slightly. "Hmm, no miracle," he said. "The bruise has lightened a bit, but I still don't think you're ready to race yet. Why don't you just stay home today? You can congratulate the boy when he passes by. He'll understand why you're not there."

"Daddy, Mommy's foot is really better, because I asked God to make it that way. Aunt Tamar said the Lord always hears our prayers, and so did Mommy." Her parents smiled at each other. Joachim agreed with his daughter that God always hears our prayers, but he added that the Lord also does things in His own time, not ours.

After the family washed, dressed and had a bite to eat, it was almost time to go to Synagogue. Joachim told his wife that if she still insisted on going to Joseph's bar mitzvah, they should leave now just in case she had to stop often. Anna would never be able to follow the procession. He still thought she should stay home, but he left the decision to her.

161

At about the time Mary and her parents began their trek to the Synagogue, Joseph had just finished dressing when he heard his uncle knock on the door. As soon as his aunt and uncle entered, Eleazer insisted on checking his nephew's head wound.

"Let me do that," Rebecca said. "I think I can bandage it a little neater than you, and no one will even be able to notice it under Joseph's cap." Rebecca carefully unwound the bandage and checked the wound. "You did a very good job last night," Rebecca said to her husband. "It's healing very nicely." She re-bandaged his head, then took his cap and gently placed it over the bandages. "There," she said. "No one will even tell there's a bandage under there."

"Your aunt's right," Eleazer said as he took the boy his prayer shawl and draped it over his nephew's shoulders.

When the boy stood up, Rebecca stepped away from Joseph and took a long, hard look at her nephew. "My, you're so handsome," she said. "Now you look like a man, and I know you'll turn the heads of all the girls in town." Joseph blushed so much that he could feel the tips of his ears burning. Before they left the house, Joseph asked his uncle for a blessing. Eleazer placed his hands lightly on his nephew's head and nodded for Rebecca to join him. When she did, he blessed Joseph in perfect Hebrew. Eleazer's lips quivered as he tried to hold back tears. The three of them left the house and started down the path to town. Joseph walked between his aunt and uncle. He had a hard time adjusting to all the additional material that hung below his knees.

It was customary for all the townsfolk to gather in the common area of the town on the day of a boy's bar mitzvah. They would then follow the family in procession to the Synagogue. The minute the candidate met the group of townspeople, the woman who accompanied her son—or in this case her nephew—was expected to drop back and join the group of women who, by custom, followed behind the men. As the boy neared the commons he could see Nabu, who was roasting several goats for the occasion. His wife had her back to them as she prepared barley cakes while their children scurried about. "Good morning, Nabu," Joseph said. The man bowed low as he touched the tips of his fingers to his forehead and then his chest. Joseph tried to duplicate the gesture. Eleazer and his wife laughed, then nodded their greeting to him and continued onward. Rebecca was prepared to drop back at this point and join the women, but Joseph asked her to stay. She was so flattered that her face radiated with joy. Eleazer held his nephew's hand, so Rebecca gently grabbed his other. She walked straight and proud next to her nephew. For the first time in her life, she couldn't care less what people thought of her, or what they'd say about her walking next to her nephew all the way to the Synagogue.

As they walked along, Joseph kept looking back. He had seen Azor and Tamar, but he was hoping to see Joachim and his daughter as well. He didn't expect to see Anna; he knew the condition of her foot. He didn't expect her to be walking for a while yet. The townspeople who hadn't gathered in the common area joined the procession as the group passed their homes. Even Zillah joined in.

They shouted out their greetings to the boy. "Congratulations, Joseph!" "May the God of our Father Abraham look favorably on you everyday of your life!" "May long life and much happiness be yours today and forever, Joseph Bar Jacob." They then joined in and marched along with the crowd.

After they had passed Joachim's house, Joseph was certain neither Mary nor her father would be joining him in today's celebration. Joseph was rather disappointed but smiled in spite of it. When they neared the Synagogue, his face beamed with joy as he saw Joachim standing by the entrance. Mary's father called out his congratulations. The blushing boy nodded toward him in a gesture of gratitude. When he entered the Synagogue to take the seat of honor, Joseph could see Anna and her daughter behind the ornamental grillework that separated the women's section from the main building. Little Mary stuck her hand through the iron filigree and waved to Joseph as Anna shouted out her congratulations. The boy tended to stand a little taller when he saw them. He sat down in his place with his uncle beside him.

The service began with spontaneous shouts of praise to the Lord and the singing of various psalms. It was a boisterous group. The rabbi carried the Sacred Scrolls to the lectern, and several men from the congregation stepped forward and read from them. More praise and singing followed, and then there was total silence. It was time for Joseph to take his place as a man, a true Son of Abraham, and read from the Sacred Writings. Eleazer stood up next to his nephew and lifted his brother's prayer shawl over the teen's head. He accompanied Joseph to the podium. The boy, with a black eye that was swollen shut, opened the scrolls to the Book of Deuteronomy and read from them in perfect Hebrew. Eleazer beamed with pride, as did Rebecca. She stood behind the metal divider and listened to Joseph's perfect enunciation of each word. When he finished reading, the congregation shouted their approval with *amen's* and *halleluiahs*. His diction was so perfect, even Zillah couldn't find anything to criticize the boy about. There was still tomorrow, though. She had plenty of time to find flaws, she thought to herself.

Joachim stood up and began to clap; the rest of the congregation joined in with him. The rabbi read the benediction, and when the women left, the men stayed behind and respectfully argued the meaning of what they had heard in today's readings. The rabbi escorted Joseph and his uncle to a small room in the rear of the building. There Joseph was briefed on the oral law and Jewish traditions one last time before he left on the morrow. By the time they were finished, the Synagogue was empty.

At sunset the Sabbath was over. The townspeople brought their torches and lanterns to the Synagogue and waited for Joseph and his uncle to emerge. It was customary to escort the bar mitzvahs to the common area of town, to the place where Nabu and his family had prepared the feast Eleazer had requested. Woman brought tambourines and other percussion instruments. They danced and played while the men sang, and others played their flutes as they led Joseph and his uncle to the banquet that Rebecca was now putting the final touches on. She had the opportunity

165

to ask Nabu to aid her with the cheese shop while Eleazer was away. He agreed to do so. She could hear the crowd as they approached, so she quickly sampled the delicacies, then ran to meet them.

Little Mary and her mother stood in their courtyard, waiting for the jubilant group to pass by. "Be careful of the pouch, and don't let go of it until we give it to Joseph," Anna instructed. She had asked her husband for one of his finest leather pouches. She lined it with a double layer of linen and filled it with barley, dates and fig cakes. In the very bottom she placed five silver shekels. Anna had taken them from the money she had been putting aside for Mary's dowry. She had plenty of time to replace them.

As the crowd passed, Anna could see Joseph and his uncle. She began to shout, "God's blessing on you, Joseph Bar Jacob!" Joachim dropped out of the group and joined his wife and daughter. They then slowly followed at the rear of the jubilant procession because of Anna's injured foot. Mary looked up pleadingly at her parents. Joachim gave his consent for her to run ahead and join the other children. Before he finished speaking, Mary was well on her way skipping toward them, joining the little girls who tried to imitate the dances that the women were doing. Mary loved it because she could twirl freely. Even if her aunt saw her, she couldn't say anything negative.

The crowd finally reached the common area. Joseph, along with his aunt and uncle, sat on mats in the center of the commons. Joseph was served first since he was the guest of honor. He felt a bit guilty, because his aunt and uncle would be the last to eat. "Don't worry about us, Joseph," Rebecca said. "This is your day; enjoy yourself. There's plenty of food for everyone." The crowd was then served.

Rebecca noticed that Zillah brought a rather large hamper with her. She kept filling it with the food, enough to serve ten people. When Zillah noticed Rebecca watching, she said, "I'm just going to bring a little something home for my husband; he wasn't feeling too well today, so he couldn't come." Rebecca just shook her head and said nothing.

After they finished eating, Joseph and his uncle stood up and began a traditional dance as the rest of the group played instruments and sang. While they danced the townspeople threw coins toward their feet. Mary, along with the other children, ran between the dancing pair and gathered the coins and brought them to Rebecca. She thanked the children and began to stack them in thirteen rows of thirteen each for her nephew. Just as the dance finished, Anna hobbled over to Rebecca and told her of all that Joseph had done for her. The stacks of coins were complete, so Joseph and his uncle returned to their places as other men stood up and group-danced. Anna presented her gift to the young man and thanked him profusely for the help he had given her, as well as for the cheese and the well-crafted crutch. Joseph graciously thanked her for her gift. Anna reached out and gave the young man a warm, loving hug. He blushed a bright red.

Joseph and his uncle prepared to sit down, when they heard the neighing of horses. Instantly the maidens, and the younger women, with their children in tow, ran to their homes. Tamar grabbed Mary by the hand and ran with her toward her house too. Everyone knew what was coming next. Zillah took off like a bolt of lightning, dropping her hamper in the process. She quickly bent over and grabbed the items, scooping them back into the hamper with the lid. *It's good enough for my husband,* she said to herself as she continued to run.

The group that was left could hear a sound similar to roaring thunder as a horse's hooves pounded on the city gate. The crowd immediately went silent. Rebecca snatched the leather pouch from Joseph and hid it under her clothing, along with the rows of coins and her husband's cup of wine. She quickly tossed across the commons the two mats that the men had been sitting on. The mats landed near each other on the other side of the square. Rebecca directed Joseph and Eleazer to go toward them.

Eliud the gatekeeper shouted, "I'm coming! I'm coming! No need to knock the gate down." What was left of the crowd pressed themselves together into a tight-knit group. Rebecca sat all by herself near the center of the street. Eliud was barely able to open the gates before the group of Roman soldiers charged into the town on their steeds.

Deputy Commander Hasid, a Syrian, shouted to Eliud, "Having a party and you didn't invite us?" He dismounted and kicked in several of the wine jars that stood next to the building. The pavement turned blood-red. "Next time you'll know better, right, Eliud?"

(Syrians were conscripted into the Roman army. The group that entered the town was stationed at a barracks just south of Nazareth. The Syrians despised the Jews since they were excused from military service. Because of their religious beliefs, they refused to fight on the Sabbath. The Syrian soldiers did everything possible to irritate the Jewish people, and usually had free rein to do so, even to go as far as raping their women. Even if news of their exploits reached the Procurator, the most they'd get would be a slap on the wrist. The Procurator wasn't too fond of the Jews either; they didn't have to follow Caesar's dictates as strictly as other Roman subjects did. They were the only people under Roman rule who didn't have to pay homage to Caesar as a god. Rome's puppet-king Herod had Caesar's ear, but since he himself was an Idumean, and not respected by the Jews, he very seldom complained about the way his subjects were treated. The Procurator, though, was careful not to step too forcefully on their toes. If word reached Jerusalem, the Jewish High Priest had his way of reaching Caesar's ear too.)

The rest of the soldiers dismounted and began to eat and drink. They just tore at the goat meat with filthy hands and shoved the meat down their throats, hardly even chewing. The Jews thought it was deplorable. The soldiers, with their mouths full of food, mocked the townspeople, spewing pieces of half-chewed food at the group as they spoke. Two soldiers lifted a large wine jar while the others stood under it with their mouths open as the wine spilled all over them. It ran down the front of their tunics, staining them deep red. Any tray of food they disliked, they just kicked over. After they were rather inebriated the commander shouted, "Where are your women? This town can't be filled with just the old hags I see around me."

Thinking fast, Asa said, "We're celebrating a special holiday for unmarried virgins in honor of one of our former judges, Jephthah. It's our tradition to send our virgins up to the hills to mourn Jephthah's daughter, who died in her virginity." It was a believable story, as the soldiers knew Jewish life was filled with all sorts of traditions.

"Why is that hag sitting in the middle of the street?" the officer asked, pointing to Rebecca.

"I'm unclean, Officer," she replied. "It's my time of month; therefore, I have to stay away from the others according to our law."

The Syrian officer wanted to make a fool of her, so he said, "Stand up so we can all see the show."

"Please don't humiliate the woman any more than she already is," Rabbi Asa said. But Rebecca was clever. She had anticipated something like this; that was why she sent the mats flying across the commons and kept her husband's cup of wine. She stood and let her outer robe fall from her shoulders to cover the coins and the gifts. She was commanded to turn around. The soldiers mocked her, and laughed as they pointed to her tunic. The idiots were so drunk, they couldn't tell they were laughing at a wine stain.

Joseph couldn't stand to see his aunt humiliated any further. He impetuously ran and stood before her and wrapped Rebecca in his prayer shawl. The officer said, "Oh! You mean to tell me there *is* a Jew with a spine—and a black eye besides." He raised his beefy arm and struck Joseph in the jaw so hard that he fell to the ground.

170

Nabu ran forward with a tray of desserts to distract the soldiers. "I have some delicious deserts for my lords," he said, bowing before them. "There are date and almond cakes, raisin cakes dipped in honey and plump figs that have been pickled in the finest wine." The officer took a fig, chewed it, and spit out the syrupy liquid on Rebecca and Joseph. He knocked the tray of desserts out of Nabu's hands.

The officer and his soldiers continued their mission of destruction by breaking the jugs of olive oil and stomping on the remaining bread and deserts. After shattering all the pottery in sight, they turned to the women and commanded them to give them all their jewelry. Rebecca removed her earrings, bracelets and necklaces. She handed them to the officer as Joseph stared at him with fierce loathing in his eyes.

"So, you haven't had enough yet?" the officer said. He kicked Joseph in the ribs several times, knocking the breath out of him. Joseph moaned in pain.

Rebecca wiped the masticated figs from her nephew's face. She lowered her lips to his ear and said quietly, "Joseph, be still; say nothing. Close your eyes and pretend you're unconscious, or else they may kill you." He did as he was told. The commander finally was satisfied that he and his fellow soldiers had humiliated the group enough. After kicking Joseph in the ribcage several more times, he signaled to his comrades to leave. In a drunken stupor they stumbled to their horses, and after many attempts, finally mounted their steeds and road through the open gate. Eliud locked it once again.

The townspeople fell to their knees and cried out to the Lord their God, asking Him to send their deliverer now. They wailed. Some tore their garments, while others bent low, scooped dirt into their hands and threw it on their heads as an expression of lamentation. Eleazer ran to his wife and nephew. He apologized profusely for not coming to their aid. Rebecca consoled her husband by telling him he'd made the right decision. "You know they would've just beaten you and a lot of the other townsmen if you had. They were just looking for an excuse to be more violent than they already were. Joseph, thank you so much for defending my honor," she said as she kissed her nephew's forehead. "But if you're ever in a situation like this again, bite your tongue, stand back, and just let it play out like the rest of the men did."

Eleazer thanked his nephew for his gallantry, but warned him to never again do what he did. He asked the teen if he was able to stand; Joseph nodded yes, so Eleazer helped him to his feet. The battered young man moaned as he tried to rise. Joachim and Nabu ran over to see if they could be of help. Anna hobbled along behind on her crutch. In a voice filled with solace she asked, "Is Joseph all right? How much more can that poor young man take?" Nabu suggested they take him home and tend to his needs. He and his family would clean up the mess. Joachim asked Anna if she could make it home by herself. She said that she could, so Joachim helped Eleazer with the battered teen.

Hobbling toward her house, Anna asked God, "Why would You, O Lord, allow such a good and pious b—" She almost said "boy" but stopped

172

herself. "…young man suffer so much abuse in such a short time?" She cried for Joseph all the way home. What she didn't realize was that God's plan is usually beyond man's understanding. As the Lord established that it would take great heat to refine gold, it also takes adversity in life to build exceptionally strong character. The God of Israel had a special use for Joseph in His Divine Plan. He needed pure gold; all the dross had to be removed.

Rebecca spent the entire night by her nephew's side. Joseph was in immense pain whenever he tried to breathe. The town physician had witnessed what had happened to Joseph, so he stopped by to check on him. He determined that two of the teen's ribs were broken. The doctor bound Joseph's ribcage tightly with wide bands of fabric. The binding helped; Joseph didn't hurt as much. He could finally breathe.

Little Mary was very pensive; she sat quietly in the dark house with Tamar beside her. She had been warned not to speak until her aunt was certain the soldiers had gone. Though the moon was starting to wane, it still painted the building in hues of silvery blue. The streets, however, were deserted, and not a sound could be heard. No light shone through any of the windows either. In the throes of fear, little Mary nestled closer to her aunt and began to tremble. It was so quiet that she could hear Tamar's breathing. Fear fed her imagination. She wanted to ask if her mommy and daddy were all right, but her aunt was stern in her warning not to speak. Suddenly Mary heard footsteps. She didn't know if it was good or bad, so she buried her face in her aunt's robe as she trembled and began to cry. She heard the slight thud of a crutch as it pounded the pavement, and then she heard the sound of a firm footstep. Her face radiated with a smile. She knew it was either Nethanel the cripple, or her mother. Mary prayed that it was the latter; her prayer was answered. Anna soon came through the door. Tamar asked, "Are my Azor and your Joachim all right? Where are they?"

Anna was slightly out of breath as she replied, "They're both fine. Azor is helping Nabu and his family clean up the mess the soldiers made, and Joachim is helping Eleazer to get Joseph back home."

"Why, what happened to him?" Tamar asked. Mary listened intently as her mother told them what the soldiers had done to Rebecca and her nephew.

"That poor young man. And my heart breaks for Rebecca too. How long must we cry out to You, O Lord, before You send us our deliverer?" Tamar asked her Maker loudly. She then asked, "Is it safe to light a candle now?"

"It is!" Anna replied. By moonlight Tamar found the flint and thatch; through her skillful hands, they soon had fire. She lit the candle and a cozy, mellow glow filled the room as Anna told Tamar what the soldiers had done. She concluded her tale by saying that Joseph was a true hero and brought honor to King David's lineage once again. Mary's ears perked up when she heard that Joseph too was from David's royal line. The little girl said nothing. She just continued to listen.

Mary's heart ached as she thought about the brutal treatment Joseph had received, and her eyes

174

misted over. She finally asked, "Why are the soldiers so mean to us?"

Before Anna could answer, Tamar replied, "Because everybody is jealous of us. God chose us above every other nation and tongue to be His people. They make fun of our laws and traditions because they'd like to have them too. That's why."

Anna shook her head in agreement. Mother and daughter then left Tamar's house with a taper of borrowed fire. As soon as they entered their house, little Mary lit the nighttime candle. Anna told her daughter it was time to go to bed. The girl asked if she could stay up until her father returned home.

"I don't think so," Anna replied. "You've had a full day, and now it's time for sleep." The little girl washed up, kissed her mother, then scooted across the bed to her place by the wall while Anna sat on the edge of the bed, waiting for her husband to return.

Mary felt her eyelids starting to close. She knew she wouldn't be able to stay awake much longer or go outside to pray, so she whispered a question to her God: "Lord, if we're Your favorite people, why did You let those bad soldiers hurt Joseph tonight? I know You can do anything. I think it's a much better idea if You just made their heads blow up before You do it to people who would just like to see You. If You did that, they couldn't have hurt poor Joseph tonight. Then maybe the bad ones would be afraid to hurt any of us again. Thank You for making my mom…" She never finished the sentence, for sleep overtook her. Anna heard her daughter's whispered prayer and just smiled. She thought that what her daughter had said did make a lot of sense, though.

As Joseph rested uncomfortably on the rim of sleep, his aunt and uncle discussed the feasibility of his trip tomorrow. Rebecca expressed her opinion that Joseph was in no condition to travel. Eleazer thought the decision should be up to his nephew. "He's really looking forward to starting his apprenticeship," his uncle said. "If I wasn't going with him, I'd try to keep him here until he heals totally, but he can just lie in the wagon until he heals sufficiently to sit beside me. The decision should be his."

"Eleazer, you should get some sleep if you're going to drive the wagon all day tomorrow. I'll sit here and care for Joseph. You just get some rest." After much coaxing, Eleazer reluctantly went to bed. Rebecca sat by her nephew's side and gently stroked Joseph's hair as the young man moaned in his sleep. She softly sang him the lullabies her mother had sung to her. Her heart ached. Rebecca realized how differently things could have been, if only she had opened her heart to her nephew earlier.

Morning came; as Eleazer awoke, he saw his wife was still by his nephew's side. He crawled out of bed and came over to her. Rebecca brought her finger to her lips in a gesture of silence. "He's still sleeping," she whispered. "There's still time before the caravan arrives. Let him sleep."

"I'll stay with him; you go and change," Eleazer said. Rebecca was still wearing the wine-stained clothes she had worn the night before.

176

She kissed her husband and whispered, "I'll bring in some fresh water and then I'll change in the shed." She gathered up her clean clothing, then picked up the water jar and headed toward the shed.

As soon as Rebecca left, Joseph awoke. He saw his uncle sitting next to him. "You didn't sit here all night, did you, Uncle Eleazer?"

"No, I didn't, son," his uncle replied. "Your aunt did, though. She stayed by your side until morning. She just left now to freshen up." His uncle expressed his and Rebecca's concerns about Joseph traveling in his condition. "It's up to you, though, son!" Eleazer said. "But I plan to go with you, if you go."

"Who'll take care of the shop while you're gone?" Joseph asked.

"Don't worry; it's all taken care of. Your aunt and Nabu will manage the place. She intended for me to go with you even before your latest injury; that's why she had you help her pack the wagon the other day."

"I mean no disrespect to either of you, but I'd still like to go to Uncle Achim's. The sooner I finish my apprenticeship, the sooner I can come back here." Eleazer replied that if that was the case, they'd both better clean up and get ready; Ali would be by about mid-morning. When Joseph first sat up he almost reconsidered his decision, because he hurt so badly; his entire body ached. His determination overcame the pain, though, so he got up and began to move around just as Mary's eyes opened to the morning light.

Mary awoke and heard her parents discussing Joseph's departure. Joachim told his wife about the pair of leather sandals he was going to take to the young man before he left. She heard her father say Joseph should've just stayed in the group with them. Joachim admired Joseph's heroism, but look what it got him. His impetuous behavior was probably due to the shame they brought on Rebecca. But if he had stayed where he was, he could've avoided the cruel treatment he received.

"Maybe if all of us were just a little more heroic, we wouldn't be pushed around the way we are," Anna said.

"What, has my mild-mannered wife turned into a Zealot?" her husband asked. "How can we stand up to a giant like Rome?"

"If my memory serves me," she replied, "didn't a little shepherd boy, who both you and Joseph are related to, defeat a giant with only a slingshot?"

"That's because the Lord was with him."

"Are you saying that He's not with us now?"

Joachim didn't have a chance to answer; Mary chimed in and asked her father if she could go with him to see Joseph off.

"I see that little pitchers have big ears even when they're sleeping. We'll see, Princess, we'll see!" Joachim said as he kissed his wife and daughter. He then left for his shop, just about the time that Ali and his caravan entered the city gates.

Joseph's grooming took a lot longer than usual. His sore body could barely move. After he prayed, he stepped outside and noticed that Eleazer had tied Joseph's father's mule to the back of the wagon. He also noticed the sturdy leather saddlebags Eleazer had filled with his brother's tools. "Uncle, why don't we just load the tools on the back of the wagon? Then the mule won't have to follow you on the way back. There's plenty of room back there. We could store the tools under the tarps and you could leave your saddlebags at home."

"The mule was your father's, and now it belongs to you, and so do the saddlebags," Eleazer said. Joseph told his uncle that he and his wife had done enough for him already. "This is what your father would have wanted, and so do I. As far as I'm concerned, the matter is closed and not open to further discussion." Joseph kissed his uncle on the beard of his chin and thanked him.

Just as Joseph finished speaking, Eleazer could see Ali coming up the pathway. He always stopped to break bread with his friend whenever he came to town. Eating with a Gentile was the only Jewish law Eleazer didn't follow. After Rebecca had poured some wine to accompany the food she'd prepared, she went to the door to greet her husband's friend. She saw Ali put his arm around her nephew's shoulder as he asked, "So what kind of super-mule kicked my young master here? No, on second thought, it must have been a stampede to do that amount of damage. I really don't know if you should be traveling in your condition." Eleazer told his friend he would be joining the caravan too.

The caravan leader welcomed the plan. When they had settled down at the table, Ali said, "This will probably be the last caravan I'll lead." He lifted the hem of his tunic to about mid-calf and showed Eleazer his ulcerated leg. "The gout is getting the best of me. I'm too young to retire, though, and none of my five sons could take over the business. Not one of them could safely lead a camel to a bale of hay that's right in front of them, let alone guide a group of people across Judea or through Galilee. So I guess I'll have to look for a new business. How about your cheese shop; I heard rumors you'll be moving to Jerusalem."

Rebecca stunned her husband by saying, "We're not moving anywhere until Joseph returns and is fully settled in his own home and has found a wife for himself." Eleazer nearly choked on his bread. Joseph's expression turned to one of shock too.

"I guess I'll just have to look for some other business opportunity, then," Ali said.

When the meal was over, it was time for goodbyes. Rebecca kissed her husband, and as he hugged her tightly she whispered, "May the God of Jacob guide and protect you my love; thank you for forgiving me. I'll prove to you I'm worthy of your forgiveness."

"You already have, my dear," her husband said as he returned her kiss. It was a more passionate kiss than he had given her in many years. She blushed.

Rebecca went to her nephew and hugged him a little longer and a little tighter than she should have. He tried not to wince from the pain. She kissed him several times on his cheek. "Joseph, in these two days, God has shown me, through your goodness, all the joy that I've missed in not treating you more like a mother and not accepting you as the son God gave me. It's an anguish I'll feel for the rest of my life. Please forgive me, Joseph," she said as tears filled her eyes.

Joseph kissed his aunt and said, "I love you, Aunt Rebecca, and thank you for everything. I really mean that!" The young man fought back his tears as his uncle moved the tarp, and Ali helped Joseph climb onto the wagon.

"Wait! Wait! The straw is too damp for Joseph to lie on." Rebecca ran into the house and brought out her favorite goatskin comforter. "Here, Joseph, put this over the straw; it should keep the dampness from getting to you." Joseph thanked his aunt. After giving his wife one last kiss, Eleazer hopped into the wagon seat and Ali sat down beside him. Rebecca waved as the wagon descended down the steep path to the lower town with the mule following behind it. Joseph kept waving to his aunt until she was out of view. He finally felt what it was like to have a mother.

Mary and her father reached the site of departure just about the time Eleazer's wagon started down the hill. Anna would've joined them, but her ankle was too swollen from yesterday. Mary heard the bells on the camels' reins as they bobbed their heads up and down, eating the hay bales Eliud had brought for them. The sound of the tiny bells reminded her of the beautiful voice she had heard. It wasn't long before Eleazer's wagon pulled in front of the entire caravan. Ali would ride with his friend and spare his leg further pain until it was absolutely necessary for him to do otherwise. When Joseph saw Joachim and his little daughter, he slid to the end of the wagon and swung his long legs to the pavement below. He went toward them to say goodbye. "Not too long now, Joseph!" Ali said.

Joachim handed the young man the new sandals. "These are for helping my wife, and for your heroics last night; you put the rest of us men to shame." Joseph didn't know what to say, so he just thanked him profusely. Mary's father extended his arms toward the young man, kissed his chin and hugged him. Joseph returned the gesture. "May the God of Abraham guard and protect you," Joachim said. Joseph returned the blessing. Just as he was about to turn around and go back to the wagon, Mary impetuously ran forward and hugged him. Joseph was a bit stunned, as was her father. Boys and girls weren't allowed to touch each other or embrace unless they were blood relatives.

Joseph didn't know what to do; he just blushed and said, "Thank you!" He then turned toward the wagon and tried to struggle back to his place. Joachim stepped forward and helped the young man up. Little Mary waved to Joseph as the caravan left; she continued to do so until he faded into the horizon.

"Why did you hug Joseph?" her father asked. "Don't you know that's forbidden?"

"I'm sorry, Daddy," Mary said. "I thought that since you are related to King David and Joseph is related to King David, it would be all right to hug him, because aren't we really cousins?"

He laughed. "I guess you're right, Princess. Very, very distant, but still cousins."

As they walked home together, Joachim tousled his daughter's hair as she laughed and said "Daddy!" She then asked, "Is five years a really long time?"

"All I can say, my dear, is that the older you get, the less time it seems." Rabbi Asa for some reason wouldn't start school until tomorrow, so Mary anxiously waited to get home so she could twirl again.

When Zillah heard that Joseph was gone, the treacherous woman set out to spread her vicious gossip to anyone who would listen. Her story went something like this: Her Joshua had gone off to join the resistance movement in the north. She'd begged him not to go, but he was too patriotic to sit idly by and watch Rome destroy our nation. Joseph, on the other hand, was a friend to the soldiers, and invited them to his bar-mitzvah party. He didn't expect things to get out of hand the way they did, though.

Joseph was uncontrollable, Zillah continued; that's why both his aunt and uncle had to do the unheard-of and walk by his side to the Synagogue. They were afraid that if they didn't, he'd bolt and run away on them. He really didn't want to go to his uncle Achim's, but Eleazer and Rebecca were used to the boy's insolence; that's why they had to send him away. They just couldn't handle him any longer. Eleazer was certain that if he didn't go along with him, the boy would leave the caravan, give up his faith, and join the Roman army. Zillah's heart bled for the couple because they were so good to their nephew and got nothing but heartache in return. You couldn't blame the boy too much, though, because ever since his father died, he had been a bit crazy.

The sad part was, even though they should've known better, some of the townspeople started to believe the lies.

CHAPTER 10

Seasons came and soon went. Seeds were sown and seedlings sprouted; they grew and their produce was harvested. There were times of joy and times of sorrow; a lot of laughter and more than enough tears. There were births and deaths, circumcisions and bar mitzvahs, betrothals and weddings. The old grew more wrinkled as the young blossomed. Traditions and customs, however, never changed among the Jews who lived in the multicultural little town of Nazareth.

It had been over five years since Mary had caused her mother to injure her ankle at the town well. The girl with the honey-colored eyes was on the verge of that mysterious transition that transforms a girl into a woman. She was taller now. Her hips had widened and her waist narrowed. Her chest was no longer flat. Lovely auburn hair, almost reaching down to her waist, framed her strikingly beautiful face and highlighted her ivory complexion. Not yet required to wear a veil, Mary turned the heads of both the old and the young men of the town. Anna anxiously awaited the day when her daughter would be required to hide her attractiveness from the townsmen's glaring stares.

Tonight, Mary awoke from a deep sleep with a sudden jerk, as if something had startled her. She didn't think she had been dreaming. If she was, she couldn't remember a thing about it. It was a rather cold night for the end of April, yet Mary felt quite clammy under her petticoat; her entire body glistened with perspiration. She felt several strange sensations occurring within her at the same time. The budding womanhood of her bosom felt a strange yet pleasant sensation as the fibers of her linen petticoat rubbed against her chest when she sat up. She had felt tingles there before, but never to this extent. A cramping sensation filled her lower abdomen and her head throbbed with pain. She regretted sitting, because the pounding in her head just seemed to worsen. She reclined again and tried to remain as still as she could in hopes that the numbing comfort of sleep would whisk away her pain, but somnolence evaded her.

Finally after many torturous and restless attempts to fall back to sleep, Mary rose from her mat and carefully slid to the head of the bed. She turned her body around and lowered her feet to the ground. With steps as light as feathers she walked across the room, located her tunic, and slipped into it. She looked to the high windows and could see tiny particles of dust dancing in the spectral light of the moonbeams. The inside air was ripe with the acrid smell of smoke from the fading embers that provided their nocturnal heat. Mary quietly made her way to the door and opened the inside latch as silently as possible; she didn't want to wake her parents. Her bare feet tingled as she

186

stepped out into the cool night air. The chill refreshed her and lessened her headache.

The full moon painted the night with a silvery glow. Thousands of stars twinkled against a black velvet backdrop. Her Aunt Tamar was right—fresh air could do wonders. The cramping ceased; the headache was gone. She reached up to the stars and pretended to grasp them between her thumb and index finger, then pluck them from the sky and place them into the open palm of her other hand. A gentle breeze played with her hair. She had never felt so full of life before. She looked up to the heavens and began to twirl slowly with her eyes wide open. She stared at the beauty of the firmament as it spun above her. Mary said, "Who but You, O Lord God, could conceive of something as beautiful as the heavens above, or of the vivid colors with which You paint the sky at sunrise and sunset. Your wonders are revealed every time we plant a seed, and You cause it to grow. You, O Lord, not only designed the beauty of the flowers, You also gave them a pleasant fragrance to delight our senses. Wherever I turn, I see the wonders of Your greatness before me."

"Who but You, my God, would think of turning the drab hills to a dusty purple when the sun sets? Or to make the earth smell so fresh and sweet after a rain? There is no one like You, O Lord, not on the earth or in the heavens above. Who can say there is no God when You surround us with the splendor of Your creation every day? For it is only from You that all good things come."

Mary felt so good that she just wanted to sit outside and breathe in the fresh night air. She sat down with her back against the wall and brought her knees up to her chest; she wrapped her arms around them as she had done when she was a little girl. Mary played her childhood game with the breeze and the rustling branches of the olive tree again. In just a few moments she fell asleep. If she had looked straight across the courtyard to the vacant house, she would have noticed the light of a single candle was now filtering through the open windows. Jacob's house had a new occupant.

Earlier last night, while Joachim and his family and Azor and his wife busily polished the leather on saddles that had been ordered by none other than the Roman Procurator, Jacob's son neared the town gate. The sun was just about to set. Joseph looked up to the claret sky above him as he heard a flock of chirping sparrows returning to their customary place to perch until daybreak. He continued to gaze at the birds. "Are you going home too?" he asked cheerily. His heavily laden mule followed him as he entered the gate. The young carpenter was finally home.

The townsmen, who were gathered at the gate, stared at the tall, ruggedly handsome stranger as Eliud the gatekeeper shuffled up to him. The old man's eyesight was now failing him. He brought his face close to Joseph's to see if he could recognize him. Eliud could not. "The town's gate is closing for the night," he said. "If you're visiting, tell me with whom; otherwise, there's a lean-to for travelers. It has wine, bread and fodder for your animal outside the gate. It's on the hillside."

"Eliud, don't you remember me?" Joseph asked.

"No! Should I?" the old man replied just as Rabbi Asa rose up from his bench and ran toward the young man.

"Eliud, it's Joseph, Jacob's son," the rabbi said to the gatekeeper as he grabbed hold of Joseph, kissed the beard on the young man's chin, and warmly hugged him. Joseph returned the customary greeting first to the rabbi, and then to the old man.

"I would never have recognized you, but then, my sight isn't what it used to be, you know," the toothless old man said. "Sometimes my vision is a little blurry."

"I almost didn't recognize him either, but I could see his father in his face," the rabbi commented. The other townsmen whispered amongst themselves, because Zillah had convinced most of their wives that Joseph had been unstable. "A little crazy" is the way they actually put it.

The young man raised his hand in greeting to the other townsmen as he said, "Shalom, may the Lord's peace be with you and your families." The men mumbled back their greeting, then huddled together. The consensus of the group was that Joseph seemed quite normal to them, so one by one they came up to him, and introduced themselves, giving him the customary greeting. When they were finished, and a few pleasantries were exchanged, Joseph said, "You'll have to excuse me, gentlemen, but I haven't seen my aunt and uncle in over five years, and I want to surprise them tonight."

189

The men looked at each other rather curiously as the rabbi stepped forward and said, "Come, Joseph, I'll walk with you."

"I'll tie off your mule and get him some straw and water too; just go with the rabbi!" Eliud said rather commandingly.

The two men walked along the street to the upper part of town. Asa put his arm over Joseph's shoulder. "I guess you didn't receive any of the messages I sent you?" the teacher said.

"No, Rabbi, I didn't," Joseph replied.

"Ever since Ali stopped leading caravans, it seems none of the nomads who took over his routes ever deliver any messages we send. Joseph, your aunt and uncle are gone."

"Did they move to Jerusalem already?" Joseph asked, his face shrouded with disappointment. "My aunt said they were going to stay until I came back home."

"No, Joseph, they didn't move to Jerusalem. They went to the Bosom of our Father Abraham."

The young man's chin dropped as a look of shock covered his face. "What? What happened?" Joseph asked with a stunned look on his face as tears welled up in his eyes.

"It was the winter sickness. It took them both," the rabbi said. "Your uncle went first, just ten months after you left; your aunt passed on two months later." Joseph couldn't believe his ears. He had so looked forward to seeing them again, and hoped he and his aunt would continue to strengthen their relationship. He'd expected a warm and happy homecoming.

190

"Joseph, the winter sickness was so bad the year you left that almost the entire upper town was taken from us. Your aunt, though, turned into a real angel of mercy from the day you left. The women of town had always considered her rather haughty, but by the time she left us, they thought she was a real saint. She cared for the homeless, the poor and the sick as well. Before your uncle passed on, the physician tried to contain the disease by quarantining the upper town. Your aunt went from house to house, feeding and caring for the sick there. On the day they brought your uncle's body down for burial, your aunt left me a clay tablet stipulating that you were to be the sole beneficiary of all their earthly goods. I was to sell the property and hold the proceeds for you until you returned. She also wrote that the beautiful wooden chest with the carved almond blossoms was to be kept for you. Your aunt wanted you to give it to the woman you would marry one day.

"I know right now is probably not the time to discuss this," the rabbi continued, "but even after I paid the funeral expenses and for the services of the priest from Jerusalem to declare the house clean, there still is a great sum of money left. I deposited half of it for you at the bank in Jerusalem, and I gave a quarter of it to the Town Elders to hold in the town's treasury until you returned. The last quarter I myself kept for you, until you came home. The beautiful chest is also at my house. Rebecca sealed it before she died and said that only you are to open it."

The young carpenter couldn't comprehend what the rabbi was telling him. After Asa told him about his aunt and uncle's deaths, the shock prevented him from thinking straight. When his head cleared a bit he heard the rabbi say, "Ali agreed to buy your uncle's property and business. Naturally, because of the disease and the quarantine, the entire product had to be destroyed. Since your aunt was no longer with us, Ali hired Nabu to teach him how to make the various kinds of cheeses."

When they finally reached the path that led up to Joseph's former home, Asa said, "Why don't we go up to see Ali? I'm sure he'd be glad to see you again."

"Not tonight, Teacher. It's rather late, and I'm sure he's asleep by now."

"Why don't you come to my house, then. You could spend the night with my family and me. It's not good for you to mourn alone, Joseph."

"I've learned something from my life, Rabbi—I'm never alone, for I know that the Lord my God is always with me; otherwise, I wouldn't have made it this far."

"Wise words for a man so young. The teacher now learns from the wisdom of his student. But I guess that's because you had such a good teacher to begin with, right?" the rabbi said humorously.

"Right!" Joseph replied. Both men smiled. The young carpenter retrieved his mule and thanked Eliud for caring for it. The two men then walked through the dark streets in silence.

By the time Joseph and the rabbi reached the young man's new home, Mary and her family had been asleep for several hours. Asa said to Joseph, "Keep your eyes open. I think someone has been using your house. Every time I'd check on it, the house was immaculate. Not a cobweb in sight, and all the tools you left behind seemed to have been oiled regularly."

"That's good. I'm glad someone made use of it."

"Just be careful, Joseph. I'll stop by tomorrow evening and go over everything with you. I'm sure your mind will be a little clearer then. Shalom, Joseph, and may you find your peace in the Lord tonight."

"Shalom!" Joseph replied. "And thank you for everything, Teacher." The rabbi left and headed for home as Joseph turned and led his mule through the front door to the stable at the rear of his house. Joseph searched his saddlebags for the candle he had bought. He found his flint and some wood shavings, and when he had fire, he lit the candle. He was surprised at how clean his house actually was. There was even an unused tallow candle that stood on his table.

After unloading the mule, Joseph walked out to the water trough beside his home and brought some water for the animal. The young man stood as he faced the Holy City and prayed. Joseph didn't ask his God why He took his aunt and uncle; he just prayed for strength and praised the God of his fathers. "My life is in Your hands," he said. "Please give me the strength to accept Your will." He could no longer hold back his tears. Joseph sobbed so loudly that he wondered if his Lord could even understand his words. Exhausted, Joseph sat at the edge of his bed and continued weeping until tears would no longer come. It was a cool night, so he didn't even remove his cloak; he just lifted his legs upon the bed, rolled onto his back, and fell into a deep sleep. The Lord smiled down on Joseph that night. God's design for the salvation of mankind was now in place. Joseph could never have imagined he would be such an integral part of the divine plan.

Suddenly, as if from nowhere, a gust of wind seemed to blow through all the homes of the little town. Joseph's candle, as well as most of the other nighttime candles, went out. The stiff wind blew Mary's hair across her face and caused her to awaken, just in time to hear the wind move through the old olive tree and call out the *"seeeffff"* she so loved to hear. Mary smiled as she rose and went into the house. She thought of Joseph whenever she heard the familiar sound. Even though the moon was near the western horizon, it still cast enough light for her to find the water jar when she entered her home.

The girl made the trip to the well twice daily now—once in the morning for her family, and again in the evening for her aunt and uncle. Mary observed the moon's position and determined sunrise was still several hours away. She still felt like walking, and even though it was very early, the town was safe. Mary placed the jar upon her head and with perfect balance tiptoed out of the room so as not to wake her parents. The girl started to walk down the street. For some reason, she was more aware of the silence of the night than she had ever been before. *Maybe it's the absence of candlelight streaming through the windows,* she thought. The town looked unoccupied without it. Mary also realized that the temperature had drastically risen. In fact, it was rather warm. *Things just don't seem right,* she said to herself.

As Mary turned the corner, her headache returned with a vengeance. She could now see the opening that led down to the well; it seemed to radiate a glowing white light. She had never seen anything like it before. At first she attributed the strange glow to her headache. Despite her pain, the luminescence still fascinated her. She approached the well, lowered the water jar from her head and set the jar on the ground. The teen sat down for a few moments, closed her eyes and prayed that the pounding headache would stop.

When she opened her eyes, the pain was gone. She stood, grabbed hold of the railing that surrounded the opening and looked down into the cavern. To her surprise, the light was so intense that it blotted out the first step. The brightness obliterated everything. Mary began to tremble, but her curiosity was greater than her fear, so she followed the railing until she reached the opening. Using her foot to trace the outline of the stairs, as her mother had taught her, she began to descend the curving steps into the surreal light. Mary could hear her heartbeat echo in her head. When her eyes began to adjust to the brightness, she was shocked to see the walls of the cavern took on a spectral sheen. They reminded her of the mother-of-pearl on a bracelet she once saw at a bazaar. She also noticed the damp, musty odor she was used to smelling was replaced by a pleasant scent. It was similar to the fragrance of the field of lilies in the meadow below town. The lovely aroma seemed to intensify with each downward step she took.

When Mary reached the last step, she saw the water in the well sparkling, as if countless twinkling stars drifted on its surface. Her fright increased; her whole body trembled. Her knees knocked together, and her stomach muscles tightened. Mary had to sit, for fear that she might fall. She wanted to run back up, but knew her legs were too wobbly to support her. Mary lowered herself down to the stone floor close to the mouth of the well, and sat there. Fear and fascination were at war within her mind. *Am I dreaming?* she asked herself. She couldn't think clearly. *Maybe I'm dead.* She pinched her arm as hard as she could; it hurt. None of this made any sense. *I wonder if I'll ever get out of here.* The light was so warm and appealing that she really didn't care. She sat there for a few minutes as she tried to figure out what was real and what was a figment of an overactive imagination. The girl put her hand in the water, but it didn't feel wet—it felt warm and silky. Mary thought she might be hallucinating or going insane.

Miraculously, instead of radiating outward, as light always does, the brightness in the cavern drew back into itself and formed its source. A being slowly began to emerge in the blinding light. The spirit who now stood before her was too beautiful to be a man, yet too handsome to be a woman. The ethereal form was transparent except for the head, hands, feet and the folds of its garments; they appeared solid. Its hair glistened like spun gold. When the apparition was fully formed, an intense light again radiated out from it. The light was even greater than the spirit itself.

The brilliance consumed everything beyond it. The figure was suspended in dazzling light, and so was Mary. There no longer were walls or a floor or anything else, just brightness and the diamond-like reflections of light where the water had been. The girl was frightened; she didn't know what to do. Her stomach further knotted up with fear when the heavenly messenger smiled at her.

Mary then heard it—the same beautiful, soothing voice that had called her name in the night many years ago. "Greetings, Mary!" the messenger said. "There is no need to fear, for you are highly favored by God. The Lord is with you, Mary. Don't be afraid!"

The girl was totally puzzled. In her nervous confusion, she sat there totally dumbfounded. She closed her eyes and bowed her head very low as the messenger spoke. When she could no longer hear the voice, she began to open her eyes and slowly raise her head. The apparition was gone; the cavern had returned to normal. The heavenly scent was replaced by the dank smell of wet stone. Mary mustered up all the strength she had, and ran up the staircase as fast as she could while her heart raced. The girl was surprised she made it to the top. When she reached the guardrail, Mary grasped it. Her legs were still shaking so badly that they couldn't support her upper body. She sat down next to the water jar and closed her eyes as she waited for the trembling to stop.

Mary didn't know how long she sat there, but dawn hadn't broken yet, and it was still rather dark. The girl eventually grabbed the railing and stood up again. She couldn't understand what had just happened. The teenager looked back down into the shaft. Now it was just a dim, candle-lit cavern. She struggled with her emotions as she tried to decide whether to go back down and fill the water jar, or come back later to do so, when more women would be present.

The young maiden pondered three possible explanations for what she thought she saw and heard. The first was that she had twirled too much

197

and her brain had finally turned upside down, just as her aunt had warned. Mary tried to allay that fear by reciting her favorite psalm. She spoke loudly so she could hear herself and be certain that she wasn't speaking backward. "The Lord is my shepherd…" She recited the full psalm, and it sounded fine to her. Twirling as a cause was ruled out for now.

The second possibility was that she actually had a heavenly apparition, but she decided it ludicrous. Out of all the Jewish people, why would God send an angelic being to tell her the Almighty favored her and she needn't be afraid? *Why would I be favored?* she asked herself. *I haven't done anything special, and what am I not supposed to be afraid of?*

The third possibility was that she was going insane. She didn't know how to prove otherwise. Finally she decided to risk going back down to the well and fill the water jar. When she grabbed it, the vessel was full to the brim. "I *am* going mad," she said aloud. "I already filled this." Mary placed the jar on her head and began to walk home just as the glow of the rising sun began to brighten the eastern sky. Tears streamed down her face as she walked.

The town began to come to life. Mary didn't notice anything; her head started aching once again, and the cramping returned. By the time she reached the courtyard of her home, her face had paled and the poor girl felt miserable.

Anna was outside. She looked up and saw her daughter approaching. "Mary, are you all right?"

"No, Momma, I'm not feeling very well."

Anna grabbed hold of the water jar. "You go inside, dear. I'll make you an herbal brew. Lie down for a while and perhaps you'll feel better." Anna began to prepare the beverage. She then moistened a cloth with water, brought it to her daughter, and placed it on her forehead. "What's wrong, dear?"

"I don't know, Momma, I've just been feeling rather sick all night." She didn't want to say anything about what she had experienced until she reached some conclusion.

"Do you think it could be something you ate?"

"No, Momma, I didn't have anything different than what you and Daddy ate yesterday. I can't explain it; I just feel miserable."

"I'll tell you what, dear—while the brew is steeping, I'll bring you some warm water and you can wash up. Maybe you'll feel better after you bathe. That always seems to work for me."

Anna placed the pitcher of bathwater in the corner of the room, in a small cubicle that was used for bathing. It was the only area in the house that had a flagstone floor. Anna left the room to give Mary some privacy. The woman returned to the fire pit and added vegetables to the lintel porridge she was making for the midday meal. She was very concerned about her daughter. There was an old wives' tale that abounded in the small town: If a girl didn't have her cycle by her thirteenth birthday, she was cursed and would be dead by her fourteenth. Mary had turned thirteen last September and still nothing. Anna didn't believe the tale, but she still prayed to her God, just to make sure. As she added the vegetables to the pot she said, "Please O Lord, don't take the precious gift You gave us away. Our daughter is Heli's and my greatest joy." Whenever she prayed, she used her husband's given name. She didn't want God to be confused as to whom she meant when she was praying.

As soon as her mother left, Mary began to disrobe. She entered the small cubicle and began to ladle the tepid water over her body. *Mother was right,* she thought. *I feel better already.* She debated whether she should tell her mother about what happened at the well. She finally decided it best to keep it to herself. There was no need to worry her mother. The girl took a washcloth and washed her face, then gradually moved down her body. When she had washed her torso and was about to wash her legs, she noticed the cloth was no longer white; it had turned a rusty red. She looked to the flagstone floor and saw deep-red droplets on the stones; she knew what it was. Now she understood—she actually had an apparition. The messenger told her not to be afraid, because she was dying. The proof was now at her feet. Before she could stop herself, she screamed. "Oh, Momma!" She realized she was nude, so she wrapped a towel around herself as her mother came running to her aid.

Anna found her daughter huddled in the corner of the small cubicle as tears streamed down her face. "I'm dying, Momma! I'm dying!" Mary exclaimed.

"What are you talking about, dear? Why are you saying that?" Anna went to embrace and comfort her daughter. As she did, she noticed the stained washcloth. A look down at the floor confirmed her suspicions. Anna hugged her daughter tightly and said,

"Mary! Mary! You're not dying, dear. Today you have become a woman." Mary looked totally confused. After helping her daughter with her personal hygiene, she explained the natural occurrence to Mary. "Now get dressed, my dear, and have a seat."

When she did so, Anna brought her the herbal drink. "Sip it slowly!" she said as she went to her hamper. Anna rummaged through the folded items until she found what she was looking for—a simple long piece of white linen. As Mary drank the brew, Anna returned to Mary's side and, with a melancholy look on her face, placed a veil over her daughter's head. When Mary had drunk the beverage, Anna draped the longer end of the cloth partially over her daughter's face. Only her eyes and forehead were now visible. "Today you have become a woman," her mother said. "And until you're betrothed, you must keep your face covered, and wear your veil whenever you are in the presence of any man other than your father or Uncle Azor. Stay here; I'll be right back." Anna ran out the door.

A few minutes later her mother came running back into the house with Tamar close behind. The old woman entered, shouting, "Congratulations! Congratulations, my dear!" Mary stood up as she ran toward her and hugged her heartily. "May God shower His blessings on you and provide you with a good husband, and children as numerous as the olive trees." The three women sat down. As the older two commiserated and shared their own experiences, Mary listened and laughed at some of their stories. Anna poured a glass of wine for herself and her sister-in-law, and the two women toasted Mary on her reaching womanhood. When they finished the wine, Tamar slapped her thighs as she always did when she was about to leave or change the course of things and said, "It's time to feed our husbands, so I better be leaving."

"We can all eat together," Anna said. "There's plenty of porridge for all of us."

"Please stay, Aunt Tamar. Please!" Mary pleaded. Tamar didn't need much coaxing. She loved Anna's porridge, and had anticipated that her sister-in-law would ask her to stay for lunch anyway. Besides, Tamar hadn't prepared anything yet.

The old woman liked being coaxed, so she said, "I really shouldn't, my dear hearts! I think I should go home now. You know I don't like to impose."

"You're not an imposition; you would be a blessing on our heads if you stayed to celebrate this wonderful event with us." Anna knew how to play her sister-in-law's game.

"You wouldn't deny us a blessing, would you, Aunt Tamar?" Mary added.

"Very well, then, your uncle and I will join you, if you insist. As surely as the Lord lives, never let it be said that I would stand in the way of God's blessings." Mary and her mother smiled at each other. "I'll go tell the men it's time to eat," Tamar said. "I can't wait to see the expressions on their faces when they see you veiled, Mary."

When Tamar returned, she helped her niece finish setting the table while Anna brought in the meal. Joachim and Azor entered the house through the stable door at the rear. The minute Mary's father saw her, he asked, "Who's this beautiful young woman who's joining us for lunch?" Joachim scooped her into his arms and kissed her forehead. "I guess it's my daughter," he said as he lowered her to the ground.

"Is my brother going blind or what?" Azor asked. "If you put ten veils on our Princess, you'd still be able to tell who she was by those beautiful eyes." Mary blushed a bright red. She didn't know what to say. They prayed and then sat down to eat.

Mary had difficulty getting the food to her mouth with the veil draped over her face. Anna reached forward and gently lowered the end of the cloth away from Mary's mouth. "You'll get used to eating with your veil on, but for now just eat with your face uncovered." Mary was overjoyed; she didn't want to walk around all day with a veil stained with porridge.

After the men returned to work, Mary said, "Momma, why don't you and Aunt Tamar go to the market now. I'll do the cleanup." The women agreed and left. Mary cleared the table. She washed the dishes and began to sweep the floor. As she did so, the young woman remembered that she hadn't brushed her hair. When she finished her tasks, Mary got her hairbrush and went to the open doorway. She sat down and began to groom her hair.

The day was rather hot and muggy. Mary was grateful she was alone, because she could remove the confining veil that covered her head. *I wonder if I'll ever get used to wearing this,* she wondered as she removed fabric. Shaking her hair free, she began to brush it slowly. Mary usually counted the strokes, but today she had too much to ponder. The young maiden still couldn't make any sense of what she had experienced this morning. *Did it really happen?* she asked herself again and again. By rote she continued brushing and was so deep in thought that she didn't notice how dark it was getting. All of a sudden, a powerful wind bent the branches of the gnarled olive tree. It was so fierce that the roof above her head creaked. The sky was streaked with lightning, and the thunderclaps were so loud that they rattled the pottery in the house. Mary jumped up in fright from the unexpected sound. Then it came—a rainstorm so mighty, it sounded as if gravel was being pelted at the house and rooftop. The cloudburst just lasted for a few moments, then turned into a steady drizzle.

Mary could hear the frantic chirping of a distressed sparrow. She walked to the doorway and saw a mother bird in panic. The nest she had built gave up its young when the strong wind hit. Her chicks lay chirping on a little island of clay surrounded by a rain puddle. The murky, ochre-colored water was rising around them. Mary forgot all about her veil as she ran to the rescue. She knew where the nest was; she had watched it being built. It was on a lower branch of the olive tree within her reach. She scooped up the chicks and returned them to the nest. Mother sparrow fluttered around in gratitude as she returned to comfort her young.

Mary was soaking wet. *This is my last chance for an unencumbered spin,* she said to herself. Besides, she loved to stand in the rain. Without looking around, she stuck out her tongue to catch the raindrops as she began to twirl. When she stopped, she opened her eyes and was shocked to see a young man staring at her from the house across the street. He had a hammer and tarp in his hands. A small section of Joseph's roof had blown off in the gale, and he was making a temporary repair. Their eyes met for only a few seconds. Her beauty enraptured Joseph. Even with her wet auburn ringlets, Mary was a vision to behold. Both of them blushed. Joseph looked down and pretended he hadn't noticed her. He then began to pound a nail through the tarp. The carpenter didn't see Mary run inside. He was so flustered that he did something he'd never done before—he struck the wrong nail. He thought that Mary might still be watching, so he didn't grab hold of his thumb as his instincts directed. He fought the desire to verbalize the word "ouch!" that was pursed on his lips. He'd wait until he got back into the house to shake off the pain in his throbbing thumb.

People may say there's no such thing as love at first sight, but Mary and Joseph would disagree. That first glance ignited a spark of love between the two of them. When Mary came back into the house, she starting twirling again as she whispered the name "Joseph" over and over. Whenever Mary said it, she could feel her heart flutter. She wanted to talk to him, but her culture forbade it. She hurriedly put on her veil and draped it across her face. Surely she could think of something she could do outside to catch another glimpse of him. Although Mary had already scoured out the porridge pot, she could always do it again. This time, though, she'd do it outside.

Joseph came down from the roof and almost tripped on the outside stairs. He was craning his neck to get another glimpse of Mary, so he lost his stride. He had to grab on to the side of the building to regain his balance. The young man was worried that Mary would see him as an oaf. The minute Joseph reached street level, he ran to the rain trough and soaked his injured thumb. The water wasn't very cold, but it still took out some of the sting. He kept his back to Mary's house. If she came out again, he didn't want her to see what a dunderhead he was. *What kind of a carpenter am I,* he asked himself. *Uncle Achim would be laughing hysterically if he saw me now.*

The young carpenter turned toward the street, and as he did, he saw Mary at the rain trough, scrubbing out a pot. Joseph ran up to his rooftop, and pretended to be fixing the tarp once again. He thought that if he left for thatch and mud to complete the repair, he wouldn't get another chance to see her today. So as Mary pretended to scrub an already-spotless pot, and Joseph knelt facing her to complete a temporary repair that was already finished, their eyes met several more times. Joseph was tempted to break tradition and go speak with Mary, but his good manners prevailed. He would be patient and wait until a family member was present and the proper introduction was made. They weren't children anymore, and a new set of rules for proper etiquette now applied. When their eyes met for about the fourth time, he did smile at the young woman. Joseph thought she smiled back at him, but he wasn't certain, because her face was partly covered by her veil.

Neither Joseph nor Mary could pretend that their projects needed further attention. Mary tried to think of something else she could do that would allow her to face Joseph's house. Joseph kept tugging at the edges of the tarp as he watched her, and in the process almost pulled it free. He couldn't think of anything else he could do either without looking suspicious, so he let go of the tarp and headed back toward the stairs. Mary could think of nothing more that she could pretend to do either, so she straightened up to go inside. Just then, Mina the matchmaker came walking toward her.

"Good afternoon, darling," the hyperactive woman said, only she pronounced it "dah-link." "Dah-link, it's a perfect day for a young maiden—a beautiful young maiden like you, may I add—to find her intended. Is your mother home, dah-link?" The woman used her hands when she spoke and fluttered around so much that Mary's neck was getting sore just trying to keep her in sight.

"No, she isn't, Mina; she and my aunt went to the market."

"Well, tell her I stopped by, dah-link, will you?" Mina didn't wait for an answer; she just kept right on talking and fluttering about as her hands moved rapidly. "How old are you now, dah-link?"

"I'll be fourteen in September," Mary replied.

"You, dah-link, should have had an intended two years ago. If you're not married by sixteen you'll be an old maid." Mary blushed at the thought of marriage.

"Tell your mother what I said, dah-link. I have twenty, maybe even thirty perfect matches for you. And tell her too, dah-link, that my husband can broker the dowry, and for a pretty woman like you, he can fix the groom's payment so that your parents will be set for life, and so will you. Tell her that, dah-link, be sure to tell her, will you, dah-link?"

"I will, Mina; I'll tell her as soon as she returns."

"You tell her the best ones go fast. Okay, dah-link?"

"I will, Mina, and shalom!" Mary said, hoping the annoying woman would leave.

"Shalom? What kind of peace can a woman with my calling have when such a beautiful young woman like you has no intended? I tell you, dah-link, I won't sleep tonight just worrying about you, dah-link. Tell your mother I'll stop by early tomorrow morning so we can talk, will you, dah-link?" Mary didn't bother to answer; she knew the woman was too busy talking to listen to anything she had to say. Mina finally stopped to take a breath.

Mary saw the opportunity and said, "I have work to do inside, Mina, but I'll tell my mother everything you had to say." Mary made her way around the matchmaker and entered the house. She tried to rub out the kink in her neck from watching the woman's fluttering about as she spoke.

After Mina left and Mary was certain the woman had gone her way, she peeked through the doorway to see if the carpenter was still outside. But Joseph had already gone inside to try and shake the numbness out of his thumb. As Mary was about to draw her head back into the house, she spotted her mother and aunt returning from their shopping excursion. Since the day Mary's mother had injured her ankle, she walked a bit slower and with a slight limp. Today, though, Anna seemed to almost run. She was signaling for her daughter to come over. Mary ran as fast as she could.

There were still puddles from the brief storm, so the water splashed against the hem of Mary's tunic, staining her garment a shade of ochre. Usually Anna would scold her daughter for being so careless, but today she didn't seem to care. The teenager could see that her mother's face beamed with joy. "Mary, Jacob's son returned to town last night—you know, Joseph, the young man who helped me at the well. Go ask your father to invite him to dinner tonight. Ask him if he could go over there right now before someone else invites him."

Mary needed no encouragement. Before Anna was done speaking her daughter was already halfway across the courtyard. She entered the shop and stood by her father as he bent over his workbench. Joachim lifted up his head and could see that his daughter's face glowed; she was absolutely radiant with joy. "Daddy! Daddy! Joseph is home! Mommy asked if you would go over there right now and invite him to dinner tonight, before someone else does."

Her father placed the threaded needle he was using into a block of soft balsa wood that he used for that purpose and said, "What! Is the carpenter only staying in his new home for one night?"

"I don't think so. Why do you ask, Daddy?"

"Then what's so urgent? If he doesn't come over tonight, there'll be other opportunities."

Joachim could see the disappointment in his daughter's eyes. He was about to tease her but thought better of it, because she looked so heartbroken. "Very well," he said, "I'll go over there right now. It'll be good to see him again. If he's home, I'll invite him over." The smile instantly returned to Mary's face.

209

"You can go with me, if you cover your face a little more," Joachim said. "Your smile is too enticing for a young bachelor to see," he teased.

"Daddy, you're embarrassing me," Mary said as she blushed and drew her veil up over her nose.

Mary grabbed her father's hand. Walking side by side, they crossed the street to Joseph's. Joachim knocked on the door and was surprised that it opened almost immediately. Mary moved behind her father when she saw the young man in the open doorframe. Joachim kissed Joseph's chin, then gave the young man a warm bear-hug. "Shalom! Welcome home, Joseph. It's so good to see you! You're a full-grown man now and even more the spitting image of your father." Joseph returned the greeting and the hug. When he leaned forward, he looked right into Mary's eyes. The embrace lasted a lot longer than Joachim expected. He then realized the bachelor lingered because he was enraptured with his daughter. Joachim forced himself to cough several times before Joseph finally got the hint and snapped out of his trance. "You remember my daughter, don't you, Joseph?" Joachim said. He stepped to the side so Mary could be seen in full view.

"Yes, I sure do, sir! It's Mary, isn't it? I knew who those beautiful eyes belonged to the moment I saw them," Joseph said without thinking, then regretted his comment. He realized how badly he bungled the formal introduction. Mary bowed her head and blushed. She was a bit too embarrassed by the compliment.

Joseph didn't know what to do or say, so he resorted to a nervous habit he'd acquired since he left. He raised both hands to his side curls and nervously kept brushing them over his ears. Joachim smirked. No matter how far back the young man pushed the dark-black ringlets, they sprang forward and coiled up like a tightly wound spring. Joseph was even more nervous when Mary raised her face to look at him. "It's good to see you again, Joseph," she said. "Welcome home!"

The young man tried to regain his composure. "I, uh—sorry, uh, I didn't mean to, uh, be rude or anything like that," he stammered. "Why don't you, I mean both of you, come in. I didn't mean for you not to come into my home. I mean, welcome to my home." Joseph realized how incoherent he must have sounded, so he decided to stop talking and choose his words more carefully before he spoke again.

"We really can't stay, Joseph. My wife and I, and I'm sure my daughter too, would like you to come over to share our evening meal with us—a kind of private welcome-home dinner in your honor."

"I'd be happy to join you and your family, sir, but I wouldn't want you to think it rude of me if I left right after the meal. Rabbi Asa told me he wanted to drop by tonight. He has several things he needed to discuss with me about my aunt and uncle as soon as possible."

"Oh, Joseph, forgive me. I forgot to express my sympathy on their passing."

"Don't apologize, sir. Over four years is a long time, especially when you face the reality of them being gone daily. I completely understand, sir."

"We'll see you at sunset, then?"

"Yes, sir! I'll be there, and thank you for the invitation. Shalom, sir, and to you also, Mary." The young maiden blushed. She loved the way he said her name. Father and daughter returned the customary farewell and left. The young woman was so happy, she felt as if she was floating on air.

Mary walked by her father's side as they crossed the street. "Go inside and help your mother prepare for our guest. Tell your mother I'll be asking your aunt and uncle to join us as well." Joachim couldn't resist teasing her a bit by adding, "And don't try to make yourself more beautiful than you already are for the young man. He already can't stop looking at you."

"Daddy!" Mary said as she moved her veil and gave her father a peck on the cheek. She then covered her face properly and ran to the door to tell her mother the good news.

Joachim laughed as he walked back to the shop. He stopped laughing when the realization struck him that his beautiful daughter might not be with them too much longer. He decided then and there that he would encourage Joseph to ask for his daughter's hand. From what he saw just now, he didn't think it would take much coaxing. If his daughter married the young carpenter, at least she'd live across the street. He knew Joseph would make a fine husband for his Mary. *No betrothal, though,* he said to himself, *at least not until my daughter turns fourteen.* He became rather despondent when he realized that birthday was only five months away. "Lord, my Mary is Yours forever," he prayed, "but she is ours for only a few seasons. It would be so hard to say goodbye to another daughter, especially my Mary. Oh! And an old man should at least experience the joy of having some grandchildren around him. Don't You think so, Lord?"

Mary ran through the door of her home shouting, "Momma! Momma! Joseph is coming to dinner. What can I do to help? Oh! Daddy also told me to tell you he's inviting Aunt Tamar and Uncle Azor too."

"Very well, then, you can make some more flatbread and some hummus. I'm roasting a leg of lamb; that should be enough for all of us."

"So how was he?" Anna asked. "Even more handsome now that he's fully grown, I suspect?"

"Yes, he is, Momma! And he's so tall that I have to stand on the tips of my toes just to see his face." Anna's smile broadened as her daughter kept talking about the young carpenter. "And he has this funny habit, Momma, it's kind of cute. He keeps pushing his side curls over his ears, and the curls just bounce right back. Oh, Momma! I almost forgot to tell you, Mina stopped by to ask if you were home. She said she has to see you."

"I expected that," Anna said. "She knows the instant a young woman is veiled. The poor dear doesn't even have to step out of her home and be seen, and Mina is already at the door. That woman literally gives me a pain in the neck."

"Me too, Momma! I had to rub the kink out after she left." Both mother and daughter shared a hearty laugh as they prepared the evening meal.

Joseph, like all the other Jewish people of his day, had a keen sense of time. They never used clocks, but relied on the position of the sun to live their day by. "After all, wasn't that the main reason God placed the sun in the heavens!" they'd answer if you asked them

213

why they didn't measure time another way. The young carpenter kept going to his front door, looking out to see the sun's position in anticipation of tonight's dinner. But no matter how often he checked, he couldn't hurry the sun's setting. On his last attempt he ran into Zillah. He tried to pretend he didn't see her and go back into the house, but she kept calling him by name in her loud, shrill voice. The young man said, "Shalom, Zillah. I hope you've had a pleasant day."

"Joseph! It's good to see you're home again. So tell me, are you enjoying your inheritance? How much was it?"

Joseph had learned from the good rabbi how to answer a question with a question, so he asked, "What inheritance are you talking about, Zillah?"

The foolish woman fell for the baited answer. "You mean your uncle left you penniless?" Joseph just shrugged. "I'm not surprised. After all, you weren't his son or anything like that. He probably considered you a burden anyway. Well, even if he didn't, I'm sure his wife did. He probably left everything to Achim. Oh! I don't know why he'd do that, though, because he never came to visit, but I guess it's better to leave it to a close blood relative than to just a nephew."

Joseph replied, "It just may be so! Shalom, Zillah! I'm very busy trying to get things organized."

"Wait! Wait!" the gossiping woman said. "Did you hear my Joshua is a renowned Freedom Fighter? He's one of the Zealots, you know. He and his men are holding the Roman army at bay, and he's going to liberate all of Israel. I really think that I may have given birth to the Messiah, or at least to one of His greatest commanders."

214

"That's wonderful, Zillah! Congratulate him for me the next time you see him. But right now, I've got to be going. Shalom!"

"Hmm!" the woman replied as she went on her way to tell everyone that Joseph was penniless.

The young carpenter went back into his house. He shook the dust from his outer cloak, then bathed again and changed into an ankle-length tunic. He oiled his hair and his beard. Joseph searched through his saddlebags to find the long piece of linen he had purchased to form a turban; he couldn't find it, so he just shook out his cotton cap and placed it back on his head. He nervously kept pushing back his side curls as he cracked open the door and peeked out again. Anxiously he waited for the sun to disappear behind the western hills. When the soft hue of twilight painted the hills a dusty purple color, he immediately left the house and crossed the street to Mary's house.

"He's coming! He's coming!" Mary said. She stood by the door and watched Joseph walking toward her house. Anna and Joachim looked at each other and started to laugh.

"Don't look so anxious! You'll scare the young man off!" Joachim said. Mary heard her father, so she flew across the room and sat cross-legged on her mat, as if nonchalantly waiting for dinner to begin.

"Don't you think it would look more proper if you pretended to be preparing dinner rather than just sitting there?" Anna asked. Mary jumped up, ran over and began to stir the hummus. "That's better," Anna said just as Joseph arrived at the door. Anna saw him pay reverence to the Law on their doorframe before knocking. With folded hands she silently thanked the

Lord that Joseph hadn't lost his piety while he was gone. Anna came up to the young man and put her arms around him, giving him a warm hug. "Welcome home, Joseph! My, how you've grown! You look just like your father now! He was a handsome man, too!"

Joseph blushed and thanked Anna for the compliments. Mary smiled at her mother as Joseph began to push back his side curls in nervousness. "And thank you for inviting me to dinner tonight. Everything smells delicious."

"Mary, aren't you going to greet Joseph?"

"Oh, I'm sorry! I wasn't thinking! Good evening, Joseph, and shalom."

"And shalom to you also, Mary!" Joseph replied.

Anna expressed her condolences to him. The three bantered about in idle conversation while Mary said nothing but kept glancing at Joseph with her haunting eyes. Joachim was amazed that in one day his little girl could have changed from a child into a woman and be shyly alluring too. The glances were not wasted on the young carpenter. Anna and Joachim noticed that while Joseph politely conversed with them, his eyes were directed toward Mary. The older couple just smiled at each other and continued to talk.

Azor and Tamar finally arrived, and after warmly greeting Joseph, they exchanged a few pleasantries with him. The group then prayed and thanked their God for the food they were about to eat. The men sat down at the low table while the women served the meal. After they did so, they too sat down and joined them. "You'll find that things have changed a great deal in our town since you left," Joachim said.

"How's that, sir?" Joseph asked.

"There are a lot more Roman army patrols bothering us than there used to be. In the past they came twice a year to collect Caesar's taxes, and once in a while you'd see a small patrol that was just looking for trouble. Now they're here once or twice a week. Although there's always been Zealot activity here in the north, Zillah has the Romans believing that her son is some great liberator of our people. Nothing could be further from the truth, though. The fact of the matter is, Joshua is nothing but a thief and a thug who runs with others just like him. I've talked to some leaders of the Zealot movement, and he's not even among their ranks. They only know he goes around extorting and robbing people in the name of the Freedom Fighters and is actually injurious to the movement. Oh, he's also dropped his first name and just goes around calling himself Barabbas. The story goes that one of the many prostitutes that follow his group of brigands thought the name sounded more mysterious. So that's how he's known today. He's the reason for the constant raids, even though he hasn't shown his face around here since the day he left."

"I was cornered by Zillah earlier, and I had to listen to her hero's saga too," Joseph said.

"Mary!" Anna said, "Why don't you pour our guest some more wine?"

"No, thank you!" the young man said. "One is my limit with any meal other than the Passover. The day after that holy day I always wake up with a miserable headache. I really prefer to drink herbal tea. It has no lasting side effects." They all laughed at his reply. Mary rose from her mat and poured him some tea that was left in the kettle from lunch. She brought it to him from behind. Joseph didn't see her as she began to place the drink in front of him, because he was speaking and gesturing with his hands. As she moved closer, he leaned back, and his shoulder touched her outstretched arm. The brief encounter was mutually electrifying. Mary became flustered. Her face turned a bright red. She nearly dropped the cup. Joseph also blushed. He stopped talking in mid-sentence, and began to smooth back his side curls. The young man stammered as he tried to continue the conversation.

Mary saw that he needed time to regain his composure, so she said, "It's tea. It's just room temperature, but I think it tastes better that way."

Joseph thanked her a bit too profusely, then quickly drank the beverage. He was still embarrassed over their contact. "I want to thank you for your hospitality. Everything was delicious, but I have to leave to meet with Rabbi Asa. If it isn't too late, may I come back after our meeting?" Joseph asked as he looked at Mary.

"By all means!" Joachim replied. "We'll look forward to seeing you later."

Joseph left Mary's house. As he crossed the street, he chided himself for stammering the way he did. *It was her touch, that's what it was,* he said to himself. *I've never felt anything like it before.* The young man couldn't wait to get back to see her again. He hoped the rabbi's visit would be a short one. Joseph would have to force himself to pay attention, because his thoughts were still on Mary.

When Asa arrived, he came with a full accounting of Joseph's inheritance and a large, heavy bag of coins he had been holding for the young man. The rabbi explained that the money was not only from the sale of his uncle's property, but also from the sale of the produce from his land. (Every homeowner in Nazareth had a field in the valley below the town, a field where they could raise crops, and have a small vineyard.)

"I thought my father's land was lying fallow. Did my uncle or you hire someone to farm it?" Joseph asked. The rabbi explained that Nabu and his family had farmed it while he was gone and gave the proceeds from its produce to him to hold for Joseph.

"That was awful nice of him, but why did he do it?" Joseph asked.

"He was so impressed by the way you defended your aunt's honor the night before you left. He said that it was the least he could do for a real hero like you." Joseph was a bit sorry he asked the question, because the compliment embarrassed him.

The young man was astonished by the amount of money that was discussed. He kept pushing back his side curls. He would have been more than grateful just for the bag of shekels and talents the rabbi had given him, but there was more. When Asa showed him the amount that was held by the town's treasury and what was in the bank in Jerusalem, Joseph was flabbergasted. He pushed back his side curls even further now; they sprang forward as he said, "What do I do with all this money?" He didn't really expect an answer. The rabbi gave none. Asa explained how he could retrieve the rest of his funds, and gave him the parchments that would satisfy his claims to it.

The young man then said, "Rabbi, the Lord has looked kindly on me, so I would like for some of what the Lord has given me to be a blessing to others as well." He took one-tenth of the coins and gave them to the rabbi as he said, "This is for the Temple in Jerusalem." He counted out another tenth and handed it to Asa. "This is for the Synagogue here. And this final tenth is for the widows and orphans. I also want a tenth of everything that's on deposit to go to each of those that I specified before."

"Your father and your uncle surely raised you in the knowledge of the way of the Lord," the rabbi said.

Joseph then counted out more silver coins and gave them to Asa, saying, "And this, Rabbi, is for you, for all you've done in handling my affairs."

"No! No! Joseph, you have been generous enough already."

"Rabbi, please permit me this blessing. I appreciate everything you've done for me. You know I can take a wife now, and raise a family comfortably on this amount, even if it takes me several years to establish my business. I realize the amount of work you had to do to settle the estate. Please do me the honor and the blessing of accepting this with my gratitude."

The rabbi reluctantly took the stipend, and was about to leave when he remembered the carved wooden chest. "Joseph, I almost forgot about the almond-blossom chest. Perhaps you can borrow a wagon and we could move it over here. My wife will really miss it, though. She polishes it often, and loves to trace the fine detailing with her fingers."

"Maybe she should keep it, then," Joseph said.

"Oh, no! Your aunt gave specific orders that the chest and its contents were to go to your future wife." Joseph said he would retrieve the chest as soon as he could get a wagon. The two men said their farewells and the rabbi left. Asa hadn't walked more than two doors down before Joseph was already running across the street to Mary's house. He was so preoccupied with seeing her again that he left the money sitting on his table. He ran back quickly, and hid the heavy bag of silver and gold coins in a pile of straw at the back of his stable. Joseph brushed himself off quickly, and anxiously ran back across the street.

The three women sat together, combing wool, while the men talked and waited for Joseph's return. Mary could hear Joseph's bare feet hitting the ground as he neared the house. When he entered, Mary said in a rather loud voice, so Joseph could clearly hear, "I meant to tell you, Aunt Tamar, Mina was here today, and she's anxious to find me a husband."

The two women looked at each other, shocked at first by Mary's audacity, then totally amused by her forwardness. They both began to laugh, then saw the look on Joseph's face immediately turn from joyful anticipation to somber disappointment. The whole town knew who Mina was. "Yes!" Mary continued. "She wants to see you tomorrow morning, Momma."

Joachim tugged at his cap and looked at his daughter as if to say, "Enough." Joachim felt bad for the young man. But even he and Azor couldn't help but be amused by Joseph's changing expressions.

"Let's talk about something else," Anna said softly. As Joseph turned to face the other men, she raised her index finger, and shook it at her daughter with a scornful look on her face. When Mary glanced over at Joseph and saw his disappointment, she deeply regretted her comment. The two men immediately began to laud the young man with plaudits on his achievements to boost his morale. Joseph spent the rest of the evening glancing at Mary with doleful eyes.

Azor began to yawn and said to his brother, "I think it's time for me to call it a night. My age catches up to me earlier and earlier. Tamar! Are you ready to leave yet?"

"I've just been waiting for you," she replied.

The couple thanked their hosts and kissed their niece goodnight. Azor whispered in Mary's ear, "Be gentle with your young man. He's crushed!" The couple wished Joseph "shalom" and told him how much they enjoyed his company. Then they departed.

Joseph stood up and said, "I hope I haven't overstayed my welcome."

"Nonsense!" Joachim said. "Stay longer if you'd like. I enjoy your company."

"No, sir, I better be going. I'm sure you have a busy day tomorrow. I do too. I've got to get my shop in order so that I can start plying my trade. Before I leave, though, I have a question to ask. Do you know who's been keeping my house clean and my tools oiled? I thought maybe since you live right across the street, you would have noticed."

Joachim said, "No! I don't. How about you, Anna?"

She shook her head. "No, I don't know either." Mary said nothing.

"I just wanted to thank whoever it was for the wonderful job they did," Joseph said. "Once again, thank you for everything. Your hospitality was a blessing, and the meal was wonderful. I haven't had a home-cooked meal like that in a long time,

Ma'am. Shalom! And may the God of our Father Abraham bless you for your kindness." The young man looked into the Mary's hypnotic eyes and said, "Shalom and goodnight to you also, Mary."

Her heart was breaking, for she could see the hurt in his eyes once again. "Shalom and goodnight to you, Joseph," she said, then boldly added, "And I hope to see you again soon." Joseph smiled so wide that his teeth glistened in the candlelight.

The carpenter's sad eyes now sparkled with happiness and restored hope as he said, "Real soon! I hope!" The young man embraced Joachim and his wife a bit too tightly. He looked at Mary one last time and wished them all shalom again. As soon as Joseph reached the street he pulled off his cap, threw it up toward the starlit sky and shouted, "Thank You, Lord!" He caught the hat and placed it back on his head. He felt like he was walking on air. The young carpenter was in love.

Joachim had stepped outside and saw what Joseph did. He laughed quietly at the young man's antics and said to himself, *The poor boy's got it bad, really bad.*

After Joseph left, Anna scolded her daughter for being a little too forward. "It's not proper for a young woman to tell a man that she hopes to see him again. And, young lady, it wasn't right to mention anything about Mina stopping by either. You'd have to be blind not to have noticed that Joseph is interested in you."

"I'm sorry, Momma, but do you really think he likes me?"

"Yes, I do! And I think he was very upset when you mentioned Mina's reason for calling. That young man has already experienced enough grief in his short life; you didn't have to add more."

"Momma, I didn't mean to upset him. Isn't he handsome, though, Momma, and he's so kind, and so tall, and so strong."

"Yes! Yes! He's all that, and I know why you mentioned Mina, but it's not proper to do so. If it's meant to be, it will be. He can't be forced into a decision on a whim. The man has to establish his business and afford a wife before he marries. Furthermore, your father will decide who is best for you. Your welfare comes before love."

"Yes, Momma! But I know Daddy likes him, and so do you, Momma."

"That's beside the point! A father has to make sure his daughter can be well provided for. I don't think Joseph could do that yet. Just never do what you did again. I think your father was a bit embarrassed too."

"I'll apologize to Daddy as soon as he comes back in. I just really like him, Momma, and I wasn't thinking when I did what I did."

"Oh, yes you were!" Anna said jovially, as she grabbed her daughter and hugged her. "I might have done the same thing," Anna confessed. Mother and daughter both laughed. "Someday he'll be quite a catch, but not until he establishes his business."

When Joachim returned, Mary apologized for her behavior. Her father said, "You really like that young man, don't you? Too bad his business isn't established yet."

"Yes, Daddy! I really do!" Mary kissed her father's cheek, then said, "I'm not very tired. I think

I'm going to go and sit outside for awhile and listen to the crickets."

"Don't stay out too late!" Anna said.

"I won't, Momma!" the young woman replied, as she gave her mother a peck on the cheek. Mary left the house as Joachim lit a fresh tallow candle for the night; he and his wife then retired.

Heavy clouds had now moved in and blocked the moon's light as Mary sat in total darkness and tried to make some sense of her day. She pondered the apparition and came up with another probable cause. *Perhaps my headache was so bad that I didn't remember filling the water jar and carrying it back up. Maybe when I sat down at the top of the well and rested, I actually fell asleep. The rest probably was just a dream. That's right; it must have been a dream.*

Mary didn't want to think about it anymore tonight. She wanted to talk to God about the way she felt about Joseph, and ask her Lord to keep him from falling in love with someone else. She didn't mention the apparition because she couldn't understand why a messenger from God would say that the Lord highly favored her of all people. She didn't think she had done anything that would have singled her out from any other person. That thought alone further convinced her the whole incident never really occurred. She liked the dream theory best. If she wasn't insane, she could give her heart totally to Joseph without reservation.

As Mary was about to go back into the house she saw Joseph's door open. The candlelight inside his house caused him to appear in silhouette in the doorframe. He wore a short under-tunic that was his nightclothes. Mary's pulse quickened as she watched him stare at her house for a few moments. He obviously couldn't see her, as there was no moonlight; otherwise he wouldn't have gone to the side of his house dressed as he was. He returned with a bucketful of water for his mule. Joseph stared at her house for a few minutes longer, then went inside. He took one last, hard look at her house and reluctantly shut the door. As soon as he went inside, Mary ran to her door, entered and closed it behind her. Her heart was still aflutter as she pressed her back to the door and waited for her heartbeats to slow down. When they finally did, she crawled into bed beside her mother and soon fell asleep.

Joseph watered his mule, then paced between the stable and his bed. The night was hot and humid. He considered sleeping on the roof because of the tightness inside the house, but thought better of it. Joseph knew he would have difficulty falling asleep with Mary's house in sight. He wasn't doing much better on the inside, though. He kept thinking of Mina's meeting with Anna tomorrow. *What if she finds someone who Joachim would consider a good match for his daughter?* he asked himself. Joseph knew that sometimes matches were made quite quickly. *No one really knows how much I inherited, except Rabbi Asa. Joachim probably thinks I'm just a poor carpenter unable to care for his daughter. What if some wealthy merchant or banker's son asks for her hand? I know what I have to do, so I better get to sleep now.* Joseph washed up quickly. He prayed and then crawled into bed. Joseph tossed and turned for several hours. He couldn't get Mary out of his mind. Finally, around midnight, pure exhaustion took over, and he fell asleep.

As Joseph tossed and turned, Mary did so as well. She dreamt that she and Joseph were walking hand in hand toward the precipice on the outskirts of town.

She felt the touch of his hand, and it made her feel warm and tingly all over. They talked and laughed as they strolled through the streets. Passersby smiled and nodded hello. Mary couldn't be happier. Suddenly, the messenger from her vision stepped between them. Their hands fell away from each other. Their hands could pass right through the messenger, but they somehow couldn't reach each other no matter how hard they tried. The being didn't speak, but he anticipated their every move. If they walked faster or stopped abruptly, he did so as well, and blocked their touch. The young couple grew frustrated. Mary was so intent on holding Joseph's hand again, she didn't pay attention to where she was walking. Joseph tried to warn her that her foot was too close to the edge of the precipice, but she was so determined to hold his hand that she didn't notice his words. Her foot slipped on the loose gravel. She slid off the side of the high ledge, and began to fall into the canyon below. She felt her hand being gripped suddenly, and her fall was broken in midair.

Mary jumped up from her sleep and in her panic she began to breathe very rapidly. She saw her mother sitting up next to her with a frightened look on her face. "Mary, are you all right? You've been thrashing around for quite a while now, and then you gasped and shot up so rapidly that you frightened me."

"I'm fine, Momma!" Mary said between rapid breaths. "Just a dream, that's all."

"I'd say it was more like a nightmare," Anna replied. "Try sleeping on your stomach; you'll

227

dream less that way. Now go back to sleep, dear."
She then turned on her side to face her husband.

Mary laid back down. She was content to know that the hand that saved her belonged to Joseph. She could see his face as he caught her in midair.

It wasn't a total nightmare, she said to herself just before she fell asleep again. She loved the way it felt when their hands touched. It was electrifying when he firmly grasped her hand to stop her fall. Just the thought of it gave her goosebumps. She whispered his name over and over until she fell into a deep sleep.

CHAPTER 11

Joseph learned to condition himself so that no matter how late he went to bed, he always awoke with the sun. This Friday morning was no different. He rose, stretched and went to the front door at the same time the cock was about to crow. He opened the door slightly to see if there was any activity in the house across the street. He hoped he could catch a glimpse of Mary. He knew she and her mother went to the well early. All seemed quiet at their house. Joseph grabbed his nearly full water jar and emptied it into the rainwater trough outside. He then prayed, washed up and resumed his vigil at the door. Joseph planned to leave for the well shortly after Mary did so he could fill her water jar and talk to her. After all, they had been properly introduced; he could at least greet her, and make some small talk. *Nothing deep or personal, though,* he thought to himself. *I don't want to scare her away.* He really liked the sound of her voice. It was soft and gentle; it reminded him of the cooing of a dove. Not only that, but he would do anything just to see those beautiful eyes he had thought of so often while he was gone. Mary's enchanting eyes appeared in his dreams many times since he first saw them.

Anna awoke before her daughter. She tapped her husband's shoulder to wake him, and then signaled for him to be quite. "Our daughter tossed and turned most of the night," she whispered. "Let her sleep; I'll go for water now. Mary can go for more later." The Sabbath would start at sunset, and enough water had to be collected today to last until after sundown on Saturday.

Joachim swung his legs off the bed, yawned, and stretched. "I don't think we'll have to warm any water today; it's unbearably hot. I'll just wash up and go right to work."

"Let me at least get you some bread," Anna said.

"No, thank you, dear!" Joachim replied. "I stuffed myself too much last night." He poured out the last of the water from the jar, and went off to wash.

Joseph's heart sank when he saw Anna leave without Mary. Impulsively, he left his house when Anna left hers, and he warmly greeted the woman. "Shalom! Good morning, Ma'am!"

"Oh, good morning Joseph, and shalom to you as well! I can see you still haven't learned to carry a water jar properly," the woman said jovially, for Joseph carried the jar by one of its handles slung over his back.

"No, Ma'am!" the young man said. "But I do believe it's a lot easier this way. It doesn't challenge my sense of balance as much."

Anna laughed as she said, "And here I thought you'd learned something from me five years ago."

"I did, Ma'am! But I'm just a little too clumsy to put what I learned into practice. I'd have more water on me and the street than I'd have in the jar."

"I don't believe that for a moment, not with a posture like yours," the woman replied. Joseph offered to carry Anna's jar for her. "No, thank you, Joseph, I've done this so often that the jar feels like it's a part of me. When I walk without it I feel as if I'm not properly dressed." They laughed together at her statement. "You know, my Mary would be happy to fetch your water for you if you like."

"I couldn't impose on her to do that," Joseph replied.

"Nonsense!" Anna said, "It's only proper for the women of town to assist a young bachelor."

Joseph tried to curb his enthusiasm at the thought of seeing Mary every morning, so he said, "If your daughter would do that for me, I would be most grateful. I would insist on paying her, though."

"We'll see! We'll see!" Anna said with a smile.

As they walked together, he wondered how he could broach the subject of Mina without sounding overly anxious or stupid. He decided to throw caution to the wind and asked, "I heard Mary mention that Mina is coming to see you today. How has she been?"

Anna was amused by his naiveté. "I really couldn't tell you, Joseph. Every time I see her coming, I try to hide." Joseph was ecstatic; Anna didn't seem to be too anxious to meet with Mina. Anna continued, "Forgive me for saying this, Lord, but the poor woman flutters about so much, my neck aches from trying to keep her in sight."

They laughed and Joseph said, "I know what you mean. She sure has plenty of energy, doesn't she?"

"Almost as much as a boulder rolling down the hillside," Anna replied. "You never know what direction it will travel in." When the woman realized what she'd said, her face turned ashen. "I'm so sorry for what I said, Joseph. My mouth was moving faster than my brain. My analogy was insensitive and rude—I mean, with what you witnessed at your father's death and all."

"No need to apologize, Ma'am. I know it's just a natural occurrence around here."

Anna, feeling a deep sense of guilt, said, "Joseph, why don't you come over for our Sabbath dinner tonight. It's your first Sabbath since you returned, and no one should eat alone during Shabbat."

"I couldn't impose on you twice in one week."

"Pshaw! Pshaw! You're no inconvenience! I have to cook for my family anyway, and what's one more mouth to feed? There'll be fewer leftovers to spoil in this heat." They laughed again. The young man kept insisting that he bring something. Anna finally told him that he could bring a dessert.

"What kind of dessert does Mary—I mean, does your family—enjoy the most?" he said, nervously pushing one of his side curls away from his face with his free hand.

Anna's face lit up with a smile. "Hmm, let's see. Mary loves the little cakes filled with pistachio nuts and covered with honey, like those sold here at the market. As for my husband and me, we like those too." Joseph was so delighted that he would have a chance to see Mary again tonight, he didn't watch where he was going and almost tripped on a large stone on the road.

When they reached the well, Joseph filled both water jars as they conversed. Somehow, no matter what the subject started out as, it ended up with

Mary's name mentioned. In a roundabout way, Anna knew Joseph was asking if Mary had any other suitors. There was no doubt in the woman's mind that the young carpenter was completely infatuated with her daughter. Anna knew then and there that Joseph soon would be asking her husband for their daughter's hand in marriage.

On the way back to their homes, Anna walked with the water jar securely balanced on her head, while Joseph, his right bicep bulging, carried the heavy jar slung over his shoulder. The water sloshed out and dripped down his back as he walked. Anna said, "Joseph, it doesn't seem that you're any better at carrying the jug over your shoulder than you would be by balancing it on your head. You're still going to be as wet as a swamp rat by the time you get home. My Mary will be your water-bearer from now on. I won't take no for an answer." Joseph couldn't have been happier.

The moment Joseph reached his door and set the water jar inside, he changed into a dry tunic. Grabbing his money pouch, the young man ran to the market. He was there a half-hour before it opened. He would be the first to select from the pastry trays and get to pick the best of the batch for Mary. Then he would go to the Synagogue to see Rabbi Asa, before the teacher conducted class. Joseph needed a big favor from him.

When the baker opened his booth, Joseph bought all of the little cakes Mary enjoyed. As he approached his house, carrying the layers of trays, he glanced at the courtyard across the street several times before opening his door. Joseph was disappointed because

Mary wasn't there. The carpenter took the pastries inside, grabbed four, and put them in a clean pouch to take with him. Joseph took one harder look across the street, and then ran to the Synagogue just as Mary awoke and climbed out of bed.

"Momma! Why did you let me sleep so late?" Mary said as she noticed her mother drawing water from a full jar. "I don't want you going to the well anymore, Momma; I should be doing that." Anna said she knew Mary didn't get much sleep last night, and she wanted her daughter to be wide awake tonight when the man she would marry came to dinner. "Momma, did you meet with Mina already? Tell me you didn't listen to that woman and pick someone out for me. Did Daddy approve of him already, Momma? Tell me he didn't. Is Daddy going to meet him tonight to accept a proposal?"

"You'll see!" Anna said. "You'll see!" Anna decided she would toy with her daughter a bit. She wanted her to experience some of the same anxiety that Mary had unnecessarily caused Joseph last night. Mary frowned and began to mope around the house. "If you keep frowning like that, no man will ever want to marry you."

"I'd rather live here and be an old maid than marry one of Mina's choices. He's probably too old to walk and probably went through more wives than King Solomon had. Do you know what Mina did to poor Leah, Momma? She tried to have Rabbi Asa and his wife agree to a betrothal to a man who was older than Leah's grandfather. She said Mina's husband told the old man the rabbi had accepted his proposal. The old leech followed Leah wherever she went. He'd sit under their sycamore tree and stare at her house constantly. He even said nasty things to her. Her mother eventually had to chase the old man away with a broom. Did you meet the man who's coming tonight, Momma?"

Anna replied that she had, and that he was a very nice man. "When did you meet him? Did Mina bring him by this morning? Momma, how could you do this to me?"

"Wait until you meet him tonight. I'm sure you'll like him as much as I do."

"Momma, you know that I like Joseph. I'm going to talk to Daddy. He'll listen to me. I know he will." Anna told Mary to take a deep breath and calm down, and that her father didn't even know she had invited the man to dinner. She told Mary to say nothing to her father until Anna had told him about the invitation.

"Go, and wash up now, and do your chores. After that you can go over and visit Leah and lament your fate. I want this to be a very special Sabbath, and I don't want anyone with a sour disposition around me today," Anna said with a mischievous gleam in her eyes. A very disappointed Mary went off to bathe.

Joseph reached the sycamore tree next to the rabbi's house and sat down under its leafy branches. It stirred up memories of his childhood. In fair weather, Joseph sat under this same tree many times as he listened to the rabbi teach. He had a full view of the teacher's house from that vantage point. The instant Joseph saw the rabbi, he'd ask Asa to join him. Joseph's stomach growled. He really didn't eat much last night because he'd been so nervous. The young man was tempted to open the pouch and sample Mary's favorite dessert, but good manners stopped him from doing so. He would wait for the rabbi. Joseph waited patiently to see some signs of life, but it was still very early in the morning, and all activities still took place within the house. Seconds seemed like hours as Joseph gazed at the closed door. Finally it opened and the rabbi stepped out carrying an armful of scrolls. The moment Joseph saw him, he ran up to the teacher. "Shalom and good morning, Rabbi! May I help you carry those?"

"Shalom, Joseph! May the Lord grant you a good day! Thanks for the offer, but these scrolls aren't heavy, just a bit bulky. I was studying them last night, and wanted to return them to the Synagogue. My little nephew is staying with us for a few days, and he finds parchment irresistible. Did you come for the chest?"

The rabbi walked toward the Synagogue as Joseph walked backward in front of him and said, "No, Rabbi, I wasn't able to get a wagon yet. I have something more important to talk to you about."

They reached the door of the Synagogue. As Joseph opened it for the teacher, Rabbi Asa said, "Why don't you wait for me under the sycamore? As soon as I put these away, I'll join you." The young man thanked him and returned to the tree. He sat under it, anxiously waiting for the teacher. Joseph nervously pushed back his side curls as he thought of what he'd say. The carpenter was so anxious that he didn't even notice how loudly his stomach was growling. Within in a few minutes the rabbi joined him. "It sounds like you're a bit hungry," Asa said. "Let me bring you something to eat."

"No, thank you, Rabbi; I brought us some of Mary's favorite cakes. I thought we could eat them out here."

"There are a lot of Marys in Nazareth. Do you mean Anna and Joachim's daughter?"

Joseph said that was the Mary he meant, as he opened the pouch and offered the rabbi the cakes.

"Mary has excellent taste," the teacher said as he took one. These are a favorite of mine too."

A pleasant breezed stirred the branches of the sycamore as Joseph replied, "I've never tried them before; my Aunt Rebecca wasn't a big believer in pastries of any sort." He and the rabbi ate the cakes. "These really are good," Joseph said. "I never knew what I was missing." The rabbi chuckled. Joseph held out the pouch to the teacher as he said, "Here, Rabbi, have another. I brought two for each of us." Asa didn't need to be coaxed.

When they had finished eating, Asa asked, "So tell me, Joseph, what brought you out to see me so early in the morning? Was there something in my accounting that puzzles you?"

"Oh, no, Rabbi! It's nothing that insignificant! I have a favor to ask of you, Teacher. As you know, I have no relatives anywhere near here, and if you'd be so kind to oblige me, I would be most grateful if you would broker an espousal between Joachim and me for Mary's hand." (In their culture, a prospective groom could never approach his future father-in-law directly.)

"I don't want to use Mina's husband, because from what I've heard, he can be very brutal with the woman's father," Joseph continued. "I'll offer Joachim a substantial sum for the dowry, and I wouldn't expect any reciprocity on his part. At dinner last night, I noticed his hands are getting stiff, and his fingers are starting to get gnarly like his brother's. He'll have to take on several apprentices soon if he wants his business to continue. That would mean he'd have to provide them with housing and food, so he'll need the money to do so. I'd be happy to pay you—no, what I meant to say is, I would insist on paying you the standard broker's fee for doing this for me."

"I'd be happy to do it for you, Joseph, but I didn't expect you to find a wife so quickly. Mary's a beautiful girl, but there's no need to rush. She isn't even veiled yet."

"Oh, but she is, Rabbi! Mina has already been over to see Anna. I'm afraid she might persuade Joachim to accept one of her client's proposals before I make my intentions known."

"Very well, Joseph, I'll go over to see Joachim as soon as I finish washing up. You caught me before I really had a chance to do so." Joseph apologized for coming by so early. "Nonsense, I didn't mean that the way it sounded. I'm glad you came to me first. As far as the brokerage fee goes, if you insist on paying me, it will just go into the Synagogue's coffers. Now tell me, Joseph, what am I to offer Joachim for your future bride?"

Asa was shocked by the amount that Joseph proposed. "Are you sure you want to offer that much?" the rabbi asked.

"Yes, I'm positive," Joseph said. "I want my offer to be too good to refuse."

"Very well then," the rabbi said. "I'll go inside now, so that I can get over to Joachim's immediately." They said their farewells and Joseph left. God heard the rabbi's morning wish for Joseph. *This is turning out to be the greatest day of my life so far,* the young carpenter said to himself as he walked toward his house.

While Joseph was talking to the rabbi, Mary was in the stable, feeding the animals and milking the goats. As she sat on the milking stool, she tried to sort out yesterday's events and analyze her frightening dream. Maybe the dream was premonitory. The Sacred Writings told of dreams that, when interpreted by men of God, revealed future events. Tonight her father might agree to an engagement with some perfect stranger. *Why, then, would Joseph save me in the dream if I were to marry someone else?* she asked herself. Maybe the apparition was real and the celestial being was telling her not to be afraid because her parents knew best and she should just trust them and not question their decisions. But if the vision were real, why would the messenger tell her she was highly favored by God Himself? Nothing made sense to her. She also knew she could never feel about anyone the way she felt about Joseph. The young woman was so disheartened that she didn't know what to do, so she prayed.

When Mary finished her chores and brought the milk into the house, Anna told her to go to Leah's. It would do her some good to see her friend.

239

Normally Mary would be overjoyed to visit her friend, but today she was indifferent. "Maybe I should just stay home and help you, Momma," Mary said. Anna replied that she really didn't need her help, and to just go. Her mother told her that when she returned she could go to the well for their Sabbath water. Mary kissed her mother and left the house. When she neared the street, she saw Asa approaching. He greeted her warmly. "Shalom and good morning to you as well, Rabbi," Mary replied. "I'm on my way to see your daughter. I'm glad I met you though, Teacher, because I have a question that I've been meaning to ask you."

"And what would that question be, Mary?"

"I've been wondering what Father Abraham, Israel, Joseph, Moses and King David had to do for God to single them out from everyone else to become such important personages. I've never heard anyone say why God chose them."

"All they did was believe God when He called them, Mary, and because they believed they were justified by Him. Their belief and trust in the Almighty was credited to them as righteousness. The Lord didn't call them because of anything they had previously done. He favored them because He knew that they had faith and would be obedient enough to accomplish His will."

Mary heard that word again—"favored." She asked, "Does that mean God could even use someone … someone from even our town to fulfill His will?"

"Mary, you were my prize student. You know the answer to that question."

"God is Almighty. He can do anything."

"Very good! See, Mary, you knew the answer to the question before you asked."

"It's just hard to understand why God wouldn't base His choice on what a person had already accomplished in life. Isn't it true, Rabbi, that only the best and the brightest can attend the Yeshiva in Jerusalem? If we use such standards, you'd think the Holy One would too. Wouldn't you, Rabbi?"

"One of the traits of the Almighty is that He is all-knowing. We select and reward people for what they've achieved. The Holy One selects people based on what He knows they'll be capable of accomplishing through His favor in the future. Between you and me, I think God has a great sense of humor. Who else would have picked a tent-dwelling nomad to become the father of a great nation, or an exiled Hebrew-born Egyptian prince-turned-shepherd, to lead a nation of slaves to freedom without an army, or turn a poor adolescent shepherd boy into a great king."

The rabbi thought the last part of his discourse would at least elicit a smile, but Mary's face remained quite somber. "Is something bothering you, Mary? You're not your usual jovial self today."

"No, not really, Teacher! I just didn't sleep very well last night, that's all."

"Well, if you need to talk, I'm always available. I really enjoy our conversations."

"Thank you, Rabbi!" Mary said. "I better be going now, otherwise I won't have any time left to visit with your daughter. Shalom, Rabbi!"

"Shalom, Mary! Remember what I said."

"I will, Rabbi!" the young maiden said as the two parted.

241

Anna was about to go and talk to her husband when she saw the rabbi crossing their courtyard. *Hmm! That's funny,* she said to herself. *Joachim didn't mention anything about the teacher coming to see him today.* A few moments later, Anna heard a knock on her doorframe. She wiped her hands on a kitchen towel and came to the door. There stood Joseph with a huge smile on his face, with enough pistachio honey-cakes to feed the entire town. She greeted him and told him to come in.

"Shalom, Ma'am! I hope you don't mind that I brought this dessert over now. I wouldn't be able to carry these trays after sunset."

"Joseph, did you buy out the baker?" Anna asked cheerfully.

"Well, kind of, Ma'am," Joseph replied. "I arrived very early, and bought all of the pistachio honey-cakes he had. You said that Mary—I mean all of you—like them."

Anna laughed as she said, "Joseph, if Mary ate even a tenth of these she'd start to get as round as me. And as for me, I just have to look at them long enough and I gain more weight." Anna saw the disappointed look on Joseph's face and realized her comments may have sounded rather crass. "But it was wise of you to go early enough to get them," she added, grinning broadly. "Usually these cakes are the first to sell out, as they were today too. Tamar and Azor are joining us for dinner, and they enjoy them also. If you don't mind, though, I'd like to give some of these cakes to the rabbi to take home to his family. He's visiting with my husband right now."

"Go right ahead, Ma'am. I know the rabbi enjoys them too. I brought him a couple this morning." Joseph realized what he had just said and began to hem and haw. Anna was a clever woman and would put two and two together. Joseph finally said, "I better be going now, Ma'am; I have a lot to do before Sabbath. Shalom!" He turned to leave, but not before Anna could tell him that Mary would be overjoyed when she saw all the cakes. She was glad to see the huge smile on the young man's face after her previous remark. She told him he didn't have to wait until sunset to return; he could come a little earlier if he'd like.

"Thank you, Ma'am! But I don't want you and your husband to tire of me on the third day that I'm home."

"Pshaw! We find your company delightful." She walked the young man to the door and gave him a light peck on his cheek. "Like I said, come a little earlier. I'm sure Mary would like that too." The young man was ecstatic. He wished the sun would set right now.

Joseph went home and sat by his partially opened door to watch for the rabbi. He was quite nervous, wondering whether his proposal would be accepted. The young man thought of the money that was still buried in the hay pile. Joseph remembered that as a child, he had seen his father remove a shill stone from the wall somewhere. His dad would store his money and other valuables behind it. Joseph would have searched for the stone at that very moment, but he didn't want to miss seeing the rabbi leave Joachim's. So he just sat by the door and kept brushing back his side curls. Finally, he saw the rabbi leave Joachim's shop; Anna came up to the teacher and handed him a wicker basket. As the rabbi crossed the street to Joseph's house, the carpenter could see Anna entering the door to her husband's shop. The anticipation was getting to the young man. His heart was beating rapidly. Joseph forced his clammy hands down to his side and anxiously waited for the rabbi. Before the teacher could even cross the street, the young carpenter threw open the door and stood in the doorway with a very nervous, anticipatory look on his face.

As soon as Anna entered her husband's shop, she asked Joachim, "So has Joseph asked for our daughter's hand?"

"Yes he has, but how did you know that's what the rabbi was here for?"

"If you'd still been in the house when I returned from the well this morning, I would've told you," Anna replied.

"Did Joseph break with tradition, and mention what he planned on doing?" Joachim asked.

"No, Joseph wouldn't do that. I'm no dullard; I could figure out his intentions just by the questions he asked me this morning. And when he told me he met with the good rabbi, it was easy to figure it all out," Anna said. "So tell me, did you give your consent?"

"Yes, I did. I told the rabbi, 'No betrothal, though, until the Feast of Booths, after Mary turns fourteen.' You won't believe what Joseph offered as a dowry."

"Well, tell me already!" Anna said. Joachim whispered the amount in her ear.

"No!" she said. "I can't believe it. Where would he get money like that from? What kind of dowry did he request from you in return? I've never heard of an offer like that, have you? It's far too much for a young man just starting out, don't you think?"

"Slow down, woman! Your questions are piling up; let me answer! Rabbi Asa said Joseph could well afford the dowry. Eleazer and Rebecca were far wealthier than anyone would've expected, and everything went to Joseph. I felt guilty in accepting the dowry the young man offered, but what was I supposed to say—that our daughter isn't worth it? Usually a prospective groom starts with a small amount and negotiates upward. I didn't know what to do when Joseph's offer started so high. I was completely dumbfounded. We'll make it up to him in our dowry on the day of their espousal even though he doesn't want anything from us. If I just make it public, as a part of the ceremony itself, good social etiquette won't allow him to refuse it."

"Oh, Joachim!" Anna said, folding her hands and looking up to the heavens. "I've been praying that Joseph would ask for our Mary's hand, and the Almighty has answered my prayers. Don't say anything to Mary, though. I told her that her future husband was joining us for dinner tonight, and she thinks Mina has paired her up with someone else. Let her be surprised when Joseph comes over for Shabbat. She'll be overjoyed."

"You never told me you intended to invite him to dinner again tonight," Joachim said. "Wasn't it a little risky to tell her something like that when you weren't sure what Joseph would do?"

"Last night I had no intentions of asking him for Shabbat, so how could I tell you then?" Anna replied.

"But as to Joseph asking for our Mary's hand, I was sure. Since his visit last night, and after our walk to the well, I've been very, very sure. I just knew it!"

When Anna left her husband's shop, she saw Mina standing outside her doorway, looking in. Anna considered going back inside before she was seen, but she knew she had to face the woman someday. *Better to do it and get it over with,* she said to herself, as she went to face the matchmaker. Surprisingly, after Anna told her that her services were not needed, and that Mary already had a proposal, the woman left rather abruptly, without even asking who the prospective groom was.

As Mary returned home from her friend's house, and turned into her courtyard, she ran into Mina as she was leaving. Her heart sank as Mina saw her and said, "Congratulations, dah-link. If it doesn't work out, dah-link, just let me know and I'll find you another, okay, dah-link?!" Mary's suspicions were confirmed—she knew that tonight she would have an intended husband. She couldn't believe her parents had allowed Mina to find her a match when they knew that her heart belonged to Joseph.

As the sulking maiden entered her house, the young carpenter's mood was quite the opposite. In less than five months he would be engaged to the woman he loved. He knew Joachim was a man of his word, and the deal was done. "I'll soon have a wife and, God willing, a family of my own," he said aloud, with great pride in his voice. Joseph, feeling a new sense of responsibility, began to search for the shill stone so he could store his money in a safer place than an animal stall. His fingernails traced the edge of each of the lower stones of the wall in search of a gap in the mortar joint. After checking out about a dozen, his nails finally sunk into a deep depression. He found the shill stone. Joseph took a pry bar and gently removed the thin stone from the wall.

He was shocked to see a Turkish water pipe, a bowl of finely shredded plant leaves and several various-sized daggers stored in the roomy wall compartment. He couldn't recall his father ever smoking. From what he knew of his dad, smoking would be out of character for him. Jewish law disapproved of the practice, and Jacob was an ardent follower of Judaism. Joseph removed the items and placed the bag of money inside. He put the daggers next to it and replaced the shill stone, then wrapped the water pipe and bowl in an old towel. He took the remainder of the cakes that he'd bought, set them in a wicker basket and fastened it and the towel-wrapped items to his mule. The young man was going to see his friend Nabu, who lived on the opposite side of town on the hillside near to the place where he grew up.

Joseph and his mule walked through the narrow streets of town toward the open market area. The young man wanted to purchase some olive oil and wine for his friend in gratitude for farming his land while he was gone. As he stood under the colorfully striped awning, and waited for the vendor's son to fill the casks with olive oil, Joseph and the vendor conversed. The man who sold fruits and vegetables in the next stall overheard the conversation. He touched his fingers to his forehead, then to his chest, as he bowed low and said, "Kind sir! I overheard you say you are going to Nabu's straight from here. Would the gracious man who now stands before me be so kind as to take my wilting produce to him as fodder for his swine?" Joseph clumsily returned the greeting and told him he would be happy to do so. The vendor brought out two very large straw baskets filled with compressed wilted greens. As Joseph secured one of the baskets to the side of the mule, the cover slipped off and fell to the ground. The smell of the rotting plant matter almost nauseated him as he replaced the lid. *No wonder we can't eat pigs,* Joseph thought.

When the baskets were loaded and the containers of olive oil and wine were securely tied off to the sides of the mule, Joseph turned to leave. The old toothless produce-vendor handed Joseph a palm leaf shaped into a cup he had filled with dried apricots. After bowing to each other several times, Joseph turned, and started his trek up the hill to Nabu's house.

As Joseph walked along, he chomped on the apricots, even rewarding his mule with a few for the heavy load it carried. When he passed the last of the outdoor booths, Joseph heard the sound of horse hooves in a slow gait. He heard a vaguely familiar voice say, "Stop at once, Jew!" Joseph slowed his pace but kept walking. As his peripheral vision caught sight of the horse's head, he felt the sensation of cold, hard steel touching his bare neck. "I could slice your neck right off with this, Jew boy!" Joseph stopped abruptly; his mule did the same.

The soldier withdrew his sword slightly so that Joseph could turn to face him. As he did so, he recognized the soldier as Hasid, the man who brought his aunt so much shame on the night of his bar mitzvah. The soldier recognized Joseph too, and tried to antagonize him to see if he had as much spunk in him now as he did in his youth. "Who are you? And where are you going? I've never seen you before."

From his years on the road with his Uncle Achim, Joseph had learned how to play the part of the humble, supplicant Jew. "I am Joseph Bar Jacob, this town's carpenter, Excellency!" Joseph said as he bowed low and kept his eyes downcast. "I didn't know to which Jew you were referring to when you called out, since this town is full of us Jews. I beg your Excellency's pardon. I'm just going to see my friend who lives on the hillside."

"Tell me, then, why haven't I ever seen you here before?" the soldier asked again.

"I have no idea, Excellency! I sure remember seeing you!"

"And what's strapped to your mule there, and how do I know you're not a Zealot?"

"Excellency! You could ask anyone in town and they will vouch for me. I'm just a simple carpenter trying to earn a meager leaving. As for what's on my mule, there's some sweet cakes, olive oil, wine, and pig fodder. Would you like some, Excellency?"

"Do I look like a pig to you?" the soldier asked gruffly as he brought the flat side of the sword to Joseph's neck once again.

"Excellency! The sweet cakes are delicious, and…" As Joseph was about to continue, a Roman centurion galloped up to the Syrian soldier. He asked the deputy if there was a problem.

249

"No, sir! I just stopped the Jew for questioning; I've never seen him around before!" The Centurion asked Joseph if that was the case.

"As I was telling your deputy, Excellency, he may not have seen me, but I sure have seen him, sir!"

The Centurion knew Hasid loved to taunt any Jew he could. To him, Joseph looked like an honest type, so he said, "You're free to go, young man, but remember, the eyes of Rome are always watching you."

"I'm used to being watched, Excellency," Joseph said. "The eyes of my God are always watching me too." The Centurion smiled at Joseph's remark and quick wit. As he and the soldier galloped off toward the town gate, he thought to himself, *You've got to give these Jews a lot of credit. They really believe in that God of theirs.*

When Joseph reached his friend's house, Nabu and his son ran out to greet him. Instead of the customary bow that Joseph expected, Nabu grabbed hold of him, kissed his beard and gave him a strong hug. "Shalom, Joseph! You look just like your father! You're really a man now!" Joseph returned the greeting. Nabu's son then greeted Joseph in the same manner.

"Shalom, Nabu!" the carpenter said. "Your son has grown into a fine young man as well."

Nabu told Joseph he had something to show him, and without any inhibitions and with an utter lack of modesty, he suddenly raised his tunic to his chest while simultaneously lowering his undergarment. "See! I'm now a man of the covenant too! Your God is my God!" Nabu said as Joseph looked away and blushed. "So is Omar! Show Joseph!" he said to his son.

"No! No!" Joseph said emphatically. "That's not necessary! I believe you!" He kept his eyes averted until Nabu had raised his undergarment and lowered his tunic. The young carpenter congratulated him and asked him what made him decide to believe in and worship the one true God.

"I've seen the faith of your—no, I mean our—people for a long time and no matter what difficulties and disappointments they faced, it seemed their belief in the God of Abraham just increased. And if the God of Israel fostered such intense loyalty and devotion, He must be the one true God. Furthermore, I could see how God's law sanctified His people, and after the night of your bar mitzvah, I knew I wanted my son to grow up to be just like you. I realized that was never the case with the gods of my—I mean my former—people. The demands of the false gods and their priests satisfied only the depraved personal pleasures of the people and their so-called priests."

Joseph blushed and thanked him for the compliment. Nabu and Omar helped Joseph unload the mule, and he reluctantly accepted Joseph's gifts. Nabu adamantly refused, however, to take any monetary compensation for farming Joseph's plot of land.

The carpenter showed his friend the water pipe and asked, "Do you know if my father ever smoked, because I found this in my house, along with this."

Nabu grabbed a few of the shredded leaves from the container and rubbed them between his thumb and index finger, then smelled them. He told Joseph his father would never have smoked, and that the substance was hashish, a very bad thing. It made you act crazy and do stupid things, he explained.

251

Jacob would never have used anything like it. Nabu suggested someone must have left it in Joseph's house when it was unoccupied.

Nabu opened the basket of pig fodder and tossed the hashish into the rotting plant matter. "Now only the pigs will act crazy, but that's what they usually do anyway." They all laughed. "Since I became a Jew, I don't take care of pigs any longer. I have swine-herders who do that for me. Besides, my family and I don't eat pork anymore. What we raise, we sell to the Procurator and his soldiers. They love it. We miss the delicious taste, and we probably always will, but that's life. Why don't you destroy that device, too, Joseph?" Nabu pointed to the water pipe.

Joseph pulled off the hoses from the sides of the pipe and flung the bowl off toward the distant hills. They all watched as it shattered into hundreds of pieces. "Good!" Nabu said. "It will never be used again!" When they finished their conversation, Joseph borrowed Nabu's wagon to get the wooden chest from the rabbi. Nabu sent his son along to assist Joseph.

As the carpenter drove the wagon through the narrow streets of Nazareth, Anna sent her moping daughter to the well for enough water to last through the Sabbath. As Mary was about to leave, Anna told her to leave the first jar she filled by Joseph's door. She had seen the poor young man struggling with his water jar this morning. The kind act could be Mary's Sabbath blessing.

All Mary had to do was to hear his name and her heart fluttered. The thought of being betrothed to another man she'd never met made her heart sink, and did nothing to improve her mood. Mary took the jar and gave her mother the slightest peck on the cheek. She wanted to be respectful, yet at the same time she wanted her mother to know how disappointed she was by her parents' decision.

"Did I just feel a butterfly flutter by my cheek? That couldn't possibly have been a kiss from my daughter, could it?" Anna asked. Mary went over to her mother and kissed her more tenderly. "Now there's no doubt in my mind; that was my daughter." The moment Mary left, Anna ran over to Tamar's to hatch her plot for tonight.

As Mary made her way to the well, she turned the corner onto Well Street and saw a mule-driven wagon approaching her. She stepped to the side to allow it to pass and noticed Joseph handling the reins. Mary saw him at about the same time he saw her. He slowed as she approached. He stopped the wagon. "Shalom, Mary! Good afternoon!"

Mary shyly lowered her beautiful eyes and replied, "Shalom! And good afternoon to you too, Joseph, and to you also, Omar!" To say more than that impersonal greeting would have been a breach of proper etiquette for a young man and unmarried maiden. They both wanted to say more, but couldn't. As Mary raised her eyes, their glances locked in a visual embrace.

Omar grinned as he watched the two of them. He finally said, "Joseph, we have to get the wagon back to my father before the Sabbath." As soon as they were on their way, the boy started chanting, "Joseph's got a girlfriend! Joseph's got a girlfriend!" The carpenter couldn't care less. He tugged the reins and the mule started to move. The only problem was that Joseph kept his head turned and continued to watch Mary. Omar grabbed the reins and said, "Whoa!" Joseph's head turned abruptly. He then saw he was driving the mule toward one of the houses.

Joseph retrieved the chest from the rabbi. Omar and he carried it into his house. Even the boy admired the intricate carvings. Joseph returned the wagon to Nabu and thanked his friend for the use of his wagon and for his son's help. He gave Omar a silver coin. When Joseph returned home, he grinned when he saw a full jar of water standing next to his door. He picked it up and carried it inside as the sun in the far western sky began to turn from blinding white to a brilliant gold. After he bathed, the young man took a clean tunic to change into. As he unfolded it, out of the folds fell the long piece of linen he was looking for the night before. Joseph formed it into a turban, then oiled his beard and opened the door to leave.

Even the sky cooperated in making this day more memorable. The setting sun gilded the underside of the dark-grey clouds with gold as they rolled across the backdrop of the vibrant, dusty rose sky. Dazzling shafts of sunlight broke through the cloud openings and dotted the western hills with ever-changing patterns of light as chirping birds sang their serenade to the waning day. The young carpenter almost couldn't control the joy he felt. If he had been wearing his hat, he could at least have thrown it up into the air again to express his joy.

Earlier in the afternoon, when Mary had gone to the well, Anna went to tell Tamar of her daughter's good fortune. She told her sister-in-law everything she had said to her daughter and about Mary's hasty conclusion. Tamar snickered and told her that was naughty. Mischievously rubbing her gnarled hands together in anticipation, the elderly woman asked what she could do to help hatch the plan. "When she brings your water this afternoon," Anna replied, "ask her if she would help you clean for Shabbat, or something like that. Just keep her busy and away from the door until after the sun sets. By that time Joseph should be over. She'll really be surprised when she comes in." The two women snickered at their little plan as they plotted further.

Joseph reached the door of Mary's home, and Anna hurriedly shooed him inside. She tugged on his arm even before he finished his customary prayer before entering. Joachim was standing at the door too. He grabbed the young man and hugged him even before Joseph could kiss his chin. "Shalom, my son," his future father-in-law said. Joseph's dark eyes lit up and a broad grin appeared on his face as he replied, "Shalom, my father. "And to you also, Mother."

As Anna hugged him, she kissed his cheek and wished him God's blessing. Joseph could see that both she and Joachim were overjoyed by his proposal. "Joseph, you go sit by the table," Anna said. "Mary doesn't know anything about your proposal or that you're having dinner with us tonight. We wanted her to be surprised, so sit with your back to the door, please."

A few moments later, Azor's head popped in the door. "Is he here yet?" he asked.

Before they could answer, Azor said, "Oh, I see he is. Shalom, Joseph, and mazel tov!"

"Shalom, Uncle! And thank you!" the young man replied. Azor went to get the women, and within moments he returned with his wife and Mary. Tamar and Azor entered the house first, blocking Mary's view of Joseph and the table. As she entered, Mary's eyes were downcast. She was quite somber. Anna suggested that she smile.

"I want you to meet your future husband," Joachim said as Tamar and Azor stepped aside. Mary looked up for a brief moment.

She saw a turbaned man sitting at the table, facing the other way. She thought she caught a glimpse of black side curls, but she couldn't be certain. The turban, and the fact that Joseph sat with his back to her, made him unrecognizable. *At least I don't think he's old and gray,* Mary said to herself. As Joachim led his daughter toward her intended, she looked up again and saw the man bring his hands up to his side curls, and push them over his turbaned ears. The curls sprung back immediately.

Mary instantly realized who the man was. She turned around and embraced her father with such force that she almost knocked him over. Mary quietly whispered, "Thank you, Daddy! Thank you, Daddy!" over and over again as she wept with tears of joy. She then ran to her mother and embraced her as well. Anna's eyes filled with tears too.

Joseph stood up and turned to face the group. Tamar and Azor congratulated the young couple as the future bride and groom beamed with joy. Anna then lit the Sabbath candles as she said the traditional prayers of Shabbat. The lovers unabashedly stared at each other the entire evening. Neither of them ate very much, even when the delectable dessert was served. In all of Nazareth you couldn't find a house filled with more happiness on the evening of this Shabbat.

When Joseph left, and as Anna and Joachim prepared for bed, Mary went outside to talk to her God. As she sat in her normal spot and gazed at the beauty of the star-filled sky, she thanked the God of Abraham, Isaac and Jacob for Joseph's proposal. She knew that all good things came from God, and with a heart filled with love and gratitude she praised her Lord. She now thought the apparition and the dream were of divine origin, to assure her she should have no fear. God would work it out so that she would spend the rest of her life with the man she loved. She didn't know why the Lord would use such extraordinary means, but she knew that God could do anything He chose to do. She was just grateful that He gave her her heart's desire.

When Mary finished her prayer, she saw Joseph's door opening. The young man headed to his rooftop to sleep. The reason for doing so, he told himself, was because it was stifling hot indoors. Mainly, though, it was because he felt he was Mary's protector now, and also, he felt closer to her when he could see her house. When Joseph reached the roof he carefully walked around his temporary repair. As he spread out his outer cloak and began to lie down, he could see Mary from his vantage point. He smiled and waved to her, and was jubilant when she waved back. While Joseph lowered his eyes to straighten out the cloak beneath him, Mary took advantage of his distraction to blow him a kiss. As if it was telepathic, Joseph immediately looked up. Mary became flustered and embarrassed, thinking Joseph might have seen what she did. She waved to him again and immediately went into her house. The young virgin leaned against the door once again until her fluttering heart slowed down a bit. Then she crawled into bed and laid next to her sleeping mother.

The next morning, Joseph accompanied Mary and her family to the Synagogue. During the service, he sat between his future father-in-law and Azor. When the service ended, Joseph lazily spent the late afternoon with Mary and her family. At sunset when the Sabbath ended, the carpenter once again dined with them. He left early, though. He could see Joachim was yawning, and Joseph didn't want to overstay his welcome.

When Joseph returned to his house, he decided to open the chest he had given his aunt to see what it now contained. He broke the wax seals and cut the cords that securely held the lid in place. At the very top of the chest was a clay tablet, written with his Aunt Rebecca's own hand, that once again asked for his forgiveness, and instructed him to give the chest and its contents to his future bride. Under the clay tablet was a lidded wicker basket filled with expensive necklaces, wrist and ankle bracelets, all types of earrings, and gemstone rings.

Joseph removed the basket and found layer upon layer of costly fabrics and priceless brocades. At the very bottom was a sizeable vial of pure nard worth over a half-year's wages. Joseph removed the expensive perfume as well as several pieces of what he considered the most-precious pieces of jewelry. He placed those articles into the wall safe, and set the vial of nard on a block of olive wood. He would give the gifts to Mary on their wedding day. After tracing the outline of the vial on the surface of the wooden block, Joseph placed the vial in the wall safe as well. When he replaced the stone, something nagged at his mind. He didn't know what bothered him.

Early Sunday morning, Joseph asked Joachim to help him carry the chest over to Mary. He explained to his future father-in-law that it was his aunt's desire the woman he would one day marry should be the recipient of the chest and its contents. When Joachim saw it, he admired the ornate carving and couldn't believe Joseph had carved such intricate details before he had ever had any professional training. They carried the heavy chest across the street while Mary was still in the animal pen, doing her morning chores.

When Anna saw the elaborately carved chest, she brought her hands to her face and said, "As sure as the Almighty lives, I've never seen anything more beautiful in my entire life." Joachim told her that Joseph had made the chest himself. Her hands still on her face, Anna shook her head in amazement. "Joseph, this is a real piece of art," she said. "It belongs in the House of the Lord, not in a simple home like ours." The carpenter told her he had made it for his Aunt Rebecca, and her dying wish was that the chest and its contents go to his future wife, so it now belonged to Mary.

"I'll go get Mary," Anna said. "Wait until she sees this." She moved toward the archway at the back of the house that led to their small stable.

Within seconds, Anna returned with her daughter. "Look, Mary, look at the beautiful chest Joseph made. It's yours now, Mary! Joseph is giving it to you!" Mary's eyes gleamed with delight as she saw Joseph. Their eyes met again. Neither of them was thinking of the chest or its contents. "Isn't it beautiful, Mary?" There was no response, so Anna repeated the question. Mary finally snapped out of her trance and looked at the chest.

"Oh! It really is, Momma!" Mary said. "Thank you so much, Joseph!" She bent down and began to finger the carvings. "These blossoms look so real," she remarked as she continued to trace the delicate flower petals with her index finger. "You really are an accomplished carpenter, Joseph." Her praise caused him to blush and brush back his side curls once again. Anna and Joachim just smiled at each other as they watched the two young lovers interact.

Joseph said that he had to leave and make the permanent repairs to his roof before another rainstorm came. As much as he would have liked to stay, he became embarrassed easily. He had a hard time accepting compliments and expressions of gratitude, so he wanted to leave before Mary opened the chest. Their eyes locked for a moment, and Joseph regretted his prior statement. He was now obliged to go. When Joseph left, Joachim said, "I better get back to work too. Poor Azor's hands are bothering him today. If I don't get back there soon, nothing will get done. Mary, I don't think any bride-to-be in this town ever received a finer gift from her future husband."

"In this town?" Anna said. "You'd be hard-pressed to find a more beautiful gift than this anywhere."

Joachim kissed his wife and daughter goodbye and returned to work. "Don't open the chest yet, Mary; I want Aunt Tamar to see it with the lid on," Anna said as she left the house and rushed across the courtyard to get her sister-in-law. Within moments, Anna returned with Tamar. Before the elderly woman even entered the house, Anna kept saying, "Wait until you see it. You won't believe your eyes. Wait until you see it, just wait."

When Tamar finally entered and saw the chest, she said, "As surely as the Lord lives, that must have been carved by the hands of angels." Mary sat down in the middle, while her mother and aunt sat on either side of her. The three women lifted the flower-covered lid. They saw the wicker basket. "Open the basket already," Tamar said. "The suspense is killing me." Mary snickered at the remark as she gently removed the lid.

Anna's eyes popped wide open as she saw the contents and said, "Oh, my, there's enough jewelry in there for a royal household. Mary, if you wore all this, people really would think you are a princess."

Mary smiled. "Aren't they just beautiful, Momma?" Let's try them on." The trio sat there, helping each other thread the pierced earrings into the holes in their ears. They also took turns trying on the necklaces, as well as the bracelets and rings. Anna had a brass pot near the winter oven, and Mary brought it over so they could see their reflections in the shiny metal. The three women really enjoyed themselves, and laughed heartily when they overly adorned themselves with too many layers of jewelry.

When they finished with the jewelry, Mary removed the wicker box and saw a plain piece of folded white linen. She lifted it out and saw a strange-looking length of fabric that seemed as delicate as gossamer. "Look at this, Momma!" Mary said. The light seemed to dance upon its surface as she held it up for her mother to see. The young woman placed her hand under the filmy weave and could almost see through the delicate fabric. Both Anna and Tamar were amazed; they had never seen anything like it. Anna carefully took hold of the fabric and veiled her daughter with it. "I can see right through this, Momma!" Mary said.

The two women were astonished—although Mary could see through the fabric clearly, they only vaguely saw her features from the other side as the light from the window cast a sheen on the filmy material. "Try looking through it, Momma," the young woman said as she draped the material over her mother's head. "You too, Aunt Tamar."

"Wait till you try this on, Tamar," Anna said in fascination as she removed the fabric from her head and gently handed it to Tamar.

The old woman placed it over her head and said, "What will they come up with next? If a woman wore a tunic made out of this, men would walk into things as they stared right through it." They all laughed. Anna knew exactly what she would use the intriguing fabric for. As the women continued to sort through the chest, they were amazed by the various textures of fabric it contained. There was even a piece of extremely expensive vibrant purple cloth, the kind that only royalty or the very wealthy could afford, as the dye was rare and very costly. The women were even more astounded when they found the expensive brocades woven with gold and silver threads. Anna already knew that on the day of her daughter's betrothal, Mary would be the most elegantly dressed woman anyone in town had ever seen.

As the women enjoyed sorting through the chest, Joseph searched the hillside for thatch to repair his roof. As he did so, he ran into his uncle's friend, Ali. The old caravan-leader expressed his sympathy at Joseph's aunts and uncle's passing, then told him of several new homes that his kinsmen had under construction on the hillside. He had taken the liberty of mentioning Joseph's name and skill to them. They were expecting him to give them a bid on installing the rafters and the thatch. "If I'm successful in landing the projects, do you think that I could rely on your sons for some muscle?" Joseph asked.

"Muscle is all I can rely on them for," Ali said. "They have strong backs and very thick heads." Joseph laughed and asked if he was being a little too hard on them. "I don't think so," Ali replied. "I couldn't trust them to lead a caravan. Now I can't even trust them to watch cheese age." They both laughed at his remark. The old caravan-leader then said, "Nabu was telling me about the water pipe you found, Joseph. I knew your uncle very well, and he talked about your father often. I just wanted to assure you that he once told me your father detested smoking and would never have done so himself. Whoever was using that pipe used it while the house was vacant. I wouldn't store anything valuable anywhere around where that pipe was found."

That's what nagged at the back of my mind last night, Joseph instantly realized. He had been so enthralled by his engagement to his beloved that he forgot about the danger of leaving his money where the water pipe had been stored. He couldn't wait to get back to his house and relocate his newfound wealth. What he just couldn't understand was why the unauthorized occupants would keep his house so clean and his tools well-oiled. To him it didn't seem to fit with the character of a person who would smoke hashish. Joseph thanked Ali for the leads, and assured him that he would visit his kinsmen later that afternoon. He bid farewell to the current cheese-maker, loaded the thatch onto his mule, and left for home at once to move his inheritance.

Joseph fixed his roof as soon as he returned home. After washing the mud and clay from his hands, he went inside and built false legs on his worktable. He then darkened the fresh wood with a solution of dirt and oil to age its appearance. The carpenter stepped back to view his work, and was satisfied to see that he couldn't tell the difference between the fresh wood and the naturally aged legs. He stored the money in the hollow legs, but because of the size and thickness of the unbendable solid-gold necklace and matching earrings, Joseph had to leave them in the wall safe, much to his dismay. Later that day, Joseph went to see Ali's relatives, and landed the jobs. His business soon began to prosper. As word of his skills spread, and Joseph's carpentry was more in-demand, he often employed Ali's sons and paid them very well. The young carpenter's cabinet-making abilities were also admired and used by the townspeople.

Time flew by more rapidly than either Joseph or Mary anticipated. Each night he had dinner at Mary's house. Though their conversation was restricted to pleasantries, the young couple's love for each other continued to grow. Joseph never came to dinner empty-handed. Anna finally had to discourage him from bringing any additional provisions, as her larder was overstocked. Each morning, Joseph woke up early so he could greet Mary when she left the filled water-jar at his door. They only exchanged the briefest of cordial greetings, but their eyes always locked into a visual embrace that mesmerized them both. Each night after leaving Mary's house, Joseph would work on the small wooden box that would hold the bottle of priceless nard. Before the couple knew it, summer had passed, and the days of the Feast of Booths were almost upon them. The young virgin had already celebrated her fourteenth birthday.

No one had yet noticed that there was a fire every night on the hillside near the stand of scrub oaks. Zaddu, the witch whom the townspeople kept driving away, had once again returned to the cave that was located near the town.

CHAPTER 12

The celebration of the Jewish New Year and the Day of Atonement had passed. On the day before the commemoration of the Festival of Booths was to begin, Mary's house buzzed with activity. Tamar kept running back and forth between her house and Anna's with last-minute details for the preparation of the betrothal that would take place in mere hours. While the two women scurried about inside the house, Joachim and Azor sat patiently in the outdoor booth that Joseph had built for the celebration of the festival.

Sukkot, the festival they were about to celebrate, was a time set aside for the Jews to remember God's care for the Hebrews on their desert journey from Egypt to the Promised Land. All practicing Jews would build temporary shelters from branches and palm fronds and live outdoors for a full week to commemorate the event. Joseph's booth was the best-constructed structure in all of Nazareth. Joachim and Azor were filled with pride as they sat in it and heard passersby comment on the fine structure. When Joachim saw someone coming, he would purposely stand up to receive their praises and then say, "Yes! My future son-in-law built this! He's a fine carpenter, you know!"

Joseph paced back and forth in his house as he kept brushing back his side curls in anticipation of the sun reaching its zenith. Today, at high noon, Mary would officially become his intended wife. He opened the door slightly and saw the activity in the courtyard across from him. Nabu and his family were already spreading out mats on the ground, on which they would serve the delicacies Joseph had hired them to prepare for his engagement celebration. The actual betrothal would take place in the town square. Afterwards a party would be held in Joachim's courtyard and the adjacent street. As Joseph nervously waited, Mary was completing her morning chores in the animal pen. Her mother was about finished embroidering light-blue stripes on the outer cloak she had made for her future son-in-law. As she did so, she thought of the day of her own betrothal. Anna wasn't even present on that day many years ago. She had been considered an old maid for four years; she was already twenty. Anna and Joachim had not even seen each other or met until their wedding day.

Joachim was the youngest son of a domineering mother, and she made sure he wouldn't marry while she was still alive. He was rather homely, so the attractive women in the town where he lived didn't pester their mothers to beseech their husbands to arrange a match. There were a few indigent fathers of homely girls who approached Joachim's father, but Naomi, his mother, would put an end to the offer rather swiftly. All Jews, rich or poor, were extremely conscious of personal hygiene, so when

Naomi learned of a possible match for her son, she would seek out the girl's mother and tell lies about her son's habits. She said that it was so difficult to get her son to clean up, his brothers had to wrestle Joachim to the ground so they could wash him and change his odiferous clothing. He smelled so bad, Naomi would say, that he had to sleep in the stable. When he did, even the animals tried to leave. No matter how unattractive or burdensome her daughter might be, no mother would have saddled her offspring with a husband like Naomi described her son to be. If that still didn't work, she would tell them he never washed his hair, and you could see lice jumping around on his head when he removed his cap. This lie definitely would halt any future interest in her son. The fact of the matter was that Joachim suffered from premature baldness, and had very little hair on his head since his late teens. He actually washed what little hair he had almost daily.

After Naomi passed away, Azor met Anna's father on a return trip from the Holy City. They struck up a friendship. After discussing their families, they decided to arrange a betrothal between Joachim and Anna. Azor accompanied Anna's father back to Sepphoris to record the betrothal in the local synagogue. Both Anna and Joachim were overjoyed when they found out they had a future mate. On their wedding day, when they saw each other for the first time, both were very disappointed. Soon, though, they grew to love each other. They no longer saw each other as the homely individuals that they were, but only as the beautiful people that their inner souls proved them to be.

Anna wanted her daughter's betrothal, unlike her own, to be a day she would always remember with great joy. As Anna continued to daydream, Tamar came running into the house with a basket full of autumn crocuses and ivy-like vines. Joachim and Azor followed close behind on Tamar's heels.

"Anna!" said Tamar. She stopped to catch her breath before she continued. "A caravan was in the commons when I came back into the city gate. Eliud said they had news for you from both of your daughters. They and their entire families, grandchildren and all, will be in Jerusalem this coming spring for the Passover, and they want you to join them. Isn't it amazing that you should hear from both of your daughters at the same time, even though they live so far away from each other? As surely as the Lord lives, this must be a sign that the Almighty will bless Mary and Joseph, and bring them nothing but joy and happiness in their life together."

Just then Mary entered the room, and Tamar again began to relay the news to her niece. They were lost in the joy of the moment as Nabu stuck his head through the open doorframe and told Joachim that the town's virgins were beginning to gather at Joseph's door to lead him to the commons. "Hurry, take these things over to Joseph," Anna said, handing her husband the new clothing she had made for her future son-in-law.

When the men departed, Anna and Tamar began to braid the autumn crocuses into the dark-green vines to form crowns. Because her hands were more nimble, Anna worked on the larger one, while Tamar's gnarled fingers worked on the smaller of the two. Anna stopped for a moment; she rose and went to the richly carved wooden chest Joseph had made. She took out the garments she had sewn for her daughter. "I think you should be getting dressed now," she said to Mary. Anna handed her the beautiful clothing she had made for her from the rare fabrics and brocades that Rebecca had left to Mary. There was a new petticoat, a long white tunic to which Anna had attached a sky-blue hem—the color of the House of David—and a blue sash of the same color. She had made Mary's outer cloak of the same blue material and trimmed all the outer clothing with various sizes of gold brocade. The beautiful earrings and the gold necklace and bracelets that Mary was about to wear were also from Joseph's aunt's treasures.

As Mary began to bathe and dress, Joachim and Azor brought the new garments to Joseph. He was surprised to see the new outfit Anna had made for him too. He greeted the men and invited them in. Since he had already bathed, he just went off to the stable area to change. His tunic now matched Mary's, save for the brocade. He proudly put on the new cloak that was striped with light blue, since he too belonged to the royal line of King David. Anna had taken a long piece of white linen and sewn a swatch of blue material to its edges. At one end she attached a piece of gold fringe. Joachim helped Joseph form the long rectangular piece into a fine-looking turban. He was pleased that his beautiful daughter would have such a handsome, decent man for a husband.

While the three men sat there talking, Tamar came running over to tell Joachim and her husband that

Mary was dressed and they should come to see her. Tamar greeted Joseph and told him how handsome he looked. She added, "Wait until you see Mary. She's the prettiest maiden this town will ever see." Joseph didn't know what to say, for he already knew that his intended was the most beautiful woman in the world.

As Joachim left, the rabbi reached Joseph's house. Anna already had placed the larger crown of flowers on her daughter's head and set the gossamer-like fabric over it. She was tall enough to place the second, smaller crown over the first to hold the veil in place. Joachim walked in the door. Tears filled his eyes as he looked at his daughter, whose lovely features were still quite distinguishable through the opalescence of the veil. Joachim came over to Mary and gently raised the thin veil over her flowery crown. He saw that Mary was crying too. "Those are happy tears, I hope?" he asked.

"Very happy tears, Daddy," Mary said as she hugged her father and mother.

"All the unmarried men in Nazareth are going to despise your future husband today, I hope you know," Joachim said.

"Why, Daddy? What did Joseph do?"

"Why? Because he's being betrothed to the most beautiful woman in all of Israel, that's all."

Mary's cheeks blushed a deep red. "Daddy! You're doing it again." Joachim kissed his daughter on one cheek while Anna kissed her on the other. Tamar and Azor did the same, then Anna lowered her daughter's delicate veil once more.

"We better be going," Azor said as he walked toward the door. "The sun has almost reached its zenith." Joachim grabbed his daughter's hand and squeezed it tightly as he went to the door. Before he could even pass through the doorframe, he heard Azor call out, "Hey! Everybody, come out here; you have to see this!"

They all went to the door to see what had prompted Azor's excitement. "No! No!" Anna said to Mary. "You have to stay inside. Joseph may see you." A very disappointed Mary stayed behind and tried to peek through the doorway to see what caused her uncle's enthusiasm, but from her vantage point she could see nothing out of the ordinary. When her mother and her aunt returned, Mary asked them what they had seen. Anna would only say, "You'll see, you'll see!" The two older women looked at each other and giggled.

Joseph emerged from his house with Rabbi Asa at his side. The young maidens who had come to lead him to the center of town envied Mary when they saw how handsome her future husband looked. Both Joseph and the rabbi were amazed at what they saw near Joachim's courtyard. Joseph greeted Ali's sons, and then he and the rabbi joined Joachim and Azor. As the four headed to the center of town, the young unmarried ladies proceeded them, dancing and playing their tambourines. While they were walking to the commons, the townspeople joined them in the procession. All the residents of Nazareth usually liked to attend these espousals. Not only did they enjoy the party that followed, but they also liked to hear what both parties offered as a dowry.

When they reached the town commons, Joseph and the rabbi stood on one side of the stone podium in the center of the square, and Joachim and Azor stood on the other. Even Eliud the gatekeeper left his post so he could try to hear what the dowry consisted of. Azor laid a fresh clay tablet on the podium. Rabbi Asa approached it and drew a line down the center of the tablet with a stylus. He said, "Joseph Bar Jacob, this day, for and in consideration of a large number of gold and silver coins, asks you, Heli, son of Matthat, for your daughter Mary to be betrothed to him as his future wife." As the rabbi said "Heli," he smiled because he could hear the crowd audibly whisper, "Who?" The group was disappointed and murmured among themselves because the rabbi didn't mention the specific amount of the dowry when he recorded it on the clay tablet. The rabbi continued: "And are you prepared to make that pledge to Joseph Bar Jacob today?" Zillah kept bumping everyone with her large basket as she inched her way toward the rabbi as he spoke. Since she was taller than him, she had no trouble peering over his shoulder to see the amount he had recorded.

Joachim and Azor approached the podium, and as Joachim spoke, his brother recorded the dowry he intended to give. "I, Heli Bar Matthat, am willing to pledge my daughter in betrothal to Joseph, son of Jacob. As a dowry I wish to give him a bolt of woolen cloth woven by my wife herself." When the women in the crowd heard this, they all said, "Ooh!" He continued, "Also, five stone jars of freshly pressed olive oil, and five stone jars of new wine." The entire crowd said, "Ahh!" As he went on with the dowry and the people kept responding with *ooh's* and *ahh's*, Joseph, from the corner of his eye, noticed six men enter the gate. He recognized the lead man as Joshua, Zillah's son.

While Joachim kept speaking, Anna told Mary it was time to leave for the ceremony. She fussed a little with her daughter's veil, then the three women left the house. As Mary stepped out into the courtyard, Nabu and his wife saw her beneath the shade of the olive tree. They were covering the delicacies they had prepared with cloths to protect them from the sun and insects. The couple bowed as she approached them. The tree's shadow allowed them to see her delicate features and her beautiful eyes beneath the veil. "Joseph is a very fortunate man," Nabu said. Mary blushed again, but said nothing, for she was too embarrassed to speak.

As Mary turned to face the street, she saw an open-air litter festooned with garlands of the same green vine and autumn crocuses that made up her crowns. The garland was entwined with white and blue strips of cloth. "It's my wife's doing," Ali said as Mary approached the litter. "I mean the garlands; the litter was mine since my caravan days and has lain idle in my shed for years. I knew one day I'd be able to use it again. It's the least I could do for your future husband since he's been so good to my sons."

The light of the midday sun caught the fibers of Mary's veil, and cast a sheen on the unusual fabric's surface, making it translucent. Mary's beautiful face could no longer be seen. She, however, could see everyone clearly from beneath the veil. She thanked Ali and told him how beautiful the litter looked. She gave him her hand, and he helped her step into the litter and sit on the upholstered chair. Mary was amazed at the comfort. She had never sat upon anything upholstered before.

"You may join her if you like, Madam!" Ali said to Anna. "It seats two, you know."

"I better not, if you want your sons to be able to walk again," she said laughingly. "If I sat on this, they probably wouldn't be able to lift it without getting a hernia or breaking their backs." The litter then made its way through the streets of Nazareth with Mary seated upon it, while her mother and aunt walked along beside it. Little girls danced before it and strew wildflowers in its path.

As the small procession neared the commons, Joachim could be heard saying, "And I deed to my future son Joseph the field adjacent to his, along with its hillside vineyard that I purchased for him and my daughter from Nathan Bar Tobias." The assembled group shouted their approval even louder than before. Just then, the litter bearing his daughter came into view. Joseph's head snapped up forward so suddenly that everyone turned around to see what he saw. The litter, and the beautiful maiden who sat upon it, enthralled them all. The crowd was silent as Ali came forward and extended his hand so Mary could descend from the chair. A lone white cloud covered the sun as she did so; now even the sky reflected the colors of David, their ancestor king. Mary's face was now vaguely visible through the veil. With open mouths, the crowd gazed upon her enchanting beauty as she gracefully stepped down and walked toward the group, with her mother on one side and her aunt on the other.

As Mary walked forward, the crowd parted to let her pass. Joseph couldn't take his eyes off his future wife. The longer he looked at her, the more his hands began to tremble. The trembling soon moved down to his legs. Eventually he could feel his knees knocking together. Joseph felt like an utter fool, but he couldn't stop the shaking. When the young virgin came closer to Joseph, the cloud moved away from the sun. Once again the veil's sheen hid her lovely face. Joseph felt the trembling in his legs lessen and finally stop. His hands, though, continued to shake. He kept staring at the veil in hopes that he could once again see through it. The young man was fearful, though, that if he were able to see her beauty for even a moment, his knees would start knocking again.

Mary took her place beside her father as Anna and Tamar stepped aside. Joseph kept looking at Mary, totally oblivious to everyone else. Rabbi Asa cleared his throat several times, hoping Joseph would hear him and snap out of his trance. When that didn't seem to work, the rabbi finally whispered, "Joseph!" That still didn't warrant a response from the young carpenter, so the rabbi called his name a bit louder.

Joseph finally snapped out of his mesmeric state and began to make his pledge. "I, Joseph, son of Jacob, son of Mattan, son of Eleazer…" He continued through his genealogy and finally reached Solomon, son of David. When the crowd heard those two names, the *ooh's* and *ahh's* were audible again. The people were impressed by his lineage. Joseph continued with his ancestors until he ended with Father Abraham. The crowd clapped at the impressive line of patriarchs as Joseph continued: "In the sight of the Almighty Lord God of Israel and in accordance with the Law of Moses and the traditions of our people, I do today pledge to take Mary, daughter of Joachim and Anna, as my future wife one year hence. This is an irrevocable promise and shall bind me to her for life. Therefore, from this day forward, I will call you Heli Bar Matthat, my father forever, and you, Anna, I will call my mother. And so in my lineage, you also will be listed as my father, and I will be your son."

Joachim, not to be outdone by his future son-in-law's lineage, began his own: "I, Heli, also known as Joachim, the son of Matthat, the son of Levi..." He continued his genealogy and reached his connection to the royal line as he said, "...and to Nathan the son of David." The crowd again responded with cheers as he continued his ancestry not only to Father Abraham but also past him through the ancient patriarchs to Seth, the son of Adam, and to Adam, the son of God. He then said, "I do today give you my daughter Mary as your betrothed in the sight of the God of Abraham, Isaac and Jacob, and according to the Law of Moses and the traditions of our people."

The crowd again applauded enthusiastically to show their approval. Joachim kissed Joseph on the chin, then took his daughter's hand and placed it in Joseph's. The moment their hands met, Joseph's trembling stopped. Their first real touch sent them both reeling as they felt their spirits soar like the birds that flew high above. The two were so moved by the warmth of their touch that they didn't even have to look at each other for their hearts to be filled with inexplicable contentment and joy.

Joachim placed his hands over the young couple and blessed them. Since Joseph had no living relative present, Rabbi Asa blessed the couple in Jacob's stead. They then turned to face each other. As they left for the litter, Joseph could vaguely see his fiancée's face through her veil. He could tell that his beloved was smiling. They both reached for the other's hand simultaneously. They then turned and walked toward the upholstered chair. With her hand in his, Joseph raised his arm to help her into the seat; he then sat down beside her while he still held her hand. "Thank You, Lord," Joseph said under his breath. *Life couldn't be better,* he thought. Ali's sons lifted the litter, and the procession to the Synagogue began. The street was filled with the sound of music and song. The young couple smiled at each other, and squeezed each other's hand a little tighter.

As the group moved toward the Synagogue, Zillah began to spread her vile lies to anyone who would listen. She told them of the unusually large amount of money Joseph had proffered as a dowry. The only reason he paid so much, Zillah told the townsfolk, was because he had his way with Mary on the day he returned to town, and Joachim threatened to report him to the Council of Elders. Joachim's dowry was a counteroffer so Joseph wouldn't get cold feet and run. It was really a forced engagement. That's why Rabbi Asa was involved. No good could ever come of their union. The only reason Anna dressed Mary the way she did was because she wanted to draw everyone's attention away from her daughter's abdomen. Mary was already in her latter stages of pregnancy.

Zillah wanted to utterly destroy Joseph's character, so she fabricated more lies. Joseph also cheated Achim out of his brother's estate by pretending Eleazer was still alive. Every so often, she said, Joseph would send his dead uncle's greetings to Achim so he wouldn't claim the money from the sale of the property and possessions he was entitled to, and that Joseph was now squandering." When Zillah met Mina, she told her the lies she had been spreading. "Hmm! So that's why there was such a quick agreement between Joachim and Joseph," the matchmaker said. "I thought something was fishy from the day I spoke to Mary about a match for her." Mina noticed the large lidded basket that Zillah was carrying. "So tell me, dah-link, what's in the basket?"

"Just a little gift for Mary," Zillah said. "I feel so sorry for the poor dear. I brought her something special." Mina tried to sneak a peek, but Zillah quickly pulled the empty basket away from her. "Now, now! I wouldn't want you ruining Mary's surprise by telling anyone what's in here. I know you're not a gossip, Mina, but if you should unintentionally slip, the surprise would be totally ruined." So the two parted, and Mina too began to spread the vicious lies to the other women in the group. The lies were now more plausible for them to believe because the women heard them from two separate sources. When Zillah reached Joachim and Anna's house, she dropped out of the procession. She waited until the group had moved far enough away that no one would see her. Entering the courtyard, she began to fill her basket, until it overflowed, with the delicacies Nabu and his wife had prepared for the celebration. Zillah quickly ran back to her own home, dropping several raisin cakes in the process.

When they reached the Synagogue, Joachim, Joseph and the rabbi went inside to enter the betrothal in the official records of the Jewish community. While they were inside, the young maidens and newly married women came up to Mary to admire her wardrobe and congratulate her on her betrothal. They hadn't heard the gossip yet. But by the time Joseph and Mary were carried back to Joachim and Anna's house, everyone had heard the lies.

Ali's sons lowered the litter to street level to allow the young couple to step out easily. He offered his hand to Joseph as he stepped out, and the carpenter thanked him profusely for the use of the litter. Joseph then gave his hand to Mary as she gracefully exited the chair. Everyone stared at her waistline to see if they could spot any signs of pregnancy. Hand in hand, the young couple then entered Joachim's house to complete the last part of the traditional betrothal ceremony.

Joseph and Mary sat cross-legged on the floor, facing each other, as Joachim poured a cup of wine and Anna brought over a small barley cake. Joseph's hands again began to tremble as he reached forward to lift his fiancée's veil. With shaking hands he raised the filmy fabric over Mary's crown as she blushed profusely. She was even more beautiful than he remembered, and for a moment he was again captivated by her honey-colored eyes. Joachim handed Joseph the cup of wine. The carpenter's hands shook so badly that the wine almost spilled over the edge of the vessel.

Mary reached out and steadied his hands with hers so he could sip from the ceremonial cup. His shaking ceased as he felt her gentle touch. He brought the cup to Mary's lips without spilling a drop of the deep-red liquid. Mary continued to guide his hands as he fed her the barley cake; she then fed the remainder to him. When the tradition was completed, Joseph rose, and offered her his hand. When Mary rose, Joseph hugged Anna and kissed her on the cheek, then kissed Joachim and hugged him as well. Mary embraced her parents too, and thanked them again for allowing her to be betrothed to Joseph. The carpenter thanked his future father-in law for the land and for the rest of the generous dowry. He smiled as he did so because, unbeknown to Joachim, they both had similar ideas.

Joseph had withdrawn his money from the Town Elders yesterday to purchase a tract of land on the hillside. He intended to build a house on that site, and then deed it to his father-in-law as living quarters for the apprentices he would need in the near future. Although Joseph didn't need the money to close the sale until the day after Sukkot, the Town Elders would not meet again until a few days after the holiday. The seller would be leaving Nazareth by then.

While Joseph lifted the veil from his beautiful fiancée, Nabu and his wife began to uncover the trays of foods they had prepared. To their dismay, they found most of the trays half-empty. At first, Nabu thought some animal had gotten to the food, and he'd have to throw away what remained since the food would no longer be kosher. But his wife pointed out to him that no animal would leave such neat rows or carefully re-cover the trays. She brought out the additional delicacies they had stored in Tamar's house. With Tamar and Azor's help, the couple began to refill the trays. When they were just about done, Joachim and Anna stepped out of the house, followed by the young couple.

Traditionally, when the betrothed young woman appeared with her fiancé, and her veil was lifted, the crowd would shout, "Mazel tov!" But only the voices of the rabbi, Tamar, Azor, Nabu and his wife, and Ali and his sons, could be heard shouting their congratulations. The others in the crowd were silent or said it in such a muffled tone that they were barely audible. The crowd was not going to congratulate a man who was guilty of such a heinous crime as rape. Joachim and Anna, and the aforementioned few others who shouted their congratulations, couldn't understand what was happening; neither could Joseph or Mary.

Joachim led the young couple to the booth Joseph had built. He took his seat next to Joseph, and Anna sat next to Mary. They waited patiently for the crowd to stream by the newly engaged couple and offer their congratulations and wishes for their future happiness. The few women who did come by spoke what Mary considered nonsense. None of them even spoke to Joseph. Instead, they were very rude to him. One woman whispered to Mary, "Some men are just animals. It's sad that you'll be saddled with one for the rest of your life." Another whispered, "I'll pray for you, my dear. The Almighty can change the worst of men." After a while Joachim stood up, and went to talk to the rabbi to find out if he knew what was happening. Asa replied that he couldn't understand it either. As the two men discussed the situation, Nabu approached them, and told the two men that his wife had overheard some vicious lies that were being circulated. When Joachim heard what was being said, he was livid. The rabbi could see the veins bulging on Joachim's temples as he clenched his fists until his knuckles turned white. "Please let me handle this, Joachim," the rabbi said. He grabbed his friend's shoulder and pressed down on it to show his concern and his dedication to righting this grievous wrong.

The rabbi loudly called for everyone's attention. "Today," he said, "for the first time since I came to reside in this town, I'm ashamed to be called a Nazarene. Vicious lies are being circulated about this wonderful young couple. The person or persons responsible for these untruths has not only sinned against this young couple, whose day of celebration has been ruined, but they also sinned against the Law of God given to Moses. They are guilty before the Most High of heinous slander by bearing false witness. In all my years as a rabbi, I have never met a more God-fearing young man of pious and impeccable character than Joseph Bar Jacob. He approached me to broker his betrothal to the young woman he loves. The large amount of money he pledged as a dowry was intended to help his future in-laws in their old age. He forbade me to ask for any reciprocal dowry, and told me to decline one if it was offered. I've never spoken to a young man, or an older one for that matter, who had more respect for the woman he was asking for in marriage. You have come here to eat his food, and drink his wine, with contempt for him in your hearts. Your Father Abraham looks down with scorn and shame on all who have been a party to this. And furthermore, this community should ostracize the person who is responsible for these vile, vicious lies."

When the rabbi finished speaking, the people, with their eyes downcast, began to leave in shame. Joseph quickly stood up and said, "Look! Neither I nor my fiancée holds any malice toward anyone of you. It's easy to fall into the grips of a skillful liar. I've done so myself. Let's all forget what happened, and please rejoin Mary and me in our celebration." The people were amazed how quick Joseph was to forgive. They now admired the young carpenter, and if anything, they didn't think the rabbi had praised his impeccable character enough.

The crowd began to chant "Joseph! Mary!" over and over until Mary stepped out from beneath the booth, and stood next to her fiancé. The people then started shouting, "Mazel tov!" so loudly that it was almost deafening. When Joseph raised his hand in an effort to silence them, the entire crowd began to clap uproariously for several minutes. They didn't stop until Joseph gently took Mary's hand and led her back into the booth. They sat down, and Joachim and Anna sat beside them once again. This time there was a continuous line of people apologizing and offering the couple their very best wishes. Anna struggled to be cordial to the people who almost ruined this day for her daughter, as did Joachim. Joseph and Mary, however, showed no animosity toward anyone.

Tamar, standing next to her husband, said, "This was all Zillah's doing. I knew she was going to start something when I saw her peering over the rabbi's shoulder. She's the one who took all that food before we got back here, I just know it! That witch was the only one carrying a basket large enough, and I never saw her at the Synagogue. I'm going to go over to her house now and wring that woman's neck."

"Calm down! You'll do no such thing," Azor said. "You're going to give yourself a heart attack, or a stroke, or something. Just relax, and let's help the kids enjoy the rest of their day."

While Joseph and Mary were returning from the Synagogue to finish celebrating their engagement, Zillah entered her house to find her son, and five of the brigands who accompanied him, drinking what was left of her husband's wine. "Joshua, you're home!" she said as she ran to him and tried to give him a kiss. He pushed her away and said, "I told you never to do that again!"

"I'm sorry, dear; it's just that I'm so happy to see you. It's been so long."

"Not long enough," Joshua replied.

"You can give me a kiss, Momma," one of his drunken comrades commented as he grabbed Zillah

286

and began to kiss her passionately while her son watched. She looked at Joshua in dismay.

Zillah finally pulled herself away from the drunken fool as her son asked, "So what's in the basket?" He didn't wait for an answer. He pulled it away from his mother, tore off the lid and tossed it aside. "Look what's here, guys. We can have some dessert while my fool mother makes us something to eat. Make us the lentil stew with a lot of garlic," he commanded. The greedy group ate everything in the basket, leaving her not a single crumb.

As Zillah bent over to grab a sack of lintels from the ground silo, she felt a hand reaching up under her petticoat. "Stop that!" she commanded.

Her son kicked her in the buttocks; she lost her balance and fell into the wall, skinning the side of her face. "Don't talk to my friends like that; that's no way to treat my guests! Do you understand me?!" After she apologized to her son for upsetting him, Zillah grabbed a cloth and wiped the blood off her face.

"What happened to the drunken fool that you married?" Joshua asked. "Did ya finally kill 'im?" That was precisely what she had done. A week ago, she killed her husband by adding a poisonous lizard to a fatal stew. She then shaved his head and beard so no one would recognize him. The evil woman stripped him naked to encourage the vultures to quickly feast on his remains. On that moonless night, with a burst of adrenaline, she loaded his corpse onto their donkey. With a honey pot in one hand and the donkey's reins in the other, she led the animal to the high precipice at the edge of town. After rubbing his colorless face with the amber liquid, so the ants would make him totally unrecognizable, she slid his body to the ground and rolled him into the gorge below. When she heard the splat, she closed the honey pot and went home. That night she slept like a baby.

"Joshua, do you really think I could do something like that to your father?" Zillah asked. "He just wandered off a few days ago, and I expect to find him sleeping in the animal pen any day now." Her son never responded.

Zillah hurriedly filled the pot with water, grabbed the lentils and beans, and went outside to make the stew. Her son's comrades frightened her. While she struck the flint to start the fire she could hear the sound of flutes, lyres and tambourines coming from Joachim's house. The exotic music made her regret not being there.

Joshua's mother was a rather attractive woman. She was in her mid-30s, yet she still maintained her girlish figure. Zillah was too vain to let anyone see her with a scraped face. *If I had known my Joshua was coming I could have pre-soaked the lentils, and this stew would have be done in no time,* she said to herself. *Now my poor dear will have to wait.* Zillah sat down on the stone bench near the fire and began to tap her foot to the festive music. "Oh, Mommy, come in here," she heard her son call. "I have a surprise for you." She wiped her hands on her apron and quickly went inside the house.

"What is it, dear?" she said as she opened the door. To her surprise, one of the men grabbed her around the waist and placed his hand over her mouth while another put a gag over it. They then pushed her to the floor and forced her to participate in the lewdest acts their depraved minds could think of. She struggled and tried to beg for mercy. Her son laughed as he watched with deranged interest while she strained to free herself from under her assailants. They carried on for hours, and their stench caused her to turn her head and vomit, but still they didn't stop. They drank more wine in between turns, and finally one by one they passed out, her son included.

Zillah removed the gag that now hung loosely around her neck, and tossed it into the pile where her clothes lay. She took a pitcher and basin, and went into the animal pen to bathe. If one of them woke up, she didn't want to be seen. She tiptoed back inside the house and put on a fresh tunic. Picking up her torn clothing, she spat at each of the five men as she went outside. The stench of their unwashed bodies still clung to the fabric. She considered washing it in the rain trough and mending it later, but she couldn't stand the thought of placing that clothing back on her body. Returning to the fire, Zillah tossed the smelly garments into the flames. She watched as the sparks rose in the cool night air. The woman considered looking for another poisonous lizard, the same type she had put in her husband's stew, but she feared her son would die. He would insist on eating it too.

While Joshua Bar Abbas was laughing at his mother's abuse, Joseph danced with Joachim, Azor and the rabbi. Mary's eyes never left her fiancé as he snapped his fingers and turned before her while his large feet moved to the rhythm of the music. Joseph turned less than the others because he tried to keep his eyes glued on his beloved too. When Mary rose to dance with her mother and her aunt, Joseph could see the envious eyes of old and young men alike staring unceasingly at his love. He considered asking Mary to cover her face again, but he knew only death or divorce could ever separate them now. The former was inevitable one day, but to him the latter was totally inconceivable. *Let them look,* he thought to himself. He and Mary belonged to each other now, and he knew in his heart nothing would ever change that. Her lithe movements, as she danced and gently tapped the tambourine above her head, were meant for Joseph alone.

Maybe it was because of the guilt they felt over falling prey to Zillah's lies, or perhaps it was because of her grace and beauty, but the crowd was overly generous as they gently tossed coins at the young virgin's feet while she danced. The children scurried between the three dancers, picked up the coins and brought them to Joseph. He thanked them profusely and handed the money to Joachim, who placed it in a large leather pouch he brought for that purpose. When Mary returned to Joseph's side, they immediately joined hands once again. Joseph squeezed her hand gently as he silently prayed, *Lord, if this is a dream, please never let me wake up again. I have no idea why I've been so blessed, but thank You, Lord! Thank You!* The celebration continued well into the night with music, dancing, and a variety of foods and plenty of wine. The waxing moon was in mid-sky before the jubilant merrymakers made their way home to their own booths, for Sukkot had started at sunset. As they walked home they passed Zillah's lean-to booth. She appeared to be sleeping.

As Zillah lay in her booth with the scraped side of her face to the wall, for the first time in her life she tried to avoid people. In the silence she began to justify her son's prior inactions. *He had to permit them to treat me the way they did if that's what they wanted to do,* she told herself. *There were five of them against one of him. He's their leader, and if they rebelled against him, what would happen to the "Cause"? No one then would stand up against the Roman army. What he's doing, he's doing for the glory of Israel. He still loves me; otherwise he wouldn't have come back to see me. He's a good man.* Long ago she started to actually believe in the story she had invented about her son's heroism, a tall tale she passed on to others.

When the streets were empty, and everyone had settled in for the night, Zillah got up and went into the house. It was hard for her to walk because she had bruised her hip when she fell, but she made her way toward her son, and sat down next to him. The woman removed his filthy cap, then lifted his head and placed it on her lap. When she was certain that he was still sound asleep, she leaned over and kissed his forehead. Zillah began to run her fingers through his greasy, unwashed hair as she softly sang the lullabies she had sung to him in his youth. She continued to do so until daybreak, when he began to stir.

Nabu and his wife were the last to leave Joachim's courtyard. The cleanup was complete, so the family prepared to settle in for the night. Since Joseph built the booth for them, and he and Mary were now engaged, he was invited to stay. The sleeping arrangements were such that Mary would sleep by the open outer wall, and Anna would lie next to her; next to her would be Tamar. Joseph was assigned his sleeping space between Azor and Joachim. Anna helped her daughter remove her crowns and veil. Mary kissed her parents goodnight, and her aunt and uncle too. She came up to Joseph, stood on her tiptoes, and gave him a light peck on the cheek as she whispered, "Shalom and good night, Joseph!" Her lips felt soft and warm. His cheeks turned bright red despite his tan. Joseph was at a loss for words, so he just shook his head up and down. He mumbled something incoherent as he raised his hands to his side curls, and attempted to push them back across his ears. Joseph forgot he was still wearing the turban. His fingers caught in the folds of linen, and he knocked the turban off his head, further embarrassing himself.

The day's activities tired the older folks, so they soon fell asleep. Joseph tossed and turned. He couldn't believe that he was lying there under the same roof as Mary. He raised himself up on one elbow to look at his beloved. Her long auburn hair glistened in the lantern light. He still couldn't believe that she was now his fiancée. As he watched her, Mary opened her eyes and smiled at him; he smiled back, but was a little embarrassed. He didn't want her to think that he was stalking her. Joseph laid back down and feigned sleep. He even pretended to snore in unison with the others to convince Mary he was actually sleeping. After a while he rolled on to his side, and partially opened his eyes. He saw Mary rise and tiptoe out of the booth. Joseph adjusted his arm under his head so he could see above Azor's sleeping form.

The silvery crescent of the waxing moon, and a sky filled with an abundance of dazzling stars, shed enough light for him to see Mary sit down and lean her back against the house. She lifted up her hands with her palms facing up to the sky as she looked up to the heavens to pray. Her very soul soared to her Maker, the Lord God of her fathers, in thanksgiving for Joseph. He was all she ever dreamed of in a husband. The apparition she thought she witnessed in early spring was the furthest thing from her mind tonight as she was caught up in indescribable gratitude to the Almighty. She thanked and praised Him again and again for His divine providence. It was the only way she could release the overabundance of joy that filled her.

When Mary returned to the booth, Joseph closed his eyes more tightly and pretended to snore a little louder. She snickered as she looked at the three men sleeping side by side. Though their heads were in a straight line, her father's feet just reached a hand span and a half below Joseph's kneecaps. The feet of her Uncle Azor, whom she always considered a tall man, ended at least two hand spans above Joseph's ankle. Mary was amazed at how tall Joseph actually was. She lowered herself to the ground by her mother's side. Joseph could feel that Mary was now watching him. He liked the feeling. Needless to say, neither Mary nor Joseph could fall into a deep sleep that night. They each tried to listen to the sound of the other's breathing over the sounds of snoring.

No couple in the entire land of Israel was happier that night than Mary and Joseph—except perhaps for an elderly couple who lived in the town of Ein Karem, in the Judean hillside, not too far from Jerusalem. Tamar and Azor's daughter, who was well beyond her childbearing years, and who had been barren all through her reproductive years, told her husband that she was with child. Zechariah, who could not speak, just smiled and shook his head up and down. His eyes filled with tears of joy as he grabbed his wife's hand and kissed it.

CHAPTER 13

It was the first morning of the Feast of Booths. As Zillah saw the sky begin to lighten, she lowered her son's head from her lap and went to pull the shades down over the windows. She was so sore that she could hardly move. Joshua needed his rest; she didn't want the light from the approaching dawn to disturb his sleep. Zillah picked up a sheet of highly polished brass she used as a mirror and took it outside to view her scraped face. It was worse than she thought. She pulled her veil further over her head to try to hide the large sore and bruise on her cheek as she lit a new fire under the pot of stew. She hadn't stirred it enough last night, so it stuck to the bottom of the pot. *I'll serve Joshua from the top,* she said to herself. *The burnt part is good enough for those other pigs.*

She re-entered her house with the pot of stew, and almost choked on the obnoxious stench that filled her home. She didn't notice the odor that much last night, as it hadn't yet permeated the house. As it had, she slowly became used to it. Breathing in the fresh outdoor air, however, cleared her senses, and now the smell was unbearable. Her son was the first to wake.

When he did, he said, "Is that stew ready yet? How long does it take for you to cook a simple meal?"

"It was ready since last night, dear, but you were asleep."

"It's morning already? Why didn't you wake me last night, you stupid idiot. You knew I was hungry!" Zillah apologized to her son and told him he had been sleeping so soundly, she didn't want to disturb him. "Once a fool, always a fool," he said as he stood up and began to scratch his hairy abdomen. "Where did you get that basket full of food from yesterday? It was better stuff than you ever made." Zillah explained that it came from Joseph Bar Jacob's and Mary's betrothal celebration. She mentioned that the young carpenter had come into quite a bit of money. He was trying to show off his wealth by impressing everyone with the money he had stolen from his Uncle Achim. She was the only one who knew about it though, because Joseph admitted it to her.

"Oh, really," Joshua said, "that's very interesting. Does he go out much?"

"Sometimes!" Zillah said. "When he's setting roof beams. But lately, he's been working from his house. He won't be home three days from now, though. He'll be using the communal team of oxen to plow his fields and Joachim's and Azor's too. I heard him talking with Silas about it. He's got the plow that day. Joseph even asked me if I wanted him to do mine—I mean ours. I'm sure he only asked because he feels guilty about you having to leave town because of him. By the way, dear, you never told me why you decided to come back home."

"I came back because I need money, and you're going to help me get it."

Zillah asked if it was for the "Cause." Joshua laughed hysterically. "Yeah, you fool, it's for the 'Cause.' We're going to get the townspeople to cough up some of their money. See that old drum over there that we brought with us? You're going to take it and beat on it as you walk through the streets, asking the people to come to the town gate for a special meeting. It's about time they paid their dues for the 'Cause,' don't you think?" Joshua continued to laugh uncontrollably.

"I can't walk through the streets with my face looking like this," Zillah said. "What will the people think of me?"

"Who cares what anyone thinks of you? Idiot! You'll do as I tell you to. Do you understand me?"

Zillah nodded as she went to her husband's hamper and took out fresh clothing for her son. "If you're going to go before the people," she said, "I suggest you and your friends bathe and put on some clean clothing. Here! Use your father's!" She handed her husband's clothing to her son. "Your friends smell so badly that no one will even come close to them if they put those clothes back on."

"So what are you waiting for? Take their clothes and wash them. The last time I looked, you still had two hands."

Zillah picked up the large pile of filthy clothing and took it outside. The stench almost made her vomit. She hung the large cauldron from the tripod above the fire pit and threw the clothes on the ground. As she began to fill it with the water from the trough, she saw Mary returning from her second trip to the well. Zillah pulled her veil closer to her face, and busied herself gathering additional kindling so she wouldn't have to look directly at her. Mary greeted Zillah as she passed by. The town gossip said nothing. Mary thought it highly unusual for the woman, since she always sought out the opportunity to engage everyone in conversation.

Zillah's door opened as Mary drew near. A rather filthy man stood in the doorway, clothed only in a very dirty undergarment. He stood there scratching his bare abdomen and his leg. The instant Mary saw him, she averted her eyes. She didn't get a good look at him, but he appeared to be a little too young to be Zillah's husband. But then again, Mary had never seen Abbas. From the corner of her eye she could see him step out of the doorframe and gaze at her. Mary could feel his eyes staring at her as she proceeded down the street. She heard him say something, but she didn't care to find out what it was. Mary increased her pace so she could get away from the stranger as quickly as possible.

"Who was that woman?" Joshua had asked.

"That's Mary, Joseph's fiancée," Zillah replied.

"Hmm! She sure didn't look that way the last time I saw her," he said as he continued to scratch himself. As he went into the house to bathe, he shouted, "You better hurry up and go get some more water so my men can wash up too. They should be getting up soon. Get moving so you can serve them some stew when they do."

Zillah picked up the pile of odorous clothes and carried it over to the rain trough. Before she soaked the items, she pulled a small knife from her sash and examined each article until she found the most sweat-stained area. The woman then cut a small, almost unnoticeable piece from each man's tunic, and tucked away the swatches into a small pouch at her side. When she submerged the garments, the fresh water temporarily masked the horrible smell. She went to fetch some soap from an outdoor storage bin. As she did, she could hear her son yelling, "Get in here right now! My men are hungry!" Zillah set the soap by the cauldron and entered the house. Joshua's friends unashamedly paraded around the house unclothed.

When Zillah closed the door, one of the men said, "How would you like to have a little more fun, Momma?" and slapped her on the buttock. She leapt forward from the shock and fell into the arms of another man. As they groped her, the men began to toss her, from one to the other, as if she was a ragdoll. Her son, the professional con-man, ignored the goings-on. During his mother's abuse, Joshua paced back and forth as he prepared an eloquent speech that would separate the townspeople from their money.

Zillah finally pulled herself free, readjusted her clothing and went to get the bowls for the stew. She dug the burnt part of the crud from the bottom of the cauldron and served it to them. She spit into each bowl. *I hope they choke on it,* she said to herself. The men ate it with relish and just demanded more. When she went to refill their bowls, she kept her arms rigid. She made sure her torso was far from them so she couldn't be groped again. Zillah told Joshua she had to wash his comrades' clothes now, if he expected them to dry before midday. The woman would then go and fetch some more water so they could bathe. She quickly picked up the water jar and exited the house.

Zillah immediately went to the rain trough and picked up the pole that leaned against it. She noticed that the smell now permeated the water. As she caught hold of each article of clothing, she transferred it to the hot water in the cauldron. She added a lot more soap than she usually did, and then went off to the well.

Mary finally reached her house and began to tell her mother and her aunt what she had experienced. She thought Azor and the others were asleep, so she spoke softly. Joseph, however, who was just lying there with his eyes closed, overheard Mary's words. He jumped to his feet and went to her side. "Mary, you're not going to go to the well alone anymore," he said. "I'm going to go with you. The man you saw was Joshua, Zillah's son. When your father and I were stating the dowries yesterday, I thought I saw him and five other men enter town. In all the excitement, I forgot to mention it to anyone. I don't trust him. I think that he still has an axe to grind with me. So please don't go anywhere alone." Mary was pleased with his gallantry. Joshua frightened her. She said that she could feel him staring at her as she walked by. She promised Joseph she wouldn't go to fetch water alone. Anna said she would go instead. The middle-aged woman didn't think Joshua would have any interest in her. "Nonsense!" Joseph said. "Mary and I will continue to do it. I'm not going to let him change all of our daily routines."

When Joachim and Azor awoke, Anna relayed the bad news of Joshua's return; the men were none too happy about it. Her husband said that if Joshua has five others with him, they all better be very careful. Joachim was convinced that in Joshua's warped mind, he probably thought he had a good reason to hate all of them. Joseph bid farewell to everyone and went home to bathe. Before he left, Anna told him to return to the booth for the midday meal. He thanked her and agreed to do so. The others also went inside to bathe and do their morning chores.

Joseph had washed up and was about to plane a board, when he heard a drumbeat. He went to the door and opened it. He saw Mary and her family, standing along the edge of their courtyard, straining their necks to see where the sound was coming from. Joseph ran across the street and joined them. He asked Joachim if he knew what was going on. Joachim shook his head and said he had no idea. Azor suggested it might be the Roman Military. They sometimes used a single drum to get the town's attention if some announcement was to be made, but their drumbeat had a more-even cadence. Before he finished speaking, Zillah turned the corner and came into view with drum in hand, beating on it as she walked. Once Tamar recognized her, she asked what the silly town gossip was up to now.

They soon heard what Zillah was shouting: "Come to the city gate at midday today!" She kept yelling it as she walked along. Tamar thought perhaps the rabbi scolded the crazy gossip enough to convince her to make a public apology for what she had caused yesterday. The elderly woman insisted on going to see what the woman was up to. Anna agreed. Azor suggested they all go. If Zillah was going to publicly apologize for her detestable rumor, Joseph and Mary should be there to hear it firsthand.

At high noon, a large crowd gathered to hear what Zillah was about to say. They soon tired of waiting in the hot sun. As they were about to disperse, Zillah, her son and three of his fellow thugs marched to the center of the commons. Joshua was gifted with his mother's lying tongue, and with the cunningness of his adoptive father, the Prince of Darkness. Before anyone could leave he shouted, "Who in this crowd is a loyal son or daughter of Father Abraham?!" As the people raised their hands, the con artist continued, "So you're all children of the promise. Right?" The people nodded.

"And the promise was that this was to be our land forever. It wasn't based on an agreement between men, but between God and Father Abraham and all of his descendants. The land we stand on doesn't belong to Caesar Augustus or even to Herod, his puppet king; it belongs to us! Now is the time for us to reclaim our inheritance!"

Azor, Tamar, Joseph, and Joachim and his family began to walk away. Joshua, who proved to be quite an eloquent speaker, continued to whip the crowd into a frenzy as he tried to convince them to donate to his fictitious cause. He told them how the Zealots needed money to continue to fight the Romans. He and the rest of the Freedom Fighters were gaining ground, but it was difficult to live the way he and his companions had to live for the sake of liberation. They needed money for food and weapons if they were to continue the struggle until victory was achieved. Success came at a high cost, not only in lives, but also with tremendous personal sacrifice. Maybe the people themselves couldn't go out and fight the enemy for their sovereignty, Joshua said, but they could invest in freedom if they gave to the cause. "Dig deeply into your purses and give generously so that you, your children and your grandchildren will forever live free of foreign rule."

Joshua was so convincing that Zillah and his fellow thugs needed additional baskets to hold all of the coins they took in. Joshua mingled with the people afterwards and promised them more folkloric tales of his achievements. He had many anecdotes to tell about his accomplishments, if they would only return tomorrow at the same time. The gullible townsfolk elbowed their way toward him so they could hug him or at least touch his hand. Many women in the crowd shed tears of pride for just being near their hometown demigod. The thug had successfully portrayed himself as a national hero and great leader. Zillah no longer cared if her neighbors saw her scraped face. To her it was a badge of honor—a sort of special marking by her wonderful son. She walked with pride next to him. Zillah now knew with certainty that her deepest desire was a reality. Her son was truly the Messiah. It was her duty and honor to serve him.

Joseph, Joachim and Azor discussed the folly of the meeting while Mary and the other two women did the same. Joseph didn't think their neighbors were so gullible. Joshua was no more a member of the Zealots than Joseph was. The three other guys looked dangerous—more like thugs than patriots. Joseph knew it wasn't right to judge people on first impressions, but he saw nothing but evil in their shifty eyes. Joachim said he saw the same thing. Azor said that it wasn't only their eyes that looked evil; their whole demeanor suggested an indescribable eeriness. The last time he felt anything like it was when he saw Zaddu the witch studying the entrails of a dead rock-badger on the path near her cave. His skin had crawled from being in the presence of such evil.

When they finally reached home, Joseph asked Joachim if he could buy a small piece of leather from him. He had an idea that he thought might interest the townspeople. It would be profitable to both of them. His future father-in-law said to just take whatever he needed. Joseph said he would only need an arm span, but insisted on paying for it. Joachim laughed as he asked the young carpenter whose arm span would be used. The cost difference could be quite sizable if Joseph's arm span was the measure, he said jokingly. The three men laughed. They went into Joachim's shop, and Joseph chose a piece of leather suitable for his purpose.

When Joseph went back home, he took some uncombed cotton Anna had given him and placed it atop a wooden stool he had previously made. He covered it with the piece of leather and fastened it in place with tacks. Joseph stood back and admired the upholstered stool. Then he sat upon it. It had the same cushiony feel that the seat of the litter had.

When he rose, he took his new creation over to Mary's house so she could try it too. When Mary and Anna saw the stool, they both were enthralled. Joseph suggested Mary sit on it. When she did, she told him it was even better than the seat on the litter. The teen told her mother to try it. Anna worried her weight would break it. Joseph said it was just an ordinary stool with some padding and leather over it; she wouldn't break it. Anna sat on the stool and was surprised at how very comfortable it was. She told Mary to go get her father, and her aunt and uncle too. They had to try out the upholstered stool. Mary went to call the others while Anna sat there primly. When Mary returned with the three others, Anna was a little reluctant to give up her seat. She finally stood up so the others could try Joseph's handiwork too. They all thought that a padded stool was a wonderful idea.

"I made it for you, Mary!" Joseph said to his fiancée.

"Thank you, Joseph," she replied, "but don't you think you should stand it out in front of your house for a while so other people can see it too? I think a lot of our neighbors would like to purchase one. You don't have to sell this one, it can still be mine, but it's something a lot of people may want to buy." Joachim agreed that it was a great idea. He told Joseph he could bring it back to Mary every night when he came to dinner. So Joseph took the stool and placed it outside his house. That same afternoon, those who passed by did notice it, and many people sat on it to try it out. Joseph received three orders for leather-covered stools that same day. He probably would have received more had Joshua not fleeced the townspeople of most of their money earlier.

In late afternoon, Joseph heard hoofbeats. The horse stopped right in front of his house. He went to the door and saw Hasid, the same Roman soldier who shamed his aunt years ago. Hasid was sitting on Joseph's creation. "Jew boy!" the soldier said. "Have you seen or heard of any Zealot activity in this town lately? And don't lie to me!" Joseph said he had not. He wasn't lying. He knew that neither Joshua nor any of his fellow thugs were really Zealots.

"You'll let me know if you do, right, Jew boy?"

"As you say, sir!" Joseph replied. He felt that his answer was noncommittal. Deputy Hasid then told him that he wanted the stool that he was sitting on. Joseph apologized and told him that the stool was not for sale. He could order one, though.

"I didn't say I was interested in buying it, did I, Jew boy? I just said I wanted it! It would serve you well to know that when a soldier of Rome wants something, it's his. Having a Roman soldier consider owning an article made by a Nazarene dog should be payment enough to a Jew boy like you." Joseph tried to contain the anger welling up within him. He'd promised the stool to Mary, and now this ignorant tyrant was just taking it from him. As the soldier tied the stool to the back of his saddle, Joseph considered grabbing hold of Hasid and wrestling him to the ground. Joachim, watching the incident from across the street, shook his head in warning. Seeing his future father-in-law's signal, Joseph calmed down somewhat, so he just turned around and walked back into his house, very disheartened. As soon as the young carpenter entered his home, Joachim showed up at the door. He told his son-in-law that he did the right thing by not antagonizing that swine. Everyone knew Hasid was despicable. Had Joseph reacted otherwise, he'd probably be dead by now. He told his future son-in-law that he was proud of him, and not to worry about the stool. Mary would understand.

That evening, when Joseph came to dinner, Mary put her hand on his shoulder, and all his pent-up anger disappeared. She told him she loved the stool he had made for her. She thanked the Lord that he was still here to make her another. Mary said she was just happy he didn't do anything that would have further provoked the heartless soldier. The Lord would deal with him. She needed Joseph to keep himself safe for her. Joseph reached up and pressed Mary's hand while it was still on his shoulder. He said that it just wasn't right that they, as God's Chosen People, were under the heel of a nation that still worshiped idols. He wondered how long it would be before God would see their subjugation and humiliation, and send His Messiah to deliver them.

"Maybe He's waiting until He knows that we can be a more righteous and faithful people, so we will recognize and follow Messiah when He does come," Mary answered.

Joachim heard the exchange between his daughter and Joseph. "Mary! How did you get to be so wise? Solomon is Joseph's ancestor, not yours, yet you spoke with wisdom that would measure up to his just now." Mary blushed and then laughed.

"Don't laugh, Mary; your father is right," Joseph said. "There was a great deal of wisdom in your words. I should never have questioned the plan of the Almighty. He alone knows the past of our people as well as our future. He not only is the God of men, but He's the God of time also. The Lord will deliver us when it's His holy will to do so, not ours." They then went out to the booth to enjoy their meal and celebrate the festival.

Joshua was very pleased with the receipts from his first charade. *These people are more gullible than I thought,* he said to himself. He was even less abusive to his mother than he normally would have been. Zillah was so pleased with her son that she went out for more wine and bought a whole lamb to roast. She stayed in her booth for the rest of the day; she couldn't stand the five men her son brought home with him. This midday, at the commons, when there were two fewer, she felt a little better, but by the time they came back to the house, the two had returned and were more abusive than ever. People came by all afternoon, asking to talk privately with Joshua. He distinctly told his mother he was not to be bothered. If anyone asked to see him, she was to say that he was in a tactical-planning meeting and could not see anyone.

As Zillah turned the spit to evenly roast the lamb, she saw Hasid in the distance. He often patrolled the streets of town, galloping through on his stallion. The minute she saw him, she flew up from her sitting position and ran into the house. She told her son to go and hide because the soldier was making his rounds. The six, who were already rather inebriated, stumbled into the stable, laughing under their breath, while they pushed and shoved each other like fools.

Zillah quickly returned to the fire pit and continued to turn the spit. The soldier stopped in front of her house and dismounted. He asked her why a woman who lives only with her husband was roasting a whole lamb today. Zillah was so used to lying that she didn't even have to think twice before she spoke. She said her neighbors were coming over to celebrate Sukkot that evening. While she was still talking, Hasid withdrew his broadsword, and with a swift sweep, cut off a section of the roasting lamb. He skewered it on the edge of his weapon in midair. He took a bite of the meat and said, "This isn't bad, not bad at all." He continued chewing as he questioned her further. "How'd you get that scrape on your face? Husband give it to ya?" She said that Abbas had a vicious temper when he had a little too much wine. "So, I understand that some Zealot activity has been going on around here," the soldier said. "Your son is a Zealot, isn't he?"

Zillah pretended to laugh. "My son! A Zealot? You've got to be joking! I would even prefer that he was one of those, rather than be the useless drunk that he is. He's just like his father. My son left six years ago, and good riddance, I say. Go inside if you don't believe me, but all you'll find is my drunken husband sleeping it off. Go ahead—go inside and check." Her lies, as always, were so convincing that the soldier didn't bother.

"If your husband is always as drunk as you say he is, maybe you and I could get together and have some fun," Hasid said.

"I'd like nothing better, but there's something you need to know first," the woman said. "My husband used to spend a lot of time with the shrine prostitutes in the hills. The physician said that what he caught from them is eating away not only at his flesh, but at his brain too. Unfortunately he passed it on to me, but maybe you won't get it." The soldier couldn't get away from her fast enough. As he rode off toward Joseph's house, she laughed at how gullible Hasid was.

As soon as he left, Zillah went back inside to check on her son. He and his five friends were sound asleep. *Better that they stay that way until the soldier leaves town,* she thought. She knew that as long as they slept, they'd be quiet. There was less of a chance that Deputy Hasid would discover her courageous son was inside. As for the other five, the longer they slept, the less time they'd have to bother her. Zillah returned to the fire pit just as the soldier rode by with a strange-looking stool tied to the back of his saddle.

By the time the festive sounds of the night's celebration began, the whole lamb Zillah had roasted was eaten. She never even had a chance to taste it. The men began to drink heavily again as she sat there while her stomach growled. As Zillah tried to leave to spend the night in her booth, one of the men grabbed her. She knew what was coming next. It hurt her deeply that her son still laughed as they humiliated her so. When they were finally finished with her, the group passed out from the overabundance of wine. Zillah found the bags of coins they had gathered earlier. She removed five gold and five silver coins, and hid them under her flour barrel. She didn't feel as if she was stealing from her son. The woman was just taking a small amount from the share of the five thugs who abused her so badly. *I really deserve a lot more than this from those pigs,* she said to herself. Zillah put her clothes back on, and as she left the house she spat on each of her son's comrades. *At least their smell isn't clinging to my clothing tonight,* she thought as she lay down to sleep. She knew their abusive treatment would continue each night of their stay. She made up her mind that a part of all the money they collected would be hers.

After Deputy Hasid completed his reconnaissance mission, he galloped out of town toward the fortress south of Nazareth, where he was stationed. Shortly after he turned on the fork that led to the plains, he had to slow his steed to a trot because the path narrowed and twisted as it followed the side of the hills. A snake lay in the weeds in his path, listening to the thunder of the horse's hoofs. The stallion sensed its presence and stopped moving. Hasid, who was used to having his way, couldn't understand why the horse froze. He kept digging his heals into the animal's sides to make it proceed. The horse began to turn in circles on the narrow path. On one of its revolutions it passed right in front of the serpent. The snake seized the opportunity; it struck and sank its fangs deep into the horse's leg, spewing its deadly venom into the animal's bloodstream. As soon as the snake attacked, the stallion reared up with such force that Deputy Hasid was thrown from his horse. His helmet came off as he flew up into the air and came down again. When he landed, his head struck a huge boulder. The serpent slithered away into the grassy underbrush. The stool Hasid had stolen from Joseph landed undamaged on the opposite side of the boulder. The soldier lay there unconscious throughout the night. Hasid's wounded horse found its way back to the fortress. The animal died from the poison shortly after it arrived.

The following morning, as Joseph awoke, he could hear Mary talking with her mother. "I'll ask Joseph, Momma. I'm sure he wouldn't mind."

Joseph slid forward from his place between Azor and Joachim, and went up to the women. "What is it, Mary?" he asked. "I heard you talking. What do you need?" She replied that her mother was out of cucumbers and melons. She was going to send her father to get some, but she told her mother that Joseph wouldn't mind going for them. The carpenter said that he had been dining with them every night, and that it was only right for him to go. He didn't mind at all. As soon as he washed up, he'd leave for the fields.

"Are you sure you don't mind, Joseph?" Anna said. "I could wait until the day after the Sabbath when we go to plow. It's just that the cucumbers ripen so quickly this time of year. When we take in the final harvest, we have so many at one time that there are too many to pickle."

"Mother!" he said. "Never hesitate to ask me if you need to have something done. Okay?" Anna nodded in the affirmative. Joseph was bolder this morning than he had ever been before. When he bade the women farewell, he not only kissed Anna on the cheek, he lightly kissed Mary's cheek as well. The teenagers blushed and looked at Anna to see what her response would be. Her face beamed with joy.

Joseph left for the fields as soon as he washed up. He tied the two large straw baskets to the side of his mule and went toward the city gate. The earthy smells of autumn filled the early morning air as Joseph approached the gate and greeted the gatekeeper. Joseph and Eliud talked for a while. As he was about to leave, Nabu's son Omar came walking up to them with his donkey beside him. "Shalom!" he said to the two men. Joseph and Eliud returned the greeting.

"Where are you going, Joseph?" the young man asked. The carpenter said he was headed for the fields. Omar said that he was going there too, and asked Joseph if he would mind if he walked with him. Joseph said he'd enjoy his company. The two made their way down the road to the path that led to the fields. When they passed the path that led to the cave where the witch lived, Joseph spat on the ground. Omar did likewise.

"Why did we just do that?" Omar asked.

"To ward off the evil eye of the witch who lives here," the young carpenter replied. "Everybody knows that she's back. I'm sure it's just a matter of time before us men will have to drive her out again."

"What's in spittle that it would do that?"

"I really don't know, but everyone does it. They say she can't cross the path over the fresh spittle of a believer in the God of Abraham." As they wound their way around the hill, Joseph was shocked to see the stool he'd made, next to a big boulder. He picked up the stool and began to tie it to his mule's saddlebags. "This is odd," Joseph said. "I made this stool, and a Roman soldier stole it from me yesterday. I guess he just threw it out over here."

Omar took a few steps forward as his friend fiddled with the stool. "Guess what, Joseph?" the boy said. "You found your stool, and I found the soldier."

Joseph walked around the boulder and saw Hasid lying against it with a huge gash on his bloodstained head. His basic instincts told him to leave him there as prey for the vultures circling overhead. Omar asked if this was the soldier who stole from him.

"He's the one," Joseph said as he knelt down next to Hasid and put his finger on the soldier's carotid artery. "He's still alive. Would you please hand me my waterskin?"

"You're not going to help him, are you, Joseph? Not after what he did!"

"No matter how I feel about him, God is the author of life, and if I just let him die, to me, it would be like killing him. I don't want that on my conscience." Joseph took off his sash to wash the soldier's wounds with. When Omar saw what Joseph was doing, he felt guilty, so he brought him the waterskin. Joseph cleansed and bandaged Hasid's head. He gave him small sips of water, watching carefully to be sure the soldier could swallow each sip. The carpenter then carried Deputy Hasid to his mule, and draped his body over the animal. "Would you do me a favor, Omar?" The boy nodded. "Go tell Mary and her family I'll be back before sunset, and not to worry about me." The boy asked Joseph what he was going to do with the soldier. The carpenter said he was going to take him back to his garrison at the fort. It wasn't far from there. Omar asked him what he would do if they accused him of doing this to Hasid.

314

"I don't think they will; the Centurion seems to be a nice guy for a Roman. I just can't leave him here to die."

Omar asked if Joseph minded if he harvested what his mother needed before going to tell Mary. "That's fine!" Joseph replied. "Mary doesn't expect me back for a while anyway." Just take your time." The two then parted. Joseph headed southwest, while Omar went toward the fields.

When Joseph arrived at the fort, he met Gaius, the Centurion who had saved him from the humiliation Hasid was subjecting him to when he first arrived in Nazareth. "I found this soldier on a path near my town," Joseph explained. "He appeared to have been thrown from his horse."

"I was about to send out a search party to look for him. His horse returned last night and died from a snakebite," the Centurion said, then added, "I've got to ask you something before you leave, young man. You Jews don't think too highly of us Roman soldiers. Why did you go out of your way to bring Deputy Hasid back here? I know he liked to give your people a hard time."

"Because, sir, I know that my God would expect me to do it," Joseph replied.

The Centurion grasped Joseph's forearm and thanked him. The carpenter had seen the gesture done enough times to know that he was expected to grasp the Centurion's forearm as well. As he did, the Centurion said, "You bring honor to your people and to your God, young man. There are few men who are as honorable as you. May your God repay you for your benevolence."

As Joseph was about to leave, he handed the Centurion the cushioned stool and said, "Excellency, this belongs to the soldier." Joseph wished Gaius "shalom" and left.

On his way back from the fort, Joseph stopped at the fields and harvested some melons and cucumbers. He washed his hands with the water from the waterskin, in accordance with Jewish law, and then he ate one of the melons. He was hungry. He had missed breakfast, and hadn't eaten anything since last night. Joseph loaded the baskets full of melons and cucumbers onto his mule, and headed back to town. *Mary and her mother will have plenty of time to sort through these before the Sabbath begins,* he said to himself as he climbed the steep path from the fields. Joseph couldn't wait to see Mary again. When he returned, she ran out to greet him. "I've been so worried about you, Joseph. When Omar told me what you were doing, I thought the Centurion might detain you for questioning."

"No, Mary, I think he must really be Jewish," Joseph said jokingly. "He was grateful, and actually was very civil with me. As a matter of fact, he thanked me for bringing the deputy back to him."

Mary reached up and kissed his cheek. "You're a good man, Joseph Bar Jacob. I'm very proud of you."

Joseph carried the food into Mary's house. Anna and Tamar complimented him on his bravery too. They started sorting the produce as Joseph returned to his house. There were still a few hours before the Sabbath was to begin. Joseph took out the wooden treasure box he had been working on as a wedding gift for Mary. He had already carved out the wooden block so that it tightly housed the vile of expensive nard. Taking up his carving tools, he chiseled away at the intricate design he was carving on the lid of the box until shortly before sunset. As the western sky turned a blazing coral, Joseph hid the box in his ground silo and placed a sack of dried lentils over it. He then slid the stone slab cover of the silo into place, and went across the street to see his beloved.

The sun had now set. It was the Sabbath. All true worshipers of the God of Abraham rested.

CHAPTER 14

On Saturday night, when the Sabbath had ended, and Joshua and his five thugs had fallen asleep, Zillah took her knife and cut a lock of hair from each of her son's comrades. Some of them stirred slightly, but she didn't care. Nothing would deter her from her mission tonight. Besides, they were so intoxicated, they wouldn't know what she was doing even if she did wake them. Zillah put each lock of hair into the leather pouch that already held the swatches she had previously cut from their clothing. The woman went to the door, silently opened it and stepped out into the foggy night. In the distance she heard a lone jackal howl as it prowled the hills in search of night prey. The milky fog was so dense that she could barely see directly in front of her. With her arm extended, she felt her way along the buildings, counting them as she passed. She had to be quiet; everyone slept outside during the festival. She finally reached the town gate, and the commons. Her steps were slower now because of the open area. Zillah almost fell into the town's water trough, but the near-accident helped her regain her bearings.

She traveled along Well Street, using the buildings that formed the city wall as a guide. The woman finally came to the end of the street at the base of the hill. There was a small opening there between the last building and the hillside's rocky base. Children often used it to exit the city undetected, so they could go play in the meadows in the lush valley below. Zillah wouldn't be going that far tonight; she just needed to make her way to the stand of scrub oaks that grew on the hillside. She was a thin woman, so by inhaling and contorting her body a bit, she managed to maneuver through the narrow passage between the building and the rock formations. When she finally reached the steep path, she swept the ground with each foot before she moved forward to make sure she didn't stray from it. An owl screeched in the distance just as her shoulder struck a rocky outcropping. In her fright she let out a muffled scream. Zillah wasn't too concerned; she was far enough away from town. No one could have heard her.

The rocky, arch-like formation was the indicator that guided her to turn right and head up the hill once more. She lowered herself to the ground, and crawled on her hands and knees through the fog. For guidance, Zillah kept her shoulder in contact with the wall of the hillside as she worked her way up to the stand of oaks. Zillah's skin began to crawl. She knew that she was close, for she could hear the shrill squeaking of rats as they scurried about. Some of them ran over her hands and shoulders. But nothing could deter her from reaching her destination tonight—nothing whatsoever.

320

Zillah began to smell a horrible acrid stench, even more offensive than that of the men her son brought into her home. As her hand reached forward, it landed on something hard, cold and leathery. She trembled uncontrollably and whimpered. The woman realized what she had touched—a human foot. The long, unkempt toenails cut into the palm of Zillah's hand. The foot felt lifeless; the woman thought it belonged to a corpse. She wanted to scream, but she kept silent. Zillah was really rattled when she heard the high, squeaky voice of the witch. "I've been expecting you, my dearie," the old hag said.

Puzzled, Zillah looked up and asked, "How did you know I was coming?"

The fog lifted a bit. Zillah noticed the deep wrinkles in the old witch's unwashed face. Her eyes were so bloodshot that they had no whites left in them. Her unkempt, wiry, slate-gray hair was entangled with bits of straw and crud. The hag opened her toothless mouth, and saliva drooled down her chin. "I knew that you'd be coming by tonight from the first night your son brought his five friends over to your home, dearie!" Zaddu said. "The badger entrails told me so. Now, dearie, give me the silver coins so I can help you." Zillah gave her two shekels. As she looked past the witch, the desperate woman noticed the glow of a campfire illuminating the fog in the distance.

"Let's go sit by the fire, dearie. I'll make you a potion so you can enter the spirit realm, and then you'll have your requests granted. I already know what they are, but you yourself have to ask the spirits for them." The hag led her to the campfire

321

and instructed Zillah to sit. The milky white haze that surrounded them mysteriously evaporated. She shuddered as she saw the witch sit down, and watched as the rats gathered in and under the hag's baggy, ragtag garment.

The witch's clothes at first seemed to be black, but as Zillah gazed at them more intensely, she realized they were just filthy from never being washed. The sorceress poured some steaming water into a filthy cup, then added some strange-looking mushrooms and other herbs to form a brew. "Let's let this steep for a while, dearie. Meanwhile, I'll go get what I need for conjuring." When she stood, the rats squeaked as they fell out of her clothing and landed on the ground. They began to scurry around her filthy feet. Some just ran up her torn clothing and nestled in her hair.

Zillah began to shake uncontrollably as she watched the witch walk toward the cave. Zaddu's body was bent so low at the waist that she looked as if she was about to topple over. A column of rats trailed behind her as she walked. The thought of sitting alone in the presence of such extreme evil frightened her to the core. In the distance, she heard a pack of jackals that were obviously fighting over the same prey. Not only could she hear their howls, but she also heard their growling and barking as they tore at each other's flesh to win the opportunity to devour the captured victim.

When the witch returned with the tools of her trade, a swarm of bats followed her. They swooped down low over Zillah's head. She frantically thrashed her arms above her to ward them off, for fear they would land on her head. Finally the winged creatures swooped upward and away as the hag sat down next to Zillah and handed her the brew.

"Drink all of this, dearie. Then you can ask the spirits for whatever you want." While Zillah drank the horrible-tasting brew, Zaddu placed statuettes of gods and goddesses around the campfire. She handed Zillah the most obscene one of them all, and said to hold it in her hand. The sorceress started to chant in sounds that were more of a cadence than actual words. She beat the ground with her staff with such force that the ground shook, forcing the burning embers to release their sparks. They floated up on the heated air and were gobbled up by the darkness above them. The sorceress began to throw fine powders on the fire, and its color changed from white to blazing orange, then to blue, then red, and finally to a sickening shade of green. Emblazoned before her, in bright red on the putrid green smoke, was the image of the obscene idol that she held tightly in her hand. Bright yellow flames shot from its mouth.

"Why have you disturbed me, and what do you ask of me?" a booming voice said. Zillah was shocked to hear the sudden question, because she was in a horrific state, entranced as she watched intently while the evil thing moved before her. "Speak! Speak now!" the voice commanded.

In fright, and with a great deal of trepidation, Zillah began to speak. "I've come to seek the destruction of Joseph Bar Jacob. If it weren't for him, my son would still be living with me today. He's a good boy, you know, my Joshua." She thought she heard laughter when she said that, but the spirit was still expressionless before her.

323

"And as to my son's five companions, I wish them the most painful of deaths, now! Plenty of tortuous suffering is what I want for them. More than the human mind can even think of. That's what I want for them; yes, prolonged, unbearable, torturous suffering!"

The sound Zillah was hearing matched the lip movement of the horrifying thing before her, but she realized the voice actually came from Zaddu's mouth. It was cold, booming, and gravelly all at the same time. It rasped out its words of venomous hate. "We spirits cannot bring harm to Joseph, for the Mighty Hand protects him from us. Only one born of a woman, as evil as he is righteous, can cause him harm, but even that will not end in his death for now. For the spells you wish to have conjured for the five, I require payment—nothing less than your soul."

She debated the offer as well as she could in her hallucinogenic state. She could not, however, rid herself of the hateful rage that welled up within her whenever she thought of her persistent abuse. With shocking resolve she shouted out, "It's yours; my soul is yours!"

The heinous voice laughed as it shouted in a growl like thunder, "Seal it in blood! Seal it in blood!" The old witch leapt up from her place and quickly grabbed the woman's hand as she drew out her knife and ran it over Zillah's four fingers. Zaddu almost yanked the woman's arm from its socket as she jerked her hand forward until it was over the fire. Zillah's blood flowed freely into the blaze. The flames turned an even-more-putrid green as they shot up around their conjoined hands. The witch turned to the woman. Zillah's nostrils filled with the

324

acrid odor of sulfur and rancid meat from the foul breath of Zaddu's toothless mouth. The witch spoke for the Prince of Darkness: "Nothing can break our bond now! You must worship me, and me alone! I now am your god!" The bone-chilling reality of that last remark filled Zillah with terror. *What have I done?* she asked herself, but it was too late. An irrevocable deal had been stuck with Satan himself.

The old witch sat down by the fire once again. "What of the five have you brought me to conjure up the fatal spell?" Zillah took the leather pouch and handed it to Zaddu. The witch worked at the knot on the pouch string with her exceptionally long, discolored fingernails. They curled up so much that they looked more like the talons of a bird of prey than nails. When she finally opened the pouch, she shrieked with glee as she saw hairs and pieces of cloth. "Good! Good! Good!" she squealed, spilling the contents of the pouch into the palm of her left hand. She dug her long claws into the glowing ashes that surrounded the fire and formed some of them into a heap. The outermost tips of her nails caught fire as she did so, but she didn't seem to notice. Zaddu gleefully spread the bag's contents over the glowing ashes, then blew out the fire on her nails.

As the strong odor of singed hair and smoking fingernails drifted on the night air, the old witch began her incantations in a strange, evil-sounding language. Chills ran up Zillah's spine as the hag banged her staff on the ground and crawled around on all fours, howling. The staff produced a loud booming noise that sounded like thunder, and then stopped abruptly. The hag spit five times into the glowing ash. The sizzling sound was amplified by the stillness of the night. Zillah recoiled in fear, as a serpent crawled out from beneath the sorceress's garment. The witch grabbed it by the head, took her knife, and with the blunt side forced it to excrete its venom onto the hot ash heap she had prepared. It caused a blinding, lightning-like flash. For a few moments Zillah could not see. When she regained her sight, she saw the witch let go of the slithery creature. It crawled back into the night as the witch resumed her incantations.

The sorceress finally finished. Zillah heard a clicking sound as the old hag rubbed her hands together, her claw-like nails tapped against each other in the process. She cackled with glee and screeched, "This is a good one, the best I've ever done, my dearie!" She laughed hysterically. Her evil laugh echoed in the still night air. The witch gathered the venomous ashes from the ground. "Now, dearie, listen to Zaddu. You must sift these ashes over the parts of their bodies on which you first want them to experience the most excruciating pain. What's left over, sprinkle over the rest of them. They will be in terrible misery until they finally die. For the spell to be most effective, you must take these idols." She handed Zillah the statuettes of the god and goddess. "You must place them somewhere prominent when you sprinkle the ashes on the five men."

"Who are these idols?" Zillah asked.

"The female idol is the goddess of fertility, Asherah; she's the one you worshiped. The other is the god Baal, whose full name is really Baal-zebub, the Ruler of Darkness, your new master!" The old witch cackled loudly again as an owl screeched in the distance. Suddenly the bird flew toward them. It swooped down and perched itself on Zaddu's hunched back while she put the cursed ashes into Zillah's pouch and handed it back to her. The witch said nothing more. Using her staff, she raised herself to her feet; the owl adjusted itself by moving up her back, more toward her shoulder, as she made her way back to the cave with the rats in tow. The bats too soon followed. The minute the witch entered the cave, the milky white fog once again descended upon everything. Zillah sat there for a moment to contemplate the horrific experience. She then began to crawl on her hands and knees to locate the path that would lead her home.

When Zillah finally found her way back, she quietly opened the door to her house and stepped inside. After setting the idols on a shelf that faced the sleeping men, she sprinkled the ashes over the bare midsection of each of the thugs. She rationed it at first to make sure she would have enough to dust each of them sufficiently. Her smile broadened, for she still had plenty left to sprinkle over their entire bodies. Before sitting down, she lit another candle to better see what would happen. Her night adventure tired her; she had to fight to keep her eyes from closing. But no matter how hard she tried, she couldn't stay awake. Zillah succumbed to somnolence and fell into a deep sleep.

CHAPTER 15

Joseph awoke. As quietly as possible, he slipped out of his sleeping space between the two other men. He walked out of the booth as he yawned, and stretched to get his body used to moving again. It was still dark as he walked across the street to his own home to wash up and change. He had a rather grueling day ahead of him. One by one the others awoke. They all wanted to reach the fields at daybreak. They still had to load the pack animals and gather together all they would need for a full day in the fields.

Joshua started to wake just as Joseph went back to Mary's to begin their trek to the fields. He slowly opened his eyes and saw two candles burning. He couldn't figure out why his mother, who was very frugal, would waste a second candle. Joshua's head pounded from an overabundance of wine as he struggled to stand up. When he did, he steadied himself against the wall, and walked toward his mother, who still slept in a sitting position close to the table. He kicked her in the thigh and said, "I'm hungry, and I need something to eat. Now!"

"Sorry, darling," Zillah said as she began to stand up and stretch her bones. "I didn't mean to sleep this long, dear. Please forgive me." Joshua blocked her view of the five thugs, who remained asleep. For the first time since they had arrived, Zillah was actually anxious to see them.

Joshua looked down at Zillah's tunic. "Your clothes are filthy. You look as if you were rolling around with pigs." She wanted to retort, "I was—your friends are just that," but she didn't want to upset her son, so instead she said she didn't know how she got so dirty, and that she would go change.

"Can't you hear me, old sow?" Joshua snapped. "I told you I was hungry. Feed me first!" She apologized for being so inconsiderate and then sliced a melon, formed some raisin cakes, and spread some flatbread with goat cheese. Meanwhile, Joshua poured himself a cup of wine and sat at the table. He waited for his mother to serve him. As Zillah brought the food over, she glanced at the thugs' midsections. To her delight, numerous pustules were forming. Joshua tore the tray from her hands and began to shove the flatbread into his mouth like a glutton. He spit the cheese-covered bread at her and yelled, "This bread is cold, you old fool! Warm it!"

"I'll make some fresh bread for you, dear," she said, wiping the bread and cheese from her face. "Just eat the other things first. I'll get the flour right now." In her haste to please her son, she didn't notice one of the thugs had extended his arm in his sleep. She tripped over it, knocking over the flour barrel. Seeing the pile of gold and silver coins she had been pilfering from him underneath the barrel, Joshua jumped up

330

from the table, seething with rage. Zillah had never seen him look the way he did now. He resembled the horrible figure she saw in the fire last night.

"You good-for-nothing old sow! You've been stealing from me!" he shouted in a voice filled with fury. Joshua moved closer to her and grabbed the wooden baking paddle. His ranting woke the others. With their bloodshot eyes they watched him advancing toward his mother.

"I'm sorry, sweetheart!" Zillah said. "I wasn't stealing from you or the 'Cause'; I was taking it from *them*." She pointed to his fellow thieves. "It was due me for the way they abused me."

"You stupid fool!" Joshua yelled. "There is no 'Cause'! Idiot! Don't you realize we're just a band of thieves and con artists?!" He tightened his grip on the paddle and began to laugh wickedly. His laughter was venomous and frightening. Zillah cowered as she moved toward the wall, and panicked when she knew she was trapped. She saw him start to swing the paddle in her direction as he continued to laugh. Zillah turned. The side of the paddle struck her in the back with such force that it severed her spinal cord. She sunk to the ground like a piece of discarded clothing. Before her upper torso hit, her neck struck a nearby wicker basket. The impact bruised Zillah's vocal cords and caused her to bite right through her tongue. She couldn't even scream. She just lay there and looked pleadingly at her son. Joshua turned to his men and said, "Sorry, fellas! We're going to have to eat cold bread this morning. Your toy is out of commission."

None of the five actually felt like eating when they saw Zillah's bloody mouth trying to form words as she tried to use the strength of her arms to drag her body to the stable. The agony of her intense pain was clearly evident on her face. When one of the men looked at her, he vomited—and not from the spell, either. Looking at his comrades, Joshua nodded to his mother and said, "I guess you guys picked up something from that fool over there." The men didn't know what he was talking about until they looked down below their navels and saw the result of the witch's curse. The moment their attention was drawn to the pustules, they began to scratch. Their skin clung to their fingernails.

"Put on some clothes!" Joshua yelled. "You're making me sick!" Then the real torment began. Their exposed flesh stung and burned so badly that the men began to moan. The moans grew louder as the sores overspread their entire bodies. They felt as if they were in the blazing flames of hell. The five began to roll around in agony, screaming, as they tried to assuage the horrific pain. Joshua was shocked to see the men's skin fall off right before his very eyes. They were useless to him now, and if their screams got any louder, the townspeople would begin to notice. In his evil, illogical mind, he did the only thing he could do—he grabbed the bakers' paddle and crushed in each of their skulls. He then sat down and finished his breakfast.

I don't need them for what I plan on doing next; I can do it myself, he thought. *All the money is mine now. I don't have to split it with anyone.* He knew nobody would notice one man going into a house, but would be likely to notice six. Joshua waited among the five corpses until sunset. He ignored his mother, who now was so weak that she could no longer move.

Joseph and Mary and her family left for the fields just before Joshua went on his tirade. The sky began to turn from a shade of gray to a soft pink. When Eliud saw Joseph and his family coming, he graciously opened the gate even though the sun hadn't yet risen. They bid him good morning and thanked him for doing so. Mary handed him two barley cakes in gratitude as she passed through. The old man thanked her profusely as he grinned at her with his toothless mouth.

The young carpenter had hoped for a cloudy day, but the sky was perfectly clear. The heat was already unusually oppressive for October, and he had four fields to plow—maybe even five if he did Zillah's. He carried two large skins of water over his shoulders while Mary, who walked along beside him, carried a large wicker basket filled with food for the midday meal. Anna and Tamar walked in front of them while Joachim and Azor followed behind, leading their donkeys that were loaded with large empty straw baskets and additional skins of water and wine. They followed the main road down the hill until it forked; then they turned left. It took them toward the narrower path Zillah had used the night before. At the stone outcropping below the stand of oaks, they could hear Zaddu cackling with glee as she once again practiced her divination on the entrails of an animal. They each spat on the path that led to the sorceress's cave as they passed.

For years the townspeople kept driving out the witch, but she always returned. Witchcraft and sorcery were against the Jewish religion. No one who truly believed and worshiped the God of Abraham would ever consider using her sorcery. They were relatively sure that in the past, Zaddu had kidnapped the babies of some of the women in town to use in her satanic rituals. But no one could ever prove it; she was too cunning.

An autumnal haze still lingered over the valley when they reached the fields near some olive trees. Joachim and Azor insisted on doing some of the plowing, but Joseph wouldn't let them. "I wore my shorter, sleeveless tunic because I wanted to get some sun," he said. It helped to compensate for the scorching heat. Another reason he wore the tunic was to show Mary his impressive biceps. He hoped that once his fiancée saw his muscles, she would feel safe in his presence, knowing he was capable of protecting her. "Besides," Joseph continued, "I have to keep in shape, just in case I land another job where heavy beams are involved." The two men let him have his way. They both felt their age, and were grateful that he insisted on doing the plowing for them. With each passing day, Joachim was more grateful to God for having a man like Joseph as his daughter's future husband.

The carpenter led the communal team of oxen from the small stable. Joachim and Azor helped him hitch the team to the plow. Joseph began digging the furrows while the other men helped the women harvest the vegetables and fruits. After all, Sukkot, the holiday they were still celebrating, was also known as the Festival of Ingathering, a time to celebrate God's providence in providing a fruitful yield. Joseph soon regretted wearing a tunic without sleeves. As the sweat dripped down his forehead, he had no choice but to let it run down his face and sting his eyes. He had nothing to mop his brow with.

By midday he had completed plowing both Azor's and Joachim's fields. Just before he finished, Anna sent Mary over to the olive grove to set out the midday meal. Anna signaled Joseph to come and eat. The five washed up as Joseph made his way back to them. He broke open several bales of hay for the oxen. As the animals ate, he removed his cap and poured the water from one of the skins over his head and body. It stung slightly as it cascaded over his sunburned neck and arms. When he felt he had rinsed off most of the perspiration, he scrubbed his arms and hands until they were clean. He rinsed his cap with water, and put it back on his head. That cooled him down even further.

Joseph then joined the group. After they prayed, Mary served the meal. She sat across from Joseph as they ate. He kept looking at Mary during the entire meal. The young couple continuously smiled at each other. Her intended was so full of compliments for the way in which his fiancée served the meal that she blushed. The two older couples grinned at each other as they listened to Joseph's unending praise of his future wife.

After the meal, Joachim told Joseph to rest for a couple hours. He was worried that if his future son-in-law returned to work too soon in the unbearable heat, he would get heat exhaustion. He suggested Joseph wait until the sun moved farther west before he started plowing again. The thought of going back out into the blinding sun was enough for the young man to take his future father-in-law's advice. After complimenting the women on the meal, he went to lie down in the shade of the olive grove.

The women sat and talked while the men slept. After about an hour, Mary noticed a single dandelion heavily covered with yellow pollen. It grew at the base of the olive tree where Joseph slept on his back with his hands behind his head. Mary got up, tiptoed to the plant and picked the flower. She sat down next to Joseph and softly brushed the blossom under his nose. Instinctively, he lifted his head just enough to move one hand and flicked his fingers toward his nose. When Anna saw what Mary was doing, she shook her finger at her daughter and mouthed, "Let him sleep. He's worked hard today." Mary was intent on being a little more mischievous, so she ignored her mother's plea. Once again she began to brush the flower against his nose.

Joseph's eyes popped open. He quickly snatched the dandelion blossom from Mary's hand. "I caught you!" he said.

"Your nose is all yellow!" Mary replied, giggling.

"Yours is going to be yellow too!" Joseph said as he raised the flower to her nose.

Before it could reach her, Mary sprang to her feet and began to run. She looked over her shoulder and said, "You'll have to catch me first!" She darted off toward the hills, running with the grace and speed of a young gazelle. Anna and Tamar laughed as Joseph began to chase after her.

Although his stride was twice that of Mary's, she was amazed that she managed to retain her lead. Each time she turned around to see where he was, Joseph was on the opposite side she expected him to be. He ran in more of a zigzag pattern to give Mary the impression he was far slower than he actually was. What she didn't realize was that he was directing her toward a cleft in the hill, where she would be trapped. When Mary turned around for the last time, Joseph was directly behind her. She had to stop running; otherwise, she would have run right into the rock formation. The walls of the cleft now surrounded her. Joseph moved toward her, arms extended, as he held the dandelion in his hand. "Oh, you're going to look so pretty with a yellow nose, and maybe yellow lips and yellow cheeks too," he said as he moved toward her, smiling. She moved from side to side, giggling as she did so, in an effort to outsmart him and duck under his outstretched arms. She didn't succeed.

Mary didn't realize that each time she darted forward, Joseph stepped a little closer and she lost ground. Soon her back was against the wall, and she had nowhere to go. Joseph gently grasped her chin with his free hand. Mary giggled and said, "No! No! Please! I don't want a yellow nose!" As Joseph was about to bring the flower up to her face, their eyes met. They both felt as if they were suspended in time. Joseph dropped the flower as he put his arm around her waist and drew her closer to him. He moved his hand and placed it at the back of her neck. He moved his head forward slowly until their lips gently met in a brief tender kiss, then he pulled back. Both felt a glowing warmth spread through them. Mary opened her eyes and saw Joseph staring into them. She took her hand and gently wiped the pollen from his nose. They both smiled. Once again their eyes locked in a visual embrace. She smiled at Joseph, and as he leaned forward again she stood on her toes and put her arms around him as well. Then their lips met again. This time the kiss was more deliberate, a little longer, still gentle, and quite tender, but also with a slight bit of passion. When their lips separated, Mary stood firmly on the ground and put her head on Joseph's chest. They wanted to stay that way forever. The young lovers realized, however, that they had to get back to her family. Reluctantly, they ended their embrace, and walked hand in hand toward the olive grove. The couple didn't speak; everything they had to say was already said in their kiss.

When they returned to the group, they both blushed profusely, as if the rest of them somehow knew what they had done. The minute Mary let go of Joseph's hand and stepped away from him, Joseph began to nervously brush back his side curls with real vigor. Joachim and Anna looked at each other and smiled. They had never seen their daughter's face glow like this before.

"I better get back to my plowing," Joseph said as he walked toward the team of oxen with a sheepish look on his face and with his eyes downcast. Mary turned around and began to busy herself by packing the produce they had harvested.

Joachim walked up to his wife and whispered in her ear, "Did we act so nervous and jumpy the first time we kissed?" They both laughed at his remark.

By sundown, Joseph had completed their fields and most of Zillah's. He stopped the team of oxen at the end of a furrow and ran up to Joachim. "Father, why don't all of you go home now while it's still light. I just have a small amount of plowing to finish. That way you can unload the harvest, and the women can prepare dinner. Just ask Eliud to open the gate for me if I don't return until after sundown. Tell him I'll knock three times, pause, and knock three times again. Don't wait dinner for me. I set aside some melons. I'll just eat them here. When I get home, I'd like to clean up and change before I come over. So I probably won't join all of you in the booth until rather late in the evening. Tell Mary not to worry about me."

"Are you sure you don't want us to wait for you? I think Mary would like that."

"No, no!" Joseph said. "Waiting for me would just be a waste of time."

"If that's what you want," Joachim replied. He reached forward to give Joseph a parting kiss and a hug. Joseph told him not to get too close because he probably smelled a little ripe. Both men laughed. As they were about to leave, Joachim told Joseph he was a very good man. The young carpenter cast his eyes to the ground, embarrassed by the compliment. The two men then parted. Joseph returned to finish plowing Zillah's field.

Just before Mary and her family returned to town, Joshua left his mother's house and went down the street to Joseph's. As he walked along, he looked for a small, rounded pebble. He finally found the one he was looking for. Picking it up, he held it tightly in the palm of his hand. When he arrived at Joseph's door, he looked around to see if anyone was watching. The street was empty, so he opened the door, went inside and put the pebble on the table. Joshua then removed the shill stone from the wall. He took out a small bag of coins as well as the golden jewelry and the knives. He sat down and counted the money in the diminishing twilight. When he was done, he lowered the tarp over the windows. Striking up a flint fire, Joshua lit a candle he stole from his mother's house. He undid the rope he had tied around his waist and looked for a hammer. He had no trouble finding one, for Joseph had several. Joshua also found an awl. His sadistic mind thought up ways he could use it. Joshua smiled as his eyes glowed with evil intent. He took the awl with him too. Then he went and sat by the door, waiting for Joseph to return home.

Joseph finished Zillah's field while the rim of the sun still lingered on the hilltop. He hurriedly unhooked the oxen, fed and watered them, and put the empty waterskin over his shoulder. He ran for the town gate, hoping to make it before the sun completely set, so Eliud wouldn't have to bother opening the gate again just for him. The carpenter felt sorry for the old man; the gates were high and very heavy. Joseph marveled at the fact that Eliud could still perform the task at his ripe old age. Joseph raced the sun. As he passed the fork in the road, he began to run faster, seeing that the gates were closing. "Eliud! Eliud!" he shouted almost breathlessly. "I'll be right there; don't close the gate yet!" When he arrived, he managed to slip through the small space that was still open. Once inside, Joseph bent over and placed his hands on his knees as he tried to catch his breath. Eliud apologized for not hearing Joseph's call. "That's all right, Eliud. It's my fault," Joseph said as he patted the old man's back. "I'm the one who's late; you were just conscientiously doing your job, as you always do."

"Let me get you some water; from the looks of the way that you're sweating, I don't think you have much left in you. And your waterskin looks empty too."

"I'd appreciate that, my friend," Joseph said. The old man brought him a bucket of water. He drank some of it and poured the rest over his head. The carpenter shook his head back and forth several times to clear the water from his face. "Sorry, Eliud!" Joseph said as he noticed the old man wiping droplets of water from himself. "I didn't mean to get you all wet. I just tried to cool down a bit. I don't ever remember it being this hot before in October."

Joseph regretted saying that the moment he said it. Eliud started one of his "I remember when..." stories that seemed to last forever. Joseph listened politely as the old man told his tale. By the time he was done, the older townsmen began to gather at the gate to talk about their day. Joseph thanked the gatekeeper again, greeted the men, and hurriedly ran home. He still felt so sweaty and dirty that he couldn't wait to get inside to wash and change. As he neared his house, he looked toward Mary's courtyard. Everyone was still inside, sorting the produce. As he opened his door, he saw a lit candle and a round pebble on the table. *Mary must have done this,* he said to himself with a smile. Joseph thought the pebble might be some sort of love token.

Living outside had helped Joshua develop a keen sense of hearing. Though Joseph wore no sandals, Joshua could still hear Joseph's large feet hit the ground as he headed toward the house. He grabbed the handle of the hammer and stood against the wall, so the open door would shield him from Joseph's view. Joshua was so used to violence that neither his breathing nor his pulse increased. He calmly raised the hammer over his head and waited for Joseph to enter.

As the door closed, Joseph immediately felt something strike his skull. A searing blast of pain coursed through his whole nervous system. Suddenly everything went blank. The carpenter's legs gave out from under him. He fell to the floor. Joshua stayed where he was until Joseph closed the door. The tyrant knew the difference between a knockout blow and a blow to kill. He needed information from his victim, so he delivered the former. After he struck Joseph with the hammer, he stood and watched him sink to the ground. He quickly bound the carpenter's hands behind him and hog-tied his feet. Joshua formed a noose and hung it around the carpenter's neck. He threaded its end through the rope around Joseph's hands.

Bending Joseph's knees to a 90-degree angle, he tied the line from the noose to the rope that bound Joseph's feet. That way, if he tried to move his arms or use his feet to defend himself, the noose would tighten and start to strangle him. The masochist gagged Joseph. He turned Joseph's head so his earlobe rested on the hard-packed clay, and drove the awl right through it. He yanked it out and took the heavy dangly golden earring the carpenter was saving as a wedding gift for Mary, and threaded the open hoop through the bleeding hole in Joseph's earlobe.

When he finished the gruesome task, he wiped his bloodstained hands on Joseph's tunic and sat on the floor, facing him, until consciousness returned to his victim. When he saw his eyes begin to open, Joshua said, "Where's my water pipe and my stash, Joseph? Everybody says you're an honorable man. It isn't right to get rid of something that doesn't even belong to you. Is it, Joseph? What would Mary think if she found out you do things like that? Huh! I'll take that gag off of you soon if you promise to be a good boy and be quiet." Joshua wanted to wait until the music and noise of these celebratory nights filled the air. They would mask any sounds or moans his victim might make.

Joseph felt a burning, stinging pain in his ear as he awoke. He started to struggle, but when he did, the noose tightened around his neck, and he found it hard to breathe. Joseph could say nothing with the gag in his mouth, but he still would have been silent even if Joshua had already removed it.

As Joshua waited for the celebrating to start, Mary made raisin and fig cakes for the evening meal. Because they spent their day in the fields, dinner tonight would consist of cold foods only—basically, the produce of their harvest with smoked fish, and raisin and fig cakes for desert. Mary couldn't understand why she was filled with so much anxiety. *Maybe it's because I've gotten used to having Joseph join us for dinner every night,* she said to herself. As much as she tried to relax, she just couldn't. She finished making the last fig cake, and told Anna that she was going out for a moment to get some fresh air. "I won't be long, Momma; I just feel so uneasy tonight, I need to walk around a bit." Anna and Tamar smiled at each other as they continued to sort through the fruits and vegetables. They thought Mary was just suffering from separation anxiety.

When Mary stepped outside, the first thing she did was glance at Joseph's house. Everything appeared to be normal. *Joseph mustn't be home yet,* she thought. *He wouldn't have pulled the shades over his windows, not in this heat.* If he was home, she reasoned, she would have been able to see light passing through his windows. She walked around the booth, but instead of calming her, doing so caused her apprehensions to grow. *He wouldn't be able to continue plowing in the dark. Did something happen to him in the field? The mountain lions and hyenas come down to feed at night.* "Oh, Joseph, where are you? I'm so worried," she said softly, and prayed for his safety.

Joachim came out and said, "Mary, I think your mother could still use your help." He saw the worried look on his daughter's face, so he put his arm around her shoulders and asked, "What's the matter, Princess? You look so pensive."

"I'm worried about Joseph, Daddy. I can't see any light coming out of his windows. I don't think he's home yet, and it's been a while since the sun set."

"It hasn't been that long, Princess. Don't forget, he had to unhook the plow, feed the oxen, and he was going to eat there too. He told me to tell you not to worry if he was late." Reluctantly, Mary went back into the house with her father just as the sounds of music, singing, and shouts of "L'chaim! To life!" filled the evening air. Father and daughter smiled at each other as the noises grew louder.

The moment the joyful sounds of Sukkot started, Joshua removed the gag from Joseph's mouth. "It's impolite not to answer a question, Joseph," he said. He kicked the carpenter in the abdomen. Joseph moaned as he tried to bring his knees up to his chest to cope with the pain, but his air supply was threatened. "Joseph, we're friends; let's forget about the water pipe. I'll forgive you for getting rid of it if you just tell me where the rest of your money is. I know you've inherited a fortune."

Joseph still said nothing. Joshua viciously kicked him again, this time in the groin. Joseph's brain warned him not to move, or he would risk strangulation, but his nerve endings overruled his reason. In his agony Joseph began to curl up again from the harrowing pain. He started choking, and his face turned blue. Joshua bent down and loosened the noose. "See, Joseph! I mean you no real harm. I know every inch of this house, because I used to play here while it was vacant, yet I can't find your fortune. Just tell me where the money is and we can part as the good friends we are." Joshua took hold of the earring he had placed in the awl hole in Joseph's ear. He twisted it as he pulled it slowly, and tore the lobe further. The tyrant continued to ask, "Where's the money, Joseph? Just tell me, Joseph! And all this could end right now!" Joseph grimaced, but he wouldn't give Joshua the satisfaction of moaning or screaming. His attacker finally succeeded in tearing Joseph's earlobe in half, but the young carpenter still remained mum.

Joshua grabbed the dirty awl and viciously stabbed it into his victim's bare biceps. Joseph moaned. "I see we're making some progress, my friend," Joshua said, repeatedly stabbing the biceps on both arms until there was barely any flesh left. Although his face contorted in agony, and his groaning grew louder, Joseph still refused to answer. Joshua then said, "You know, Joseph, I never complimented you on your choice of a fiancée. She's a real beauty, that one. She's a pure, lovely girl who probably takes pride in her virginity. Wouldn't it be a shame, Joseph, if early tomorrow morning when she goes to the well, me and my five friends would help her lose it, hmm?"

That was all Joseph needed to hear to break his silence. "The rest of the money is hidden in the legs of my worktable. There's a pry bar along the wall."

"Why, thank you, friend!" But don't call me Joshua any longer—just call me Barabbas. Doesn't that name sound bad, Joseph? Hmm!" Joseph didn't reply.

Mary was very nervous now; she couldn't keep her mind on the sorting. She hadn't stopped praying since

346

she returned to the house. Mary started putting the smaller melons in the same bin with the cucumbers. She prayed unceasingly for Joseph's safety.

Joachim noticed how troubled his daughter looked, so he went over to her and said, "If Joseph isn't home by the time we finish with the produce, I'll go over to his house to see if everything is all right." Mary felt a little better, but she still couldn't rid herself of the apprehensions that haunted her.

When she finished with the basket of produce, she thought to herself, *I'll go outside again to see if any light is coming from his windows.* As tears began to well up in her eyes, she prayed, *Holy Lord God of Israel, please let Joseph be inside when I do.*

Joshua tore at the table legs with the pry bar like the madman he was until he destroyed the faux legs. He finally found what he was looking for. He removed the bags of coins from their hiding place and put them on the table next to the pebble. From the corner of his eye, he saw a pocketed leather apron. He replaced Joseph's gag, then took the apron, put all the loot into the pockets of the garment and laid it on the table as he removed his outer cloak. Joshua went to the stable and brought several bales of straw to the center of the room, setting them close to where Joseph lay. He took a stick, wrapped one of its ends with cloth and dipped it in the melted tallow that welled up in the center of the candle. His plan was going smoother than he had anticipated.

Barabbas slipped into the deeply pocketed apron and replaced his outer cloak. *If anyone notices me, they'll probably think my clothing is a bit bulky,* he thought as he laughed. He lit the torch, raised it in the air and set fire to the thatch on the ceiling that was farthest from the door. "Bye-bye, Joseph!" he said. "Thanks for the jewelry and the money!" He walked to the door and opened it slightly to see if anyone was watching. When he had assured himself the coast was clear, Barabbas slid the small rounded stone into the furthest end of the inside door latch until the metal bar remained upright.

As the flames ate away at the tinder-like thatch, unimaginable brightness filled the room. The roaring yellowish-white tongues of fire leapt across the ceiling, gluttonously searching for anything they could consume. Joshua looked up at the hungry flames and smirked. He threw the torch into the straw bales he had brought in. As he stepped out into the night, he slammed the door shut behind him. The pebble fell to the ground, and the latch fell into the metal slot. The door locked, keeping everyone out, and Joseph trapped inside while the insatiable flames started to lick away at the tarps covering the windows.

No one noticed Joshua as he made his way back to Zillah's house. Though the leather apron was very heavy, his shoulders still moved up and down in rhythm to various tempos that filled the night. He almost felt like dancing. *This sure has been a great day,* he thought as he reached home. When he entered, he struck flint and lit the nighttime candle. He was shocked to see that while he was gone, Zillah had regained some of her strength and managed to use her hands to slide halfway to the door. "Oh no you don't, Mommy!" he said, dragging the woman back to the remotest part of the

348

stable. He stomped on both her hands until he heard her bones break. "You're not going to spoil my day by inviting anyone else to my party," the spawn of Satan said, laughing hysterically.

Barabbas poured himself a cup of wine, and prepared something to eat. He sat at the table and ate amongst the fleshless rotting corpses of his fellow thugs. He didn't want them to think him rude, so he raised his cup of wine to them. "L'chaim! To life! My good friends! L'chaim! And from now on, it's going to be a great one for me."

After Barabbas left, the heat and smoke from the burning straw caused Joseph's eyes to water. As the tears streaked down his face, his nose began to run. His parched throat was dry and raw; it pained him as he struggled to breathe and swallow. It felt as if the fire itself was raging in his very throat. The flames kept eating their way across the thatch above, and his exposed skin stung badly from the intense heat. He closed his eyes in an effort to protect them, for fear of going blind. As the fire licked at the moist layer of clay above the thatch, billows of dark-black smoke began to descend upon him. Joseph coughed repeatedly; the gag that was still in place over his mouth muffled the sound. His burning lungs could no longer cope with the acrid vapors or the lack of oxygen in the room, and his breathing became laborious. *Holy and Mighty Lord, forgive me my sins, and show me Your mercy,* he prayed. *Please watch over Mary for me too.* Then he sunk into the dark void of unconsciousness.

As the flames from the burning hay moved closer to Joseph, Mary, lost in thought, put the last small melon into the cucumber bin. She was so anxious that she couldn't think straight anymore. "Daddy! I'm going outside to see if Joseph is home!" Her instincts told her to go and check this very moment. She ran to the door and stepped outside. Panic gripped her as she screamed, "Daddy! I smell smoke! And I think it's coming from Joseph's house!"

Joachim went to the door; he almost had to shout to be heard over the celebratory sounds that filled the evening. "Probably just the smoke from cooking fires, Princess."

"No, Daddy, it's coming from Joseph's house! I know it! Please do something! I know Joseph's inside, Daddy! I just know it! Please! Please!" the frightened girl said.

As soon as Joachim stepped outside, Mary's suspicions were confirmed. "Azor! Joseph's house is on fire!" he shouted. "Mary, you stay where you are, and don't move! Don't cross the street for any reason!" Still shouting, he instructed the other two women, "Anna! Go and get the physician! Tamar, let everyone know that Joseph's house is burning! Azor, come with me! I think Joseph is inside!"

Had Joseph not lost consciousness when he did, he would have heard a sound like thunder shaking his door. Joachim threw his body against it. Azor, with his tunic raised above his knees, kicked at it. Tamar ran through the streets, screaming, *"Fire! Fire! At Joseph Bar Jacob's!"* Her voice was so loud that it could have raised the dead. Anna ran in the opposite direction, yelling the same thing. The music and laughter stopped immediately as the townsmen ran, filled buckets with water and ran to Joseph's house. Mary stood right where her father commanded. She put her hand to her mouth and bit her nails, trembling. She watched in horror as the haphazard pandemonium that only a fire can cause played out before her tear-filled eyes. She hadn't stopped praying since she first suspected something was wrong with Joseph. Glistening tears ran down her cheeks as the flames leapt up and illuminated the nighttime sky.

A small section of roof at the back of Joseph's house collapsed. The lambent flames now began to crawl up the window shades. Mary shuddered at the sight, thinking Joseph might be trapped inside. She watched as her father and uncle frantically tried to break down the door. Suddenly she remembered the message of the heavenly being: "Do not be afraid!" Those words of comfort echoed in her head. She felt an amazing calm fill her as she stopped biting her nails, and lowered her hands to her sides. Mary's breathing returned to normal as she quietly said, "Your will is to bless us, not to do us harm." Mary recalled the words of one of the psalms. *"I will depend on You my God alone, I will put my hope in You, for You alone can save us."* When she finished whispering those words, the door to Joseph's house miraculously flew open.

The pounding force of Joachim's body against the door, and Azor's constant kicking, sent vibrations through the iron door-latch, causing it to rattle and slide up at last. Fortunately, it was Azor's foot, not Joachim's body blow, that was the *fait accompli*, or else Joachim would have gone flying through the doorframe right into the inferno within. The heat from the raging fire almost seared their eyeballs. The townsmen drenched the two men with buckets of water to hold back the consuming flames. The younger men acted as water-bearers. The older men mounted the stairway to the roof and formed a bucket brigade. They provided a constant supply of water in an attempt to douse the flames that now flared up through the opening of the collapsed roof section.

Joachim grabbed the end of his cloak and raised it over his head to shield his face from the burning heat as he moved toward Joseph; Azor did likewise. When they reached him they saw his blood-stained body. He appeared lifeless. Because the carpenter was so covered with perspiration, and had drenched his cap, clothes and head with water earlier, the fire hadn't leapt to him yet. Joachim still carried his harvesting knife in a sheath tied to his waist. When he reached for it, the skin on his fingers stung and blistered; the intense heat had already transferred itself to the metal. But his adrenaline wouldn't allow him to react to the intense pain until after he had cut the cord of the noose that encircled Joseph's throat. Azor and he carried Joseph out into the street. The two men coughed so badly, they could barely catch their breath.

Anna arrived with the physician just as the two men set Joseph's body down in the middle of the street while Mary watched and prayed. The girl trusted God completely; she knew Joseph would be all right. Anna grabbed her face between her hands and shook her head as she cried, "No! No! Lord!" She was certain Joseph was dead. The physician wasted no time. He told Joachim and Azor to move to the other side of the street, where the air was fresher, and breathe deeply; he would check them later. The doctor then knelt by Joseph and tore open the upper part of his tunic. After pinching Joseph's nostrils together and breathing several deep breaths into his mouth, he placed his fingers on the young man's neck, over the carotid artery. He couldn't feel a pulse, so he put his ear on Joseph's bare chest, over his heart. After listening for a while, he shook his head. The physician repeated the entire procedure several more times with no results. He placed his ear to Joseph's chest once again, and kept it there for quite a while as he listened carefully. He shook his head again, and then stood up to make the dire pronouncement.

All of sudden the physician heard a gasp. At first he thought it had come from Anna. When he heard it again, he knelt down next to Joseph and placed his ear on Joseph's chest yet again. The doctor placed his finger in his opposing ear to block out all other sounds. This time he heard it—a very faint, irregular heartbeat. He backed his head away as he observed Joseph's chest struggling to rise and fall.

"He's alive!" he said to Anna. "Just barely, though!" The physician stopped two of the stronger water-runners and told them to move Joseph away from the building just as Tamar returned. She hugged Anna and they both wept.

"Take him to my house," Anna said. "We'll care for him there. Mary, start boiling some water. Joseph's alive and his wounds need to be cleansed."

As they had been directed to do, Azor and Joachim were sitting in the booth under the olive tree, breathing heavily and still coughing. Mary had just brought them some water for their parched, stinging throats. "I know Joseph's going to be all right. I put all my trust in the Almighty," she said to her father just as she heard Anna call out to her. She ran into the house and filled a kettle with fresh water.

Joachim still coughed as he ran for the flint, and started a fire as Azor ran for tinder. Mary's father grabbed the kettle from her and hung it over the new flame. "Go to him, Princess! I'll take care of this. I think he needs to hear your voice right now." Mary needed no coaxing. She had wanted to be by Joseph's side from the moment he was carried from the inferno, but she didn't want to get in the way of the physician or the water-runners. Furthermore, she had thought that if she did run to him then, it would show a lack of faith and trust in God's providence.

There was total bedlam in the streets as the fire raged. Barabbas counted on it to make his escape. The bucket brigade had to pass right by Zillah's house as they went to refill their buckets at the well. The route they all took passed right by the locked town gate. Eliud had abandoned his post to participate in the brigade. Barabbas grabbed his mother's bucket and followed the townsmen, acting as if he intended to head toward the well. When he reached the town gate, he feigned stumbling. In their continued effort to bring water to Joseph's house, none of the men noticed him. Barabbas lifted the timber from the slots in the gate and opened the huge doors. When he was sure no one could see him, he slipped through the gate into the night. No one saw the devil's spawn leave.

The flames had consumed virtually every particle of combustible matter in Joseph's home. As a result, his mule died of smoke inhalation. The water and lack of fodder turned the flames into glowing embers, then into columns of thick black smoke. As they carried Joseph into her house, Mary ran to his side. She cried when she saw his bloody face and arms. "Joseph! Joseph! It's me, Mary!" she shouted. "Please don't give up! I need you, Joseph! I love you!"

The moment the two men set Joseph down, the physician began barking orders. He told the two to lower the shades to prevent the smoke from further entering the house. Then he called out for all the items he needed. Mary ran to get a needle and thread, while Anna looked for a bolt of unused linen. Tamar ran home to get her apothecary bag and all the balms she had. "Is the water boiling yet?" the doctor called out to Joachim.

"It's just simmering," Joachim shouted back.

"Bring it in anyway! I need to get started now! And close the door behind you to keep the smoke out."

Joachim carried in the steaming water while Azor followed close behind, still coughing. Tamar made it into the house just before the door closed behind them. As soon as she entered, the elderly woman spread out all of her herbs and balms next to the doctor. She quickly rattled off what they were. The physician ordered the women out of the room so Joachim and Azor could bathe Joseph before he started his procedures. When they left, the doctor moistened a small piece of cloth and squeezed it into Joseph's parted lips. He watched Joseph's neck carefully to see if his Adam's apple moved. It did. He lifted Joseph's head and poured a little more water into his mouth. Joseph swallowed without too much difficulty.

"He's dehydrated," the physician said. "See to it that someone gives him very, very small sips of water day and night. He's running a fever, and he needs water regularly. Whatever made the puncture marks on his earlobe and his biceps was probably dirty. I think he may be fighting a serious infection too." The doctor then began to add Tamar's powders and herbs to one of her balms. He stitched Joseph's earlobe back together and then began to rub the balm he'd prepared into all of Joseph's wounds.

After the doctor finished, Joachim and Azor wrapped Joseph's body in the bolt of unused linen, as directed. The women were told they could come back in. Mary hurried to Joseph's side. The physician showed Anna and Tamar how to prepare a healing brew that was to be administered three times a day. Mary raised Joseph's head and cradled it in her lap. She kissed his forehead and then began to gently stroke his face. As the doctor prepared to leave, he whispered to Joachim and Anna, "I don't think Joseph will live. I did everything I could, but I think it would take a miracle to save him. His lungs might have been singed. His breathing is too laborious. His heartbeat is too weak and irregular to expect a recovery at this point. All I really could suggest is that you make him as comfortable as possible. I'll check on him in the morning but, to be honest, I don't think he'll make it through the night. The only thing the poor man has going for him is the love of your family, and his age. All any of us can do at this point is pray." Joachim and Anna thanked him and tried to pay the doctor for his services. He refused to accept anything. "This has been a terrible tragedy for Joseph and your entire family. I couldn't live with myself if I capitalized on such an unfortunate set of events."

When the physician left, the rabbi came over and sat with the family. Mary stayed by Joseph's side through the entire night, placing cold compresses on his forehead, giving him small sips of water, administering the herbal brew and running her fingers through his thick black hair. "Joseph, don't worry!" she whispered as she leaned her head close to his ear. "I know that the Holy One is with us. He doesn't want us to be afraid. He will heal you; He will bind up your wounds."

Just before sunrise, Joseph opened his eyes and stared at Mary. The whites of his eyes were blood-red from the smoke. In his delirium, and with a hoarse, raspy voice, he said, "Mary, no well, don't go, Mary! Don't go well, Mary, no!" The five others who were still there ran to his side just as his eyes closed again, and he slipped back into unconsciousness.

"None of you women are going to go to the well alone for a while," Joachim said. "The monster that did this may still be around." Azor wholeheartedly agreed.

"We all know who did this," Tamar said. "It was Joshua, that devil incarnate." The rabbi, who usually found the good in everyone and always tried to defend them, said nothing. None of the others in the room seemed to disagree with her statement either.

As dawn finally broke, there still was no improvement in Joseph's condition. He was able to swallow tiny sips of water and the lung-worth brew that Mary administered to him, but there was no real change in his condition. The rabbi left to go home and freshen up just as the physician arrived. He checked Joseph's heart and breathing, shaking his head as he did so. The doctor unwrapped Joseph's biceps, took the dressing off his earlobe and shook his head again. Anna had kept a kettle of water boiling throughout the night just in case it was needed. The doctor used it to re-cleanse Joseph's wounds.

Mary still sat with Joseph's head on her lap. The physician knew better than to ask her to leave. After he salved the wounds and dressed them, he said, "Joseph's wounds are severely infected, and they seem to be getting worse. His fever is still very high. I still can't believe he made it through the night, but his heartbeat seems to be a little stronger and more regular today. That's a very good sign. I would feel a lot more optimistic about his recovery if he would start coughing. That would indicate that his lungs are beginning to clear. I'll be back later in the day to check on him again." The doctor left.

Earlier, before the sun rose, as Eliud was about to open the city gates he saw the town physician heading toward Mary's house to check on his patient. "Doctor, how is Joseph doing?" the old man asked with a look of deep concern on his face. The physician replied that it was touch-and-go for the young man. His life now was in the Lord's hands. "Poor Joseph," Eliud said. "In his short life he's experienced more sorrow than most people four times his age."

"It's a real shame," the doctor agreed. "His life so far has been that of a modern-day Job."

As they were about to continue their conversation, someone began to pound on the gate. "I'll be there in a minute!" Eliud shouted, then said, "I may be needing your services before you know it, Doctor. Last night I could swear I locked the gate at sunset, when Joseph returned from the fields. Funny thing is, though, when I came back from the fire, the gate was wide open."

"I wouldn't worry too much about it, Eliud. Confusion reigned last night. Our minds can play some pretty strange tricks on us when it does."

The pounding got louder and more urgent-sounding. The physician bid the old man farewell and started to walk toward Mary's house as Eliud yelled back at he top of his voice, "I hear you! I'm coming!" He shuffled his feet as he made his way to the gate and lifted the crossbeam from its brackets. Three men slipped through the opening as soon as there was enough room for them to do so. "What's so important that you couldn't wait until the gate was fully opened?" Eliud asked.

"We're Zealots, and we're looking for a place to hide out for a day," the leader said. "Our spy told us there are Roman troops combing the hillside, looking for us."

Eliud thought the Romans had learned that Joshua was in town, and he mentioned it to the men. "That fool!" the Zealot said. "He never was in our movement, but that con artist sure is convincing. He's duped a lot of folks in this northern region. He's just a common thief and swindler who makes all of us Zealots look bad. Our movement hasn't even received a copper coin from him, yet he tells such convincing stories that people contribute to him heartily. He's not interested in the liberation of our people; the only thing he wants to liberate is the poor from what little money they may have."

Eliud hadn't contributed to Joshua's "Cause" because he just didn't trust him. The thought of him duping all his fellow townspeople irked him no end. "There's a tunnel under my quarters that leads outside of the gate just in case the soldiers enter the town while you're still here," he told the Zealot. "Not too many people know about it. I'll give you shelter and food if you'll tell the townspeople what you just told me. Maybe some of them can still get their money back from those swindlers since Joshua is still here." The group leader said he would be most willing to do so. Perhaps that would restore some honor back to their Zealot cause and expose the cheat once and for all.

The gatekeeper picked up his ram's horn and blew it three times. It was a signal to the townspeople to gather in the commons. His fellow citizens soon began to arrive, some still yawing and partly dressed from being awakened so early in the morning. When a sufficient number had gathered, Eliud introduced the Zealots. The leader relayed how Zillah, Joshua and his comrades had duped them. Several people in the crowd now understood why some of their valuables were gone when they had returned from Joshua's meeting. "I thought I'd just misplaced the new knife I purchased for a sizable amount of money," one man said. Another added, "Me too. I had two gold denarii missing from my house." Others began to mention what they were missing. The crowd soon whipped itself up into a frenzy when they realized what Joshua and his band had done.

360

People ran home and returned with pitchforks, hoes and clubs. The Town Elders, instead of trying to restore calm, had also been duped, so they too joined the mob. Asa, who arrived at the scene a little later, couldn't dissuade the crowd from getting their revenge. They shoved him aside as they stormed through the streets until they reached Zillah's house. Kicking open the door, they found the five rotting corpses, and Zillah three-quarters of the way to the door, struggling on her elbows to drag herself forward. The stench in the room was unbearable; the men who had entered were already gagging. One man spotted the idols on the shelf. There was no need for a trial. Zillah was not only guilty of robbing them; she was also guilty of idolatry. The punishment was death by stoning. Zillah couldn't speak; her tongue had swollen so much that her face was distorted, and her vocal cords were still badly damaged. She tried to plead with her arms while her broken finger flapped loosely in the air. Tears filled her eyes as she begged for mercy. The crowd had none. Some of the townspeople dragged her body to the precipice at the end of town. It was the same place where Zillah had disposed of her husband's body over a week ago. They threw her into the gorge below and stoned her until there was no life left within her. Her dead body lay next to the corpse of her late husband, whose remains were no longer recognizable from that height.

The townsfolk who stayed behind at Zillah's house searched for Joshua but couldn't find him. They had no idea whether one of the corpses was his or not. When their search ended, the people began to carry in bales of dry straw and thorn branches. The angry men laid the flammable matter in the center of the room. One of them took a stick and knocked the idols off the shelf into the heap of combustibles. There were still hot coals in a nearby fire pit; a little fanning soon produced a flame. They tossed the fire into the straw bales and watched for a few seconds as the greedy flame spread and began to consume everything within its reach. They left the house and shut the door tightly.

So ended the life of Zillah the murderous gossip; none of her possessions were left either. The only thing that remained of the vile woman was the devilish son she had spawned. He was still alive, and more willing than ever to perpetrate more evil acts on the people of the land.

Last night, when Joshua crossed the path that led to the witch's cave, Zaddu cackled in an eerie, high-pitched voice. She looked down at the rats that nestled in her filthy clothing and said to them, "My dearies, there's finally someone more evil than me!" She began to laugh hysterically. The creepy sound of her frightening laughter echoed throughout the hills. The townspeople never heard it, though; they were too busy fighting the fire at Joseph's house.

CHAPTER 16

There is a saying that "time heals all wounds," and so it was with Joseph's. He finally was able to cough and breathe more easily. The physician and all of Mary's family members had almost given up hope, but Mary never did. She trusted in her God to heal Joseph, and her trust and confidence in the Lord was rewarded by his total recovery. It was a slow process, but Mary never left the side of her beloved until he regained consciousness and was able to sit up by himself. When he reached that point in the recovery process, Mary would spend her nights at her aunt and uncle's while Joseph stayed with her parents until his house was repaired.

When Joseph's wounds had completely healed, Mary helped him regain the strength he had lost in his biceps. She assisted him in lifting small boulders at first, then graduating them in size and weight until full strength was restored to his arms. The young couple talked and laughed together as they planned their future. During his period of recovery, they grew closer with each passing day. Mary finally admitted to her fiancé that she was the one who cleaned his house and oiled his tools while he apprenticed with his uncle.

She also told him she couldn't wait for his return. By the first week of December, during the height of the winter's rainy season, Joseph was as physically fit as he was before the robbery. Unfortunately, his financial situation had deteriorated badly.

Barabbas had robbed Joseph of more than half of his inheritance, as well as everything he had earned through his carpentry work. The seller of the hillside property Joseph had agreed to purchase was heartless. He demanded of the Council of Elders that as long as Joseph still lived, the contract was in effect. He could care less that the money Joseph intended to use as payment was stolen from him. The seller insisted on the full price Joseph had agreed to pay; otherwise, according to the law, he was entitled to Joseph's home and fields. The Council, which was made up of a group of honest men of high moral character, had to follow the law and agree with the seller. When the Chief Elder came to regretfully notify Joseph of their decision, the carpenter was distraught. Joachim and Azor told Joseph they would pay the seller. Their future-in-law could repay them at his convenience from the inheritance that was still on deposit in Jerusalem.

The townspeople rallied together to help Joseph as much as they could, but Barabbas had robbed them too—not only by his con, but also by his thugs who stole their personal property while Joshua delivered his speeches. They brought what little they could to aid in the rebuilding of Joseph's home, but Joachim and Azor had to dig deeply into their savings once again to pay for most of the supplies. Mary did her part too. She gave all of the jewelry Rebecca had left to her, as well as the expensive purple fabric and brocades, to Nabu. He was going to Sepphoris, a much-larger town than Nazareth. She asked him if he would be so kind as to sell her things there, where the market for such items was much more lucrative and would bring a higher price. Nabu did as Mary requested, but the items didn't sell for as much as Mary had hoped.

Joseph had asked Rabbi Asa, who was going to Jerusalem for the Feast of Hanukkah, to withdraw the balance of his inheritance and bring it back to him when he returned. The good rabbi agreed to do so, but didn't expect to be back until mid-January. The weary young man began to question his decision to marry. His beloved deserved more than an impoverished carpenter. After Mary left for her aunt and uncle's one night, Joseph asked Joachim if he thought it would be best for his daughter to give her a writ of divorce. "Mary is too wonderful to waste her life sharing it with a poor carpenter like me. I'll have to spend most of what I have to repay my debt and re-establish my business."

Joachim was shocked by the statement. "Do you love her, Joseph?" he asked.

"You know I do, Father, now more than ever."

"And she loves you, Joseph! I don't think my Mary could ever give her heart to anyone else. If you two love each other, every obstacle in life will cause that love to grow and not diminish. Together, and with faith in the Almighty, you can overcome any hardship that life may bring your way. Believe me, Joseph, if you have the right woman at your side, even the direst of circumstances will be a source of amusement to you both in your old age."

When the rabbi returned from the Holy City with the rest of Joseph's inheritance, the carpenter still insisted on giving the rabbi the tithes he had committed himself to on the night when they first discussed his inheritance. The rabbi tried to dissuade him based on his current circumstances, but Joseph said, "The money was promised with the Lord as my witness, and I have to fulfill my obligation. Otherwise, my word means nothing, and neither does my faith in the Lord." Rabbi Asa reluctantly took the money and distributed it as Joseph had requested.

That night, Joseph paid Joachim and Azor what he owed them. There was still a small amount left with which he could complete his house and buy new tools, as the fire's intense heat had warped most of his saw blades. Before returning to her aunt and uncle's for the night, Mary took Joseph aside and handed him the money she had earned from the sale of the jewelry and the expensive cloth. "Joseph, I know what you're going to say, so just don't say anything. This money is not mine; it's ours. Use it however you see fit. It'll help us rise above this calamity. And I don't want you worrying about our future, for our God will provide for us." Joseph reluctantly took the money and kissed his fiancée on the forehead. He realized how foolish he was to even consider giving this wonderful woman a writ of divorce. He knew he couldn't live without her.

The next morning, Joseph went back into his house for the first time since the fire. The townsmen had even whitewashed the walls to conceal the char marks. Joseph immediately went to the ground silo and lifted the stone lid. He reached into the hole and removed the bag of lentils. The dried legumes absorbed most of the water that was used to put out the fire on that disastrous night, leaving the treasure chest relatively undamaged. Now more than ever he wanted to finish his special project for his love. Every spare moment Joseph had was spent working on the beautiful little chest.

By the beginning of March, Joseph's carpentry business was thriving once again. He, Mary and her entire family were to go to Jerusalem to celebrate the Passover. Joachim, with a little of Azor's help, had a lot of leather products he wanted to take to the Holy City. Hundreds of thousands of people would converge on Jerusalem for the celebration. Joachim knew he could sell most of his inventory there. Joseph too had made several leather-upholstered stools, wall shelves and hand-carved items. Mary convinced him to take those along. Besides, Joseph would have the opportunity to meet Mary's sisters and their families, for they too would be in Jerusalem for the Holy Festival.

At the end of the first week of March, when they gathered for dinner to discuss the trip to Jerusalem, Azor started coughing. At first Mary thought her uncle was choking on his food, but he waved his hand to signal to the group that it was only a cough. Shortly thereafter, he lost all the color in his face. Mary, who sat opposite him, became very concerned. Tamar said to the group, "He's been coughing like this for weeks, but he won't let me call the physician."

In truth, Azor had been feeling poorly ever since he assisted his brother in rescuing Joseph from the fire, but he said nothing to the others. He always seemed to be short of breath. Last October, when he and Joachim were sowing the barley and wheat, he became so dizzy that he had to sit down right in the middle of the field. Azor had tried to muffle his coughs, but he couldn't conceal them as much as he would have liked to. Tonight Joachim could see large beads of perspiration pouring down his brother's forehead, and his eyes were dull and watery. "Azor," Joachim said, "you have to see the physician before we leave. You can't walk all the way to Jerusalem when you're feeling the way you do." Azor waved his hand in front of himself again, as if to silence everyone. He continued to cough while Tamar shook her head in utter frustration.

Throughout the next week, Azor's condition worsened. "I'm going to get the physician," Tamar said. "I don't care what you have to say about it, and I'm going right now." Tamar then realized how sick her husband actually was, because he didn't protest.

By the time the doctor arrived, Azor was running a high fever. After listening to his heart and lungs, the physician whispered to Tamar, "I think your husband has a delayed case of the winter sickness. He won't be going anywhere for quite a while. I recommend complete bed rest." He told Tamar what herbal brews to administer to her husband. Tamar followed all the recommendations, but Azor's health deteriorated.

When Joachim came to see his brother, he informed him that he and his family were canceling the trip. Azor was furious. "You're not going to miss seeing your daughters and your grandchildren on my account. Tamar will stay with me. We have the doctor here if we need him. What by you staying here with me could possibly change things? If the Lord wills it, I'll get better, and if He doesn't, I've got nothing to complain about. I've had a good, long life. You and your family just go to Jerusalem." There was no arguing with Azor once he made up his mind.

That night, when Joseph came over to have dinner with Mary and her parents, the topic of their conversation centered on Azor and Tamar. "I'd feel just awful if something happened to Azor while we're gone," Anna said.

"He'd never allow you to stay home, and take care of him," Joachim remarked. "He got so upset when I told him that we were going to cancel our trip that I was afraid he'd have a stroke."

"Daddy!" Mary said. "I could stay here and help Aunt Tamar. I don't think Uncle Azor would say anything if I stayed behind. Not once in my life has he ever scolded me or given me a cross look. That way I could help Aunt Tamar take care of him." Mary looked at her fiancé and saw the disappointment in his eyes, so she added, "If that's all right with you, Joseph." The carpenter nodded in agreement and said that he wouldn't go either, just in case Azor needed to be lifted.

"Aunt Tamar and I can do that, Joseph," Mary replied. "He's always been a thin man, and he's lost even more weight in the last couple of weeks.

Besides, Father could use your help, and you have your goods to sell too. Aunt Tamar and I will do just fine by ourselves." Reluctantly, Joseph and her parents agreed to let Mary stay behind.

On the day of their departure, Azor seemed to have rallied a bit. He even got up and went to the door to say goodbye. When he learned Mary wasn't going, he pretended to look a little cross. He always hoped that when it was time for him to leave this earth, the three people he most wanted by his side were his wife, daughter, and Mary. He knew it was impossible for his daughter to be with him now. Azor was very content to know that at least two of the three women he loved so dearly would be with him if he died.

Joseph, along with Mary's parents, bid Azor and Tamar a sorrowful farewell. Mary walked with Joseph toward the caravan that had gathered at the gate. Her father would drive the wagon with Anna by his side. Her heart was breaking; she had been with Joseph every day since the fire. She couldn't bear the thought of being without him now. Her lips trembled as tears began to run down her cheeks. Joseph's face was filled with emotion too as he took Mary in his arms and kissed her forehead while fighting back his own tears. Mary put her head on his chest and wished his embrace could last forever, but she knew he had to leave. She heard her father say it was time to go. Joseph kissed her forehead again and reluctantly ended the embrace. Mary took his hand and walked with him toward her parents. As she hugged them and kissed them goodbye, she still held on to Joseph's hand. "Give my sisters and their families my love. Tell them that my heart and my thoughts will be with all of you."

Their touch soon had to end. Joseph gently squeezed her hand and unwillingly Mary let go. He then jumped onto the back of the wagon as he said, "I'll miss you, Mary!" She waved goodbye as the caravan moved through the town gate. Joseph kept looking at his fiancée and waving to her until the caravan vanished into the horizon while Mary blew farewell kisses to her beloved.

A disheartened Mary walked back to her uncle's house. Her heart ached as she dried her tears and tried to put a smile back on her face. When she entered the house, she saw that her uncle had returned to bed. For the next week Mary cooked for the older couple and kept both homes spotless. Mary could see her uncle's health was failing more with each passing day. In her free time during the week that followed, Mary would sit on the floor by her uncle's bed and retell the same stories he had told to her when she was a little girl. Amazingly, she remembered them word-for-word. Occasionally he would try to smile, but some days he barely had the strength to do even that. Tamar tried to bolster his will to live by pretending to be a bit ornery with her niece. She would purposely disagree with Mary's version of the story. When she did so, Azor would try to raise his trembling hand and point to Mary, indicating that her version of the story was correct. Whenever they saw his finger start to move, they would nod at each other and smile.

It had been over a week since Mary's parents and left for the Holy City. She knew that they should have reached Jerusalem days ago. Tonight all Jewish believers would celebrate the Passover, and then for seven days thereafter, the Feast of Unleavened Bread. Mary was melancholy. She missed Joseph and her parents terribly. She always loved the Passover Seder and so looked forward to celebrating the Seder meal with Joseph for the first time.

Nabu had invited the rabbi and his family to join them for the Passover meal. As Nabu and his family were recent converts to the Jewish faith, Asa felt it would be encouraging if he and his family attended. So the rabbi, his wife and two daughters, and future son-in-law reached Nabu's hillside home as the full moon appeared on the eastern horizon. Even though Nabu knew the severity of Azor's condition, he still extended an invitation to Mary and her aunt and uncle. He knew, though, that they wouldn't be attending. The whole town was aware that Azor was on the verge of death.

There would be no celebrating in Tamar and Azor's house tonight, for it appeared Mary's uncle wouldn't live through the night. The physician had been by earlier in the day and told Tamar that it was just a matter of hours. "I really don't think Azor has much fight left in him," he said regretfully. "I truly believe that he will be resting in the Bosom of Father Abraham before the cock crows tomorrow."

As Tamar sat with her husband's head upon her lap and Mary sat on the floor next to his bed, stroking her uncle's hand, Nabu and the other celebrants in his home drank the first of four ceremonial cups of wine required in the Seder ritual. His son Omar, with great pride in his voice, asked the first of four required questions. "Rabbi! Why is this night different than any other night?"

Azor's face now had a grayish pallor, and his lips were turning blue. His labored breathing would stop occasionally. Mary and Tamar thought they had lost him several times earlier that afternoon. Now it seemed that the time between breaths was even longer and more labored. Tamar asked, "Mary, would you mind leaving us for a while, dear? I'd like to be alone with your uncle before he leaves us. I have a lot of things to say to him yet." Mary understood. When Joseph was on the verge of death, there were so many things she wanted to say to him in private, but there were always too many people around for her to do so. The teenager tearfully hugged her aunt. She then went up to her uncle and kissed him tenderly on his forehead. Mary said what she thought would be her final goodbye. While she gently stroked his cheek, Mary's tears streamed down her face. Her uncle already felt cold.

As Mary prepared to leave her uncle's side, Zaddu walked to the fire pit with a bowl full of beetles pressed against her wrinkled, dried-up breasts. Between her index finger and thumb, the old hag held a toad by its foot. It struggled to free itself from her grip. Her other hand clung to the staff that supported her hunched body. The sorceress tried to walk as quickly as possible so that she could flick the beetles, which were now crawling on her hand, back into the bowl. She was hungry tonight. She didn't want her dinner running away on her. When the witch reached the bonfire, she lowered herself to the ground and put down her staff. With her free hand she shooed the bugs back into the bowl with her claw-like fingernails. Zaddu took the live toad and popped it into her toothless mouth. She gummed its warty flesh. The sorceress scooped up the bugs in her claws and dropped them into her mouth too. The witch chomped on them as drool ran down the sides of her chin. Zaddu loved the nights when the moon was full. When it shone above her, she often worshiped it. When the silvery orb was most intense, she would get down on all fours, crawl about and howl at it just like a jackal. Tonight, however, she sensed something was about to go awry. She didn't even relish the taste of the toad or the beetles as much as she normally did.

In the hillside home of Nabu's family, the rabbi told the age-old tale of Israel's release from Egyptian bondage. The convert to Judaism wasn't a good storyteller, so he deferred the honor of the act to Asa. The group listened intently as he told them of how the Angel of Death passed over the houses of the children of Israel and slew the firstborn of the Egyptians, even the son of Pharaoh. Expressions of both fear and wonderment could be seen on the faces of those listening as the story unfolded. While Asa relayed the marvelous events to his listeners, Mary stepped out into the moonlit night.

As soon as her niece left, Tamar closed the door behind her, and went to lie next to her husband. She

374

placed her hand under his head. With her free arm, she drew his near-lifeless body to herself. Tamar pressed her tear-stained cheeks to his face and kept kissing him. She told her husband how much he had meant to her for the past 63 years. The tears from her eyes not only flowed down her cheeks, but ran over his as well. Tamar knew in her heart that the Angel of Death would soon be visiting them that night.

The early-spring night was quite chilly. Mary shivered a bit as she walked across the courtyard to her house. The grass was damp and cold under her bare feet. Once again the full moon shed its silvery light over the entire town. As she walked in the blue-velvet shadows beneath the olive tree, she was a bit maudlin thinking of what life would be like without the uncle she loved so dearly. She prayed to the Lord, "*Your will be done in all things,*" as her tears flowed freely. Mary considered going back to the house and building a fire in the winter oven for her aunt and uncle. But she thought better of it. The girl believed that her uncle had very little time left, and it would be best if they were left alone. By the time Mary reached her doorway, thick black clouds suddenly covered the nighttime sky and blocked out all of its light. Mary now stood in total darkness.

Zaddu too saw the clouds blot out the moonlight as she gummed the beetles. The sky above suddenly turned pitch-black. She sat there and noticed that not a single star was visible overhead. Suddenly the flames of the fire shot high into the air, and in them the hag could vaguely see the figure of Baal-zebub himself. The horrific image of the Prince of Darkness formed in totality as the witch's body fell backward and she began to convulse. Her face contorted as greenish foam filled her mouth and ran down its sides. Instead of black irises, glaring red eyeballs now appeared in her sockets as her eyes rolled back into her head. The evil one and his demons took possession of her body once again. They needed her vocal cords to communicate with each other. As soon as they did so, Satan's bloodcurdling, growl-like scream filled the still night air.

Asa stopped the story in mid-sentence as a roaring, heinous howl-like wail tore through the night. No one could tell if the terrifying scream was animal or human. The men ran to the door and looked out into the night, as the women and children huddled together in the corner of the room, trembling. They could see nothing because of the impenetrable darkness. Before Asa began telling the story again, Nabu drew down the heavy leather shades and tied them off so they couldn't be opened easily. The rabbi then continued to tell the account of the Exodus. The uneasy group sat closer to each other, shaking with fear, as the story of deliverance continued. Even the light of the tallow candles seemed to dim a bit, as if they too could sense evil.

Mary was frightened by the sound too. The young virgin's hands shook as she opened her door. Knowing the location of everything in the room, she immediately found the flint, struck it, and had fire with which to light the night candle. She was so maudlin that she didn't even lock the door. Mary expected her aunt to come by any moment to inform her that life had departed from her dear uncle. The teenager removed her veil. She was too tense to sleep, so she decided to pray. After brushing her hair, Mary still needed something to do to deplete her nervous energy. She sat down next to the basket of wool and began to comb out the strands of the tangled fibers.

Tamar pressed her face even closer to Azor's. Her head lay so close to his that their gray hair intertwined. One would never be able to tell where her hair ended and his began. She could feel how cold his face felt. Tamar reached for his hand and kissed it; it was cold too. She told Azor how blest she was to have him for a husband. The woman smiled as she recalled and reminded him of the joys and sorrows they had experienced in their long life together. Thinking the Angel of Death was very close to their door, she said, "I don't know how I can go on without you, my love." As she stroked his hand, it felt colder by the minute. "No matter how many people will be around me, I'll still be alone without you. You knew how to make me happy when I was depressed. You, my dear, could make me laugh, even when I was angry and beside myself with rage. If you leave me, my heart will be hollow and empty, for it always has and always will belong to you, my dear, sweet husband. I don't want to live without you by my side. How can I? You are my life!"

Azor tried to move his lips. "There, there, my love," Tamar said. "There's no need to speak. I know what you're thinking, my dear. We've been together so long, we know each other's thoughts. It won't be too long." She said through heart-wrenching, almost inaudible sobs, "And we'll be together again. Then you can tell me everything you wanted to say to me now." The old woman's body heaved as her sobbing intensified. A light, brighter than anything Tamar had ever seen in her life, now filled the room. The old woman knew that it must be the Angel of Death. She pressed her lips to her husband's cheek and waited with dread for the angel who would take his soul. "Maybe, since I've seen his light, he'll take me too," she said aloud hopefully.

As Mary sat and combed through the wool, she felt a sudden calm come over her. She had never experienced such a soothing feeling of peace before. Her sense of smell detected the aromatic fragrance, much more pleasing than even the scent of lilies; it was pleasantly overpowering. She recognized the intriguing smell. Mary knew what was about to happen even before the room filled with the dazzling light. The virgin had no fear this time as she watched the light form into the image of the angelic messenger appear before her. Mary waited in joyful anticipation of hearing that lovely, mystical voice once again. The angel and the light were brighter than human eyes should have been able to tolerate, yet Mary had no trouble looking directly into the glorious, radiant face of the heavenly being.

The angel bowed low to Mary as he said in his beautiful, melodic voice, "Greetings, Mary, highly favored daughter of the Most High. The Lord is with you." As she bowed to the angel in reciprocal greeting, Mary once again wondered why he addressed her the way he did. The angel continued, "Do not fear, Mary, for you have found favor with the Most High. You shall conceive and bear a son and give Him the name Jesus. Great will be His dignity and He will be called the Son of the Most High God. The Lord God will give Him the throne of David His father. He will rule over the house of Jacob forever, and His reign will be without end."

Mary was puzzled, so she asked the angel, "How can this be, since I have not known any man?"

The angel answered, "The Holy Spirit will come upon you and the power of the Most High will overshadow you; therefore, the Holy Offspring to be born of you will be called the Son of God. Know that Elizabeth your kinswoman has conceived a son in her old age; she who was thought to be sterile is now in her sixth month, for nothing is impossible with God."

Mary was overcome by wonder and sublime joy. She bowed so low in submission to God's will that her forehead touched the floor. "I am the servant of the Lord. Let it be done to me as you say." Mary was now in such a state of ecstasy that her spirit soared as the power, the wonder and the omnipotence of the Almighty filled her and coursed through to her very soul. Then the angel left her and the light faded. Had Mary not been so enthralled and ecstatic by the glory that surrounded her; the virgin would have felt an ever-so-slight twinge on her lower-right side. It was soon followed by a slight tingle just below her navel as the sacred embryo entered her womb and implanted Himself therein. This time, even though the angel departed, the heavenly fragrance remained.

379

Everyone at Nabu's trembled uncontrollably as they once again heard the eerie, rasping sounds echoing through the hills, shattering the stillness of the night. The sound had the cadence of human speech, but with the abrasive shriek of an injured wild animal. The rabbi tried to continue the story, but everyone could hear him stammer with apprehension and fear in his voice. They too could feel that same terror in the pit of their stomachs.

Zaddu's body flew through the air and landed with a thud. The furious-sounding voice that now possessed her shrieked loudly, "The virgin has surrendered herself to His will. The Almighty has already begun to take on human flesh."

The witch was levitated once again. Her body was suspended in midair as another voice came from the witch's mouth, shrieking, "We need this old sow for our sorcery; don't kill her yet! You know that we communicate best through her!"

The old hag's body freefell and draped itself over the branch of a scrub oak. It looked as if she was folded in two. Her head spun in circles as her mouth formed the Prince of Darkness's screaming words, *"Don't tell me what to do!"* He caused the witch's body to fly upward off the branch and then fall to the ground with an earth-shattering thud.

A third, gravelly voice said, "Why are you concerned? They'll just stone the virgin. They'll think she's an adulteress. Joseph has never had relations with her. He won't stand to be humiliated so."

The hag's body convulsed again as Satan screamed, *"Joseph is a fool! We can't break him! Nothing that we've done so far has worked."*

Another demon caused the sorceress's lips to move and blurt out, "What do you fear? Human flesh will weaken Him. He will be a child of the Fall. After all, we found no resistance to evil in Adam or Eve. You can tempt Him with earthly wealth, power, and glory too."

Still another voice blared in, "My liege, why are you so concerned? There's always Zaddu, Herod, the Romans, and the people of the region. The Jews believe the Messiah will be a great political leader who will topple the Romans, and they're certain the children of Israel will rule the world. When He shows them His love, compassion and mercy, they'll never believe who He really is. They see God as vengeful, quick to anger and slow to forgive. The people will never believe He is God when they see Him seeking and reaching the lost. I say leave Him be for now. He will hang Himself! Our top priority should be to spread evil and dissent among those who can reject Him. That should cause His human heart to break."

All the voices seemed to agree. "So be it!" Baal-zebub said. He couldn't resist levitating Zaddu's body and crashing it back down into the earth a few more times. Her mouth dropped open, and hundreds of serpents crawled out of the foam that filled it. Satan and his demons left her. The snakes slithered off in every direction, looking for souls that would be susceptible to doing evil. The Prince of Darkness himself slithered off toward the town of Nazareth to start his destructive work there.

Mary still sat with her forehead resting on her knees. She contemplated all that she had experienced in the last few moments. Her soul was still enraptured and lingered in the glory of her God. The 14-year-old was to be the mother of the Messiah, the Promised of Ages. "I will not be afraid; this is all in the hands of the Almighty," she whispered. "Why should I fear?" Mary decided then and there to tell no one what had just happened. Her destiny was in God's hands. The virgin had never felt such joy and peace; her entire being was filled with sublime contentment.

Bang! All of a sudden Mary heard her door fly open and slam into the wall. The stillness was broken. Before she could react to the sound, someone grabbed hold of her hand and jerked her to her feet while pulling her toward the door.

Zaddu had difficulty standing after the possession. Her entire body ached from the pounding she had just experienced. As she spat into the fire, she muttered, "So this is the thanks I get for being his loyal servant?" She should have known better than to speak against the evil one, for as soon as she said it, the fire began to sputter. Hot glowing embers flew toward her head. She tried to run from them before they struck her, but she wasn't fast enough. Her skin sizzled as the coals burned deep craters into her face. Some of them landed in her matted grey hair and set it afire. She rolled around on the damp earth, screaming at the top of her lungs as she tried to pick the smoldering embers from her unkempt, tangled mane with her curving nails.

The Seder supper at Nabu's had ended. The rabbi sent his wife and daughters home under the protection of his future son-in-law. The four ceremonial cups of wine made all of them a little woozy. None of them ever drank that much in such a short period of time. Asa stayed back with Nabu. The clouds had parted. Once again the full moon bathed the hills in tints of silvery blue. The two men planned to scour the hillside to see if some animal had attacked a person or group of people. If that was the case, perhaps they could locate the victim or victims. If they were already dead, they at least could provide a proper burial for them. From the sound of things, the poor doomed souls seemed to have suffered quite a bit. The two men climbed the hillside until they reached the summit. They both turned slowly as they scanned the moonlit hills. The only unusual thing they could see was the illumination from Zaddu's fire, bathing the branches of the scrub oaks in a yellowish light. "I heard that she was back," the rabbi said.

"I don't know why she can't find someplace else to live," Nabu replied. "How many times does she have to be driven out from a place before she realizes she's not wanted?" The disheartened men finally abandoned the search and returned to Nabu's house. His family was already asleep when they arrived, so the rabbi didn't go back inside. Asa thanked his host for the Seder supper. He hugged Nabu and kissed his chin as he wished him, "Shalom!"

As he walked home, the rabbi pondered all that had happened on this strange night. His shadow moved along beside him in the eerie silence. The full moon once again bathed the streets in silvery light. *I should stop at Azor's to see if the women need anything,* he said to himself. As he came upon their courtyard, he feared the worst. Since the front of both of their houses faced the street and the doors of both homes faced the courtyard, he saw Mary's door first; it was wide open. *She must have left in haste,* he thought. *Azor must be resting with his fathers already.* When he turned from the street and entered the courtyard, he saw that Azor's door was wide open too. He paid his respects to the Law on the doorframe and then knocked.

"Shalom! And please enter," said a deep male voice that sounded like a younger version of Azor.

With great trepidation the rabbi stuck his head inside the house. He couldn't believe what he saw. Azor was sitting at the table, eating, while Mary and his wife sat on either side of him, looking up at him lovingly with their arms draped over his shoulders. He immediately noticed how radiantly beautiful Mary looked.

"Good evening, Rabbi," Azor said. "Maybe you can help me out a bit here. Ever since I got up, my wife and my niece won't let go of me. I can hardly raise my hands high enough to get food into my mouth." The rabbi just stood there wide-eyed as he watched the old man eat.

Both Tamar and Mary greeted the rabbi. Tamar then started talking. When she did, no one could stop her. She relayed the story of what had happened that evening, without even taking a single breath. "...and Rabbi, I tell you as surely as the Lord lives that I was convinced the light I saw was the Angel of Death, but instead it turned out to be the Angel of

384

Life. I was certain that my Azor breathed his last breath as the light disappeared, and then he sits up like he was never even sick. He says to me, 'Tamar, I'm hungry! What do we have to eat?' Then he just gets out of bed like he hasn't been sick for a day in his life, and goes to sit at the table. So, Rabbi; I can't believe what I'm seeing, so I run over to get Mary and she's sitting there sleeping with her head resting on her knees, mind you. So I grab her hand, yank her up and practically drag her to my house. Mary thinks I'm hysterical, because I'm so out of breath I can't speak. So she comes in, and she can't believe what she sees either."

Tamar finally stopped her tale and took in a deep breath. Azor said he didn't think he was as sick as his wife said, and asked the rabbi what he thought. Asa and the two women laughed heartily while Azor looked at them, rather puzzled. He resumed eating. After the three explained to Azor how close to death he actually was, Mary and the rabbi left. When Azor finally stopped eating, he hugged his wife and affectionately kissed her.

The rabbi walked Mary to her door; when they were about an arm's length from it, the rabbi said, "Mary can you smell that? There's a strong fragrance, almost like lilies, but it's too early for them to be blooming."

"Yes, Rabbi, I do. It sure smells heavenly; doesn't it?" The rabbi nodded in agreement. As Asa walked home, he couldn't figure out why Mary looked so radiantly beautiful. She had always been very attractive, but tonight there was something majestic and regal about her. *Maybe it's because she wasn't wearing a veil, and her long auburn hair just added to her beauty.* Or maybe it was the peace and contentment he saw in her face. *Whatever it was,* he thought, *she looked absolutely stunning.* He would remember this night as long as he lived. What a dichotomy—the bloodcurdling sounds, and a house filled with fear during the Seder, and now indescribable joy, and a miracle besides.

When Mary returned home and closed the door, she thanked the Lord for sparing her uncle's life. She then pondered the sacred mystery she was now a part of. Mary remembered every word the angel had said. She, a fourteen-year-old girl from a small town far from where her faith was centered, would be the Mother of the Christ, the Anointed One. She lowered her hand to her abdomen and said, "Thy Kingdom come."

CHAPTER 17

Almost two weeks had passed since the angel appeared to Mary. Today, her parents and Joseph would be returning home. Mary was feeling awful. For the last two days she had been experiencing morning sickness. Tamar told Mary not to worry; it was probably just anxiety. She told the virgin to try not to think about Joseph's homecoming and to just imagine how wonderful it will be when he and her parents finally return home. Tamar and Azor were both worried about their niece, for although her beautiful eyes sparkled like they never had before, dark circles had developed under them.

Mary ran to the bluff that overlooked the fertile Jezreel Valley to see if she could spot the caravan as it approached Nazareth. Strong spring winds blew her veil; it billowed out like the sails of the boats that drifted on the Sea of Galilee, which appeared as a tiny, shining mirror in the distance. She walked to the very edge of the bluff, from where she could see the lead mule of the caravan and its rider in the valley below. A knot formed in the pit of her stomach as she thought of Joseph and how he would react when he learned she was pregnant. She loved him so much. Mary imagined his face when he discovered that she was with child. "His heart will probably break," she said aloud and began to weep. "Everything makes me cry lately. I don't know why; I should be overjoyed at what God has done for me, but all I do is cry." The girl chided herself for her erratic emotions.

As Mary turned to leave, she saw a serpent at her feet. She almost recoiled in fear, but her keen mind stopped her; she realized where she was. Had she stepped back even a little, she would have fallen off the bluff. The serpent arched its ugly head and hissed; it was poised to strike. Mary prayed as she slowly raised her heels off the ground while keeping her eyes focused on the snake. She leapt forward just as the snake struck.

Joseph couldn't wait to see his love. As soon as Joachim's wagon reached the foothills of Nazareth, Joseph jumped off and ran like a young stag toward the town gate. Soon the caravan leader was far behind him. Even though the young carpenter's parched throat burned and his lungs felt as if they were about to burst, Joseph made up his mind that he wouldn't stop running until he reached Mary and held her in his arms. As he entered the gate, he saw Eliud. Joseph grabbed hold of the old man and quickly kissed him on the chin. Without even breaking his stride, he said, "Shalom, Eliud!" He continued running toward Mary's house. The gatekeeper chuckled as he watched the breathless Joseph continue to run through the town's streets. *If I had a fiancée as beautiful as Mary, I guess I'd be running home to see her too,* he said to himself. Eliud returned to the gatehouse to await the arrival of the rest of the caravan. On further reflection, the old man thought, *I don't think I'd ever let her out of my sight to begin with.* He chuckled again.

Joseph finally reached Mary's door. He pressed his hand against the building and leaned back as he tried to catch his breath. The carpenter touched the sacred box on the doorframe and prayed while he tried to steady his breathing. He wiped his dripping forehead in the sleeve of his tunic and then knocked on the door. There was no answer.

Azor saw Joseph enter the courtyard. He came out to tell him that Mary had gone to the bluff to watch for the caravan. Kissing Azor's chin, he said, "Shalom, Uncle! You're looking great!" Joseph's breathing was so loud that he wasn't sure what Azor had just told him, so he asked, "Where did you say Mary was, Uncle?"

"She's at the bluff, Joseph."

The young man turned immediately and ran for the cliff. As he did, he saw Mary coming toward him. Her arms were moving in front of her as if she were running a marathon. She screamed, "Joseph, a snake! A snake! The back of my tunic! A snake!" Joseph caught up to her and stopped dead in his tracks. He reached around Mary and saw the serpent that clung to her garment. Its fangs were caught up in her hem. He grabbed the snake by the tail and snapped it, pulling it free. Its fangs tore through the fibers of Mary's garment. Joseph tossed the reptile off the side of the hill. A tearful Mary threw her arms around her fiancé. She clung to him tightly. "I'm so glad you're home," his intended said through her tears. "I've missed you so much."

"You should've never gone up to the bluff alone," Joseph said. "You could've fallen off, and who would've been the wiser. Promise me you'll never go there by yourself again." Mary's fiancé couldn't have known that she wasn't alone, that the Lord her God was within her. Joseph was so intent on seeing his love that he hadn't said anything to Azor about his son-in-law when he greeted him in the courtyard. Since Mary was so upset by the incident with the serpent, Joseph didn't think he should say anything to her yet about her cousin's husband. The couple walked hand-in-hand to the house.

Joseph tried to quiet Mary's uneasiness by telling her about the beauty of the Temple and about her sisters and their children. "They seemed to like me, Mary; your eldest sister said I'd make a good father someday, because of the way the kids took to me. They were hoping to see you too. Both of them were disappointed that you couldn't make it, but they said they understood. By the way, Mary, Uncle Azor really looks great. You must've taken good care of him. Your mom and dad are fine too." Joseph noticed that Mary was unusually quiet. He was surprised that his fiancée hadn't inquired about her parents before he mentioned them.

Mary and Joseph reached the house just as Joachim and Anna did. Mary ran to the wagon and hugged her mother the moment she stepped down from the seat. Before either of them could say a word, Tamar came running out of her house with Azor close behind. Tamar said, "Anna, you wouldn't believe what happened while you were gone." She proceeded to tell Anna and Joachim the same story that she had told to the rabbi on the night her husband was miraculously healed. Mary's parents had no trouble believing Tamar's story. They saw that Azor looked healthier than ever.

Joachim hugged his daughter, then walked over to his brother and hugged him too. "If you should ever have that angel visit you again, brother, send him my way," Joachim said. "You look about ten years younger." Azor laughed.

"As long as you're both here, I have some sad news to tell you," Joachim said. "Your son-in-law seems to have had a stroke when he was performing his priestly duties at the Temple during the Day of Atonement services. We heard that he came stumbling out of the Holy Place disoriented. He was unable to speak. All he did was wave his hand in the air and gesture irrationally until they took him back home. His neighbors said he continues to make pottery, but he still can't speak. They haven't seen Elizabeth since the day they brought him home. Because he can't speak, no one is certain about his condition. We would've gone up to see your daughter, but we only found out about the tragedy the day before we were scheduled to leave. It was the Sabbath, so we would've exceeded the travel restrictions had we done so."

Mary wept as Joachim gave them the sad news. Tamar held her face in her hands and shook her head. "My poor son-in-law, and my daughter, she has no one there to console her."

"We have to go to her at once!" Azor said. "Who's to say he won't have another stroke soon? They usually come in clusters. The caravan should be retuning to Jerusalem in three days, and Ein Karem is less than a half-day's travel from there."

"But Azor, you're just getting over your illness," Joachim said. "And face it, brother, you may look younger since we've returned, but you're still the same age. You and Tamar can't make the trip by yourselves."

"I'll go with them!" Mary said. "I'm concerned about them too. Elizabeth shouldn't have to face this alone." The women were shocked by her statement. She was engaged now, and she shouldn't have offered to go without consulting Joseph first, but Mary held her ground. "I'm certain Joseph won't mind, do you, Joseph?"

His fiancée had backed him into a corner; what could he possibly say? So he said, "I don't mind," even though his heart panged at the thought; he wanted her to stay with him. They'd been separated long enough. "It's all right with me if your parents approve." In his heart Joseph really hoped her parents would say no, but they didn't. He would've insisted on going along, but he didn't want to insult Azor by agreeing that he was too old to travel without another male family member. Besides, even though he did well in Jerusalem, the money he made there wouldn't last forever; he needed to get back to work. He experienced firsthand that the new caravan leader was as competent as Ali had been. He knew Mary's safety would be assured.

In three days there was another tearful departure as Mary and her aunt and uncle bid farewell to the people they loved in Nazareth, and headed for the Judean hillside town of Ein Karem. It would be almost three months before Joseph would see his beloved again. It gave him plenty of time to complete the hand-carved treasure chest he was making for his future wife.

The long, arduous trip was taxing for Mary. Morning sickness caused her a great deal of discomfort. Azor and Tamar blamed themselves for allowing their niece to accompany them. The couple sat by their campfire one night while Mary went off to commune with her God. "Azor, we shouldn't have let our Mary join us on this trip," Tamar said. "We knew that she had been feeling poorly before we left. We're in no-man's land without a physician, and she's been sick every day since we've left."

"I think it may be just what you said before, my dear. It's just a bad case of separation anxiety. If Mary's health doesn't improve by the time we reach Jerusalem, we'll stop there and find a good physician to examine her. There are plenty of good doctors in the Holy City." His solution quelled Tamar's anxiety.

The morning of what was supposed to be the last day of their journey started out beautifully, mild and pleasant. Mary awoke to a blazing-red sunrise. *Oh no!* She thought, recalling what her mother had said about 'red skies in the morning.' The caravan leader passed through the makeshift tents of the travelers, waking the still-sleeping sojourners. "Wake up! Hurry! Hurry! We'll never make it to Jerusalem before the rain hits unless we leave right now. Hurry! Pack up your belongings!" He prodded them with his staff.

Azor sat up and stretched, then he gently shook his wife's shoulder. Tamar raised herself up on one arm as she asked, "What's the hurry? It's still rather dark, and we don't have that far to go."

"Red skies!" Azor replied. "We've been blessed so far; after all, this is still the rainy season." Mary greeted the two as they stretched the kinks from their bodies. The young woman looked surprisingly healthy as she packed up their supplies and rolled them in the goatskin they used for their nighttime tent. She tied it with their identifying cords and carried it to the wagon that held the supplies for the travelers who made the journey on foot. The caravan resumed traveling as soon as the risen sun could be seen on the eastern horizon. The leader expected the group to reach the Holy City by midday.

When they were about an hour away from Jerusalem, a strong wind from the west drove dark, foreboding clouds across the Mediterranean Sea; they soon blocked out the sun. Their scout looked for shelter as lightning flashed, tearing the dark sky asunder. Loud peals of thunder shook the earth, scaring the pack animals; they reared up in fright. The caravan leader led the group into a nearby cave just as a torrential downpour began. It would last way into the night. Mary and her relatives were stranded there till morning. They wouldn't reach Ein Karem until midday tomorrow.

The next morning, Mary and her relatives broke from the caravan just before they reached Jerusalem. By skirting the city they could save at least an hour of travel time. As they passed Jerusalem's massive fortress-like walls, they saw the magnificent Temple of Herod rising high above them. The impressive edifice had been under construction for almost two decades now and wouldn't be complete for another half-century. The trio stopped, raised their hands and prayed as they faced the sacred structure. Azor told his niece that they would stop in the Holy City to visit the Temple on their return trip.

The trio finally reached the hillside town of Ein Karem as the sun was at its zenith. Prompted by the Spirit of God, Mary broke free from her aunt and uncle. She ran up the hill to her cousin's house that was located at the highest point in town. "I'm glad we didn't overreact to Mary's illness," Tamar said. "There doesn't seem to be anything wrong with her now. She runs like a swift gazelle."

The young woman reached the courtyard of her cousin's home and saw Elizabeth sitting on a stone bench, mashing figs. The out-of-breath teen called out, "Elizabeth! Elizabeth! It's me! Cousin Mary!"

The moment her elderly cousin heard Mary's voice, she grabbed hold of her abdomen. The child within her womb leapt with joy as he was filled with the Holy Spirit. Elizabeth laughed as tears of jubilation ran down her cheeks. She ran to her cousin and cried out, "Blessed are you among women!" She hugged Mary tightly. "And blest is the fruit of your womb. But who am I that the Mother of my Lord should come to visit me? The moment that I heard your greeting the baby leapt in my womb with joy. Blessed are you, Mary, for you trusted that the Lord's words to you would be fulfilled."

Mary drew back from her cousin's embrace. The teenager raised her hands high above her head in praise to the Living God. As she looked up to the heavens, Mary could feel the presence of her Maker dwelling within her body. She saw the thin, white cirrus clouds gliding across the cobalt-blue sky. As they rose higher and higher, her soul seemed to soar with them. She could no longer contain the joy that welled up within her. In a state of ecstasy, Mary began to twirl very slowly as she sang a prophetic song. "My very being proclaims the greatness of the Lord, and my spirit finds such joy in God my Savior." She crossed her wrists and extended her hands toward Elizabeth. As her cousin took hold, they both leaned back and twirled very slowly.

The old and the very young were bound together in the shared experience. Elizabeth could feel the presence of the Holy Spirit, and now the Divine enraptured her too. The exuberant fetus in Elizabeth's womb leapt again as Mary continued her song. The embodiment of God's promise to His people now grew within her very own body, so she sang praises to the glory of her God, as His Spirit directed her. The words that came from her mouth made the young virgin stop singing and spinning as she realized what she actually had been prophesying. Still holding her cousin's hands, she looked at Elizabeth, bewildered by the magnitude of the honor God had bestowed upon her. "All generations shall call me blessed!" Mary said in amazement. "God, who is mighty, has done great things for me! Holy is His name!" She finished her canticle of joy while still holding Elizabeth's hands.

When Mary's song faded, the two women fell into each other's arms as the power of the Holy Spirit departed from them. Drained by the mystifying experience, the two women wept with joy as they clung to each other. Elizabeth broke the silence. With a voice filled with excitement the elderly woman said, "Mary, we will live to see the Days of Messiah! And you, Mary, will nurture Him. You are His Mother!"

The young virgin whispered in her cousin's ear, "Elizabeth, please don't tell anyone what you know. I trust in the Mighty One. He'll reveal His plan in His time, not ours." As soon as Mary finished speaking, Elizabeth's parents came into view. They couldn't believe their eyes when they saw that their elderly daughter was pregnant.

Mary stayed at her cousin's until Elizabeth gave birth to a son. Her husband Zechariah named the baby John at the circumcision. On that same day, his speech was restored, and he began to prophesy to all who were present. At the end of his canticle, Zechariah said that his son would go before the Lord to prepare straight paths for Him. Light would now shine on those who sat in darkness and in the shadow of death. Mary and Elizabeth smiled at each other. After the guests left, he told Mary and his family about how God's messenger announced John's future birth at the Temple, as he was about to burn incense to the Lord. The entire group praised God.

Anxious to return to Nazareth, Mary knew that her aunt and uncle wanted to stay behind and enjoy their new grandson. One evening, when Zechariah was sitting at his pottery wheel, Mary entered his shop and asked if he could make arrangements for her departure. She asked him because she knew her aunt and uncle would feel duty-bound to return home with her if she told them.

"It seems rather coincidental that you would ask me about this today," Zechariah replied. "A wonderful family from here is leaving for Sepphoris with the next caravan the day after tomorrow. That's the town just north of yours. I'm sure they'd be happy to have you join them. Although we'd love to have you stay with us until your aunt and uncle leave, I know that you must be longing to see your fiancé and your parents by now."

After a tearful farewell and many blessings and good wishes for a safe journey, the young virgin left the town of Ein Karem. She wouldn't have a chance to enter Jerusalem to see the Holy Temple this time either. For now, the walking, living, breathing Temple of the Most High God just saw the magnificent edifice from a distance once again, as she carried her Lord and Savior back to their Nazarene home.

Every time a caravan from the south entered the town, Joseph was there, waiting for his beloved. About a month after she left, Joseph received word, through a reliable caravan leader, that Mary would not be back until the end of June. Joseph anxiously awaited her return. Each night at dinner with his future-in-laws, the young carpenter would opine the reasons for her delayed return. One night he would worry about Mary's well-being; the next night it was Azor's. "You don't think anything could have happened to her en route, do you, Father?" Joseph asked Joachim when Anna had stepped outside.

"No, I don't, Joseph," Joachim said. "It's more likely related to Zechariah than to anyone else. His condition may have worsened. They've probably extended their stay for Elizabeth's sake. Kind of like, you know, for moral support, maybe." He wanted to say, "Don't worry, son; she still loves you," but he didn't want to embarrass the young man.

On the last day of June, as the deep-blue shadows of the hills crept over the small town, Joseph stood talking with Eliud. "Joseph!" he said. "Maybe I should retire already and you can take over my job. You've been here almost as much as I have since Mary left."

"What! Are you tiring of my company?" the carpenter asked jovially.

"Never!" the old man said with a look of concern on his face. "Joseph, I hope you know I was just joking. You're always welcome here."

"I know. I just thought one good tease deserves another." Both men laughed.

Joseph walked toward the open gate. In the distance he saw the lead rider of the caravan. "Please, Lord, let Mary be with them," he prayed, while he waited and nervously brushed his side curls over his ears. His smile beamed across his face as he saw his love approaching the gate. Mary had never looked more beautiful than she did now. He noticed that her face was a little fuller than he remembered it, but that just enhanced her beauty. As soon as Mary passed under the archway, Joseph ran to her and lifted her up in his arms. She was just a little heavier, it seemed. She didn't linger in his embrace as long as she had when he returned from his trip. *Maybe she's just overtired,* he thought. "Where are Uncle Azor and Aunt Tamar?" he asked with real concern in his voice.

"They stayed behind," Mary said. "I have so much to tell you and my parents, but let's get home first. Before we do, though, I'd like you to meet my traveling companions. They've really been good to me." She introduced them to her fiancé. Joseph thanked them profusely and ran to a market booth to buy them some dates and tangy dried apricots. Shortly after he returned, the caravan left for Sepphoris. Mary and Joseph walked hand-in-hand to her parents' house. When she reached the courtyard, her mother and father ran out to greet her. Anna immediately noticed there was something different about Mary. She looked healthier and had a certain glow about her. When she hugged her daughter, Anna's rounded abdomen rubbed against her daughter's. She could feel that her Mary had gained a little weight in the midsection. *Elizabeth must be a good cook,* she thought. Joachim hugged and kissed his daughter, and the four went inside the house.

The moment they sat down, Mary began to tell them about Elizabeth and Zechariah's experience. She ended it by saying the elderly couple had a baby boy. "They named him John," Mary said, "and he will be the precursor of the Messiah, according to the angel and Zechariah's prophetic canticle." Anna clasped her hands and held them to her bosom as she praised the Lord. The men sat with their mouths partially opened as Mary concluded her story. They too praised the Lord God of Jacob.

400

That evening, Joseph noticed Mary was a little distant. Anna noticed it too. Before her trip, Mary would purposely put her hand closer to Joseph's so he could reach and hold it. She didn't do so tonight. *Maybe she just needs some rest; the trip was grueling,* Anna thought. She knew how tired she felt when she returned from the Passover celebration. That night, when Mary and her parents retired for the evening, Anna feigned sleep. When she thought her daughter was sleeping, Anna raised herself up on one elbow and looked down at Mary's midsection. Her petticoat clung to her body. Anna's worst fears were realized. Mary's rounded abdomen was quite evident under the white fabric. *Tomorrow is the full moon, and it should be her time of month,* Anna thought. *I'll watch Mary closely. If she doesn't have her cycle, I'll go and talk to Joseph.* She couldn't believe the pious young carpenter would have taken advantage of her daughter before they were wed. *He sure fooled me,* Anna said to herself as she fell asleep with tears in her eyes. She didn't know that her daughter was just feigning sleep.

Mary had been praying silently when she felt her mother stir. She could feel Anna's eyes looking down at her. The teen's heart ached. She wanted to tell her mother everything, but she thought it would be a lack of trust in her Maker if she did. Mary had told the angel that she was the Lord's servant and that the Almighty should use her as He desired. "You are my refuge and my strength, O Lord," she continued to pray silently in the words of the psalmist. "It's in You that I trust." Mary could hear her mother crying. She wanted to comfort her, but she didn't want her mother to know she was awake. When Anna finally stopped

401

crying and Mary was certain that her mother was asleep, she put her hand on her tummy and rubbed it gently as she whispered, "I feel so badly, Jesus; we made Your grandma cry." Misty-eyed, the young virgin finally surrendered to sleep.

Two weeks after the full moon, Anna was sure that Mary was pregnant. It was time for her to go see Joseph. She walked across the street and knocked on his door. When Joseph saw Anna standing there, he went to hug her, but she pulled back. "Come in, Mother," he said. "Is something wrong?" Anna started to tremble as she broke down in tears. Joseph stepped forward to comfort her, but Anna pulled back even further. "Now I know there's something wrong. What is it, Mother? You can tell me!"

Anna wiped the tears from her eyes as she said, "Joseph, you're a wolf in sheep's clothing! How long did you think it would take before I noticed Mary is pregnant? If you want to regain some standing in this family, take Mary as your wife now and spare her any further shame. No wonder she went to Elizabeth's; she knew you weren't honorable enough to leave her alone. You tell my husband! I don't want to be the one to break his heart." As soon as she finished speaking, she turned around and left, slamming the door behind her.

Joseph stood there with his mouth open. He was in complete shock. The carpenter began to tremble as his face turned bright red. He slammed his fist into the door but was unfazed by the pain; the anguish in his heart was far worse than anything he felt in his bloody, skinned hand. The intricately detailed treasure

402

chest he had carved for Mary was within his reach. He picked it up. With all of his strength he slammed it into the wall. He heard the wood crack, and the damaged chest fell to the ground. Joseph walked to his bed and reclined. He covered his face with his strong hands and wept. "She's pregnant." He couldn't even say her name. "And the baby's not mine. I hope she doesn't try to say that a couple of kisses caused this; everybody knows better," he said. "She can't blame me." His sobs grew louder and louder.

Anna returned to her house. Mary could see how upset her mother was. She asked, "Is everything all right, Momma?" Anna just raised her hand and quickly lowered it in disgust. She never answered. Mary knew that Anna knew she was going to be a grandmother. The two women didn't speak to each other until that evening.

Joseph just lay there. He lowered his hands from his face, but the light from the window shone right into his eyes. He was so depressed. All he wanted to do now was sleep. The carpenter wanted to numb the pain he felt, but then there was the possibility of nightmares; he didn't know which was worse. He draped his arm over his eyes; it blocked the light, but he couldn't stop the nagging thoughts of Mary's betrayal from haunting him. Anger still churned inside him. He couldn't sleep. Knowing what he had to do, he shot up from his bed. The carpenter washed his bloody hand and wrapped it in some cloth. He then stepped over the damaged chest that was still on the floor, and opened his door. Joseph impulsively ran down the street toward the Synagogue.

It was a beautiful day, so Rabbi Asa was holding class under the huge sycamore tree when he saw Joseph approaching. The young carpenter realized the rabbi was busy, so instead of stopping, the tormented carpenter walked toward the precipice. *Where's that serpent now?* Joseph asked himself. *If it were here, I'd antagonize it so it would strike me and end my sorry life.* But there was no need for the snake; evil is always close at hand. Satan, the great deceiver, has a way of entering the thoughts of the disheartened.

You should throw yourself off this precipice. Your life is ruined. Should you bear the shame for that woman's folly? She duped you! Do you want to raise someone else's child? Have you no pride left? Do something! Act now. Joseph walked closer to the edge.

Go ahead, Satan continued. *Just one more step forward and all this will be over with. The pain you might feel won't be any worse than the pain you're feeling right now. One more step, Joseph; that's all it would take. Just one more step forward, and all the pain will end forever. Your life has been nothing but misery and sorrow. It will never end. God won't blame you for your actions. Go ahead, Joseph; do it now. Jump! Jump! Jump!*

Joseph looked straight down and saw nothing but empty space below him. He stepped back quickly as he repeated the words of a psalm he remembered, *"You, O Lord, are my defender. I will never be defeated."* He chastised himself for even considering the temptation to leap. He still believed what the Scripture said, that the Lord holds us in the palm of His hand. The disheartened carpenter sat down. The beauty of the fertile valley in the distance calmed him somewhat. Joseph began to toss small pebbles into the barren gorge below as he waited for the rabbi to finish teaching. He soon tired of it and sprawled out on the rocky surface under the heat of the scorching summer sun.

Asa tried to rush through his teaching session without depriving his students of the wisdom that the Scriptures and the Law contained. He saw how dejected Joseph looked. As soon as he dismissed his pupils, he ran into his house, briefly explained the situation to his wife and started to leave.

"Wait!" his wife said, quickly putting some bread, dried fish and a small flask of olive oil into a large napkin and tying its ends together. "You and Joseph need to eat something." The rabbi thanked his wife, kissed her, and then grabbed a full waterskin as he hurried off toward the precipice. He felt fortunate to have such a loving, understanding wife. When he reached the bluff, he saw Joseph lying dangerously close to the edge of the rocky ledge, with his arm over his eyes. Asa didn't want to startle the young man, so he softly called his name several times. Joseph lowered his arm. He squinted at the bright midday sun, and rolled toward Asa. Joseph stood up and greeted the teacher.

The two men sat down well away from the sheer drop-off. "My wife, the thoughtful person that she is, packed us a small lunch, Joseph," Asa said. "Shall we pray first?" Joseph nodded. The rabbi led them in prayer as they faced the Holy City. He then untied the ends of the napkin and spread the meager meal before them. Asa noticed that Joseph barely picked at the food. "Tell me, Joseph, what did you do to your hand?" the rabbi asked as he finished eating. "And why do you look so troubled?"

At first Joseph just rubbed his wrapped hand against his thigh, then he started to brush back his curls as he said, "I just scraped it on a very large piece of wood." He wasn't lying; he just didn't want to share the whole story. "Teacher, my friend has this moral dilemma. He's engaged to what he thought was a good, pious woman. Well, it seems that he found out she's expecting a baby and he isn't the father. What would you advise him to do?"

The rabbi held his bearded chin in his hand as he looked down and thought for a moment. "The Law says she should be stoned to death." He saw the tortured look on Joseph's face. "But," he continued, "the Law at times doesn't consider God's mercy. The Almighty forgives the penitent sinner, and in the case you presented, there are two lives to consider—the mother-to-be, who is the guilty party, and the innocent life she is carrying. To take the life of the innocent would punish the child for the sin of the mother. In my opinion, that would be an injustice, and in opposition to God's call for justice tempered with mercy. But, if her fiancé decided to have her stoned, according to the letter of the Law, he would be fully justified in his decision. Does he know who the father is?"

"No, I—I mean he—no, he doesn't know who the man is," the flustered carpenter said as he stumbled on his words and nervously pushed back his side curls.

406

The teacher was a very clever man. At first he thought Joseph might be the so-called friend he spoke of, but when he mentioned adultery, the rabbi just couldn't believe Mary could be guilty of that act. Asa saw how distraught and confused Joseph was. He knew this would be the ideal time to establish who the characters in Joseph's story really were, so he said, "You know, Joseph, sometimes when people are traveling in caravans, they can be taken advantage of, especially a young attractive woman. Do you think Mary could've been raped?"

Joseph looked shocked as he said, "I never thought of that!" He then realized he had just confirmed that Mary was the adulteress.

The rabbi placed his hand on the young man's shoulder and said, "Joseph, I've seen Mary with you. She adores you. It's hard for me to believe she would consent to have relations with anyone else voluntarily. Have you talked to her about this yet?"

"No I haven't, Teacher. Anna just came over a few hours ago and accused me of taking advantage of Mary and getting her pregnant. I haven't seen Mary since."

"Before we discuss your options, Joseph, just think of how our nation as a whole sinned, and has been unfaithful to God and His laws. Our forefathers brought idols into the Temple, the very dwelling-place of God's name. They burned incense before those graven images, and worshiped them in the Lord's own house. They covered the sacred walls with pagan symbols and sacrificed their children in fire to Moloch and Baal. Yet God in His mercy didn't completely destroy us. Instead, He sent us into exile and saved a remnant that acknowledged their sinfulness and repented. He then brought us back to the land He promised to our fathers. Look at your ancestors David and Bathsheba. According to the Law, she and the king should have been stoned. And if they had been, you wouldn't be here today. In my opinion, there shouldn't be one law for royalty and another for us common folk. God sees no difference between us and loves us all the same. We must always be willing to temper justice with mercy, for God is merciful with us. So, my dear friend, let's consider your options. The first would be to go to Mary and find out what really happened. If she's been raped, you could either marry her or issue her a writ of divorce and send her away.

"Another option would be to go to the man who impregnated her and offer to issue Mary a writ of divorce. Then he could marry her and her life would be spared. If he chooses not to, you could still divorce her and send her away. Or if you found it in your heart to forgive her, just marry your fiancée with no questions asked and raise the child as if it was your own, claiming legal parentage. The most regrettable, in my opinion, would be to publicly accuse Mary of adultery and have her stoned to death. None of these are easy decisions, Joseph. Pray to the Almighty to guide you, and He will show you the way. Don't make a rash decision, whatever you do. There are two lives involved. Come talk to me, day or night, if you need to unburden yourself. I'm always available, Joseph. Just don't despair. Promise me."

The rabbi knelt, and put his arms around Joseph as the carpenter wept bitterly on his shoulder. When Joseph could weep no longer, the two men stood up. As they walked toward the Synagogue, Asa placed his arm around Joseph's shoulder. When they parted, the rabbi said, "Remember, Joseph, I'm always here for you. You're a good man, Joseph Bar Jacob; God will direct you to do what's right in His sight."

The rabbi headed back home, but instead of going inside, he decided to go to the Synagogue. He couldn't believe that a gentle soul like Mary would willingly consent to adultery. *It can't be true; Mary's too sweet and innocent,* he thought. *She wouldn't hurt anyone, especially Joseph. She's too much in love with him to break his heart like this. It just can't be. Something isn't kosher.* Asa faced the wooden cabinet that contained the Holy Torah, and bowing low, he prayed to God to shed His light on the situation these young people faced. "O Lord, Joseph is such a righteous young man, and Mary is such a pious, wise, obedient, God-fearing young virgin." When he said those words, something clicked in his mind. He remembered the night of Passover, the garish sounds of evil. Tamar's claim of seeing the Angel of Life, Mary's glowing as if she had stood in the very presence of the Almighty Himself, and the heavenly scent. Asa stood erect; he opened the cabinet and looked for the scrolls of the prophet Isaiah. He finally found them.

A candle constantly burned before the cabinet that contained the holy writings. Asa took a taper, held it to the flame, and lit the lamp that stood on the reading table. He spread the scrolls out and began to search for a certain passage. His finger scanned the Hebrew words and stopped abruptly. The good rabbi found what he was looking for. Asa read it aloud. *"'Therefore the Lord Himself will give you a sign: The virgin will be with child and will give birth to a son, and you will call Him Immanuel.'"* The rabbi scanned more passages, and his finger stopped at these words: *"For a child is born, to us a son is given, and the government will rest upon His shoulders. And He will be called Wonderful Counselor, Mighty God, Everlasting Father, Prince of Peace."*

Asa searched further and found the passage. *"'A shoot will come up from the stump of Jesse; from his roots a Branch will bear fruit. The Spirit of the Lord will rest on him.'* I think Mary is carrying the Anointed One," Asa said aloud in amazement. "Isaiah confirms it. Both Mary and Joseph are from the royal lineage of David, and Jesse was the king's father." Chills ran down Asa's spine. He continued to read the other prophets as well. The only thing that countered his supposition was the location of the Messiah's birth. A passage written by the prophet Micah stated that the Anointed One was to be born in the same place as King David—the town of Bethlehem. Mary and Joseph lived in Nazareth.

It was past dinnertime when the rabbi's wife called out to him as she stood behind the grillework that separated the court of women from the Synagogue proper, "Asa, are you going to study all night? Your dinner is already cold! Come into the house, dear. You can study further tomorrow, when the light is better."

410

"Wait for me, dear; I just have to put these scrolls away and then we can walk back to the house together." So his wife waited for him in the waning moonlight.

It had been a hot summer day, but now the evening was pleasantly cool. The sliver of the moon that hung in the sky above allowed the stars to glow even brighter than they normally did. As Asa came through the darkened archway of the Synagogue, his wife said, "Look to the east, dear! There's a falling star."

"You and I will see more wondrous things than that, my love. I believe that we will be blessed enough to see the days of Messiah."

"Are you sure, Asa?" she asked excitedly.

"I'm almost positive, dear! Almost positive!" The couple walked back to the house hand-in-hand. Asa finally ate his dinner.

Mary was somber as she sat at the table with her parents. Her mother hadn't spoken to her all day. When she would ask her mother a question, Mary would receive a one-word answer at best.

"Why isn't Joseph coming to dinner tonight?" Joachim asked.

"A man has to work to earn a living. With so much daylight at this time of year, he's probably finishing one of his many projects," Anna said abruptly. "Besides, he doesn't have to eat here every night, does he? They're not married yet, you know." Joachim was surprised at his wife's sharp tongue; she never had spoken to him that way before. She usually fawned over Joseph. He couldn't understand her attitude this evening. Mary wasn't herself either. Joachim knew when to keep his mouth shut, so he continued eating and said nothing else. All that could be heard in their home that evening was the clanking of utensils as Anna served the meal in agitation. Mary ate very little.

When Joseph returned from his meeting with the rabbi, he stared at the empty courtyard across the street before entering his home. He wouldn't be joining Mary and her parents for dinner later. Anna had bruised his pride; besides, he had to decide what to do. The carpenter immediately went to his bed and laid down. It was late afternoon, and there were still many hours of daylight left before sunset. He could've done some carpentry work, but he worried that he wouldn't put forth his best effort, and Joseph was a perfectionist. He put his arms behind his head and closed his eyes.

Satan once again slithered his way into the young carpenter's thoughts. *Have her stoned to death. Look at what she's done to your reputation. Remember the rumors Zillah spread on the day you were betrothed? Now people will believe them. Everyone will see you as an out-of-control pervert. She's made a fool of both the rabbi and you. Remember how he defended you on that day? How long do you think it'll take before even he starts to question your moral character? Have her stoned to death! The sooner the better! That way you'll be vindicated. If people then give some credence to Zillah's story, Mary will be the aggressor, not you. You're perfectly justified to point that out to the public. Go do it now—there's plenty of daylight left. Even the rabbi said that it's in accordance with the letter of the Law. You deserve the justice that the Law demands. She's nothing but a lying, cheating...*

412

Joseph jumped up from his bed before the thought could be completed. He hurried to the stable room and began to brush his donkey. "I have to keep myself busy so this won't get to me," he said aloud. "I can't let myself keep sinking lower and lower like this." The donkey turned its head and looked at Joseph with its sad eyes, as if it understood the predicament the carpenter was in. Joseph couldn't go on grooming the donkey forever, or else the poor animal wouldn't have any coat left. He put down the brush and finally picked the chest up off the floor. When he lifted the cover, it split in two, right through the center of the lilies he had carved deeply into the wood. It was now flawed, just like the fiancée he had so cherished and respected. The flask of expensive perfume, however, was undamaged because of his skill. Joseph had carved out a depression that perfectly matched the shape of the flask.

When Joseph lifted the perfume from the chest, the wooden bottom also split. "Broken dreams! Broken promises!" he shouted as he set the flask of nard aside and reached for the flint. He placed it over a pile of straw that was still in his winter oven. *Let them think I'm crazy for cooking inside on such a hot day. Why should I care anymore?* he said to himself. When the straw caught fire, he put the four pieces of the chest over it and sat down with his back to the wall. The greedy flames ate away at the wood. Like his hopes and dreams, he watched as all his effort went up in smoke and disappeared. All that remained of the chest, and his plans for the life he hoped to have with Mary, were a few glowing coals and a pile of ashes. The disheartened young man watched the glowing embers.

413

The night's darkness crept over the town. Joseph's heavy eyelids closed in sleep. With it came his childhood nightmare. It was almost the identical dream he'd had just before he left for his apprenticeship. *It started out in the same peaceful way with him and his father going out to fell the cedar tree. Except for his Aunt Rebecca, the same characters were there, and it followed nearly the same sequence. Instead of his aunt coming down as a bat and beating him, though, Anna had the broom, and she kept whacking him with it. When he crawled to the edge of the cliff to try and help his father, Joseph saw Mary there instead, covered with blood. Her hand was extended upward toward him as she pled for help, while the townspeople kept stoning her.*

The trembling young man awoke screaming, "No! No! Stop it now!" Sweat poured from his face. He trembled so much, he was afraid to stand. Joseph raised his knees to his chest and buried his face in his hand. "I could never let them do that to her. I still love her!" he said as he began to sob deeply. "Lord, what am I to do?" Joseph pleaded with his Maker for a solution to his dilemma. When the trembling stopped, he stood up and went to the door. It was now night. He kept brushing his side curls back as her walked through the dark, empty street, contemplating the options that were still open to him. Stoning, he knew, was definitely out of the question.

Mary sat in her courtyard with her back to the wall. She wondered why no light came from Joseph's windows. "Maybe he's left us," she said to her unborn son. "I think Grandma told him about You, Jesus. But we can't blame him, can we? He's such a good, pious

414

man, and You know what he probably thinks. My heart is breaking with the hurt he must be feeling. I still love him so much, but no one would believe me if I told them what really happened. And if I did, You wouldn't be able to grow up like a normal child. Even Grandma and Grandpa would treat You differently. I want You to be able to run through a mud puddle, do somersaults, and chase after a butterfly. If our neighbors found out, they'd probably expect You to turn water into wine when the grape crops do poorly, or make it rain during droughts, or at least make our crops multiply. And they'd always be watching You. We're just going to have to let Your Father work this out for us. I know He won't let anything happen to You or me."

When Mary finished talking, she saw Joseph's door open. She watched as he walked down the darkened street. "He's still here, Jesus. See, Your Abba will take care of everything." Just as Mary told her baby that His Daddy would take care of things, she felt a flutter in her abdomen. She smiled her first smile in days. Mary sat there for a while longer. She saw Asa come up to Joseph's door. He knocked and then stepped inside. "I think the rabbi knows about us too," Mary said to the child within her womb.

As Joseph sat watching the flames eating away at the chest he had carved, the rabbi laid next to his wife; he was so excited, he couldn't sleep. With tears in his eyes he praised the God of Jacob for letting him live to see the Days of Messiah. He couldn't understand how a virgin could become pregnant without knowing man, but he knew nothing was impossible with God. Could the Almighty actually be the Messiah's Father? Asa remembered Mary's question about what the great patriarchs had done to have God choose them from all others for His divine purpose. He remembered his response to Mary about being favored just because God chose to do so. *Did Mary, the favored one, somehow know way back then that she would be the mother of the Messiah?* Asa asked himself. He also recalled the wonderful fragrance coming from Mary's house when he walked her home on the night of Passover. When he inquired about it, he recalled Mary saying something about the smell being "heavenly." His excitement intensified when he realized that he, Asa Bar Simeon, might some day teach the Messiah the Sacred Scriptures and the Law. The rabbi rolled out of bed and gently tapped his wife's shoulder. "I've got to go see someone right now," he whispered.

"Asa, it's nighttime. Who would be up at this hour?"

"I'm positive that the person I'm going to see will be," he replied. He kissed his wife and left. As he walked through the darkened streets, he asked himself, *What if Joseph has done something already? I've got to tell him what I know before he makes some rash decision that he'll regret later. I know he's a rational, righteous man, but when somebody gets hit in the head with a load full of bricks—and that's what Anna's accusations must have felt like to him—who could blame the man if he went a little crazy? Wait a minute—maybe Joseph gives Mary a writ of divorce and sends her away, and that's how she gets to Bethlehem. But then I'll never be able to be Messiah's teacher. He just can't choose stoning. I've got to warn him. He just can't do that.*

416

When Asa arrived at Joseph's house, he didn't notice Mary in the courtyard across the street. He stepped into the dark house and softly called Joseph's name. There was no response. A few embers still glowed in the winter oven, so the rabbi felt his way to the stable. He found a piece of straw, placed the end of it on the hot ember and gently blew on it. The tip caught fire, and he lit Joseph's night candle. Asa waited for about an hour, but Joseph didn't return. The embers had since turned to ash. The rabbi rummaged through the heap and found a piece of charred wood the fire hadn't totally consumed. He grabbed it gingerly. When he was sure it was cool, he found a small piece of wood in Joseph's shop. He wrote on it in Aramaic, "Don't harm the Messiah or God will never forgive you." He stood it up on its end over the winter oven, where he thought Joseph would see it. At that very moment, Asa decided to return to Joseph's the first thing in the morning. If the carpenter still wasn't home, he'd ask Eliud if Joseph had left town.

Mary saw the glow of candlelight through Joseph's windows shortly after Asa entered. "I wonder what the rabbi's doing there?" she said to her son. "We should go inside now; the wind seems to be picking up." So Mary entered the house and went to sleep.

When Asa left Joseph's house, the door slammed shut. The vibration knocked over the small board that Asa's message was written on. It fell to the floor and landed face-down near the oven. If Joseph had found it and read it, he wouldn't have understood what it meant anyway. The rabbi realized that fact as he crawled back into bed.

Joseph, for the past couple of hours, sat on the hillside where he spent his boyhood years. He stared up at the starry sky and felt lifeless and lonely. The hollow sound of the pebbles he tossed down the hillside added to his feeling of solitude. He reviewed his remaining options over and over without reaching any real conclusion. He slowly walked back to his house, eliminating one option after another. When he entered his home, he removed his outer clothing and sat on the edge of the bed. Joseph didn't remember lighting the candle before he left, but it was a troubling day, and he thought he could have done so. *Who else would have done it but me?* he wondered. He was sure that it wasn't Mary—not tonight, at least. Not after she knew that he knew of her pregnancy. The carpenter noticed a small board on the floor. Without bothering to turn it over, he picked it up and put it on his workbench.

After much soul-searching, Joseph finally decided what to do. Tomorrow morning he would go over to Mary's and give her a writ of divorce. He'd also give her the small amount of money he had saved and send her away into confinement. She still had some distant relatives in Sepphoris. Her parents wouldn't have to travel that far to see her and their new grandchild. *I'll send her more money when I can,* Joseph said to himself. His heart was still heavy, but at least Mary would live and be able to raise her child. The baby wouldn't have to pay for the sin of its mother, either. He prayed the words of a psalm, *"'Help me to do Your will, for You are my God, and lead me in the right path, for Your spirit never deceives.'"* Then the brokenhearted carpenter swung

418

his long legs up onto the bed and fell into a deep sleep. Surprisingly, he had a very pleasant dream—or was it reality? Joseph would never know for sure.

The carpenter woke at daybreak, sitting on the edge of his bed. He took a deep breath and filled his lungs with the mildly fragrant air. He opened his door slightly and saw Mary returning from the well. When her back was to him, he opened the door a little more and saw that she already had filled his water jar. Hurriedly, Joseph washed up and dressed. He wanted to catch Joachim before he went to his shop. He needed Mary and both of her parents present when he was to do what he planned. Joseph was very neat; he couldn't stand anything out of place. Seeing the small board on his workbench, he picked it up and was about to return it to the woodbin. When he grabbed it and turned it over, he saw the note. As he read it, he smiled. The rabbi was wrong; Joseph *did* understand what Asa meant. Instead of placing the board back where it belonged, he left it face-up on his dining table, then ran across the street to Mary's house.

Mary had just returned to the room after milking the goats when she heard a knock on the door. Joachim was sitting cross-legged at the low table, eating; he was about to rise when Anna said, "I'll get it." Wiping her hands in her apron, she went to the door and opened it. Rather than hugging Joseph like she normally did, she simply stepped back and said, "Shalom!" She wouldn't even speak his name.

Joseph had started to lean forward to hug Anna, but when he saw her reaction, he thought it best not to do so. "Shalom, Mother! Is Father still home?"

Joachim put the bread in his hand down on his plate. He stood up and said, "Shalom! And good morning to you, Joseph! We missed you at dinner last night." He walked toward his daughter's fiancé and kissed his chin.

Joseph returned the greeting and immediately said, "I have to talk to you and Mother; it's very important!" He saw the look of concern on Joachim's face as he addressed Mary for the first time and said, "Why don't we sit down at the table? Mary, please sit next to me." Joachim was intrigued; he had never heard Joseph speak so commandingly before. The carpenter didn't want to look into Mary's beautiful eyes. If he did, he knew he would lose control of the situation and start stammering again. He was so confident in what he was about to do that he didn't even brush back his side curls when he sat down.

Mary took her place next to Joseph; Anna sat down beside her husband at the opposite side of the table. "Shall we begin?" Joseph asked. Mary lowered her eyes and looked down at the table. She didn't know what to expect.

Rabbi Asa overslept. His class was supposed to begin in about a half-hour. "Why didn't you wake me, dear?" he asked his wife.

"I thought that after your late night you could use some extra sleep. You don't have to teach the Law the first thing every morning, you know. I was planning to school the children with reading and writing first, and then when you awoke, you could do your instructing."

"Excellent idea, my dear!" the rabbi said as he jumped out of bed and did more of a ritualistic ablution than a thorough washing. "I think they could benefit immensely from a full day's session on those two subjects alone. I've got some life-saving business I have to take care of first thing this morning. Would you be willing to teach the class all day?"

"Of course! Just go do what you have to do."

The rabbi kissed his wife and flew out the door, chomping on a couple of dates as he ran toward Joseph's house. When he got there, he knocked on the door; there was no answer. The rabbi entered anyway. He saw the board on Joseph's table and chastised himself for not leaving a clearer message. *I foolishly wrote that with foreknowledge of the facts that I learned,* he thought. *How could I have possibly thought that Joseph could understand this with his limited knowledge of the situation? I'm supposed to be a learned rabbi, but my message sounds as if a dunce wrote it.* He left the house and ran toward the town gate to question Eliud.

By the time he reached the old gatekeeper, Asa was winded. He was breathing so deeply he could hardly speak.

"Rabbi! What is it?" Eliud asked. "I've never seen you panting like this before."

Asa still didn't regain his regular breathing pattern. Between deep, heavy breaths, he managed to ask, "Did you ... see Joseph ... leave town ... yesterday or today?"

"No, Rabbi! I haven't. Why? Did something happen?"

421

"Not yet, I hope!" Asa said, finally regaining his breath. "I just have something very important to discuss with him."

Joseph sat across the table from Joachim and looked him straight in the eye as he said, "Father, I would like to move our wedding to tomorrow evening. Mary is expecting. The sooner we do this, the better it'll be for all of us." Mary looked up at her fiancé with even more admiration and smiled at him. Her baby fluttered several times too. The young carpenter was prepared for a tirade, but instead he thought he saw a smile forming at the corners of Joachim's mouth.

He tried to sound like the stern father, but the love of a prospective grandpa made his voice mellower than he intended. "Very well, then. We can have the wedding supper here. No big or elaborate gathering, mind you! Who will your witnesses be?"

"I'll be asking the good rabbi and Nabu," Joseph replied.

Joachim's eyes welled up with tears from the knowledge that he soon would have a grandchild to actually bounce upon his knee and watch grow. "Have them bring their wives and families too," he said. "I think Mary and Anna could handle that." The two women nodded in agreement.

"Thank you, Father!" Joseph said as he went over to embrace Joachim. He was surprised when Anna came toward him and gave him a big hug too.

Mary's mother whispered in his ear, "You've done the right thing, Joseph Bar Jacob."

He squeezed Anna a bit harder as he said, "I know I have, Mother. Thank you for telling me about the baby." Anna was shocked that Mary hadn't told him anything, but then, Mary had never told her, either. Joseph said, "I have to go and ask the rabbi and Nabu to be my witnesses." He bid farewell to Anna, and Joachim. Mary grabbed his hand and walked him to the door. He didn't squeeze it like he normally did.

As he was about to leave, Mary stood on her tiptoes and gave Joseph a kiss on the cheek. "Thank you! Joseph, the Lord will bless you for what you're doing," she whispered.

The carpenter backed away slightly. "Shalom, Mary! I'll be back at dinnertime." Joseph didn't know how to act in the presence of the mother of the Messiah. He was afraid to even touch his fiancée.

Mary watched Joseph leave as she whispered, "See, Jesus! Your Abba worked everything out." The young virgin then turned and entered the stable through the courtyard. Today was the day of the week that she had to muck the animal stalls.

As Joseph was crossing the street, he heard Asa calling out his name. The young man turned and saw the out-of-breath rabbi running toward him. "Joseph, you've caused me to get more exercise than I get from a trip to Jerusalem."

The carpenter laughed and said, "I've heard it said that exercise is good for your health." He grabbed hold of the rabbi and gave him a hearty hug. "If you have time, would you please come inside? I'd like to talk to you, Rabbi."

"I was hoping you'd say that," Asa replied. "I've got a lot of things to tell you too."

When they entered Joseph's home, the two men sat on the floor, facing each other. Asa said, "First I want to apologize for the message I left you last night. I was excited and not thinking clearly when I wrote it. I assumed a lot when I did."

"No need to apologize, Rabbi. I didn't read it until this morning, and it made perfect sense to me when I did. If I had read it last night, though, I wouldn't have understood it at all."

"What do you mean, Joseph?"

"Well, Teacher, after a long walk and a lot of soul-searching, I finally made up my mind to divorce Mary and send her away." Joseph could see the disappointment on Asa's face. "I was heartbroken, but kind of glad at the same time, because I finally knew what I was going to do. You see, I sat for a while on the hillside by Ali's house where I grew up. I remembered how difficult it was for Aunt Rebecca to accept me. I wasn't related to her by blood, so she resented me terribly, God rest her soul. I thought that if I were to take Mary as my wife, her child would be a perpetual reminder of her infidelity. I might have ended up taking out my misery on her son or daughter too. I knew what that felt like. I couldn't do that to Mary or her child; it'd be just too cruel."

"Joseph, you can't just send her away, not if you know what my message really meant."

"Wait, Rabbi! I haven't finished my story yet. Anyway, I went to bed, and I don't know if it was a dream or if it just seemed like one, but I never remember having smelled anything in either of my past dreams or even my nightmares. Yet in this one, I definitely smelled a sweet fragrance. *It was almost like the room was filled with flowers or something that smells nice like that. I hear this great-sounding voice calling my name, 'Joseph, Joseph, son of David.' So, I swing my legs to the floor, I sit at the edge of my bed and start rubbing my eyes because the room is so bright, it's like looking directly into the sun. Then some of the light forms into—into like an angel—I think that's what he was, anyway. I could see right through him, yet I saw him completely. I know that doesn't sound like it makes too much sense, but that's the best way I could describe him."*

Asa leaned forward and seemed to listen even more intently as Joseph continued. *"Then the angel comes and sits down next to me on my bed right over there; he puts his arm around me,* like this." Joseph leaned forward and demonstrated how it was done. *"And the strangest thing is that even though he's like a spirit, I can feel his arm resting on my shoulder, and I feel this calm come over me. The angel says, 'Have no fear about taking Mary as your wife. It's by the Holy Spirit that she's conceived this child. She's to have a son, and you're to name him Jesus, because He'll save His people from their sins.' We sit there for a while just saying nothing. It felt so peaceful that I didn't want him to leave.* The next thing I know, he's gone, and I wake up, sitting on the edge of my bed. The funny thing is I could still smell a bit of that fragrance in the air when I awoke."

The rabbi sat there wide-eyed and said nothing. "So, this morning, Rabbi," Joseph went on, "as soon as I washed up and dressed, I went over to Mary's and asked Joachim if I could take Mary as my wife tomorrow night, and he agreed. I also told him he was going to be a grandpa. Unlike Anna, he seemed a bit happier with the news, even though I know he didn't want to show it. I could still tell. What I'd like to ask of you, Rabbi, is, would you do me the honor of being a witness to our wedding?"

"The honor would be mine, Joseph. I never dreamed that I, a small-town rabbi, would be so blessed as to be in the presence of the Messiah before He's even born."

As soon as Joseph left, Joachim said to his wife, "So that's why you were so upset last night; you knew Mary was expecting. Why didn't you tell me?"

"Because I didn't know how you'd take the news, that's why!" Anna replied. "And I really didn't want to believe that our innocent, sweet Mary and a righteous man like Joseph would be intimate with each other until they were married. You know how vicious people can be. Really, I guess I just didn't want to face it myself."

"When did Mary tell you?"

"Funny thing is, she never did. I went over and confronted Joseph yesterday. Today he thanked me for letting him know. I guess he didn't know either. It hurts me to think she wouldn't have told me. We were always so close. Maybe it's her shame."

"Shame! What shame?" Joachim said. "Anna, Anna, you know in our culture it's the betrothal that binds a man and woman for life, not the wedding. A man can't end a betrothal without giving his fiancée a writ of divorce. In many of the towns right here in

426

Galilee and in Judea too, the couples live together and have relations with each other from the day of their betrothal. They consider the wedding as a day to celebrate the fact that they've worked out their differences and can now live together in a negotiated peace for the rest of their lives. Joseph's injuries drew the two of them into an emotional vortex. When people are caught up with such deep feelings and they center on a person you already love totally, I would think that yielding to each other physically then comes very easily. It just naturally follows. Intimacy is a surrender, my dear, be it emotional or physical. And it's hard to define where one ends and another begins."

"Joachim, you're right!" Anna said. "I think I was too hard on Joseph yesterday. I need to apologize; I didn't even greet him properly when he came over this morning. Maybe I should go over to his house right now and do so."

"Why don't you wait until this evening, when he comes to dinner? There's no rush! Meanwhile, you have a wedding to plan, and I'm going to go buy a whole lamb for the wedding supper. Just think, Anna—we're going to have a grandchild that lives right across the street from us. And we're sure going to spoil that little one too." Anna smiled at the thought. Then she kissed her husband as he left for the marketplace.

After Joseph finished his story, the rabbi told the young carpenter about the Messianic prophesies of Isaiah he had discovered. He didn't mention anything about the prophet Micah and his prediction that Bethlehem would be the town of the Messiah's birth. Obviously, the Almighty's plan was unfolding just as He had intended. The Lord didn't need Asa's help to have the prophecies fulfilled. Naturally, he was rather curious as to what would cause Mary to travel to that town. After the rabbi and Joseph parted, the young man ran to Nabu's house to ask him to be a witness to his marriage also.

The following evening just before sunset, both of Joseph's witnesses and their families gathered in Joachim's courtyard. Nabu assisted Mary's father; they removed the roasted lamb from the spit as the groom crossed the street. The guests followed Joachim into the house, as was the custom; the groom entered last. Because of the haste of the nuptial, none of the town's virgins were invited to lead the bridegroom inside, as was the tradition. Joseph took his place beside his fiancée. Mary looked radiantly beautiful even in her plain clothing. Her beauty dominated the room. He smiled at her as he sat cross-legged on the floor next to her. The group ate heartily, and toasted the young couple several times during the meal. When the supper was nearly over, Joachim handed Joseph a cup of wine while Anna placed a small bowl of honey and a single piece of flatbread in front of the young couple. Joseph divided the bread in half and rolled up each piece. He then handed one to Mary. They simultaneously dipped the bread into the honey and fed it to each other. Joseph was a bit nervous. His shaking hand left a drop of the amber liquid on her chin. The bride smiled as she wiped the droplet with her finger, then turned her head and

428

licked the golden liquid from her hand. The honey caused her chin to glisten in the candlelight. Joseph dipped the edge of a napkin in the wine and wiped the shiny spot with the moistened cloth. The guests laughed as they watched the couple interact. Joseph then took a sip of wine and handed the cup to Mary; she just moistened her lips with the claret liquid. The group shouted, "Mazel tov!"

The couple stood up and walked hand-in-hand to the door with their guests following close behind. The spouses of both Nabu and the rabbi formed a cradle with their arms and lifted Mary off the floor. The bride draped her arms over the women's shoulders. Joseph's two witnesses did the same for the young groom. They carried the couple to the threshold of their home. Anna lit a taper; shielding the flame with her hand, she led the group to the newlyweds' house. When they reached the door, Joachim extended his hands over the couple and gave them his blessing. Anna then handed Mary the lit taper, a tradition symbolizing their prayer that the Almighty would shed light on their path throughout their life together. The young carpenter opened his door and led Mary over his threshold. He closed the door behind them as the group outside shouted, "Mazel tov!" Joseph and Mary were now husband and wife.

As the guests returned to Joachim's house to celebrate further; Mary lit the night candle in her new home. Her husband never looked directly at his bride after he closed the door. She thought it might have been because Joseph thought she had been unfaithful to him. Mary wondered why Joseph had

429

married her with no questions asked. She had no way of knowing her new husband viewed her as the Ark of a New Covenant no one should touch. He knew more about her baby than she imagined. Joseph pointed to the bed and said, "Sleep there, Mary. It's more comfortable. I'll sleep on the floor."

The young bride removed her veil and smoothed her hair with her fingers as she said, "I love you, Joseph! You'll never know how much our wedding meant to me. You're a wonderful man!"

The newlywed blushed as he removed his cap and said. "I love you too, Mary." He then reclined on the floor, silently pleading with his God to give him the strength to resist carnal temptation and to instead do His will.

When Mary was certain her husband had fallen asleep, she slid to the edge of her bed and reached over the side. The young bride softly touched her husband's black curls as he slept on the floor beside her bed. Mary's other hand rested on her abdomen as she said, "I think Your Abba found the most righteous man in all of Israel for us, Jesus." Her baby turned within in her womb as she said those words; Mary knew that her son agreed.

The next day, when the townsfolk saw Mary entering and leaving Joseph's home, some of the women snickered. It wasn't as bad as Anna thought it would be, though. "That's what happens sometimes when a very handsome man and an exceptionally beautiful young woman live in such close proximity to each other when they're betrothed," one woman said. "Things sometimes happen!" It would have been far worse for the couple had Zillah still been alive.

CHAPTER 18

Joseph could hear the autumn rains pounding his rooftop. He was glad he had completed plowing and sowing his fields before the fall rains began. It was mid-October, over a year since he and Mary had been betrothed. He rose from the floor, stretched and looked down at his beautiful wife. She slept on her side near the edge of her bed with her lovely auburn hair fanned out around her. Joseph still couldn't believe she was his wife. He didn't want to wake her. Mary was very tired lately. The young man suspected his wife was in her last trimester. She had never told him when her child was to be born, and he never asked. He too trusted in the God of Abraham. Joseph knew that Anna had tried to calculate a date based on when she suspected Mary had conceived, but his wife was mum on the subject. The baby had grown considerably. He didn't think she had much longer to go before she delivered.

The rain only lasted a couple of hours, but it came down heavily enough to top off the water jar Joseph had placed outside. He knew it would save Mary a trip to the well today. While he carried the heavy jar into the house, Mary stirred. "You sure

431

slept well," Joseph said to his wife as she sat up in bed and rubbed the sleep from her eyes.

"The baby had a restful night, so we both had a good night's sleep," Mary replied. She asked if it had rained last night.

"More like early this morning," Joseph said. "So we have plenty of water. You don't have to go to the well today."

"You're obviously having trouble with your vision, my love. With all the weight I'm gaining, I could use all the exercise I can get. I'm as big as a house."

"You're not gaining weight; the baby is. Anyway, I thought pregnant women were supposed to lie in bed all day eating dates and figs."

Mary laughed as she said, "In what town, Joseph? Tell me, please! And take me there right now." They laughed together. Mary walked over to her husband, stood up on her toes and gave him a peck on the cheek. "I forgot to tell you good morning."

"I bet you never forget to say that to all of your other husbands," he said jokingly, and then realized what an insensitive remark he had just made. "I'm sorry, Mary! I didn't mean to imply anything by my stupid comment."

"Joseph! You're much too sensitive; I knew full well that you were joking. I know you know that you're the only man I love. I could never love any man as much as I love you." Joseph wanted to sweep her up in his arms and kiss her, but he still refrained from touching her. Instead he just blushed and played with his side curls as he replied that he loved her too.

Mary sat down on the edge of the bed and told Joseph to sit beside her. She took his hands in hers and looked into his dark, gentle eyes. "Joseph, I suspect you know who the father of my baby is. Do you, Joseph?" He nodded.

"Is that why you won't even hold my hand anymore?" she asked. The carpenter nodded his head again. "How did you find out?" she asked.

Joseph explained everything. He told her about the decision he had reached to send her away, and about the angelic dream that caused him to change his mind. He also told her what the rabbi had learned from the Scriptures. Joseph apologized for not believing in her when Anna broke the news to him. Then he told her about his childhood and the way that his Aunt Rebecca felt about him and that he didn't want to feel that way about her child.

"Joseph," Mary said, "promise me you won't tell anyone else what you know. I want this baby to have a normal childhood and not be hounded by the rabbis or priests, or anyone else, until God Himself is ready to reveal who He is. The Lord has handled things so far, and I know He'll continue to do so."

"I promise, Mary. I'm sorry about the rabbi, but I had to talk to someone. And he figured everything out even before I had the dream. But I trust Rabbi Asa, and I know he won't say anything to anyone."

"I've another question for you, Joseph. When the baby is born, who will the people think his father is?"

"Me, I guess!"

"And will you bounce Him on your knee and hold His hand when you go to the Synagogue and kiss Him goodnight? Maybe you'll even sit by the fire at night while He puts His sleepy head on your chest as you tell Him a bedtime story."

"I suppose so, Mary; I'll try to be a good father to Him."

"If you're going to do that with the Son of God, why won't you hold my hand? I'm just the wrapping, Joseph; *He's* God's precious gift." Mary smiled as Joseph clasped her hand as tightly as he had on the day of their betrothal. When he let go, she rested her head on his chest, and took his hand and put it on her abdomen. It was the first time he felt the baby move.

"Wow!" Joseph said as he laughed. The moment that he felt the baby stir, he felt a paternal relationship with Mary's son. "Doesn't it hurt when He kicks like that?" he asked. Mary was about to answer when they heard a sound that caused the tiny hairs on the back of both their necks to stand on end. It made them recall the terror of last fall.

While Mary and Joseph sat talking on the edge of the bed, the Roman centurion and his *aide-de-camp* came riding into town; twelve soldiers on foot followed close behind. The Centurion believed in treating all people with respect and never abused his power. He and his aide dismounted and tied their steeds to the hitching post. Gaius greeted Eliud warmly, then asked if the gatekeeper would summon the Senior Elder. Eliud liked the way the Centurion treated him, so he bowed and said, "Yes, Excellency!" and hobbled off to the Elder's home.

Boom, boom, boom. The sound of a single drumbeat echoed through the streets of town. The voice of the *aide-de-camp* could be heard shouting in Aramaic, "By order of the Emperor, Augustus Caesar, all heads of households must appear before the Centurion Gaius at the town gate at midday today to hear a decree from his August Majesty, the Emperor of Rome." The doors of the homes began to open as the townspeople stepped out into the street and began to inquire of each other what new hardship the Emperor was about to burden them with. Children hid behind their mother's skirts as they watched the two soldiers parade through the streets.

Joseph opened his door too. He saw his father-in-law standing across the street and went to join him. After they greeted each other, Joachim said, "For a moment there, when I heard the drumbeat, I thought Zillah had been resurrected from the dead. It sent chills down my spine."

"Mary and I felt the same way too, Father. I wonder what they're up to now."

"Only the Lord knows. I think that Augustus has nothing better to do than make our lives miserable. By the way, Joseph, how is Mary doing?"

"She's doing fine, Father, and so is your grandchild; He was just doing His exercises for us."

"Pretty sure it's a boy, are you?"

"I'm positive, just by the way He kicks." Both men laughed.

"I think I'll go over to the gate right now and try to find out what's going on," Joachim said. Joseph said he would join him. He'd just let Mary know where he was going. When he came back out to join his father-in-law, the rabbi was talking to Joachim. The three men made their way to the gate to see what they could learn. Most of the other townsmen did likewise.

The Centurion saw Joseph approaching, so he excused himself from the Senior Elder and walked over to the young carpenter. "Joseph!" he said. "I'd like to talk to you, if you have a moment."

"Certainly, sir!" Joseph replied. He excused himself and took his leave from the two men. Gaius walked toward the gatehouse. Joseph followed.

When they reached the wall and were away from most of the crowd, the Centurion said, "I just thought you'd be interested in knowing that the wounded soldier you brought back to camp survived, and he's doing fine now. He also won't be bothering you anymore. Deputy Hasid has been transferred to the Southern Division stationed in Jerusalem. Once again I want to thank you for what you did for him. My men are like sons to me. No matter how uncontrollable they sometimes get, I'm always concerned for their welfare. By the way, Joseph, where is your ancestral home?"

"It's Bethlehem, King David's birthplace. Why do you ask, sir?"

"Are you able to read Hebrew, Joseph?" The carpenter said that he could. The Centurion walked over to the gatehouse and returned with a scroll. "Turn and face the wall as you read this. I don't want the others to see it quite yet."

The carpenter read the decree. The Centurion could see the look of concern on his face. "My wife's pregnant, and the baby is to be born right around that time. Are there any exceptions, sir?"

"None, I'm sorry to say. The Emperor wants an accurate count by age groups, and everyone has to comply. He considers himself to be merciful by scheduling it during the winter so it won't interfere with your planting and harvests. By dividing the census into two separate age groups, none of your towns will be completely empty during any given month; that way your livestock won't suffer. Your age group will have to register during your month of Tebeth, the month we Romans call December. I wish I could do something for you, Joseph, but there are no exceptions to the Emperor's decree."

Joseph returned the scroll to the Centurion and thanked him for letting him see it before the other townspeople. He then returned to his father-in-law and the rabbi just as the *aide-de-camp* read the decree in four languages. Asa was the only person in the crowd who didn't grumble when they heard what the soldier read. The rabbi had a big smile on his face. The decree was posted on the town gate in Aramaic, Greek, Hebrew and Latin, and then the Centurion and his soldiers left.

As they walked home, Joseph and Joachim lamented their fate. The rabbi just kept smiling. "We can't even travel together," Joachim said to his son-in-law, "and Mary will probably be due when you have to travel. Mother and I have to register in the month of Kislev, and you and Mary can't register until the following month."

"It's probably better that way, Father," Joseph replied. "At least we can take care of each other's homes and animals." This made Joachim feel a bit better about the divided trip. When the three men were about to part, the rabbi told Joseph that if he had some time, he'd like to show him something.

"Sure, Rabbi!" the young carpenter said. "I have time right now!" So the two men walked toward the

Synagogue. Joseph was surprised the rabbi didn't seem upset by the inconvenience of the census.

When they reached the Synagogue, Asa said, "When you see what I have to show you, your opinion of the census will totally change." He went to the cabinet, withdrew the scroll of the prophet Micah, and brought it to Joseph. He spread the parchment on the reading table and pointed to a specific passage of the prophecy. "Read this, Joseph!"

Joseph began to read: *"'But you, Bethlehem-Ephrathah, too small to be among the clans of Judah, from you shall come forth for me one who is to be ruler in Israel; whose origin is of old from ancient times.'"* He looked up at the rabbi in amazement.

Asa pointed to the next passage. Joseph continued to read, *"'Therefore the Lord will give them up, until the time when she who is to give birth has borne, and the rest of His brethren shall return to the children of Israel. He shall stand firm and shepherd his flock by the strength of the Lord His God; and they shall remain, for now His greatness shall reach to the ends of the earth; He shall be peace.'"*

"You see, Joseph, the census wasn't Augustus's idea; it was God's," Asa said with a chuckle. "God has a sense of humor. He used a pagan to fulfill His will. The Lord had to get Mary and you to Bethlehem some way."

"I'm not questioning the wisdom of the Almighty or anything like that, but you know what, Rabbi? If the angel had told me to take Mary to Bethlehem, I would've done so. Then there wouldn't have to be a census."

"God works in strange ways, Joseph," the rabbi said, and the two men laughed.

438

When Joseph returned home, he told Mary about the census and about the prophecy that the rabbi had him read. "See how amazing the Almighty is," Mary said. "The most powerful person on this earth is still subject to God's will. He's doing God's bidding without even knowing it." Joseph nodded in agreement.

It was chilly that night as Mary and Joseph sat together by the fire that burned in the winter oven. The young carpenter, of his own volition, held his wife's hand. "Joseph, I think it's time I told you how all this came to be," Mary said. She proceeded to tell him the whole story, from the very first time that she heard her name called in the night, to her visit to her cousin's house. "That's why I had to leave and go see Elizabeth," she explained. "I felt like God's Spirit was prompting me to do so." Joseph had listened to his wife's entire story without interrupting once. Only glowing embers were left when Mary finished her tale.

Joseph said, "You know, Mary, it's strange—the fragrance you described in your vision is the same as the one I smelled when I had the dream. It makes me wonder even more if I was actually asleep when the angel spoke to me." Mary said she didn't think he'd been dreaming. She rested her head on her husband's chest, barely able to keep her eyes open. Joseph too felt his eyelids getting heavy. "I think it's bedtime, don't you?" he said. Mary gave her husband a tender kiss on the cheek, and the two prepared for bed. Joseph still slept on the floor. That night, a thick heavy fog covered the town like a pall blocking out the bright starlight and what little light was left of the waning moon.

It was way past midnight as Zaddu sat fireside, drinking the cup of thick, crimson liquid. She shook from head to toe as the slow-moving fluid ran down her throat. It wasn't as if she never drank the likes of it before, but she detested this kind. It didn't taste coppery like it was supposed to. It was sweet and pure; the witch couldn't stand it. Two distinct voices once again came from the hag's vocal cords. The high-pitched one screamed, "I can't drink any more; it's sickening! If I do, I'll vomit."

The gravelly, booming male voice said, "Drink all of it, old sow! You have to leave tonight!"

"But it's choking me!" the witch's voice shrieked as she lowered the cup from her lips and added more branches to the pyre. She ducked as the red-hot embers spat their glowing coals at her in retaliation.

The deep, eerie booming voice shouted, "No, you fool! Don't add any more wood. It destroys the sweet savory smell; let it smoke. Now, drink! Drink!" The crone gagged as she swallowed the remaining thick, crimson-colored liquid while the thunderous laugh of the Prince of Darkness echoed through the dark hills.

Mary awoke and shot up in her bed; she could hear the terracotta plates rattling in the small cabinet. The clatter was drowned out by a horrendous noise, like that of rolling thunder. Even with the night candle burning, the darkness of the night was overwhelming. Joseph too sat up from his place on the floor. He also heard the ghastly sounds. The hairs on the back of his neck stood up as the noise grew louder and continued. Mary reached down and touched her husband's shoulder. He jumped, then heard her say, "Joseph! What do you think that awful sound is? It's so frightening!"

440

"At first I thought it was just peals of thunder, but I don't know what it is. Maybe it's a mild earthquake, the way things are rattling around." Joseph didn't dare tell his wife what he was truly thinking. To him, the sound was so grotesque, it was what he imagined Satan's laughter would sound like. Finally the eerie noise stopped. When it did, the night didn't seem as dark to Mary as before. She slid all the way over to the edge of her bed. She turned on her side and lowered her hand back down toward her husband. Mary slept throughout the night with her hand touching Joseph's shoulder. She had no way of knowing that her husband was as frightened as she was.

Early the next morning, a hysterical woman who had recently given birth ran through the street, dressed only in her petticoat. "My baby! My baby!" she screamed. "My baby is missing!" She ran from house to house, yelling hysterically, trying to solicit the help of the townsfolk in locating her newborn. Her dumbfounded husband, clad only in his short tunic, stood at their door, his mouth wide open in disbelief. The townspeople immediately knew who was responsible. Joseph ran out of his house shortly after the screaming woman came to his door. He grabbed his pitchfork and ran to the town gate, where a posse had assembled. They carried clubs and all sorts of implements that could be used as weapons. Eliud intended to join them, but they convinced him to stay behind and stand guard. They ran down the road and took the fork that led to Zaddu's cave.

When they entered the darkened cavern, the men thrust their pitchforks in every direction in an attempt to kill the rats that normally roamed there. Neither the witch nor the rodents were anywhere to be found. Zaddu had been sent to southern Judea; her rats followed the decrepit hag. One of the men who had the forethought to bring a torch ran to the fire pit. He tried to find a glowing ember that he could coax into a flame to light the cave. Joseph went with him to see if he could help, because the cave was overly crowded.

That's when the young carpenter saw it. Tears filled Joseph's eyes as he pointed to the charred cartilage the fire hadn't consumed. Grabbing his tunic at mid-thigh, he poked a hole in the fabric with one of the prongs and stepped out of the circular piece of cloth. He gently picked up the remains with the cloth and wrapped them in it. "I'll place these in my family's ossuary," Joseph said. "No one needs to know about this gruesome scene, especially the baby's parents. Let them still have some hope in thinking that their child may still be alive. They don't have to know that their baby was a victim of a horrific satanic sacrifice."

Joseph carried the remains to the hillside tomb of his family members. He rolled the stone away from the entrance and stepped inside. His hands trembled as he opened the stone ossuary within the burial chamber and placed infant's remains among the bones of his family members. "Take good care of this little one," he said aloud to his loved ones who were interred there, especially to the mother he never knew. Joseph replaced the limestone lid over the rectangular box as he prayed to the God of Jacob, "Lord, show this little one Your glory and help his parents find peace and solace in You." When the emotional carpenter returned home, he fell into his loving wife's waiting arms and cried like a baby.

442

CHAPTER 19

Mary and Joseph had planned to leave for Bethlehem on the first day of Tebeth; her parents, however, hadn't returned until the end of the first week of that month. The painful arthritis in Anna's ankle delayed their travels, for they had to walk both ways. She had refused to let her husband take a wagon, because the roads were overcrowded. Anna didn't want to ride on their donkey, either. Her biggest fear was that the animal would lose its footing on the steep inclines because of her excessive weight.

Mary sat on the edge of her bed as she rolled diapers and sleepers into rectangular pieces of heavy cotton swaddling cloth for the trip to Bethlehem. Her husband entered just as she was tying the roll with wide bands of fabric. "Joseph! Have you packed the salt?" she asked. "We have to rub Jesus with it when He's born, before we swaddle Him." Joseph asked why they had to do that. "Momma said that's what has to be done to every newborn if you want the baby to be healthy," she replied. He asked how much they would need. "A few handfuls, I suspect," Mary said, forgetting for a moment the size of Joseph's hands. "On second thought," she added jovially, "two of your handfuls should be enough." She recalled how encompassing his hand was when he held hers. Joseph smiled at his wife as he reached for the container of salt.

When Joseph finished, he went and sat at Mary's feet. He leaned his back against the edge of her bed as he said, "Mary, do you ever get anxious when you think of who you are carrying?"

"I try not to, Joseph; every time I do, I think of what the angel said about not being afraid. So I try my best to trust in the Lord," Mary replied, as she played with the dark black curls at the nape of his neck.

"No wonder God favored you above all others."

"Joseph, Joseph! When will you realize that I'm no more favored than you are? I may be carrying the Holy One, but haven't we both been chosen to raise Him? He chose you from among every other man who ever lived to be the earthly father of the Messiah. You'll be His role model and protector. If that's not being favored, I don't know what is. Didn't you tell me the angel also told you to have no fear? The Almighty will give us all the help we need to do His holy will."

"I guess you're right; I just always considered myself to have more brawn than brains. I would've thought the Lord would've picked someone a lot smarter than me to be one of the early teachers of the Messiah Himself."

"My dear! Did you ever think the Lord chose you because He wanted His Son to be raised with love, and with an example of righteousness? He knew that you were the best one to provide that for Jesus. Neither you or I are the most brilliant people in all of Israel, but neither of us is the most thickheaded either. If the Lord had wanted brilliance, He would have chosen a learned rabbi. Instead, He chose you and me. And I agree with the Almighty—I think you're one of the smartest men in all of Nazareth."

Joseph blushed at his wife's compliment; he was always amazed by her wisdom. At just fifteen she had more intelligence and logic than most women three times her age. "Mary! I think you should have been a rabbi," Joseph said. "You can teach Messiah all He needs to know." Mary laughed as she placed her hands over his cap and moved his head from side to side. "Ooh, that feels good!" Joseph said cheerily. "My neck was kind of stiff, but you're loosening it up." The couple then just sat there in silence, enjoying a quiet moment together.

Mary and her husband went over to her parents' house for dinner that night. The young virgin had already packed dried fish, fruits and flatbread for the trip, but Anna insisted they take more. She had prepared a large canvas sack filled with additional foodstuffs for their journey. It was a tearful parting; Joseph and his wife would begin their journey at sunrise. With the census in full swing, there was no need to wait for a caravan, since the roads were filled with sojourners, and campsites dotted the roadsides.

When Mary and her husband returned home, the rabbi stopped by to wish them God's blessings on their journey. As he was about to leave, Asa kissed Mary's hand, an act that wasn't common practice in their culture. "Blessed are you among women," he said. "And may the Almighty give you a safe journey to and from Bethlehem. I look forward to the day when I can see the Messiah for myself."

Mary then did something very unusual. "Rabbi!" she said. "Would you care to feel Him move?" Joseph smiled as Asa nodded. Mary took the rabbi's hand and placed it on her abdomen. The teacher began to praise the Lord of Heaven as the Messiah kicked and turned within the virgin's womb. Asa left their house with continued praise to his Maker for fulfilling His promise to His people Israel.

That night Joseph filled two skins with water. He then took a long piece of leather he had bought for his stools and rolled it up tightly; he did the same with his goatskin blanket. The young man placed his saddlebags near his donkey and moved the rest of the traveling supplies closer to the animal as well. Joseph left his wife's comforter so she could cover with it, as the night was cold. Mary could also drape it over herself as they traveled toward Bethlehem in the nippy winter air. Everything was now ready for their departure, so the young carpenter reclined on the floor next to his wife's bed. He prayed to the God of Israel to give them safe passage. The carpenter drew his feet up under his cloak for warmth and fell asleep.

Zaddu found another cave she could use as a temporary home for herself and the rats she so loved. She would stay there until the time was right. It was located about two days' journey from the town of Nazareth on the road to Jerusalem. She sat by the pyre in the blackness of night, once again choking on the thick crimson liquid she was forced to drink. A sound like rolling thunder could be heard as she did so. Mothers with empty arms mourned for their missing infants in every town the witch had passed on the way.

That same night, Deputy Hasid returned to the barracks of the Fortress Antonia in Jerusalem. He sat on his leather-covered stool as he removed his armor and prepared for bed. He had received his orders earlier that day. The soldier was being sent further southwest to a small town once again. It was a minor promotion; he would be in charge of a half-dozen soldiers who were overseeing the census there. Hasid despised the people of Jerusalem, because they were haughty and disrespectful. They were unlike the people in the smaller towns and villages who cowered in fear at the sight of him. In Jerusalem, the soldier couldn't retaliate because of the power of the High Priest, so the anger just festered within him. He would take his leather-covered stool and his indignation with him when he left tomorrow.

As Rabbi Asa always said, "The Lord moves in strange and mysterious ways."

It was still dark and quite chilly in the one-room home when Mary awoke. She slid down to the bottom of the bed in order to clear her husband's body when she stepped down to the floor. With her abdomen the size that it was now, maneuvering was quite difficult. Last night, Joseph had placed a partly filled water jar close to the winter oven so his wife would at least have tepid water to wash with when she awoke. As she sat on the edge of her bed, Mary looked down at Joseph. She rubbed her abdomen as she spoke to the child within her, "See how Your Abba has blessed us. There's no finer man He could have chosen to be Your earthly father. And he's as handsome as he is righteous; he'll raise You to be like him. Yes, my little one! You're going to have an earthly father that You can be proud of. And he'll protect us as long as he lives." Mary kissed her fingertips and would have touched them to Joseph's sleeping head, but her large abdomen wouldn't allow her to bend that low. So she just blew the kiss to him, and went off to bathe.

When Mary finished washing, she walked over to her husband and softly called his name several times. He didn't stir, so she called his name louder. He was so soundly asleep that he still didn't hear her. She couldn't bend, so she gently nudged her husband with her foot. Joseph shot up from the floor and shouted, "What! What's wrong?"

Mary smiled as she said, "Nothing, sleepyhead; it's just time for us to leave."

Joseph rubbed his face in his hands as he yawned and asked, "Are you sure it's morning? It feels like it still should be the middle of the night."

"Yes, I'm sure!" Mary said. "By the time we reach the city gate the sun will be up." The carpenter stood and stretched as his wife came to him. She stood on her tiptoes and kissed his cheek. Joseph grabbed her hand and squeezed it gently, then he went off to wash up.

When they stepped out into the cold early-morning air, Joseph lifted his wife onto the back of the donkey. One could hardly call the animal a beast

448

of burden, for now it carried the Promised of Ages and His mother. They reached the gatehouse just as the sunlight conquered the early-morning darkness. Eliud was in the process of opening the huge wooden doors of the portal. The Centurion still allowed the old man the dignity of tending the town gate, even though Roman soldiers were stationed there to monitor incoming travelers and supervise the census. Eliud shuffled over to Joseph, kissed the beard on his chin and wished the man and his wife a safe journey. With tears brimming in his eyes, he came over to Mary, grabbed her hand and said, "I'm going to miss you and your husband. Sometimes the younger people of town think I've been around too long; they treat me more like an old worn-out fixture than the person that I am. You and Joseph have always shown me respect. I hope to see all three of you very soon. Shalom, Mary! And may the God of Jacob go with you and your husband." The old man had no way of knowing that the Lord of Hosts was riding with His mother atop the donkey. Joseph hugged his old friend; it would be the last time he'd do so. Eliud would be resting in the Bosom of Father Abraham by the time they returned to Nazareth. The gatekeeper would never see the Messiah walk the streets of his town.

And so the young couple passed through the town gates and entered the valley below as they headed for the town of Bethlehem. Mary sat wrapped in a goatskin comforter. Joseph, staff in hand, led the donkey to join other weary sojourners on the dusty road south. After a full day's travel, the entire group of travelers encamped for the night. Campfires soon dotted the darkening roadside. Using his goatskin comforter and the long piece of leather he had brought, Joseph formed a pup tent for his wife. The young couple had an overabundance of food, so they shared some of their provisions with fellow Jews and Gentiles alike who were in need. Mary begged Joseph to sleep inside the narrow tent, but he refused. Instead, he packed the remaining space with their provisions. "Joseph! You keep my comforter then!" Mary said. "The tent should hold in the heat. You'll be out in the cold without anything to cover with."

"I've slept out in the open before, Mary; I'll be fine. It's more important that you and the baby stay warm." He tucked his wife in under the comforter and lowered the tent flap.

Joseph found a stone that would make a suitable pillow. After removing his sandals, he used a little bit of water to wash his dust-covered feet. The carpenter laid down in front of the tent's opening and fell into a sound sleep. When Mary could no longer hear her husband's breathing, she slid to the edge of the tent and covered him with half of her comforter. She arched her body as much as she could to still remain within the confines of the tent. She always awoke before her husband. So while the eastern sky was still pitch-black, she pulled the cover back into the tent and covered herself with it. Mary laid back down; that way Joseph wouldn't suspect she had kept him covered during the night.

The carpenter rose at sunrise. After finding fodder to feed their donkey, he reloaded the animal. The young couple was on their way once again. A

450

strong cold wind blew in from the Great Sea. Joseph's olive-colored skin now turned vermilion as blowing dust from the hillside and the cold winter's air stung his face. His mouth filled with sandy particles, and his teeth ground against the gritty matter every time he tried to swallow. He grabbed the end of the fabric that covered his head and pulled it over his face so that only his red, stinging, eyes were visible. He kept looking back at Mary to make sure her veil still covered her face. They plodded along; finally, in late afternoon, the wind subsided.

That evening, as the sun began to set, they reached a place suitable for camping. Joseph helped his wife down from the donkey. Mary demanded that before they did anything else, she wanted to wash the dust from his eyes. He leaned back as she poured cold water over them and wiped them with the sash that she now had to wear just below her breasts. "Take off your cloak and your tunic too, so I can shake the dust from them," Mary said commandingly.

"But I'll only have my undergarment on then," Joseph replied.

"You're my husband, aren't you? And I already saw your bare arms and legs when you were plowing the fields."

"So you looked, did you?" Joseph asked in playful banter as he began to disrobe. He laughed to himself, because his wife had sounded just like her Aunt Tamar when she demanded something of her husband Azor.

Mary shook her head as a sheepish grin crossed her face. She took the goatskin comforter and draped it over her husband's shoulders as she said,

"Stay covered, now, so you won't freeze. I'll shake the blanket out later." When Joseph was fully dressed, he set up their campsite. The celestial starlight was bright enough for Joseph to find sufficient fuel for a fire and fodder for the donkey. A bright glowing fire in the upper distant hills hinted at life among the barren rocks.

Though the young couple camped a considerable distance from the other travelers, the children with whom they shared their food with last night had no trouble finding them. There was still plenty of dried fruit left in the sack Anna had packed, so Mary shared it with the little urchins. "Only take one each," she said. "That way there'll be some left for tomorrow night too." Either the children didn't understand her dialect, or they were hungrier than she realized, for each child took a handful. The canvas sack was only a quarter-full when they had finished. Mary walked toward Joseph and said, "The children sure did a good job of nearly emptying Momma's sack of food."

"From the looks of some of them, I think they needed it. You've packed enough for us anyway, and we haven't had to touch that yet," Joseph said.

"I know! My heart went out to them, too; some of them were all eyes," his wife said. She then began to prepare their simple meal of dried foodstuffs.

The couple sat and ate by the fire while the cold winter air descended on the valley with a vengeance. It wasn't long before they could actually see their vaporous breath. "It's going to be a cold one tonight," Joseph said. "I've found some boulders that I'm heating by the fire. I'll put them inside the tent. They'll keep the chill out of the air for you tonight." Mary knew it was useless to argue with her gallant husband, so she said nothing. She planned to cover him up again with part of her comforter once he fell asleep.

As Mary snuggled up under her goatskin blanket, Zaddu finished speaking to her rats. The old hag then began to scrape the sandy soil onto the fire with her long curving nails to extinguish it. She didn't want anyone to follow her back to the cave when she completed her mission, just in case she had to run back to that location. The hunched-over sorceress then descended into the valley below. Occasionally, she would turn to see if any smoke still drifted up from her fire pit. It didn't.

When Joseph lowered the tent flap, he began to settle in for the night. The carpenter brought the donkey to the front of the tent, tied its tether to a large boulder and coaxed the beast to lie down. Mary had a craving for dried apricots before she retired, so Joseph left the sack Anna had packed inside the tent with his wife. He slept with the rest of their provisions between him and the tent. Joseph was cold and overtired. He stretched out next to the donkey, hoping the animal's body heat would give some warmth. The flames in the fire pit still danced in the cold darkness.

Mary awoke screaming. She shot up, swinging her arms wildly about. Something was crawling all over her. The shrill squeaking noise she heard made her skin crawl. Joseph leapt up, grabbed his club and entered the tent. The light from the fire lit the interior. Astonished to see rats crawling everywhere, Joseph arched his body over his wife's to keep the rodents away from her; suddenly everything went dark. The moment Joseph went inside, the witch stepped out of the darkness. With amazing speed and dexterity that even surprised the old hag herself, Zaddu swung her staff and knocked over the tent's support. The hides fell, covering the young couple. The donkey brayed as the witch stabbed at the full waterskin with the knife she held in her other hand. She turned quickly, grabbed the full bag of food and draped it over her shoulder. As she was about to stab at the moving forms beneath the tent, the donkey stood, bucked its hind legs and sent the witch flying through the air. The hag was amazed at how agile she had become. She rolled over and immediately ended up on her feet. The evil creature ran toward the darkened hills.

Mary and Joseph tried to free themselves from the tangle of leather and goatskins while still fighting off Zaddu's rats. The rodents disappeared as suddenly as they'd come when the old hag departed. The couple was left with only the small amount of food that Mary had inside the tent, and one useable waterskin with less than a half-day's supply of water in it. The astonishing thing, though, was that no matter how much food and water Mary and Joseph consumed, there was always the same amount left in their respective containers when they finished.

In a few days the young travelers reached Jerusalem. They camped in the Kidron Valley, just outside the city walls. Joseph had promised his wife he would take her to the Temple so she could see the magnificent structure firsthand and worship the

God of Jacob there. His plan was to take Mary to the Temple early the next morning and show her some of the other places of interest within the Holy City too. They would then leave for Bethlehem and would arrive at their destination by late afternoon.

The next morning, the couple rose early and packed their supplies. They tried to enter Jerusalem, but were told that travelers could not bring their animals into the city today by order of the king. Herod's son, Prince Philip, would be welcoming his future bride and her retinue tomorrow; all the streets were being cleansed for the festive occasion. Joseph had to pay the gatekeeper to leave his donkey outside the city walls. Joseph and Mary walked to the Temple.

The couple entered the Temple compound by the Sheep Gate and proceeded through the colonnade called Solomon's Porch. Mary looked from side to side in awe of her surroundings. She who bore the Messiah couldn't enter the Temple proper, but instead had to stay in the Court of Women while Joseph went inside to pray. They then walked through the streets of the Upper City, beholding all the architectural wonders. As fabulous as the other buildings were, they paled in comparison to the magnificence of God's holy dwelling-place. The couple finished their tour when the sun was far west of its zenith. The carpenter claimed his donkey, and the pair began the last leg of their journey.

Mary and Joseph had to circle the northern and western walls of the city before they reached the road to Bethlehem. Had they been allowed to bring their donkey into the city proper, they could have exited at the road that led directly there, saving considerable travel time. When they were about an hour from Jerusalem, the couple stopped for a bite to eat. Most travelers were midway to their destination by this time of day, so there were very few passersby when Mary and Joseph sat by the roadside and ate. When they finished eating and as Joseph hoisted his wife up onto the donkey, Mary's water burst. The puzzled carpenter looked at the puddle at his wife's feet. With panic in his voice he asked, "What just happened? Are you all right? Are you having the baby now, Mary? What should I do?" The nervous young man lowered his wife onto the donkey's back and began to brush back his side curls as he paced around the animal.

"Joseph, the baby and I are fine. Momma said this happens sometimes. Why don't we start traveling again? I'll let you know when I think the baby is coming."

"Maybe we should just stay here and wait it out," the young man said.

"No, Joseph, you know what the prophet said— our little Jesus has to be born in Bethlehem."

Joseph smiled from ear to ear at his wife's statement "our little Jesus." *It's the first time my wife referred to her baby that way,* he said to himself. Joseph liked the way it sounded. The carpenter grabbed the donkey's reins and started walking again with a hastened pace. With every second step he took, Joseph turned to his wife and asked, "Are you and *our little Jesus* all right?" Mary nodded. She didn't want to alarm her husband, but now she was experiencing rather severe cramping in her lower back.

The eastern sky began to darken as Mary and Joseph passed several elaborate tents and a very expensive-looking covered litter standing nearby. Intricately designed handmade carpets were spread on the ground as slaves and women-in-waiting scurried about, doing their various chores. Blazing braziers and torches surrounded the campsite as the smell of freshly roasted meat filled the air. Joseph nodded toward the campsite as he said, "Must be Philip's intended. They're camping here for the night." As he looked at his wife, Joseph could see the pain on her face. "Are you okay, Mary? Should we stop?"

The young virgin shook her head from side to side as she tried to stop herself from moaning; she was experiencing her first real labor pain. When the sharp contraction subsided, she said, "I think my labor has started, Joseph."

The young carpenter could see the town of Bethlehem in the distance. "We don't have much farther to go, Mary," her anxious husband said. "Not much farther at all! Not much further!" The nervous carpenter kept repeating that statement as he increased his pace to a trot. The bouncing movement only heightened the teen's labor.

Future generations would call this miraculous, holy and historic night "Christmas Eve."

CHAPTER 20

Rabbi Asa walked to the precipice on the cold December evening as daylight surrendered to the approaching darkness. He could see his breath and shivered as he raised his prayer shawl over his head for warmth. Asa didn't know why he felt so compelled to look toward the eastern horizon, but tonight, he was mesmerized by it. His wife, with her winter shawl draped over her head, came out to join her husband. "Asa! You're going to freeze out here! Why don't you come home with me now?"

"I'll be home shortly, my dear," he replied.

"What are you looking for out there?" she asked. "I've been watching you stare in the same direction ever since you left the house."

"I can't explain it, my love. I just feel compelled to watch the eastern sky. I don't know why myself."

"Please come home! You're probably chilled to the bone. If you're not careful, you might catch the winter sickness. I'm freezing cold, and I just came out here now."

"I'm fine! Just go inside. I'll be home before you know it.

"Promise me you won't stay out here too much longer." The rabbi agreed and told his wife to leave before she caught a cold. "Your daughters are expecting you to tell them a story tonight. Please don't disappoint them."

"I won't, I promise!" She kissed her husband on the cheek and returned home while Asa continued to stare toward the east. When he saw it, he knew why he was so compelled to stay out in the cold for so long. He fell to his knees. Filled with an overabundance of joy and wonder, he raised his arms to the heavens. His eyes brimmed with tears and his heart soared as he praised the God of Abraham, Isaac and Jacob in thanksgiving. He knew that the Messiah, the Promised of Ages, would be born sometime tonight.

That same evening, Zaddu sat at the mouth of her cave near the town of Bethlehem, piling thorn branches over a newly lit fire. She saw it too. The witch began to curse and moan as she rocked back and forth in horror. The old sorceress knew what would happen next. Her body was levitated and thrown mercilessly to the ground several times. Multiple voices then began to shriek from her mouth. The old crone was being tossed around like a ragdoll. Her eyeballs rolled back in her head, and green foam flowed freely from her mouth. The hillside echoed with the sounds of hellish rage.

Meanwhile, Deputy Hasid sat on his leather-covered stool near a writing table in the watchtower. From that vantage point, he could see the eastern sky through the window in the room. Hasid couldn't believe his eyes either. He walked closer and looked out through the opening. The soldier had never seen anything like it before. He stared at the strange phenomenon. The deputy looked down for a moment and saw the line of travelers waiting to register. They were turning around to stare at the heavens too—everyone, that is, except for a tall, dark-haired man and his wife at the end of the line. The young man was oblivious to his surroundings. He was only concerned about his pregnant, suffering wife and her baby. She sat upon the donkey with her body arched in pain. The deputy could tell that she was in the throes of labor. Hasid watched as the carpenter tried to bypass the line and enter the town gate. The people who were ahead of the couple began to shake their fists at him and curse.

A soldier left the registration table and directed the carpenter to return to the end of the line. When Joseph tried to explain that his wife was in labor, the soldier drew his broadsword and ordered him back to where he was. When the soldier returned to the table, he noticed that his comrade had left his post to confer with the deputy inside the tower. When his fellow soldier returned, he walked to the end of the line and said to the young man who had tried to bypass the waiting group, "You can enter now, but you must come back and register tomorrow morning. Do you understand me?" Joseph nodded and thanked the soldier profusely. With his broadsword drawn, he escorted the young couple past the complaining registrants to the town gate.

A lady-in-waiting ran into the tent of the princess-to-be and said, "My Lady, you must come outside for a moment to see this strange phenomenon."

The young woman rose from her divan. "What is it, Miriam?"

"A strange and wonderful occurrence is taking place in the heavens. Maybe it's a sign that the God of these people is blessing your impending engagement." The lady-in-waiting covered her mistress with a lavishly embroidered fur-trimmed cape.

The young woman stepped out into the surprisingly bright night. "Why is it so bright out here with only a half-moon?" she asked. Miriam pointed to the eastern sky and said to look up. The woman raised her eyes to the heavens and saw the celestial wonder. A huge, brilliant star sparkled like a diamond, with a tail similar to a comet's. The dazzling light, however, didn't trail behind it; instead, the gleaming tail fanned out perpendicular to the earth. The wondrous star moved very slowly in a westerly direction while the rest of the heavenly bodies appeared to remain stationary in the firmament above. The young woman kept staring at the wonder until her teeth chattered from the cold and her neck began to ache. "Tomorrow, I'll ask Prince Philip to inquire of the king's astrologers as to what this wondrous sign might mean," she said to her lady-in-waiting.

"It can only be a blessing for you, my Lady, a sign that you and the prince will have a happy life together." The women walked back to the elaborate tent. Periodically, they returned outside to see the wonder. At the early part of the second watch of the night, they noticed the unusual star stopped moving when it reached the nearby town of Bethlehem.

As Joseph and Mary neared the small rowdy inn, a recognizable voice shouted, "Halt!" Joseph turned and saw his nemesis standing before him. The carpenter was prepared to plead his cause to the deputy, but Hasid said, "There's no room for you in the inn. All the stalls are filled, and the courtyard is full too." He pointed to the hills as he continued, "There's a cave at the end of the road there that's used as a stable. I don't think it's any dirtier than the inn, and you'll have some privacy there."

Joseph bowed to the deputy and thanked him profusely, as did Mary. When the hardhearted soldier saw the beautiful woman, he said in a voice more compassionate than his usual, gruff tone, "Go now, before your wife gives birth atop the animal." So the young couple headed toward the stable as Hasid returned to his post. For the first time in his life the deputy felt some inner peace. Mary's contractions now came at regularly spaced intervals. With the excitement of the impending birth, neither Mary nor Joseph noticed the bright new star.

When the couple finally reached the cave, Joseph lowered his wife to the ground and tried to make her as comfortable as possible. He covered her with the goatskin blankets. "I'll start a fire so I can see what's inside. There should be a lantern or two in there." In his rattled state he reached into the wrong side of his saddlebag for the flint; his hand touched something cold and hard. With all the excitement in his life since the day he found out that Mary was pregnant, he had forgotten he had placed the vile of costly nard

463

into his bag several months ago. Joseph searched the other side of his saddlebags and finally found the flint; he struck it over some wood shavings until he had a live spark. As the fire blazed, the nervous father-to-be carried a lit twig into the cold, dank cavern and searched for lanterns. He found three and lit them; finally the cave had some light.

The pungent smell of ammonia and animal waste stung his nostrils. Joseph's eyes watered. *What kind of father am I going to be, if this is the best I can do for my wife and her son?* He asked himself as he worked at a feverish pace to muck the cave. *Messiah shouldn't be born in a place like this.* Both of the oxen watched with curiosity as Joseph pushed the damp, odiferous straw out of the cave's entrance and into the fire. The sheep and goats often got in the young man's way and bleated, voicing their disapproval at being disturbed. Joseph could hear his beautiful wife groaning in pain. "I'll be through in a minute, Mary! Just hang on! I'm almost finished!" He heard his wife's heavy breathing. He was concerned that the obnoxious smell would sicken her and make matters even worse. The carpenter broke open several bales of fresh hay and spread them on the floor. Running to his saddlebag, he grabbed the vile of nard and doused the walls of the cave with the priceless perfume. He then ran outside to get his loving wife.

Mary was in the middle of a strong contraction when Joseph bent over to lift her. With her fists and teeth clenched, the young woman shook her head from side to side, indicating she didn't want to be moved just yet. When it was over, Joseph lifted her and carried her inside. Upon re-entering the cave, he was amazed. The fragrance of the nard mingled with the acrid odors in the cave and created an altogether different, pleasing scent that was familiar to him. The entire cavern smelled like a field of lilies. Even the animals seemed pleased with the aroma. The donkey had followed Joseph into the cavern and joined the other beasts as they watched the miraculous drama that was unfolding before their very eyes.

Joseph lowered Mary to the floor, opened her covers, and mounded up some hay for her pillow. Beads of perspiration formed on Mary's brow; she grabbed his hand and squeezed it with all her might as she bore down again. "Joseph, I think the baby is coming now," she said through clenched teeth. "Put your hands under His head and shoulders to catch Him." She let go of her husband's hand and raised her tunic. He knelt down in front of his wife, nervously brushing his side curls over his ears as he waited. The fifteen-year-old virgin pushed with all her might, clenching her teeth and grunting. Joseph's jaw dropped in amazement as first the baby's head, and then His shoulders, were delivered. He placed his huge hands under the baby and caught Him as He was born. Soon he held the newborn Messiah in his calloused hands. *I'm the first person to hold Him,* the astonished young carpenter thought to himself.

"Grab Him by the feet, turn Him upside-down and tap His bottom," Mary said.

A confused look came over Joseph's face as he did as his wife requested. He could hear the baby gasp for breath, then cry. "I think I hurt Him, Mary! He's crying!"

"No, no, Joseph! Momma said that's what we have to do. He's supposed to cry. Now hold Him the right way and tie off the cord, then cut it." With trembling hands, the nervous carpenter did as he was told. The moment Joseph lowered the infant back into his arms, the baby stopped crying and opened His eyes to look at His earthly father. Joseph handed the baby to His mother. "Isn't He beautiful, Joseph?" As Mary looked at her son, she was overcome with joy. She still found it hard to believe that the infant she was holding actually was hers.

The young man smiled as he stood up and said, "He looks just like you, Mary!" Joseph went to get the swaddling cloths and salt. "You did a great job, Mary; you're amazing! Really amazing!" The couple cleaned up the infant, rubbed Him with salt, and swaddled little Jesus. Mary cradled her newborn son close to her breast and prepared to nurse Him.

Joseph left the cave to finish burning the pungent-smelling straw and find some kindling for the fire. He also looked for some boulders that he could heat to keep his wife and her son warm. The new father was surprised at how bright it was outside with only a half-moon. He finally looked directly overhead and saw the source of the strange light. It was the Star of Bethlehem, shining over the cave where the Christ Child lay. "Wait until I tell Mary about this," he said aloud as he went about gathering the things he needed.

When Joseph re-entered the cave, Mary was sound asleep. Little Jesus, however, wasn't. Joseph could see His hands and feet trying to wiggle within the swaddling cloths. It reminded him of a butterfly struggling to leave its cocoon. The young man walked over to his wife's side and picked up the baby. "Why don't we let Mommy sleep; she's very tired after the workout You gave her. ... Oops! No wonder You're wiggling like that, little fellah; You're soaked. Everything seems to be in working order," he said jovially. The baby smiled at the carpenter as he carried the newborn to the manager, laid Him on the sweet-smelling hay and began to change Him. When the carpenter unwrapped the infant, His tiny hand reached out and grabbed hold of Joseph's finger. In that moment, he bonded with the baby. The righteous young man felt as if Mary's son was asking him to be His father. Joseph couldn't hold back his tears.

When Hasid returned to the watchtower, there was only one family left to register. He walked up to the two soldiers that were seated at the table. Standing between them, he placed one of his meaty hands on each of their shoulders. They were shocked; Hasid was always a loner. The closest he ever got to anyone was a sword's length away, and to be that close usually meant his sword was through someone. He surprised them even further when he said, "Both of you soldiers go get some sleep; you've worked hard today. I'll take the night watch." In the past, the deputy had never cared how long or how hard his soldiers had worked. He wouldn't have taken night duty unless he was ordered to do so by a superior officer.

As the soldiers helped the census-taker clear the tabletop of the documents, Hasid patrolled the silent, deserted streets. The star still amazed him.

He noticed it no longer moved—it remained stationary over the cave were the young couple were lodging. His trek finally took him past the inn. He followed the road until it became a worn footpath that led to the cave. The night was cold and still; he could see his vaporous breath.

As the deputy neared the stable, he could hear the clinking sound the boulders made as Joseph set them around the fire. Hasid fought with himself. He was in the throes of an emotional conflict that was new to him. The warrior was starting to develop a conscience. His hardened heart began to soften. No matter how hard he fought with himself, he still felt compelled to go and thank the young carpenter for saving his life and to pay him for the stool. He started to follow the footpath, but when he finally caught sight of the entrance to the cave, he saw the carpenter go inside. *I won't disturb them now,* he thought. *His wife is probably still in labor. I'll wait until tomorrow.* The soldier turned around and headed back to his post at the town gate. It was so quiet, he could hear his armor move against his skin as he walked.

While Hasid spoke to his men at the gate, Zaddu came crashing down to the ground one last time. The harsh gravelly voice that came from her vocal cords said, "Kill the old sow now, and we won't have a chance to rid us of the trio tonight! She's our only hope. Only human hands can take the life of the God-man." Another, more evil-sounding voice, that of the Prince of Darkness himself, asked how many times was he to allow her to fail. She had botched ever opportunity he had given her.

"Give her one last chance. Empower her with additional strength and dexterity, then perhaps she'll succeed," another voice said. "If she fails again, you can stop her heart. You're still the author of death, so what's there to lose in one more try?" All at once a myriad of voices came from the witch at the same time, affirming the proposal to give the hag one last chance. When they stopped using the old sorceress to communicate, she sat up slowly and wiped the green foam from her mouth into the sleeve of her filthy garment. Her head ached. All she could hear was a ringing in her ears from the abuse that her body had just suffered. A sudden burst of energy shot through her. She jumped up into a standing position and reached down for her staff. When her long, curved fingernails touched it, her talon-like claws went right through the wood. She shrieked with laughter as she danced with glee around her campfire. The rats looked curiously at their mistress; not a single one of them had ever seen her with such strength before.

Meanwhile, the beautiful young woman and her lady-in-waiting stepped out of her lavish tent for one last time that night to behold the wondrous star. It was noticeably brighter, but it had remained in the same position for over an hour now. "My Lady, I think you should get some rest now," Miriam suggested. "Tomorrow is a big day for you; your future subjects should see you at your finest, refreshed and alert."

"You're right, Miriam! I can always look at this strange new star tomorrow night with Prince Philip. Perhaps we can find some meaning for its appearance then." So the young woman and her lady-in-waiting re-entered the tent. Miriam prepared her mistress for bed. Once again the princess-to-be reclined upon her divan while the older woman covered her with richly embroidered quilts. She then busied herself arranging the various cosmetics that the young Idumean woman would use tomorrow when she awoke. Miriam then went to lie down on the carpeted ground at the foot of her mistress's divan. Before she did, though, she looked down at the glamorous girl. She was so delicately beautiful. Her only drawback was that when she slept, she always kept her mouth wide open.

Hasid returned to the watchtower and got his stool. He sat down by the gate in the cold night air, enjoying the peaceful silence. Suddenly, in the distance, he heard a mystifying sound. It was a chorus of the sweetest, most beautiful voices he had ever heard. He wasn't able to make out the words of the song, though, as it drifted on the night air. Hasid felt as if he was privy to some supernatural event that was unfolding almost within earshot of him. He opened the heavy wooden gates and went out to stand on the low bluff near the town's entrance. In the distance he saw a huge expanse of milky white light that hung over the not-too-distant hills. It seemed to expand in size as more of the mystical-sounding voices joined in the supernatural chorus. The wondrous melody brought tears to the hardened soldier's eyes. He stood there entranced by the mysterious glow and the captivating heavenly sound. He hoped that the singing would never stop.

470

Zaddu swung from ridge to ridge as she made her way toward the cave where the newborn baby lay. The witch looked like a scrawny ape swinging through the air. Her curved brown nails were now as hard as steel. She was able to dig them into the hardest rocks to keep from falling into the gorge below. Had her ears not been ringing, she too might have heard the heavenly chorus. If she had, she probably would have just cursed at it anyway. Amazed by her revitalization and increased strength, the old hag cackled in her high-pitched voice as she swung closer and closer to the entrance of the cave. She realized she was reaching her destination too quickly. *Maybe they're still awake,* she thought. *It would be better to strike while they're asleep.* The witch stopped swinging, and dug her fingernails into the underside of a jutting rock formation. From a distance, she looked like a huge vampire bat hanging above the gorge below.

The deputy watched until the milky white light faded and the singing stopped. Reluctantly he left the bluff and locked the town gates once again. He sat on his stool, his head buried in his hands, trying to sort out his strange new feelings and the mysteries that had been unfolding around him. Hasid didn't know how long he had sat there in deep thought, when suddenly he was startled by a sound that tore through the stillness. He heard someone relentlessly pounding on the gate. He leapt to his feet. Normally he would have ignored the sound, or even cursed at the person, telling whoever it was to go away. Tonight was different, though;

471

the soldier walked toward the peek-thru. The squatty, muscular man opened the small door and looked through the opening to see who was frantically knocking at this late hour. The deputy saw a group of rather shabbily dressed men. Even if he hadn't seen the young man with an injured sheep draped around his neck, he would have recognized them as shepherds by their odor. "What do you want at this hour?" he asked rather gruffly.

The oldest shepherd, who stood at the head of the line, said, "Forgive us, Excellency, but we were out tending our flocks, minding our own business, when we saw the angel of the Lord. We weren't drinking wine or anything like that; we all saw the same thing. The angel told us, 'Do not be afraid'; he came to bring us good news, tidings of great joy to be shared by everybody. 'For today in David's city a Savior has been born for us, the Messiah, the Lord.' He told us that it would be a sign to us that we would find the babe wrapped in swaddling cloths and lying in a manger. Then, Excellency, the sky above us was filled with what must have been a whole army of angels, and they praised God, singing, 'Glory to God in the highest, and peace on Earth to those on whom His favor rests.' Believe me, Excellency! I'm telling the truth!" All the shepherds now gathered around their leader and nodded their heads in agreement.

Hasid then did something he never would've done before. He removed the heavy timber from the gate and allowed the shepherds to enter. "A young woman who was in labor and her husband are in the cave over there," Hasid said as he pointed to the location. "Its entrance is just below that bright star overhead. Be careful—the path that leads to it is quite narrow, no more than two abreast. The man has a fire going near the entrance; you can't miss it." The shepherds bowed to the deputy and thanked him repeatedly as they passed through the opened gate. They smelled just awful. As the motley band walked toward the cave, Hasid closed the gates. He sat back down on his stool. "You're getting too soft-hearted," he chastised himself. "Soldiers need too be strong and authoritative. We're supposed to be able to kill without emotions. I don't know what's happening to me. I believed everything the yokel said to me." In the distance, he thought he heard a screech owl; it almost sounded as if the nocturnal bird was laughing.

Joseph had just finished wrapping the infant in a fresh swaddling cloth when he heard a tapping sound. He left the infant in the manger as he went to see who it was. The group of shepherds had gathered around the gate, and they were peering through the openings between the boards. Joseph approached them. "Are you here to retrieve your sheep?" the carpenter asked.

"No, sir! Neither the sheep nor the goats are ours. The angel of the Lord told us to come here to pay homage to your newborn son, the Messiah." Joseph was amazed by what the old sheepherder said.

"Let me wake my wife, then you may come in." Joseph went over to Mary and gently tapped her shoulder. The overtired new mother smiled and nodded in agreement as Joseph explained what they wanted. Mary grabbed hold of Joseph's hand and stood up. He led her to the manger and helped her sit down beside it. When the shepherds entered, they fell on their knees before the child and praised the Lord God of Abraham. Joseph saw what they were doing. When he realized the child before him was being adored as the Messiah, it struck Joseph that maybe he too should adore the child. The young carpenter had been so involved with the child's birth that he hadn't thought of it before. Joseph knelt down and bowed low to the infant. Mary smiled at her husband; she'd have to have a talk with him after the shepherds left. The eldest of the group of worshipers recounted the story of their encounter with the heavenly beings to the young couple. They listened intently as the old shepherd spoke. Joseph lifted the babe from the manger, and handed him to his wife so the men could have a closer look at their Deliverer.

The shepherds left the cave rejoicing and praising the God of Abraham. When they tried to tell others about what they had experienced, no one would believe them. Why would God inform poor itinerant shepherds that Messiah was born? Surely He would have announced such monumental news to the High Priest first; he in turn would then notify the entire nation of Israel. It was ludicrous to even remotely consider that the God of Creation would entrust a nineteen-year-old carpenter and his fifteen-year-old wife with the task of rearing the Messiah. They had forgotten that centuries before, God chose an adolescent shepherd boy named David to be Israel's greatest king.

When the shepherds left, Mary padded the mound of hay next to her with her free hand and asked Joseph to sit beside her. He sat down next to his wife and son. "My darling husband," she said, "I know it can be overwhelming when we think of whom the Lord has given us to raise, but I don't think that the Almighty wanted us to go about adoring Jesus just yet. Do you? We'll have plenty of time to do that when His Heavenly Father reveals that He's the Messiah to all of Israel. Do you really think that He could experience life the way it should be if we did that? My parents would be afraid to even hold Him if we told them who He actually is. His Kingdom will last forever. We'll have plenty of time to venerate Him then. If the Lord wanted us to worship our son now, He would've had me give birth to Jesus in the Most Holy Place of the Temple, not in a stable. We have to raise Him like any normal child until God is ready for Him to begin His mission, whatever that might be. Otherwise, people will treat Him as if He's odd or something. If you weren't personally involved in this divine mystery, would you have believed that we would've been chosen to be His parents? I certainly wouldn't have. I'm sure as our Jesus grows up, we'll have to set parameters for Him just like other parents do. I don't think we could do that too well while kneeling before Him. Do you? And you should know firsthand what happens when a child isn't properly disciplined—or have you already forgotten about Joshua Bar Abbas. We know that He's God's Son, but He is also the son of our father Adam, the son of man. Right now, neither of us knows what that means. So I think we should raise Him the way a normal child is raised. If that's wrong, I'm sure Jesus or His Father will let us know otherwise."

"Everything you just said makes perfect sense, Mary. When I was holding Jesus and changing Him, I didn't think too much about who He really is. To me, He seemed like any other baby, except that He's ours to raise and love. But when I saw the shepherds worshiping Him, the reality overwhelmed me. I kind of asked myself, *What are you doing standing here when you're in the presence of the Son of God?*"

"I know how you feel, Joseph. When I first held Him in my arms, I realized how favored we really are. But I'm not going to be afraid to ensure that He's raised properly, like any other child," Mary said. "Did you notice, Joseph, that this stable smells just like a field of lilies? It's the same fragrance I smelled every time the angel appeared to me." Joseph said that it was the same scent he smelled when the heavenly messenger visited him too. Only this time, it was just the scent of nard that mixed with the smell of the stable. He told her that it stunk badly in the cave before he sprinkled the walls with it.

"Where on Earth did you get the nard from?" Mary asked. Joseph told his wife the whole story. She smiled at him and said, "So you were that angry? I can't blame you, though; I think I probably would have done the same thing. This beautiful scent doesn't smell anything like nard, though. Perhaps it smells this way because the angel of the Lord has been with us all this time to watch over the Lord's own Son."

"It's possible, Mary. Oh! I almost forgot to tell you about the star."

"What star?" Mary asked. Joseph described the strange phenomenon to his wife.

"I want to go out and see it," she said.

"You're still rather weak. Why don't you wait until tomorrow night, when you're stronger? I'm sure it just won't disappear overnight."

476

"You're right! Why should I go out and see a star when I can look at the Son?" the virgin said with a smile on her face.

Joseph caught the play on words and smiled at his wife. "Am I going to be able to live with you?" he asked. "Motherhood sure has made you witty." Mary laughed.

Hasid opened the town gates as the shepherds approached. He counted them to ensure that the same number that had come in was now leaving. The deputy noticed how different the men acted. There was a peaceful serenity about them he didn't detect before. The youngest of them said, "Thank you, Excellency, for allowing us to see the Messiah with our own eyes." Hasid just nodded his head, but said nothing. Before he closed the gate entirely, he peeked out at the shepherds as they walked back to their fields. Their hands were lifted up to the heavens, praising their God as they returned to their flocks.

Joseph's former nemesis went back to his stool. He removed his helmet and ran his fingers through his thinning hair as he tried to make some sense of what had happened tonight. The deputy had heard that the people of this strange land were always looking for their promised deliverer, a king who would establish an everlasting kingdom. People everywhere would be subject to Him. The Messiah was a threat not only to Caesar, but to King Herod as well. What if news of this child's birth reached Herod? The old fool was nuttier than a pistachio tree at harvest time. If Herod killed his wife and sons the way he did, what would he do to this newborn Messiah?

If Hasid told Joseph and his wife to leave the country now, it would be repayment enough for Joseph's saving his life. Yet if he did so and kept mum about what he knew, he could be accused of treason against Caesar and Rome. Hasid put the helmet back on. He didn't know what to do, but he knew he had to do something. The soldier walked back toward the end of the street. He paced back and forth before the curving path that led to the cave while he tried to decide what to do. In the distance, he could hear the carpenter pounding on something. He knew the young man, and perhaps his wife, was still awake. The deputy continued to pace as he pondered his options.

A stiff winter wind began to blow. Mary shivered; she brought her son closer to her bosom to keep Him warm. Joseph noticed and immediately ran to get her the other goatskin comforter. Her husband wrapped her and the baby with it. Joseph told her that he would go and check if the boulders were hot enough to bring inside. The carpenter also decided that he'd fasten a sheet of leather over the entrance of the cave to keep out the cold wind. The boulders were barely warm. Joseph found a good-sized branch and broke it into pieces. He whittled one side of each into a pointed wedge. Grabbing the sheet of leather, he poked holes into it at one end and draped it over the wooden frame of the entrance. He then pounded the wedges between the timber and the stone.

As Joseph entered the cave, he immediately felt the difference. He then latched the gate behind him. He turned and saw his wife still sitting where he had left her. "Joseph, I think that our son is going to have a hard time learning how to be a carpenter."

"Why do you say that, Mary?"

"Every time He heard you pounding, our little Jesus jumped. He opened His eyes and pouted. I thought He was going to cry."

"I'm sorry about that, Mary, but I think I cut down on the draft quite a bit by shielding the entrance from the wind."

"I know, Joseph. I was just teasing you," Mary said. "I don't think there's another man on this earth as kind, considerate and loving as you. How could you have known that Jesus would react to pounding that way? I thank God every day for giving me a husband like you."

The carpenter blushed as he said, "Thank you, Mary! I thank God for you too! Why don't you lie down and get some sleep now; you deserve it. If the baby wakes, I'll take care of Him—as long as He's not hungry. If He is, I can't do anything about that." They both laughed at his remark. Mary adjusted herself to a more comfortable position and then cradled the infant in her arms. The baby awoke, and His wide, deep-amber, mesmerizing eyes gazed up at His mother as she said, "I'll nurse Him again; maybe we'll all be able to sleep through the night then." Joseph told her that while she was doing that he'd go check on the boulders again.

The strong, cold wind wouldn't allow the boulders to absorb heat properly or as rapidly as Joseph would have liked. He walked around the fire, rubbing his arms with his hands as he did so. *Mary needs a little privacy,* he thought. His teeth began to chatter as the wind blew up under his woolen tunic. It was so strong that even a tall, muscular man like him had difficulty standing erect. Joseph lifted the leather sheet he had hung over the entryway and stood between it and the gate so as to stay the winter wind's stinging bite.

While Mary nursed her son, she pondered the sacred mystery that had unfolded on this holy night. She looked down at her newborn son, kissed His tiny head and asked Him and His Father to guide her in her decisions concerning Him. The young mother trembled with the impact of the realization that the God of Creation was actually nestled in her arms. Suddenly she wasn't as sure as she had been whether to worship Him now or not.

When Joseph thought that Mary was finished nursing, he turned, faced the battered gate and opened it. He looked lovingly at his wife and her son as she slept with her newborn cradled gently in her arm. The goatskin covering had slid off of her back when she readjusted her clothing after nursing. Her entire back was exposed to the chilly air inside the cave. Joseph quietly moved toward the sleeping duo. He knelt beside them and adjusted their covers. Mary opened her eyes and smiled at her husband.

"With the strong winds, I don't think the boulders will ever heat up enough to give us any warmth tonight," Joseph whispered. "As a matter of fact, I think that it's going to blow the fire out."

Mary raised herself up on her free arm and gently kissed her husband's forehead. "Thank you for all you've done for us, Joseph," she whispered. "Come and lie down next to me; we can put little Jesus between us and keep Him warmer that way. You need to think of yourself once in a while too.

Your lips have turned blue from the cold." She lifted the covers. Joseph still shivered as he reluctantly lowered himself to the ground, being very careful not to disturb the sleeping baby. Mary covered her husband with the remainder of the blanket, then she reclined and draped her arm over Joseph's hip. Her hand now rested at the small of his back. Joseph timidly placed his arm over his wife's shoulder. He half-expected Mary to pull away from him; instead, she pressed her forehead even closer to his face. He could smell the fresh clean scent of hay that clung to her hair. They laid there; content to finally be in each other's arms. As they drifted off to sleep, the baby opened His enchanting eyes. Jesus looked at His parents and smiled.

Long ago, when Mary was only eight, she had asked her mother if she would ever be a queen. Anna told her daughter it would be preposterous to believe that a girl from the small town of Nazareth could reach such heights. What Anna couldn't possibly have known at the time was that her daughter's title would be far greater than the most exalted title of any woman who had lived or ever would. Her daughter would forever be called the Mother of God, the virgin who bore the Prince of Peace, Lord of lords, King of kings.

EPILOGUE

In the hills of Ein Karem, Tamar slept with her six-month-old grandson by her side. Elizabeth had no objections; she knew that her parents would be leaving in a few days to return to their home in Nazareth. Let her mother pamper baby John as much as she liked. At their age, her parents probably would never see their grandson again.

Meanwhile, Zaddu the witch finally reached the precipice where the cave that was used as a stable was located. Her hard, claw-like nails dug into the soil of the path that led to the cave's entrance. With her newfound strength she hauled her body up to the pathway and sat there, dangling her bony legs over the steep rise. She would sit there until she was sure the trio inside was sound asleep. The crone had to be patient; when she completed this mission successfully, she would prove how valuable she was to the Prince of Darkness.

Hasid had stopped his pacing and decided to head back to the watchtower. The cold, piercing wind had forced him from his position on the path. He would build a fire in the brazier at the town wall and warm himself. The soldier still couldn't decide what he would do. He mumbled his options to himself as he walked. By the time he reached the town's inn, he had finally reached a decision.

Zaddu swung her bony legs up onto the path. She stood as best she could with her bent frame. The old hag circled the fire pit; the howling winds had already extinguished the flames. Strong winds pushed the witch forward toward the cave's entrance. Her ears were still ringing, so she couldn't hear its sound. The strong gusts kept the leather curtain firmly plastered against the gate. Every time she pulled the tarp away, the wind blew the covering back. Soon her claw-like nails tore through the leather, shredding it to ribbons.

The gate was too high for the witch to reach over it, so she slipped her nails through the opening between the boards. She slid them along the side of the weather-worn plank as she tried to release the inside latch. Splinters of wood flew through the air. *Just one more try,* she thought to herself. She was convinced that if she moved her nails up just a bit slower, the latch would release without making too much noise. Zaddu reached for the dagger in her sash. Suddenly her eyes glowed like rubies and her tongue split in two. She hissed loudly as she felt something encircle her neck and jerk her backward.

Hasid's newfound conscience forced him to do what was right. He would go see Joseph right now. If he were asleep, he'd wake him and thank him for saving his life. The soldier would ask his forgiveness for the wrongs he had done and pay him for the stool. Hasid would also tell him how insane Herod actually was, and suggest that Joseph protect his family by fleeing the country until the king died—just in case the good news that the shepherds had received reached the palace. The cold no longer bothered Hasid; his resolve warmed the soldier's heart.

The Deputy reached the path that led to the stable. He was unfazed by the strong wind gusts; his squatty stature kept him solidly planted on the ground. As he approached the cave, he saw the old hag struggling with the leather curtain. He recognized her at once.

"Halt!" he said commandingly. The witch seemed to pay no attention to him as she struggled to open the gate. He saw her reaching for the dagger in her sash. With lightning speed, Hasid placed her in a headlock and tried to pull her away from the entrance. The hissing sound she made almost caused him to lose focus, but he held his ground. With Herculean strength the hag tried to break from his grasp. Her hands flew through the air, slashing at his armor. Hasid could feel her nails tear through his leggings and rip through the flesh of his legs. But the battle-hardened warrior kept Zaddu's head locked in his arm as he struggled to bring the old witch down.

Even though he wore his helmet, Zaddu succeeded in digging her razor-sharp nails into his cheek. Blood flowed freely from his facial cuts and streamed toward his eyes. He finally brought the evil, superhuman creature to the ground. Locking his legs around her, he was able to use his free arm to start rolling with the hag to the edge of the cliff. He could no longer see. The blood had flowed into both of his eyes. The hissing form within his grasp began to buck like a bronco as she tried to free herself from his clutches. Her curved nails found the unprotected spot between his metal arm-cuff and his shoulder. She dug her fingernails in so deeply that when she pulled her hand forward, a good-sized chunk of his arm stuck to her hideous claws. The sound of the hollowing wind masked his loud moan. Racked with unbearable pain, the soldier rolled one last time. He and the witch both fell into the gorge below.

Hasid died instantly; his debt to Joseph was now paid in full. The old hag's body was twisted every which way, but her heart still beat rapidly. Her head was twisted backward from the fall. The witch's heartbeat began to slow as she gagged uncontrollably. It slowed even further as the serpent slithered over her forked tongue. When the entire snake had crawled out of her mouth, the hag's heart fluttered one last time, and then stopped beating. Zaddu was dead.

The serpent slithered off toward the road and followed it until it reached the elegant tents of Philip's future fiancée. It had no trouble winding its way over the terrain and slipping under her tent unnoticed. The serpent moved past Miriam and slithered up the gold lamé sheet that covered the divan. The beady-eyed reptile stared at the young woman's opened mouth as it flicked its forked tongue in and out.

Baby John's eyes opened wide as he raised his tiny arms above his head and clenched his fists tightly. His entire body went rigid. Tamar awoke as her grandson gasped for air. He began to cry, and his arms and legs moved about wildly as he trembled uncontrollably. John's grandmother feared he might be convulsing, so she placed her little finger in his mouth to prevent him from swallowing his tongue. Tamar called out for her daughter to come and help.

Miriam could hear her mistress gagging. She rose quickly to help the young woman. Although her whole body heaved, she still slept. The lady-in-waiting saw her charge's eyes moving rapidly beneath her eyelids. *She definitely is dreaming, but why is she gagging so?* she asked herself. The young woman finally stopped choking and settled down. *I wish she could learn to sleep with her mouth closed. It's not only unsightly, but only the gods know what could crawl in there when she sleeps,* her handmaiden thought. Miriam checked on the young woman once more before she returned to her place on the carpeted ground and fell back asleep.

With looks of genuine concern on their faces, the parents and grandparents tried to figure out what could possibly be wrong with baby John. As they did so, Philip's future wife dreamed.

Philip's fiancée saw herself lying on her divan in a palatial room. The young woman was much older than she was now, though. Her future brother-in-law, Prince Antipas, was making passionate love to her while her future husband, Prince Philip, sat at the edge of the divan and wept bitterly. The adolescent girl, who looked very much like her when she was just thirteen, watched the pair as they made love. When they were done, Antipas slid off the divan, and whispered in the woman's ear, "Herodius, tell your daughter Salome to dance for me. I'll give her up to half of my kingdom..."

Baby John, the prophet, grabbed hold of his neck with his chubby little hands; he screamed and began to cry uncontrollably. None of the adults could figure out what was bothering him. But then, that's another story.